SCORCH

MOUNTAIN MAN PROTECTORS SERIES

GEMMA WEIR

Scorch
Montana Mountain Protectors #2
Copyright © Gemma Weir
Published by Hudson Indie Ink
www.hudsonindieink.com

Cover Design by Kirsty-Ann Still, Pretty Little Design Co.
Formatting by LJDesigns

Also by Gemma Weir

*Creating unreachable expectations for
women the world over ;)
It's time for the next Montana Mountain
Protector*

* * * WARNING * * *

My heroes are assholes. They are not PC. They are, at times, morally ambiguous, behave like cavemen, and sometimes they'll do whatever it takes to get their heroines pregnant.

Please, please, please don't read this book thinking I'm exaggerating about how OTT and alpha these characters are because you'll hate the book and then write a scathing review saying both me and my characters are psychopaths.

My mountain men are controlling, manipulative, cruel, and sometimes cold to the point of being glacial. If alphaholes are not your jam, then please stop reading now.

All of my heroes are over-the-top, jealous, unreasonable, possessive assholes.

If you consider unapologetic alphaholes unacceptable or feel their behavior is in some way abusive, then this isn't the book or series for you.

If you're a naysayer who thinks what I write is romanticizing domestic violence and abuse, then please, please stop reading now. You will not enjoy this book!

This book isn't a guide to dysfunctional relationships; it's fiction. My books are fantasy; this isn't real life. It's a romance novel and should be read as such.

We all know in the real world, throwing a woman over your shoulder, messing with her birth control, or stalking her and letting yourself into her home is a one-way ticket to either a restraining order or the mental hospital.

Nothing I write is based on real life, it's pure fantasy, so it's okay to agree that the dysfunctional relationships between my characters are sexy as fuck. Please do not kink shame me or my enthusiastic readers for finding these extreme alphahole behaviors hot. Maybe if you read this book with the pinch of romantic salt it was intended to come with, you might like it too.

Please heed this warning. My books will make you question your feminism, so I suggest you leave it at the door while you live in the world of my creation for a little bit, then pick it back up on your way out. It's okay to like this kind of story because that's all it is. A story, a few hundred pages of fantasy intended to titillate and excite, not to change your life.

If you're easily offended, this isn't the book for you.

But if, like me, you love a guy who is so obsessively in love with his girl that he will manipulate, coerce, control, and obsess over her until she gives herself to him completely, then read on and welcome to the world of the Montana Mountain Protectors. ;)

For a full list of trigger warnings for each book, please check out my website www.gemmaweirauthor.com.

Chapter One

Nero

How the fuck have I ended up in this situation?

My feet move on autopilot as I carry the millionth box of Tori's things into the house I apparently now live in... with her. I don't have anything specifically against James's friend per se. No, that's a lie. I do have an issue with her specifically.

I don't like her.

She talks too much. She's too loud, too shrieky, too female, and far too perpetually happy. I'm not sure how this happened or if I even agreed, but from today, I'll be sharing space with her and if I didn't love my brother so much, I'd be pretty pissed at him for forcing me into this god-awful arrangement.

The problem is that I do love my brother. Right now, while I'm lugging boxes full of God knows what, he's in

Las Vegas getting engaged to James, the woman he's fallen head over heels in love with, and for him, I'll keep my mouth shut and move into a house with *her*.

"I swear I didn't have this much stuff when I moved to town. Boxes are like rabbits; they multiply and now just look at all this. Thank God we have a spare room. I can use it for storage while I go through each of these and get rid of everything I don't need. Although I guess it would have made sense to do that while I was packing instead of when we'd already hauled them up here." She laughs. Slapping me on the bicep, she steps past me, her arms full of rainbow-colored throw pillows. She dumps them onto the black leather couch I ordered when Buck dropped the "you need to move out so I can move my girlfriend in" bombshell, then smiles widely, passing me to head back out to the truck.

For about a minute after Buck announced that I needed to share a house with a complete stranger so his new girlfriend would agree to move in with him, I didn't think it would be too bad living with Tori.

Then I met her.

She reminds me of one of the crazy rainbow dolls little girls in kindergarten have. The ones that make your eyes hurt just to look at them. Only Tori doesn't have rainbow hair or even dress that brightly. She just has an exceptionally rainbow-like disposition and everything about her smiling, cheerful, upbeat personality makes my soul wince.

Glaring at my new couch, that's now drowning in garishly bright throw pillows, I think about demanding she shift all the mismatched cushions off my Italian leather La-Z-Boy. I can imagine her smile finally slipping away; how the outrage and hurt would look on her face, but instead of saying anything, I stay quiet, silently vowing to move them all the first chance I get. She can make her bedroom look like a unicorn threw up all over it, but the shared spaces need to stay calm and neutral.

Dutifully, I stack the box in my arms with the others in the spare room I'd been hoping to use as a gym, then silently head back to Buck's truck to get the last few things out of it. If she's noticed that I haven't spoken a word to her since I arrived at the house she and James have been sharing, she hasn't mentioned it. But I've come to the conclusion that as long as she's talking, she's happy, and she doesn't seem to need anyone to talk back.

"Are you hungry? The guys mentioned ordering pizza and helping me unpack," she asks.

I grunt, neither agreeing nor disagreeing. The guys she's talking about are my teammates. Buck thought it would help James to feel like more of a part of our world if she got to know the rest of our team, and of course he asked Tori to tag along too. I guess he assumed if both women knew the other people who they'd be living up on the mountain with, it'd help them agree to move up here.

The rest of our team took an instant liking to both girls, so now, not only am I living with Tori, but both her, my brother, his new fiancé, and the rest of my teammates expect me to socialize with her too.

Hell. On. Earth.

I could handle it if everyone was just being polite, but the team genuinely seems to adore Tori. So much so that they've even added her to our social group text. Now the chat that used to consist of monosyllabic questions, like *video games? Movie? Beer?* Or *Bar?* Has now been replaced with gossip, chitchat, and entire conversations made up of hearts, smiley faces, and flame emojis.

Despite my annoyance at being forced out of my home and into a house with a stranger, I'm happy for my brother and James. According to him, the first time he saw James, he knew she was his and pursued her relentlessly until she succumbed to his charm. They haven't known each other long and it hasn't been smooth sailing for them, but judging by the picture of them on the giant Ferris wheel on their Vegas strip, with his ring on her finger, it's clear they've gotten things settled and I'm getting a new sister.

Right now, the happy couple is on a plane on the way back to Montana. So, I've officially moved out of the house I've shared with Buck since we came to Rockhead Point a little over a year ago and into the house next door with a woman I barely know—and really don't like.

I could've—and maybe should've—moved in with one of my teammates. But honestly, I like the idea of living with one of them about as much as I want to live with *her*. Ultimately, not creating a rift with any of my team was more important than me disliking my new roommate, so I'm going to give living with Tori a chance for a few months. If it doesn't work out, I'm going to speak to Hal about buying a piece of land and building myself a house somewhere on his property.

"Earth to Nero. What do you want on your pizza?" Tori asks, her hands on her hips, her lips spread into a slightly forced smile.

I recognize the look. It's the way my ex, Miranda, used to look at me, especially in the last couple of months when I refused to fall in line with her plans for me. "Pepperoni," I snap curtly, turning and heading for the stairs before she can talk to me again.

With all of Tori's stuff in the spare room and James's things now in the room that used to be mine next door, I head upstairs to my new bedroom. It only took me about ten minutes to move my furniture and pack all of my stuff into two boxes. I've always traveled light, and even though we've been in Rockhead Point for over a year, I guess I haven't really put down enough roots to think about buying more stuff yet.

Because my brother is a control freak who was determined not to give James an excuse to delay moving in with him, he arranged for a contractor to redecorate the master suite in his house while he was in Vegas, and I had them come in and paint my new room too. The moment I close the door behind me, I exhale, some of my annoyance falling away. My walls are a deep blue, the floor natural wood, and the ceiling white. My linens are navy, and as I sit down on my bed, I let the Egyptian cotton soothe away some of my stress, breathing easy for the first time since Tori opened her mouth today.

I honestly don't know what it is about her that annoys me so much. She's not an awful person, or at least not as far as I know. There's just something about her that is too much. Like she absorbs all the air in a room, and after spending two hours with her this morning, living in a shack on the side of the mountain sounds like a better option than being surrounded by her all of the time.

Lying back on the bed, I kick off my shoes and lift up my legs. Closing my eyes, I inhale deeply, then push the breath back out slowly, forcing my muscles to relax one by one. I know that the whole situation with my ex, Miranda, has fucked up my view of women right now. I'm not as angry or bitter as I should be after what happened, but I am a little resentful over how everything went down with her, and maybe I'm projecting that onto Tori.

But, Jesus, if she'd just shut up for five minutes, maybe I'd be able to tolerate her a little more.

My cell beeps and I sigh, knowing exactly who it is. My ex and her two boyfriends, Ethan and Mark, have been messaging me relentlessly since I told her we were over. Miranda told me when we first met that she loved romance books and dreamed of having a whole group of guys all panting over her.

Looking back, she never lied to me. She told me right from the off that she was dating multiple men. She confessed her biggest fantasy was to be in a polygamist relationship, where she could be the center of the group. I guess I just didn't realize how serious she was about making her fantasy turn into real life.

When we first started dating, she seemed like the perfect woman and I was happy that she wasn't looking for a serious, committed relationship. The demands of my job make it hard for me to find enough time to keep a woman happy, so it wasn't a problem that she was dating other people who could pick up my slack.

A part of me just assumed that, at some point, we'd

get more serious and take things to the next level. Maybe become exclusive, or book a vacation or something. But after we'd been dating for six months, instead of focusing on me and her, she started talking more and more about the harem idea and including the other guys she was dating too.

When I told her that wasn't something I was interested in, she backed off and things continued as they had been for a little while until she started mentioning the other guys again. She kept suggesting that I should meet them, that we should go on dates as a foursome, that I should give us all a chance to see if this alternative lifestyle could work.

In hindsight, I should have seen the red flags she was waving at me, but I thought it was all just a sex thing, that she got off on the fantasy of being a part of a group. A few weeks before we broke up, I picked her up for a date and when we got to the restaurant, I found out she'd arranged for her other two guys to be at the table waiting for us.

Apparently, I was the only one who didn't know this wasn't just a fantasy for her. It turns out that Mark and Ethan were both totally okay with a group dynamic, and the three of them had been in a happy throuple for a while but were ready to make it a happy quad... with me.

The truth is, if being in a harem—or what-the-fuck-ever you want to call it—makes them happy, then all power to them. But I know it's not my thing because I'm not the type of guy who would be willing to share a woman that I considered mine.

It wasn't until I was confronted with Mir and her band of merry men that I realized I didn't think of her as mine. I wasn't jealous of the other guys she was sleeping with or angry that she was picking them over me, so when I broke things off, I was confident I was doing the right thing.

Unfortunately, Miranda and her harem aren't content to just let me walk away, and ever since that day, I've been receiving almost constant texts, calls, pictures, and videos from them. I blocked Miranda's number a while back, but they don't seem to have any issue finding disposable cells to contact me from.

Maybe when I was an idiot teenager, I'd have just sat back and enjoyed the free porn, but accidentally clicking on a video of my ex being spit roasted between two guys I don't know while all three of them call your name is fucking messed up. Half the things they've been doing in the clips they've sent me are things Miranda and I never even talked about her wanting.

She said anal was a hard pass for her, but I've received several up close and personal pictures and videos of dicks slamming into her ass in the last couple of weeks. Honestly, there's nothing sexy about watching another dude rail the woman you thought you could have had a future with.

The whole situation is making me sick to my stomach. I'm not jealous or angry that she and her harem seem to have a super active sex life. I'm pissed that despite me telling them all that I have no intention of becoming guy number three in their group, they won't accept that I'm not interested.

I wouldn't call myself vanilla, and my sexual tastes lean toward the kinkier side of sane, consensual fun. But I never in a million years considered that she'd actually make her fantasy into her day-to-day life and try to get me to be a part of it.

Deep inside, I'm a little embarrassed that I wasn't enough for her, that I wasn't enough man to make her happy. But if they'd just leave me alone, I could accept that my male pride has taken a hit and move on. Instead, I'm being bombarded with dick picks and sex tapes and then, on top of that, I'm now being forced to live with the loudest, most annoying female on the planet.

Chapter Two

Tori

My new house is kind of awesome, but my new roommate is an asshole. James is on her way back from Vegas, and I'm so glad that she and Buck got things sorted out and that he loves her enough to put a ring on her finger. No one is more deserving of a man who sees how special she is than James. But as pleased as I am for her, a part of me is a little pissed that Buck's stolen her from me and that my new roomie is Nero freaking Henderson.

On a scale of one to hotter than Hades, Nero is sex on legs. But he has the personality of Grumpy Cat. Seriously, I'd lay money on the fact that there were more enigmatic cavemen. I have no idea how I'm going to tolerate living with this dude.

When Buck and James first suggested I move out of

the house I've been living in for the last five years to live in the middle of nowhere on the side of a mountain, I agreed. Because I knew if I didn't, James wouldn't have agreed to move in with Buck.

But now, a part of me wishes I'd said no. I could have found a new roommate or paid the full rent myself at a push. Either of those options would have been better than moving in with someone who clearly dislikes me.

The sound of his bedroom door shutting echoes through the house and I sigh, glancing around at my new home. It's a nice enough house. Three bedrooms, two and a half baths, a relaxed open-plan kitchen, living and dining space, and a cute backyard with a patio area.

If I was living here alone or with James, I'd be over the moon. But being here with Nero has put a serious dampener on my excitement. I've only known him for just over a week, but from the very first time we met, he's made it pretty damn obvious that he barely tolerates me.

What I don't get is why. I don't like to blow my own trumpet, but I'm a likable person. People like me, they always have. In high school I had loads of friends and when I went to culinary school, I was the person everyone wanted to work with on group projects.

When I graduated and started looking for a job, I was inundated with offers, and I had my pick of restaurants and bakeries to work in. It was my choice to move back to Montana and work for Mrs. Yates at her cake shop. But even here, all of my customers adore me, coming back again and again for every celebration, event, and occasion.

So, I just don't get why Nero doesn't like me.

My cell pings and I know without looking it'll be the smoke jumpers group chat. Buck, Nero, and the other five guys in their team are all specialist rural firefighters who get dropped into inhospitable areas to fight wildfires. I met Oz, Danny, Warrick, Anders, and Knight at the Barnetts' barbeque a couple of weeks ago and we all immediately hit it off. Before we left, they invited me to a video game and pizza night and added me to their social group chat.

I know a lot of the friendliness was because Buck is their boss, James is his girlfriend, and I'm her bestie, but still, it's clear they all like me enough to want to have me as part of their group, and I like them all enough to want to invest some time into new friendships.

We'd all been settling into a new fun group dynamic until James and Buck hit the first roadblock in their relationship almost a week ago when Buck went AWOL. I asked the guys to help find him and they ghosted me. However, now that their boss and my bestie are fully loved up and engaged, the guys have been messaging me nonstop in an attempt to make things right and I'm happy to let them grovel—at least for a little while longer.

Torrrriiiiiiiii

DANNY
We're bringing pizza

ANDERS
And ice cream

OZ
What's your favorite flavor.

WARRICK
You seem more like a cookie kind of a girl

DANNY

Come on, sexy, you know you forgive us, stop making us work so hard.

KNIGHT

We didn't do anything wrong. You've sent her six texts in less than a minute, most people don't type fast enough to reply straight away.

ANDER

We ignored her when the chief and his woman had their misunderstanding. That wasn't cool of us.

DANNY

And we've apologized.

WARRICK

More than once.

Giggling, I read the messages. I get why they ignored me; I even understand it. They picked their teammate and buddy's side, and I get it. I'd do the same to defend James. I forgave them almost immediately, but it's fun watching them try to get me to talk to them again.

Taking pity on them, I type out a message.

ME

I want ALLLLL the meat on my pizza, extra cheese, and I like cherry and chocolate ice cream. Nero wants Pepperoni.

A reply pops up immediately.

WARRICK

Cookies?

ME

If you bring the ingredients, I'll make some. Store bought cookies suck ass.

Shoving my cell into my pocket, I grab an armful of stuff and head upstairs to my room. Opening the door, I allow my eyes to graze over the new bedroom set that was delivered earlier today. Honestly, it's the bed of my six-year-old self's dreams, but when I saw it in the small antique store in town, I knew I had to have it.

It's a wrought iron four-poster, with ornate twists and flowers and patterns adorning the posts that rise into the air, with similar, smaller versions running up the headboard and footboard. Right now, it's bare, with just my mattress placed in the frame, but I can already envisage how it'll look once I've twined twinkle lights around it and draped almost translucent voile panels over the top.

I grew up about an hour away from here, not far from Boseman, which is the closest city to the small town of Rockhead Point—the place I've called home for the last five years. After I graduated, I moved here and worked for a couple of years as a private chef, but pastry has always been where my heart lay.

Part of the reason I accepted my current job in a small-town bakery was that when I interviewed for the position, the owner, Mrs. Yates, told me that she planned to retire and was looking to employ someone who would potentially be interested in buying the business when she stepped down.

We both knew that with my culinary arts degree, references from some of the top restaurants and academies in the country, and my skill in patisserie and pastry, I was extremely over qualified to make birthday cakes in rural Montana. But I've bided my time, gradually making small changes when I can, waiting for my chance to buy her out. Two days ago, it finally came.

Mrs. Yates pulled me into her office and told me she and

her husband were retiring and moving to Florida. As soon as the paperwork is signed next week, Yates Bakery will be all mine and I'll rebrand the store as Le Petite Patisserie. Not even Nero's Grumpy Cat personality can dull my excitement at finally having the free rein to bake and sell all of the things I've been dying to for years.

My business plan will maintain the bespoke celebration cakes I spend most of my time doing now, but I'll be able to fill the shop counter with things that are a little more exciting than muffins and snickerdoodles.

Kicking off my shoes, I grab the box marked bedding and start to make my bed, pulling sheets onto the mattress and comforter, then adding all the soft and fluffy pillows I simply had to have the moment I bought the bed. Once I'm done, I step back and smile widely. The bed is white perfection. Crisp white linens with a dozen throw cushions in a mix of fabrics, from ultrasoft faux rabbit fur to fleece, knit, and even silk.

The urge to shed my clothes and dive into the bed naked is almost too strong to resist, but I refrain, reaching for the next box and opening it. An hour later, the sound of noise downstairs alerts me to the presence of the others in the house, and I pause, pushing my hair back from my face with the back of my hand.

Almost all the boxes that Nero loaded into my room are empty and my new—much larger than I've ever had before—closet is full of my clothes and shoes. My makeup, toiletries and girly things are all placed neatly in the bathroom, and the majority of the knickknacks I brought with me, including my framed pictures and childhood teddy, are placed on the two small wall-mounted shelves.

The only boxes that are still sealed are the ones that are full of my books. I'm a reader. I have a Kindle, of course, but some books are so good that you just need to hold a physical copy. So, I have several boxes of books, some romance, some fantasy, and some practical cookbooks. Then I have my bibles. These are the hand written recipes that I've perfected over the years and my notes from culinary school. If I lost those, I honestly don't know what I'd do. I'm thirty, and I started my first notebook at the age of eight after I fell in love with baking when I spent the summer with my grandma in Louisiana.

My bibles hold a lifetime of knowledge and they're my pride and joy. Unfortunately, the one thing my new room lacks is any bookshelves, so, for now, the boxes will have to stay in the spare room until I can buy or make some storage to fit them all.

"Tori," someone calls out before the sound of feet pounding up the stairs echoes through the house. A moment later, two huge men barge into my bedroom, taking over the space and filling it with their larger-than-life presence.

"Hi Danny, hi Oz," I say in greeting, watching as the macho men take in my princess bed.

"Holy shit, your bed is like a prepubescent girl's dream." Danny snickers.

"I know, right?" I smile, not even slightly ashamed at his assessment. "I love it so much and eight-year-old me would be so jealous."

"It looks…soft," Oz says, his lips curled into a grimace.

"I guess it could be worse. It could be pink." Danny

shrugs.

"Let me guess, you guys have black or gray bed linens?" I ask, arching my brows at them.

"Navy," Oz admits.

"Black." Danny shrugs.

"Boring! Juvenile or not, my new bed is beautiful and I love it."

"After the explosion of rainbow-colored carnage you decorated the sexy new couch with downstairs, I expected it to be an ugly explosion of color up here too. So I guess the white could be worse." Danny smirks.

Sticking my tongue out at him, I roll my eyes. "Whatever. Why have you barged your way into my room without knocking?"

"Pizza's downstairs, come and eat. Has Nero set up the TV and his gaming system yet?" Oz asks.

"No clue, I've been up here unpacking," I say, not wanting to admit that Nero hasn't said more than a handful of words to me since the day we met. Or that he's basically ignored me since he arrived at my place this morning, then retreated to his room the moment the truck was empty.

"We brought beer too," Oz says.

"Cool. Let me just have a quick shower and get changed. I'll be down in five. Make sure you save me some pizza."

"Hurry up, I'm fucking starved," Danny says, turning and heading for the bedroom door.

"Get out then," I snark, playfully shoving at Oz's back as he shuffles after Danny and out of the room.

Five minutes later, I'm clean and wearing my comfy shorts and cropped sweater with my fuzzy socks. I may be surrounded by sexy-as-fuck firefighters, but I need to be comfy to eat pizza and drink beer. I still look cute, but dressed down and without makeup, I know I probably look closer to twenty than I do thirty.

I'm kind of a midget at five-three, with enough curves that it's clear I eat the cakes and goodies I bake. My hair is a mousy brown with natural blonde highlights. It hangs past my shoulders and is wavy in a way that always looks kind of a mess. My skin is a sea of inconvenient freckles that refuse to be hidden no matter how much concealer I use.

I'm cute but not sexy. Curvy but not voluptuous, and pretty but not gorgeous. Basically, I'm average, a healthy six out of ten, that can get to a seven and a half with a great dress and killer heels.

What I do have is great skin, great tits, a great personality, and the confidence that shows I actually like myself. I know I'm fun and bubbly and an awesome friend, which is why people like me. Well, most people, except of course for my new roommate.

Sliding my cell into the pocket of my shorts, I rush downstairs, my feet slipping a little on the hardwood floor when I hit the foyer.

"Here she is," Anders says loudly. "I saved you some pizza."

"Thanks." I smile, sidling up beside him and grabbing a slice of cheesy pizza straight from the box. "Mmmh, this is good," I say after the first bite, my mouth full of cheese, red sauce and chunks of meat.

Anders laughs, curling his arm around my neck and pulling me into his side. "Jesus, Tori, I fucking love watching you eat. You really don't give a fuck. It's awesome."

Not bothering to acknowledge him, I take another bite of pizza, humming happily at the greasy deliciousness. Danny hands me a beer while Warrick pushes a box with more pizza toward me across the counter. Several minutes later, when my stomach is full of greasy goodness, I spot Nero standing beside Knight on the other side of the kitchen, watching me with a scowl etched across his handsome face.

Ignoring my sour-faced new roomie, I glance around the room at all the hot firefighters. Six scorching hot men to stare at and use as bean-flicking material—who bring me beer and pizza.

Maybe living up here won't be as bad as I thought.

Chapter Three

Nero

What is it with this girl? My teammates are enamored with her and for the life of me, I just don't get why. Sure, she's pretty enough; short, with big, full tits and a perpetually happy personality that's so fucking peppy. I'm starting to wonder if she's mainlining coffee or just one of those freaky, permanently chipper people.

We moved into the house a week ago and when I went back to work, I was relieved to get away from her and her stiflingly cheerful aura. I've spent four peaceful days away from her, but now I have to go home and back to the house we share.

The moment I step foot through the door, it's clear that in my absence, she's made the house even more of a home. Her home.

The multicolored cushions she dumped on my couch the day she moved in have been moved. Now, all that remains are half a dozen throw pillows in various shades of reds, oranges and yellows, which look bright against the stark black leather. There's a large candle in a hurricane lamp on the coffee table and a rug with slashes of complimentary reds and oranges covering the floor.

Dropping my bag by the couch, I walk into the kitchen, finding the sides filled with more kitchen equipment than I've ever owned in my entire life. According to Buck, Tori works at the bakery in Rockhead Point, and when the guys came around the day we moved in, she made cookies that had Danny down on one knee proposing to her, so I guess they must have been good.

The house that was empty and heartless only days ago now feels like her home, and everything about that pisses me off. This isn't just her house, and she can't just claim all the space and make it her own.

Striding back over to the front door, I kick off my shoes, ignoring the shoe rack that wasn't there when I left for work four days ago, and leave them on the floor beside it. Inhaling sharply, I scowl at the sweet, cinnamon-apple scent that fragrances the air from a candle that's burning on the dining table and stomp angrily into the kitchen, opening the refrigerator and staring at the shelves full of food I didn't buy. "What the fuck is all this?" I snarl angrily.

"Food," she says from behind me.

Whirling around, I scowl. "You couldn't have left me a shelf to store my food?" I demand.

"I'm sorry, I guess I just assumed we'd take turns buying

groceries and eat them rather than label our own stuff like we're in college," she says dryly with an amused smile.

Gritting my teeth, I manage to swallow down the words that threaten to come out. Even though I wish I could, I don't tell her that I happily shared food with my college roommates because I actually liked them and wanted to live with them, *unlike her*.

"Look, Nero, I'm a baker and a chef. I like to cook. When I lived with James, I used the kitchen at the store to do my test bakes, but being so far up the mountain, it's harder for me to run to the bakery every time I get an idea for a new dessert. So how about I clear out the top shelf for you, and we agree that unless something has specifically got a label on it, I'm happy to share anything that's in there?"

She's being so fucking reasonable and instead of placating me, she's only making me angrier. "Whatever," I hiss, closing the refrigerator and straightening but not turning fully to face her.

"I was going to make some pasta for dinner. I'm craving carbs. Do you want to join me and we can set some housemate rules and boundaries," she suggests, smiling widely.

"I have plans," I growl, marching past her and up the stairs like an angsty teen running away from my parents. Stepping inside my bedroom, I close the door behind me before I take a full breath. I don't have any plans tonight, but I need to find some because I know I can't spend the night here with her and her happy fucking smiling face.

Stripping out of my shirt and pants, I flop down onto the mattress in just my boxers and socks. Leaning over the side of the bed, I pull my cell from my pants pocket and open up the group chat for my teammates. Normally, by now, someone would have posted about heading to a bar or something. Instead, there's a stream of messages between the guys and Tori, discussing plans for a *Call of Duty* death match at Danny's place tonight.

"Fuck," I hiss, dropping my cell to the comforter and staring up at the ceiling.

How has she managed to infiltrate every aspect of my life in such a short amount of time? She's living in my house, socializing with my friends, and filling my refrigerator with food that I can't eat.

I hate how much I hate her. I hate her smiling face and her bouncy tits, and how I noticed that she's not wearing a bra beneath her slouchy shirt when I tried my hardest not to look at her.

Buck's happiness is incredibly fucking important to me, he's my brother and my best friend, but right now, I almost wish he'd never met James, just so I could get rid of the ray of annoying fucking sunshine downstairs.

The moment I think it, I know I don't mean it. I like seeing my brother in love and happy, and even though I hate that James's ex-husband and ex-family-shaped baggage caused my brother so much pain, I like James too. I just wish that she didn't have to have an annoying sidekick that I'm now forced to live with.

My cell screeches out a sound that makes me groan. I changed the tone for any unknown numbers and now it blares out a warning siren anytime anyone I don't know calls or texts me, so I know to avoid answering. I know without looking that it's more than likely Miranda or one of her men. With Tori downstairs and Miranda refusing to leave me alone, I need to get out and find a distraction.

Forcing myself upright, I head for the bathroom and step into the shower the moment the water starts, not bothering to wait for it to warm. Washing myself quickly, I wrap a towel around my waist and head back to my room. Luckily, Rockhead Point isn't the type of town where you have to dress up to go to the bar, so I pull on some jeans and a plain white T-shirt, then sit down on the edge of the bed to pull on my socks and sneakers.

My hair is almost military short, so I just rub my hand over the short strands and call it good. I know what I look like. I'm tall, physically fit and attractive. I've never struggled to find female company, and that's what I need tonight to take my mind off all the changes that have taken place in my life in a short amount of time.

Shoving my cell into my pocket, I head down the stairs and out the front door, not even looking behind me to see if Tori is watching me go. Normally, I'd hit up my teammates to join me for a drink, but I don't want to risk one of them inviting Tori when she's who I want to avoid. So, instead, I unlock my car and slide behind the wheel.

When we first moved here, I didn't bother to bring my car, instead choosing to keep it in storage in Washington State, where we used to live. Since we're used to living and working together, I've been pretty happy sharing Buck's truck, but a few months back, I decided if this place was going to be home, I needed to ship my Shelby GT350R out to Montana.

If I hadn't pursued my desire to be a firefighter, I think I would have ended up working on cars in some capacity. I'm a self-confessed gearhead and the moment my butt hits the butter-soft suede seats, a sense of calm starts to settle over me.

I've always loved vintage American muscle cars and even a year after I first saw it, I still sigh appreciatively at Huck Barnett's Pontiac GTO whenever I head up to their place to see Juni. But I enjoy the comfort and convenience of a new car and my Shelby gives me the best of both worlds.

Pushing the button to start the car, I moan audibly as the engine burbles to life beneath me. Closing my eyes, I take a moment to appreciate the purr of the V8, allowing it to fill my soul with a feeling that only a true car lover can appreciate.

Eventually, I open my eyes and pull away from the house. The Shelby handles the winding mountain roads like it's riding on rails and I take the scenic route, driving for the sake of driving, until I eventually park in a space a block down from Barney's.

It's midweek, but the bar is still fairly busy, with music pouring from the old-fashioned jukebox in the corner. Sliding onto a seat at the bar, I nod to Barney, and he lifts a finger, telling me he'll be with me in a minute.

I want a shot of Jack Daniels, but I know I can't have one. There's only a handful of cabs in town and none of them will want to take my drunk ass back up the mountain, so when Barney ambles over to me, I order a beer, sipping it slowly and knowing I'll have to switch to soda after I've finished.

"Hi," a sultry-looking woman with fire-truck-red hair says as she slides onto the stool beside me.

"Hey," I say, running my eyes up and down her assessingly. I have no problem with assertive women. In fact, when I'm looking for a hookup, I enjoy being hit on or propositioned. In a long-term relationship, I think I'd probably end up falling into a more dominant roll, but tonight, all I'm looking for is distraction.

"I'm Nina." She smiles, holding out a hand with black-painted, pointed fingernails.

"Nero."

"I know who you are." Her eyes rake over me and when they lift to my face again, she licks her lips and exaggeratedly crosses her legs. Her outfit is pretty casual, with tight blue jeans and a tank top that's cropped just below her tits, showcasing her toned, flat stomach.

"You do?" I ask, flirting with her a little.

"You're one of the new firefighters."

"You've got me all figured out, huh? Can I buy you a drink?"

"Sure, I'll have a vodka, cranberry please."

Tipping my chin to Barney, I order Nina a drink and we make small talk for a while. She asks about my team, commenting several times about how hot we all are and how we should do a firefighters calendar, posed naked with just the fire hoses hiding our junk.

Her hand ends up on my arm, her pointed nails scraping up and down my bicep. "I love this," she says, curling her palm over my muscle and squeezing.

"Being physically fit is all part of the job."

"Do you have a six-pack? Can I see?" she asks eagerly.

"I have some definition," I admit.

Her hand grabs for the hem of my shirt and I stop her. "I'm pretty sure Barney wouldn't be impressed if you start trying to get me shirtless."

"My place is just around the corner. Why don't we head there and you can show me your abs and... any other muscles you'd like me to see?" Her wink is playful and flirty, straight to the point, and I have to appreciate her candor. She's clearly down to fuck, and even though she's on the verge of being too forward, hooking up is exactly why I'm here.

Lifting my glass to my lips, she watches me with hopeful eyes. Placing one talon-like nail under the bottom of my glass, she lifts it, tilting it until the last of my beer slides into my mouth.

Lifting her own glass, she downs the entire contents in one long gulp, then places the empty glass on the bar, slides off her stool and purses her lips. "Ready?"

Honestly, no, I'm not, but I place some cash on the bar for the drinks, then follow her to the exit.

For the last year, Miranda and I haven't committed to being exclusive, but I've only ever been a one-woman man, so while she might have been dating multiple men, I was only seeing her. She's the only woman I've had sex with in a year and, honestly, it feels all kinds of wrong as I take measured steps behind Nina. Her confident surety reminds me a little of Mir and I swallow down the lump of annoyance that I'm thinking about my ex as I follow this stranger to her home to hook up.

I don't feel like I'm cheating on Miranda. I know things are over between us and that I won't be betraying her by being with someone else. But still, it feels wrong. This isn't my first one-night stand. In my early twenties, I was a dog, making a game out of bagging women left, right, and center, but it's been years since I engaged in completely meaningless sex with a stranger.

Like she promised, her apartment is less than half a block from the bar and when she opens her door, I step inside, wrinkling my nose at the strong tobacco smell that permeates the air.

My dick is soft and the only thing that's brewing inside of me is a strong sense of revulsion. Objectively, Nina is an attractive woman and I'm sure plenty of men would love to be where I am right now. But despite her lithe, fit physique and overt sexuality, I'm not interested.

I have never been more grateful to hear the sound of the unknown number warning tone screeching from my cell phone than I am in this moment. Pausing in the hallway of the apartment, I pull my cell out, offering Nina a grimace. "I'm sorry, I have to take this."

Her brow furrows and a frown pulls down the corners of her lips, but she dutifully takes a step farther into the apartment while I stay where I am. Pressing the red button on my screen to decline the call, I lift my cell to my ear and talk into the silent phone.

"Hey." I pause, like I'm listening to someone speak. "Seriously?" I pause again. "No." Pause. "Fine. Okay, whatever, but you're seriously going to owe me one." Pause. "Fine, I'll be there in thirty minutes. Bye."

Nina turns around to face me. Like having her back to me prevented her from hearing every word I just said. Crossing her arms over her chest, she pouts.

"I'm sorry," I say with as much sincerity as I can. "Fitzy's had a situation and they need me to go to base and cover for him."

"You're seriously leaving?" she asks, shock clear on her face.

"I'm sorry."

I'm expecting her to nod or even tell me I'm an asshole, but instead, she shrugs out of her jacket, then pulls her shirt up and over her head, flashing me her very fake tits with a smirk. "Why don't you stay?" she says in a deliberately seductive tone.

"I'm sorry," I say again, shrugging.

"Seriously?" Nina says incredulously. It's clear she's not used to being turned down when she's half-naked.

Turning, I open the door, offer her a two-fingered wave and then leave, pulling the door closed behind me. The moment I'm back on the sidewalk, I inhale a deep breath of cool night air. Guilt hits me for a split second, but it's gone before it even really registers. Nina didn't deserve to be ditched the way I just did, but I'm guessing in ten minutes, she'll be back at Barney's looking for someone else to replace me with.

I could get in my car and find another bar, but the peace I found in the idea an hour ago has been ruined. Instead, I climb into the Shelby and form a plan to drive out of town and toward the mountain lake Cody Barnett told me about a few months ago.

Unlike the bigger, more accessible lakes, this one is small and kind of a pain to get to, but it's beautiful and hopefully quiet, which is exactly what I want right now. Stopping at the grocery store, I get a soda, then grab a burger and a piece of pie from Granny Annie's diner before jumping in my car and heading for the lake.

Just like I hoped, the gravel parking lot is empty when I get there, so I grab my food and drink and start the short hike to the water. Unlike the bigger lakes, there're no picnic areas or amenities, so I sit my butt down on the grass and watch the still water while I eat.

It doesn't take long for the calm of the lake to settle over me and when I exhale, my shoulders relax and I lie back, staring up at the inky blackness above me speckled with twinkling stars.

I love Montana. I didn't think I would, but I love the endless sky, mountains, and forests. Everything about living here makes my soul settle and I need it in a way I didn't appreciate until we moved here.

It's late by the time I collect my trash and walk back to my car. Jumpers Row is dark and silent when I climb out at the curb outside the house. Silently, I slide my key into the lock on the front door, then head for my bedroom, refusing to even glance in the direction of her room as I pass.

Chapter Four

Tori

My new roommate is an unmitigated asshole. After I suggested dinner and conversation, he declared he had plans and disappeared. Then he came back in the middle of the night and was still asleep when I got up and left for work this morning.

I doubt he'll comment on it, but I emptied half of the refrigerator after he left last night. I honestly don't understand why he was so pissy about there being food in there, but at least the guys all appreciated the snacks I took with me to Oz's place.

They all asked me what the matter was when I got there for our video game session, but I told them it was nothing. I'm not going to be the girl who bitches about her roommate to his friends. Instead, I ate junk food, followed by a cake that I mentally tweaked the recipe for while I was eating it, and then pretended every person I killed in Call of Duty was Nero.

The bout of violent, computer-generated warfare was surprisingly therapeutic, and I went to bed a lot less annoyed with Nero than I was earlier in the night. Hopefully, once we can get some clear ground rules set in place, we can avoid any more situations like yesterday. If not, then I might have to consider moving into the small apartment above my store.

Right now, it's just being used as storage for the old kitchen equipment Mrs. Yates no longer needs but refuses to throw away. Once the store is officially mine, I'll be having a serious cleanup. The tiny apartment has a bathroom, a small kitchen living space and two bedrooms, one of which Mrs. Yates currently uses as an office.

It wouldn't take much to make it livable and as I bought the building along with the business, I wouldn't have to worry about paying rent or commuting to work. Being so far away from James would suck, but she basically has to drive past the shop twice a day on her way to work, so it's not like we wouldn't see each other. Although it wouldn't be as often as when we'd been living together or next door to each other.

I'm meeting with my lawyers next week to finalize all the paperwork and sign my life away on the large loan I've taken out to be able to afford to buy the store and the building it's housed in.

Luckily, it's not as big a loan as it would have been if I hadn't gotten a large inheritance from my grandma when she passed. It seems fitting that the woman who inspired my love of baking also gave me the opportunity to be my own boss and own my own business.

Sliding the key into the door at the back of the building, I push it open and step into the storage room behind the kitchen. Hannah will have been in early to collect the pastries and cakes we supply to other local businesses, but the store itself won't open for another couple of hours.

When I first started working here, we used to stock the same things at the counter that we supplied to other local stores, but I changed that, and now the only place to get our most popular goodies is right here in the shop. Stepping into the kitchen, I switch on the lights, then move down the row of commercial ovens, turning them on one by one until everything is set up and ready for me to get started.

Baking, for me, is therapeutic. It's my happy place, and an hour later, when I'm pulling the second batch of cupcakes out of the oven, I'm smiling and singing along to the radio I have on in the mornings before the shop opens.

Mrs. Yates employs a handful of counter staff, but until I came along, she ran the kitchen single-handedly. For about six months, we worked side by side. Then she confessed she'd lost her love for baking and the store, which was why she'd employed me.

Being the only baker is tough, and the first thing I plan to do after I take over is to employ someone to make the basic cakes and cookies. Then, I'll be able to concentrate on the more complex patisserie items that I plan to start selling the moment the business is officially mine.

Right now, I batch cook the night before my days off,

and Mrs. Yates just frosts the cupcakes in the mornings before the store opens. I hate knowing that on those days, the products aren't fresh, but I'm only contracted for forty hours a week, so unless I want to work for free, there's nothing I can do.

It's another two hours before the counter is full of delicious-looking goodies and I smile to Daniel, who's busily setting up the till before I head up to the roof for my break with a cup of coffee in my hand. A gentle exhale falls from my lips as I push the door open and step out onto the roof. I brought a few lawn chairs and a rickety table up here a while back, and now it's where I spend all my breaks when the weather is dry. As soon as the building is officially mine, I want to start a small roof garden up here so I can grow fresh herbs and plants rather than buying them.

The sun is bright and I sit down, propping my feet up on the table. Tipping my head back, I close my eyes, trying to absorb as much vitamin D as I can while I cradle my mug of coffee in my hands. It's quiet up here, even though the street below is busy with tourists milling around and discovering the treats Rockhead Point has to offer.

My family lives less than an hour from here. My parents divorced when I was younger, but they stayed good friends and co-parented me and my four brothers like a well-oiled team. They got back together about five years ago, which is weird but works for them. I knew after culinary school that I wanted to settle in Montana, and Rockhead Point is close enough to go and visit them when I'm not working.

Unlike me, my brothers are all spread over the country. I'm the middle child between two sets of twins. My older brothers, Atticus and Felix, are three years older than me, and my younger brothers, Jude and August, are three years younger. We're all single, and every time any of us speak to my mom or dad, they ask us when they should expect grandbabies.

Atticus is a tattoo artist and Felix is a sculptor. They both live in California. Jude and August are professional hockey players playing for Nashville. I don't really tell many people that they play hockey for a living because once people find out you have professional athletes in the family, they change, and I've been duped more than once by women befriending me just to get close to them.

I miss them all, and I'm hoping eventually all of my brothers will move back to Montana so we can be closer again. We have a sibling group chat and video call at least once a week, but it's not the same as being around them in person.

Drinking the last of my coffee, I stand from my seat and head back downstairs to get started on the three-tier wedding cake I need to make. When the cake is baked and on the rack to cool, I head for Mrs. Yates's office.

Since we agreed on a price and started the paperwork for me to buy the business and property, I've been meeting with her for a couple of hours each afternoon so she can—in her words—*Teach me the business side of running a store*.

This is basically her spending two hours a day showing me how to run inventory, order supplies and pay taxes. I don't have the heart to explain that I already know how to do all of these things because, at the end of the day, I don't want to piss her off before the final signatures are on the sale agreement. Plus, she's a lovely lady and she's trusting me to take over a business that she's poured years of her life into.

When my eyes are heavy, I wave goodbye to her and leave her office, heading back to the kitchen. I'm supposed to finish at three because I came in at seven. But I spend half an hour wrapping up the wedding cake I'll decorate tomorrow and then prep ingredients for the morning.

The key to being a successful commercial baker is organization, and I like to make sure I have things set and ready to go for the next day, so I don't have to waste time in the morning when I get in.

My mind is twitching with the need to experiment, and as I grab my jacket and purse, I turn toward the grocery store instead of my car. The moment I lift up a basket, I remember Nero's angry expression last night and sigh wearily. I'm not sure I want to piss him off any more than I already have, especially when I don't have anywhere else to live, at least not for a few weeks.

Starting to lower the basket to the pile again, I pause, step to the side and pull out my cell. I'm in a group chat with all of Buck and Nero's teammates, but I also have all of their numbers. Danny or Oz wouldn't have a problem with me using their kitchens, especially if I let them eat the results of my experiments, but I'll also have to deal with their company, and for me, baking is a solitary experience.

So, instead, I pull up a number I haven't used before and hit dial.

"Yes," Knight answers. No greetings or platitudes, just straight to the point.

"Hi Knight, I hope it's okay that I called. I was actually

hoping for a favor."

"What do you need?"

This is why I called him. I wouldn't say we're exactly friends, but then I get the impression Knight isn't the type of man who has many close female friends.

"I was wondering if I could use your kitchen. I'll clean up after myself and I'll cook you dinner as a thank-you afterward."

"You have a kitchen," he says simply.

"I do, but I don't think Nero will appreciate me using the kitchen for experimental baking for work."

"I'm not good company," Knight states with a hint of something that sounds almost close to regret in his tone.

"That's fine. I'm not looking for company, just a kitchen space to use."

"Okay. I don't have baking things though."

"I'll bring everything I need. What's your favorite meal? I'll make it for you."

"I don't have a favorite."

"Okay, well, what do you enjoy?"

"Food," he says simply, like it's the most obvious thing in the world.

"Okay." I smile. "I'll make good food then."

"Fine."

"Fine," I say back. "I'm just at the grocery store. Would it be okay for me to come to yours in about an hour?"

"Okay."

"Thank you, Knight. I really appreciate this."

"Goodbye." He ends the call before I have a chance to speak again.

His bluntness reminds me of my brother Felix and as I start to pick up ingredients, I'm smiling the entire time.

Just over an hour later, I'm knocking on Knight's door. He answers it immediately like he has been standing behind it waiting for me to arrive. And if he's as similar to Felix as I think he is, he probably has. "Sorry I'm late."

"Come in."

He doesn't bother to offer to take the large box full of ingredients and baking equipment from me and I don't expect him to. Instead, I push the door closed behind me and follow him into the kitchen.

I've been inside Danny and Oz's houses, and they've both made the places their homes, with pictures and personal items, but Knight's place looks like it's waiting for someone to move in.

The walls are all white, with no paintings, pictures, or adornments and the room looks bare except for a black leather couch and a TV on the wall. The kitchen counters are entirely empty and it's so clean it looks brand new.

"Do you need anything?" he asks, his hands in his pockets.

"No, thank you. What time do you usually have dinner?"

"Nineteen hundred."

"Okay, I'll have it ready for that time."

"Are we eating together?" he asks, his brow furrowed.

"That's entirely up to you. Dinner is my gift for you allowing me to use your kitchen. I'll make enough for both of us, but if you prefer to eat alone, I can take mine home with me."

"We can eat together," he says.

"Okay. Do you eat at the table or the breakfast bar?"

His brow furrows again like he's confused, so I smile. "My older brother, Felix, is very particular about how, when, and where he eats. You remind me of him, so I thought I'd ask you what I'd ask him."

"You have a brother?"

"I have four brothers, two older, two younger."

"I eat at the breakfast bar."

"Perfect." I smile.

"This isn't a date." His gruff tone only makes me smile even wider.

"No, this isn't a date. This is a thank-you and hopefully the start of us being friends."

"Nineteen hundred," he says with a nod, then turns and walks away.

Two hours later, the tray of white chocolate and passionfruit tarts looks decadent and delicious while the scent of rich cheese, garlic, and chicken fills the air. Just like I expected, Knight reappears and seats himself on a stool at the breakfast bar at exactly nineteen hundred hours, and I place the plate of chicken parmesan with roasted broccoli and brussels sprouts in front of him.

"Beer or water?" he asks, getting up from his seat to get drinks.

"Beer, please," I say, sliding onto the stool beside his and waiting for him to return.

A moment later, he hands me a beer, then sits back down and doesn't look at me again before he starts to eat. I wait a minute, then when he doesn't comment or spit it out, I start to eat too.

I gave Knight a large portion, but he easily clears his plate. "There's more chicken in the pan if you want it," I tell him.

Standing, he takes his plate to the pan and serves himself more chicken and more veggies before sitting back down and continuing to eat in silence. I guess to some people, the lack of conversation would be awkward or disconcerting, but I'm used to it. In fact, I find his quiet company incredibly relaxing.

By the time he's eaten his second plate, mine is empty. "Was that okay?"

"You can use my kitchen anytime you need. I like mac and cheese. But you can cook this again too."

"I make great mac and cheese and an even better roast lamb."

He turns to look at me, his expression neutral. "When do you want to use the kitchen again?"

I smile, and a soft chuckle bursts free. "How about the day after tomorrow?"

"Good." He nods.

"Good." I nod back. "Would you like to try one of the tarts I made? The recipe's not a hundred percent yet, but I think they'll be pretty good."

"Yes, please." He nods.

Jumping up, I take our plates to the sink, then put a tart on each of the dessert plates I'd already set out, adding a scoop of whipped cream on the side of each before passing one to Knight and sitting down beside him again.

Just like before, I wait for him to cut off a bite and eat. For me, half the joy of baking is watching others enjoy my food. It makes me feel like I've achieved something to know I've created a cake or tart, or whatever, that people enjoy and want to eat. If I was feeding someone other than Knight, I'd probably ask them a hundred questions about the texture, flavors, and overall appeal. But I don't do that now. I just sit quietly and watch him devour it, smiling widely to myself, my heart full.

He finishes the first tart in a couple of moments, then turns to me, his eyes glancing to the tray of six other small tarts sitting on the counter.

"Help yourself," I tell him.

He moves faster than I expected, putting another tart on his plate and a large scoop of cream.

"You like it?" I ask tentatively.

"Yes," he says quickly. "Do you sell these at the store you work at?"

"No, not at this minute."

"Why not?" he asks between bites.

"Mrs. Yates likes to stock muffins, brownies, and pastries. She thinks that's what people want."

"I want another of these," he says, lifting the last bite into his mouth.

"You like them that much?" I ask.

"Yes." He nods.

"I told you to help yourself." I gesture to the tray and he takes another.

"You should put these in the store," he says confidently.

"Can I tell you a secret that no one else knows?" I say, feeling the need to confide in this man, who isn't quite a stranger but not yet a friend.

"Yes," he says, his eyes turning serious, his full attention focused on me.

"I'm buying the store where I work. The business and the building it's in. I'm signing the final sale paperwork next week."

For the first time since I met him, Knight smiles, and his face changes from intense and brooding to gorgeous and light. I've always thought he was attractive, but when he smiles, he's blindingly good-looking. "Congratulations. If you sell these, I'll buy them."

"Thank you." I smile back.

Chapter Five

Nero

After I woke up this morning, I opened one of the kitchen cabinets, searching for coffee filters, and found it full of cooking equipment. Machines I've never seen before, more baking pans than anyone could ever need, and just about every piece of cooking paraphernalia that you could ever own.

A part of me wishes I could bitch her out for filling the kitchen, but each item is carefully arranged and organized with nothing haphazard or messy and one double cabinet has been left entirely empty. After I got up, I went down to town and bought groceries. After paying for my food, I started feeling like an asshole for the way I treated Tori last night, so I stopped by the store she works at, hoping to see her and apologize, but she wasn't in the front serving like I expected.

Yates Bakery is a small place with a counter full of cakes, Danishes, and sweet treats. The guy behind the counter smiled widely when he served me, but if Tori was there, she must have been out back or taking a break and I didn't bother to ask for her, intending to speak to her when she got home.

I was in the yard when she got back from work, and when I heard the door close, a part of me assumed she'd seek me out, but she never even glanced around or looked for me. Peering around the door, I watched her pull a box from somewhere before she loaded it with things from the kitchen cabinets.

When I stepped inside, she looked at me, smiled, then turned and left again, not bothering to speak. Curious, I watched through the window as she grabbed some bags from her car, put them in the box with the other stuff, then walked three doors down and knocked on the door.

That was three hours ago. What the hell is she doing at Knight's? And why is she still there? Knight doesn't do girlfriends or dates. Hell, I don't think he even does one-night stands. He's weird, cold, almost emotionless, but he's a damn fine smoke jumper and a good dude once you get past the fact that he barely speaks and sometimes doesn't get social cues.

If she'd gone to any of my other teammates' places, I'd get it. They like her and she likes them. But Knight? It doesn't make any sense.

Could they be dating?

I don't know why that thought pisses me off, but it does. Tori and Knight would be totally wrong for each other. He barely speaks and she never shuts up. She'd drive him crazy and when he lost his shit and told her to stop talking, she'd cry.

No. Just no.

I've almost made the decision to go and knock on his door, just to find out what the fuck is going on, when the front door opens and Tori strolls inside, still carrying the box.

She jolts in shock when she spots me standing in front of her. "Oh, fuck, you scared me," she gasps. "Why are you lurking behind the door?"

"I wasn't," I snap, annoyed at her and Knight and everything.

Sidestepping me, she walks into the kitchen and starts to unpack the things from the box, placing them carefully back into the cabinets while I hover behind her.

"Dinner," I snap.

Ignoring me, she lifts the last thing from the box.

"Dinner," I say again, louder.

Standing, she turns to face me. "I'm sorry?" she says, confused.

"Have you had dinner?"

"Oh." Her expression clears. "Yes, I've eaten. I'm sure you've seen it by now, but I cleared off the top shelf in the refrigerator for you and some of the cabinets. I'll make sure not to take over all the space in here again. Feel free to use any of my cooking equipment, but if you break anything, please just let me know. I've ordered some racking for the garage and as soon as it comes, I'll move everything out there. I know it's all consuming the kitchen right now."

"That's—"

"I'm used to living with James and she didn't really use the kitchen, so I kind of just claimed it as mine. I'm sorry, I wasn't thinking about how things would be different living with you. I'll be more considerate going forward."

"I—" I start.

"I have to be up early, so I'll see you later." Then she leaves, taking her box with her, without letting me say anything.

She really doesn't ever shut up. I was trying to speak and she just talked over me, then had the audacity to just leave without even giving me a chance to say what I needed to.

Part of me wants to go after her. It's not late, barely even nine p.m. She won't actually be going to sleep. But then I realize she's probably going to her room to get away from me, or at least so I can't be an asshole to her again. Guilt lies heavy in my stomach and instead of following her upstairs, I go back to the living room and stare blankly at the show that's playing on the TV.

She's gone again by the time I get up the next morning, and I resolve to make peace with her today. Living with a virtual stranger is hard enough without us actively trying to avoid each other.

After showering and eating a bowl of cereal from the box that's now stored in the kitchen cabinet Tori emptied for me, I head next door, knock, then open the front door. Even though it's only been a few days, I miss living with my brother. I know most siblings couldn't stand to work and live together, but Buck and I have never behaved like typical siblings.

Sure, at times, we drive each other crazy, but we're close, and it's weird feeling like I have to knock on the door of the house I shared with him a week ago. "Bro," I shout, taking a step through the door and then pausing in the hall.

"In here," Buck calls from deeper in the house and I head for the kitchen, assuming he'll be in there. "Coffee?" he asks. "And did you knock?"

"I don't live here anymore," I remind him.

"Yeah, but you knocking is just weird."

"You wouldn't be saying that if I walked in on you fucking James on the couch."

"I'd cut your fucking eyes out," he growls.

"Exactly." I laugh. "So, from now on, I'll knock."

A growl comes from him as he slides a mug of coffee across the counter to me, and I roll my eyes and laugh. "So how is almost married life?"

"Fucking perfect, but it'll be completely perfect once I actually marry her."

"What's the rush?" I ask. "You've only known her for a month and you've already got your ring on her finger."

"Because she's mine and I want the entire fucking world to know."

Blinking, I stare at my brother. I knew he felt this way. He told me before he chased James to Vegas and came back engaged, but seeing the ferocity on his face is a little shocking. I've never felt so sure about a woman that I wanted the entire world to know she was mine. Even with Miranda, I never worried about her dating other men, although at times when she wasn't available when I wanted to see her, I did think it might be nice not to have to share her.

His surety only makes me more aware that Mir wasn't ever going to be my *one*, and a tiny pang of something that feels a little like jealousy taps at my heart. I'm not jealous of him and James. She's nice enough, but not my cup of tea. But I think, maybe one day, I might want to find someone who makes me so confident that she's the one for me.

"So, how're things with Tori?" Buck asks, pulling me from my inner thoughts.

Dragging in a deep breath, I exhale audibly.

"Fuck, that bad?" Buck asks, his eyes wide.

"Not *that* bad."

"But bad?"

"It's not great, to be honest," I admit.

"Tori's great. What exactly is the problem?"

"She's loud."

"Really?" he asks, his brows pulled together.

"She's taken over the house with throw pillows and rugs and all her stuff everywhere."

"Throw pillows and rugs?" He snickers.

"Yes. All over my brand-new couch. And the kitchen is full of cooking stuff."

"Well fuck me, bro. How fucking dare she put cooking equipment in the kitchen? The nerve of the woman."

"When I got home the other night, the refrigerator was completely full of her food," I say emphatically.

"Food that was specifically hers?" he asks.

Pausing, I purse my lips. "Well, no."

"So, she bought food for you both and you're offended by that?" His confusion is clear and it only makes me feel like more of an asshole.

"I mean…" I trail off.

"Did she label stuff… or?"

"No, she said I was welcome to anything," I confess sullenly.

"Nero, I'm going to be honest. I don't really know what your issue is. She stocked the refrigerator. It's hardly an inexcusable offense. Honestly, it sounds pretty good; else, you'd have gotten off shift to an empty house and had to go and buy groceries before you could eat."

"Fine. Whatever," I snap.

"Bro, explain it to me because I'm struggling to see the problem."

"I just…" I swallow, then sigh. "I just don't like her. She's so fucking—"

"Nice, attractive, funny, easygoing?" Buck interrupts me, trying to fill in the blank when I struggle to find the right words to describe her.

"Sunshiny," I say finally.

"You have an issue with her being too… sunshiny?" he asks slowly. "Have you turned into Knight and I didn't notice?"

"Fuck you," I snarl. "And Knight definitely doesn't have a problem with her. In fact, I think they're dating."

"You think who are dating?"

"Tori and Knight."

"Wow," Buck says slowly, his expression turning pensive before he shrugs. "It wouldn't have been my first guess, but I get why he might be interested in her."

"You do? Because I can't see it. Knight hates loud, he

hates disorder, he hates most things."

"Why do you think they're dating?"

"Because she spent three hours at his place last night."

My brother turns pensive again, then shrugs. "Good for them. If it works out, maybe she'll move in with him and you can have next door to yourself."

"Seriously," I blurt. "That's all you have to say? It's Knight. I've never seen him with a woman, and honestly, I wouldn't be surprised to find out he's still a virgin, and you're just okay with Tori sliding into his life and taking advantage of him?" I hiss angrily.

"Take advantage of him?" Buck laughs. "Knight is a thirty-seven-year-old man. He's not a fucking virgin and he's more than capable of holding his own and deciding who he wants to spend time with."

"How do you know he's not a virgin?" I demand.

"Because he's one of my team and I talk to him," Buck hisses.

"You talk about his sex life?"

"Of course not. But he did explain a little about himself, including his sexual orientation and a little about his background, when he interviewed for the job. But we both know this isn't about Knight. This is about Tori and your issues with her. I've never known you to take an instant dislike to someone, so what's really bugging you about her? Are you attracted to her? Is it a sex thing?"

"No," I scoff. "It's not a sex thing. I just don't like her."

"Bro, you're not home half the week. Can't you just be polite and avoid her the rest of the time? She's at work all day, so it's only a few hours on the evenings we're not on shift that you have to cohabit in the house at the same time. Maybe if you give her a chance, she'll grow on you."

"I shouldn't have to tiptoe around her when it wasn't my choice to share a house with her in the first place," I snap.

Sighing, Buck scrubs his hand over his eyes. "I know. I'm sorry. This is my fault, but I knew having Tori up here would make it an easier move for James. I need her with me. I can't stand the idea of being away from her and I can't move down to town and be thirty minutes from base if there's an emergency. But you're right. I forced this on you. Why don't you move back in here and I'll see if I can find something for me and James halfway between here and town."

"No," I exhale, feeling like an asshole again. "It's fine. It's only the first week. I'll give it some time. I'm sure I can make it work next door with her."

"No, it wasn't fair of me to just expect you to move in with a complete stranger just because I wanted James here."

"Look, it's done now. If it doesn't work out, I was already planning to try and buy a piece of property and settle here when I retire from the service. I can bring that plan forward and build myself a cabin."

Buck doesn't look convinced, but he nods cautiously. "You plan to settle here?"

"Juni isn't leaving. The Barnetts are Rockhead Point through and through, so what better place to live than close enough to family that I can be a part of our nieces' and nephews' lives? I don't want to be the uncle they only see at Thanksgiving."

"I get it. I want my kids to grow up with Juni's and the rest of the Barnetts too. Imagine how great a childhood it would be to have all your cousins around you."

"You want kids?" I ask, a little surprised.

"As soon as I can. James will be pregnant the moment I give her my last name if I have my way."

My brows lift so quickly it feels like they touch my hairline. I have never heard my brother talk about getting married, settling down, and having kids before. But then I guess he's never been serious about a woman before either. I'm pleased for him, but at the same time, it feels like he's moving on with his life and leaving me behind.

"Fuck." I snicker, then sober. "I'm happy for you."

"Thanks." A dry laugh falls from his lips and he smirks. "Beau thinks the Barnett love at first sight legacy has moved on to the jumpers now all the Barnetts are wifed up, so maybe you'll be next."

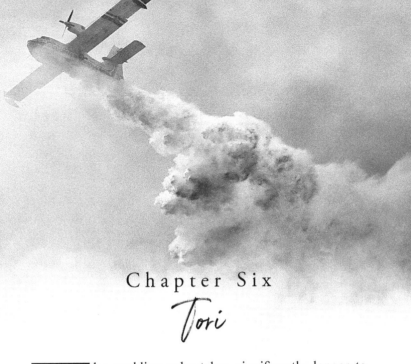

Chapter Six

Tori

The wedding cake takes significantly longer to finish than I anticipated and it's late when I slow my car to a stop outside the house. My fingers are sore from making icing flowers, my shoulders ache from being hunched over the marble counter all day, and my stomach is growling and empty.

I definitely consider myself a perfectionist, and there was no way I was allowing the Lowenstein wedding cake to leave the store until I was one-hundred-percent happy with it. There are some cakes that allow you to hide imperfections or even incorporate them into a design. But a white-on-white cake doesn't allow for even a slight margin of error.

Mrs. Yates told me to go home, but, for me, the small details are what sets us apart from all the other cake stores. I go the extra mile to make our customers' celebration cakes as perfect as possible, and they notice. It's why repeat clients on custom cakes have increased by two hundred percent since I started working at the bakery.

Climbing out of my car, I pad wearily to the front door, unlock it and step inside. Kicking off my shoes, I place them on the rack, taking my purse with me as I head to the kitchen.

The TV is on and Nero is sitting on the couch, a bottle of beer in his hand and a bowl of popcorn on his lap. "Hey," I say as I move past him, putting my purse on the counter before opening the refrigerator and pulling out the ingredients to make a quick pasta dish.

"You're late," Nero says.

"Yeah," I answer. I don't have the energy to fight with him right now. I just want to make my dinner, then take a bath and go to bed.

"Where have you been?"

Glancing over my shoulder, I jolt when I find him on the other side of the breakfast bar.

"Work."

"You have my number. Text if you're going to be late so I don't end up calling the cops thinking you've gone missing or crashed your car halfway up the fucking mountain," he growls.

Blinking, I shake my head. "I'm sorry. What?"

"You heard me. It's common fucking decency to let your roommate know if you're going to be late." He walks away before I can even process his words.

What the hell was that? Was that his way of telling me he was worried about me? Or is he just finding another reason to be an asshole to me? I honestly don't know. For the most part, I'm an easygoing person and I consider myself a great housemate. Sure, we had the issue with the refrigerator, but I've been mindful about clearing space for him and even ordered racking for the garage so my cooking equipment isn't taking over the kitchen.

But it feels like no matter what I do, he's finding reasons to be a dick, and I'm just not sure why. I'm still contemplating his behavior as I pour my pasta onto my plate and start to eat, leaning against the counter.

When my cell beeps, it's a text from the Lowensteins telling me how over the moon they are with the cake. All of my perturbed thoughts about Nero dissolves, replaced by the sense of achievement that always accompanies a happy customer, and I'm smiling widely when I head upstairs, passing Nero as he heads for his bathroom.

The house is dark and quiet when I pad into the kitchen the next morning. Setting the coffeepot to brew, I whip up a quick batch of eggs and eat them at the breakfast bar while I text with James.

She only lives next door, but I haven't seen her at all since Buck's been off shift and at home with her. I don't blame them for wanting to spend all of their time together, but after living with her for the last three years, I miss her.

Opening up the shop, I stow my stuff and get to work with renewed vigor after last night's success with the wedding cake. Turning the radio up loud, I dance around, singing along to the music as I cream, stir, and whisk, filling cupcake tins and trays with soon-to-be delicious treats.

An hour later, the kitchen smells of cinnamon and apple

from the cupcakes I've just pulled from the oven, and the comforting smell only makes me even happier.

"Good morning, dear," Mrs. Yates says, turning the volume down on the radio as she passes through the kitchen and toward the stairs to her office.

"Good morning, Mrs. Yates. Did you have a good night?"

"Yes, thank you, dear. Mr. Yates and I did a virtual tour of the condo we're going to be living in when we move to Florida.

"Oh, that's exciting." I smile.

"I can't wait. No more Montana winters. Sunshine and warm days all year round."

"Sounds lovely, but I think I'd miss the snowy mornings and frosty nights."

"Were the Lowensteins happy?" she asks. "The cake was stunning, as always."

"Very happy. They texted me last night to let me know how pleased they were." I beam.

"Wonderful. Something smells delicious, what is it?"

"Coffee and walnut muffins. It's been a while since I made them and the produce guy convinced me to try his new nut guy."

"Lovely." She nods absentmindedly, reaching up to open the door to the stairs and disappearing through it.

If I thought she was interested, I'd explain how I plan to start introducing not only a muffin of the day but also a matching themed drink too. Normally, we only sell basic filter coffee, so we're not in direct competition with Wake Up and Go Go, the coffee shop down the street. But I think if we just offer one drink a day, matched to the theme of the treat of the day, then we won't encroach onto their sales and vice versa.

With Mrs. Yates safely ensconced in her office, I turn up the radio and get back to work. By the time I'm pushing through the doors to the roof on my break, I can't keep the smile from my face. Some days are just good days, and today is one of them.

I'm still smiling as I skip out the door and head down the street to the grocery store at the end of the day. Knight texted me this morning to ask me what time I'd be getting to his place, and when I told him I'd be there at seventeen hundred, he sent me back a thumbs-up emoji.

He said he likes mac and cheese, but I saw the excitement in his eyes when I mentioned roast lamb, so I've decided to make that instead. I want to try out some mini mousse cake recipes for the store so I can make them while the lamb roasts.

I have to go to three different stores to get everything I need, but I'm still home earlier than I expected, just after four p.m. The house is empty when I open the door, but Nero's car is parked on the street, so he must be around somewhere.

Armed with the box from the other day, I start sorting through the cupboards, grabbing all the things I need. Sliding my KitchenAid across the counter, I grunt when the full weight lands in my arms. It's too big to be hauling around, but I know I won't be happy with the consistency of the mousse if I don't use it.

I'm paused by the front door, debating how Knight will

feel about me arriving early when the handle turns and the door swings inward. Taking a step backward, I try to avoid getting hit by the door but end up stumbling, landing on my butt on the floor, the heavy box in my lap.

"What the hell are you doing?" Nero growls.

"I fell." I giggle.

"Why are you laughing?"

"Because I fell on my butt," I say through a laugh.

Stomping over to me, he effortlessly lifts the heavy box off me, then clamps his hands on my waist, hauling me off the floor and back onto my feet like I weigh nothing.

"What are you doing with this stuff?" he demands gruffly.

"I'm taking it with me," I say, still giggling despite his furrowed brow and serious expression.

"Taking it where?"

"To Knight's."

"Why?"

"So I can make us dinner." Bending down, I haul the box into my arms again and head for the front door. I'm still early, but I'm hoping it won't be too much of an issue for Knight. If it is, I can always drop the stuff off and then go back at five to start cooking.

Nero follows me out the door and to my car, pausing at my side when I open the trunk and grab the bags of groceries. Adding them to the already heavy box, I balance it precariously in my arms, walking cautiously and trying not to fall again before I make it to Knight's.

"Stop. For fuck's sake, you're going to end up on your ass again," he snaps, snatching the box from my arms and almost making me fall when he throws me off balance. Storming past me, he slams his fist against Knight's door, shoving the box into his chest the moment he opens it.

Knight's expression is bewildered as Nero turns on his heel and storms down the path and back into the house we share, slamming the door behind him.

"You're early," Knight says.

"I know. Is that okay?"

Knight pauses, clearly thinking about it for a minute. "It's fine. Come in."

Just like the last time I was here, Knight leaves me alone as soon as my things are in the kitchen, and I don't see him again until exactly nineteen hundred hours when he appears silently and slides into his seat at the breakfast bar.

We eat side by side, drinking beer from the bottle and it's… nice… peaceful.

"Tell me about your brother," Knight says, surprising me as he eats his second helping of lamb.

"Which one?"

"The one you said I reminded you of."

"His name is Felix, he's three years older than me and he's an artist."

"What kind of art?"

"Sculpture mainly, although he paints too, he just doesn't sell those."

"Is he famous? Would I recognize anything he's sculpted?"

"He mainly sells to private collectors, but he's done a few exhibitions and installations at galleries. His pieces are beautiful." I smile. "I have some pictures of work he's done on my phone if you'd like to see."

"I'd like to see," Knight says, leaning into me when I pull my cell from my pocket and show him some pictures of the abstract creatures Felix creates.

"What is it?" he asks.

"Apparently, this one is a male sea creature, but it just looks like a well-endowed merman." I laugh. "He's been in a mythical underwater creatures phase for the last six months. Before that, he did animals. Horses, unicorns, dragons, that kind of thing."

"I don't really understand art," he confesses.

"Me either, but I love my brother's mind and that he can create these things with his hands just from his imagination."

Knight nods. "Tell me about your other brothers."

"Felix's twin is called Atticus. He's the oldest by six minutes and he's been talking about how important that is his entire life. He's an amazing tattoo artist and a great brother. My other brothers are twins too. Jude and August are professional athletes. I don't get to see them as much as I wish I did. I miss them."

"You're close." Knight says, a statement more than a question.

"Very. We video chat at least once a week, but I wish they all lived closer so I could see more of them. Do you have any siblings?"

"No," Knight says, his expression becoming even more shuttered than normal.

"I made a few varieties of chocolate mousse cakes that we can have for dessert. Chocolate and black cherry, chocolate, peanut butter and white chocolate peppermint."

"Yes," Knight says.

"Which did you want to try?"

"How many did you make?"

"Four of each."

"Then one of each," he says, his mouth pulling up at the corners.

Laughing, I pull the small mousse pots from the refrigerator and watch as Knight devours them all. When we've finished and Knight has convinced me to leave all the leftover mousse cakes for him, I wash the dishes, then load all of my cooking stuff into the box I brought it in.

"Are you using my kitchen to avoid Nero?" Knight asks, shocking me.

"He's not my biggest fan." I smile. "Thank you for letting me cook here. I sign the papers for the store next week, so I can use the kitchen there to experiment instead."

"Is he being mean to you?" Knight asks, his tone raised and as close to angry as I've heard from him since we met.

Pausing, I turn to look at him, considering his question. "Not mean exactly. But I know us living together wasn't his choice. Buck sort of forced me on him so that James would move up here. It just feels easier if I stay out of his way. He's only there less than half the time, but it's still awkward sharing space with someone who clearly doesn't want me there. But my store comes with an apartment above it, so I might move in there once the sale goes through."

"You can use my kitchen as much as you like."

"Thank you, Knight, I appreciate that."

"You still have to make mac and cheese," he reminds me.

"Well, if I move in above the store, you can come and have dinner at my new place. I'll make mac and cheese and you can taste test the new dishes I plan to start selling in the store."

"Okay."

"Okay." I smile. "Stay safe over the next few days."

"I always do," he says, like it's the most obvious statement in the world.

Saying goodbye, I slip out of the door and make my way back to my house, balancing the box on my hip as I turn the key in the lock and push it open. Nero is sitting on the couch, watching me as I step into the house.

"Hey," I say politely, heading to the kitchen to unpack my cooking supplies.

"What are you doing with Knight?" Nero snarls, prowling toward me, his enormous frame looming over me in the dimly lit room.

"Excuse me?"

"You heard me. What are you doing with Knight? If you're fucking him, the others need to know. We don't share women and we don't allow them to fuck with our team." His voice is so hard, it's like jagged shards of glass.

Blinking, I stare up at him, then shake my head and bend down to slide my KitchenAid into the cabinet.

"I'm serious. I won't let you screw Knight over and then think you can move on to Danny or Oz. Our team is a family and I won't let you fuck us over like that."

A disbelieving scoff falls from my lips as I straighten and turn to face him. "Firstly, what I do or do not do with Knight is absolutely none of your business. Secondly, are you seriously suggesting my plan is to have sex with the members of your team and then tick them off a list like I'm playing bingo and their names are part of a full house? Is Buck the bonus number? Do I win a prize if I fuck my best friend's fiancé?"

His lips part, but I have no interest in hearing anything he has to say. He's made it very clear what his opinion of me is.

"I don't get what exactly I've done to make you dislike me so much. I'm likable and not—like you've suggested—because I have sex with every person I'm nice to. You've been a sullen asshole since the first day I met you and I don't get why. I know that us living together is not exactly the dream for either of us, but with my job and yours, we barely have to tolerate each other for a couple of hours a day, a couple of days a week, and yet for some reason, you still seem determined to be as much of an asshole to me as you can."

His mouth opens and closes like a fish, but he doesn't say anything. "Seriously." I laugh, the sound manic and high-pitched. Turning, I move to step around him and head for my bedroom, but his hand on my ponytail stops me, and before I even know what's happening, his lips are on mine and he's kissing me.

Nero is kissing me!

Firm, unyielding lips devour mine while his tongue forces its way into my mouth, demanding entry and submission. I don't even know if I kiss him back before he's gone, and not just pulled away, but gone. His back is to me as he storms up the stairs, the echo of his door slamming shaking the house and my very core.

"What the fuck?" I whisper, lifting my trembling fingers to my lips and touching them to test if any of that was real. Nero just kissed me. We were arguing and then he kissed me. He basically accused me of having sex with Knight, with the intent of then moving on to one or multiple guys on his team. He implied I was a slut, and then he kissed me.

Nope. It doesn't matter which way I think about it. It just doesn't make any sense. He kissed me. He hates me. Maybe hate is a strong word. Possibly, he deeply dislikes me might be more accurate.

But no matter which way you look at it, we're not friends, and definitely not kissing friends. I think suggesting we're friendly acquaintances might be pushing it. So why did he kiss me?

A part of me wants to march upstairs, bang on his door, and demand to know what the hell just happened. But my sensible side is telling me I might not want to know what prompted his bizarre change of direction.

My lips tingle as I finish unpacking the box of stuff, and I manage to make it to my bedroom before I have a mini meltdown, staring at myself in my bathroom mirror and admiring the slight puffiness of my lips.

Nero is a beautiful man. Tall, thick, and incredibly attractive. If he'd been a bit nicer since I met him, he'd totally be bean-flicking inspo. But his attitude toward me has meant I've kept his sexy ass out of my fantasies and firmly in the "sexy but ruins it by being an asshole" pigeonhole.

Tasting his tongue has changed everything. He's still an asshole, but now he's an asshole who made my knees weak and my panties damp. Stripping out of my clothes, I drop them into the hamper, then turn on my shower. I wait for the water to heat before I step in, soaking my hair while my mind replays the kiss on a loop in my head.

My hands move on autopilot as I wash my body then shampoo and condition my hair. My nerve endings feel hypersensitive, my nipples are taut peaks, and my pussy aches with emptiness. I'm single and almost thirty years old, I have a vibrator and a couple of other toys to help me get through nights like this, but right now, I don't want a fake cock. Pulling the showerhead from the hook on the wall, I move it between my thighs, aiming the torrent of water at my sex.

The pressure and heat feel amazing and I close my eyes, bracing one hand on the tile wall while I slowly move the showerhead around, massaging my clit and entrance. I swear I don't intend to think about him, but an image of Nero pops into my head and my internal muscles clench appreciatively. His hair is wet, freshly out of the shower, and his expression is that perpetual scowl he's had since the first time we met.

Lust fills his eyes, and then he's kissing me, his fingers twisted tightly into my hair, holding me in place as he dips down and takes my lips, claiming them as his. Heat bursts to life in my stomach and I come on a gasp, my muscles grasping at nothing as pleasure barrels through me.

Panting, I ride out my orgasm, exhaling weakly and blinking open my eyes as I fall forward, resting my head against the cool tile while I catch my breath. How can my body react so strongly to the memory of a single kiss with him when my last sexual experience left me cold and impassive?

It takes me longer than I want to admit to turn off the shower and rehook it on the wall. My legs feel weak and the type of exhaustion I only ever feel after great sex washes over me, making me lethargic and floaty. Wrapping a towel around my body and another around my hair, I stumble to the bed and flop down into my pillow pile, allowing the mix of soft fabrics to cocoon me.

Not even bothering to change into my pj's or brush my hair, I fall asleep, dreaming of the roommate from hell, who dominates my thoughts.

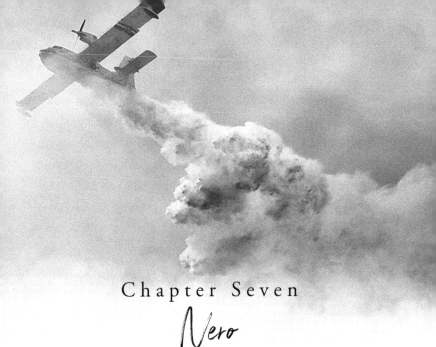

Chapter Seven

Nero

What the actual fuck?

What the fuckity, fuck, fuck, fuck?

I kissed her.

I don't even know why I did it, but it was like I just couldn't not, so I grabbed her and kissed her.

One minute she was talking. Berating me might be a more accurate description, and then the next minute, my mouth was on hers and she tasted like the most decadent type of forbidden. I've kissed plenty of women in the past, but none of them have ever tasted the way she does. Like she's a black hole ready to devour me.

I don't even know if she kissed me back. She didn't push me away, but she's not mine. I think she's Knight's and I just kissed her.

Fuck.

Shame hits me like a Mack truck. I kissed my friend's girl. I'm an asshole! There's not even a good excuse for my behavior. She didn't come on to me. She didn't encourage me in any way. In fact, it was all me. I fisted her ponytail, dragged her to me, and took what I wanted without thought.

Sighing, I drag my hands through my hair and rub at my temples tiredly. I don't want to, but I need to go and speak to Knight. If he and Tori have something going on, I need to confess that I kissed his girl and apologize for my moment of madness. This was all me, not her, and I owe them both an apology.

The idea of telling Tori that I'm sorry I kissed her and that it won't happen again rankles something inside of me. Admitting to her that I was wrong feels almost unfathomable, and not just because I don't feel like touching her was a mistake.

Opening my door, I sigh, eyeing her bedroom for a moment before stepping past it, only to freeze on the spot when a muffled cry breaks the thick silence. Backing up, I stand outside her door and listen.

A second noise filters through the wall, and this time, I'm almost positive I know what it is. Tori. My pest of a roommate, my sexy, infuriating, annoyingly desirable roommate, is getting herself off.

I know it's wrong to stay here, but there is nothing in heaven or hell that could wrench me from this spot right now. Pressing my head gently to the door, I listen as soft moans turn into gasping cries and closing my eyes, I imagine how she looks.

The sound is too quiet for her to be on her bed, so she

must be in the bathroom. Maybe she's bent forward over the counter, rubbing her clit with her fingers, or fucking herself with a toy. My dick hardens and I reach down and cup myself through the fabric of my pants, squeezing my length as a new image of her pops into my mind. I can imagine the way she'd look squatting on the floor, riding a dildo she's suctioned to the tiles and getting herself off while her tits bounce up and down as she searches for relief.

Pushing my hand past the waistband of my pants, I stroke myself slowly, imagining how she'd look. Gripping the basin with one hand, her knuckles white as she holds on tight, her other hand between her thighs, fucking herself hard and fast with her fingers.

A keening cry filters through the door and I know she's coming. My dick twitches beneath my fingers, and I follow her over the edge, hot spurts of cum exploding into the fabric of my briefs like a teenager who can't control himself.

I wait for the shame and guilt to hit me, but all I feel is need, want, and desire. Instead of going to Knight's, I turn around and go back into my bedroom. I toss and turn for hours, and when I finally fall asleep, my dreams are filled with all the hundred different ways Tori could make herself come while I listened, watched, and gave her a helping hand. Or tongue. Or dick.

By the time my alarm goes off the next morning, I'm a mixture of disgusted with myself and horny as hell. Of all the women in the world I could be lusting over, Tori should be at the bottom of the list. It's not that she's not attractive—beautiful, really—because she is. But because she belongs to my teammate. She's my friend's woman, and until now,

I've never even considered crossing that line. It's one of my unbreakable rules.

I should have gone straight to Knight last night and confessed what I did, but the moment I heard her in her room, I knew any apology I gave him would be a false platitude at best or an all-out lie at worst. And I'd rather say nothing than tell him a load of bullshit that I don't mean.

Tori's an early riser. I don't know her exact hours, but for the last four days, she's been up and gone well before I've woken up. However, this morning, I can hear the sound of her moving downstairs.

My head is telling me to take my time getting showered and dressed so that by the time I get down to make breakfast, she'll be gone, but my dick has other ideas. My cock is eager to see her again, to kiss her again, maybe even touch her, but that can't happen.

Even if she wasn't starting something with Knight, she's still not at all my type. She's too loud, too cheerful, too constantly happy, and she'll drive me crazy… just the way she has in the week and a half we've been sharing a house.

No. Tori Hoffman is not the type of woman I'd consider for anything more than a one-night thing, and uncomplicated sex is completely impossible with someone so interconnected with the other important people in my life.

Deciding not to be a pussy, I take a quick shower then head downstairs.

"Good morning," she singsongs, so brightly I actually cringe at her enthusiasm.

"Morning," I growl, heading for the coffee machine and pouring myself a mug.

"Do you want breakfast? I was just about to warm through a croissant," she asks, her back to me as she does something at the stove.

"No thanks, I'll just have some cereal," I mutter, keeping as much distance between us as I can manage in the small kitchen. With my bowl in one hand and my mug in the other, I opt to sit at the dining table rather than at the breakfast bar, hoping she'll pick to stay in the kitchen. I sigh when she eyes the breakfast bar with longing before taking the seat opposite me at the table.

The smell of buttery croissant fills my nose, and I glance at her plate, wishing I'd said yes to her offer to warm one for me. The pastry is huge, a golden color and dripping with chocolate spread.

Her fingers pull off chunks, and somehow, I manage to stop myself from looking at her when her hums of enjoyment border on pornographic. My cereal tastes like ash, and my dick is hard enough to slice a hole in my pants. If I look at her now, I know I'll kiss her. Fuck, I'm envisaging licking chocolate spread from her lips and fingers. Her tits, her clit.

No. Nope.

Last night was a mistake, one that I have no intention of repeating. Ever. And apparently, I'm the only one being affected because she's not acting like a horny teenager. In fact, she's just being her annoying, sunshiny self. Clearly, she knows me kissing her was nothing more than an aberration, never to happen again and nothing we need to discuss or even think about.

With a renewed sense of determined calm, I eat my tasteless cereal, pointedly ignoring all the moans of pleasure

Tori makes while she finishes her own food. I eat so fast I'm confident I'm going to either puke it back up or have indigestion for the rest of the day, but the need to get away from her is strong enough that I practically throw my dish into the dishwasher in my haste to get out of the kitchen.

I don't breathe again until I'm in my bedroom with the door closed behind me. Only then do I look down and acknowledge the steel bar in my pants. I'm hard. No, I'm rock hard and I didn't even look at her.

It's official. I'm fucked.

For a long moment, I consider heading for the bathroom to take care of my problem, but I don't. She's Knight's and if that means I have to deal with a hellacious case of blue balls this morning, then that's my penance for betraying my friend and lusting over his girl's sex phone operator foodgasm.

Shoving clothes into my bag, I force myself to focus, making sure I have everything I need for my four-day shift. The routine of packing is so familiar that it barely holds my attention, and my thoughts wander back to Tori.

I wonder what she'll be doing while Knight is away. If they'll be texting or sexting. If she'll make noises like she did last night as she thinks of him, or if she'll be louder when I'm not here to hear her.

My fingers clench into fists and unbidden anger rushes through me. Why does thinking about her like that piss me off so badly? Last night, when I was standing at her door like a creeper and listening to her come, it made me harder than I've been in my entire life.

Shaking my head, I angrily finish my packing, zipping

my bag and throwing it over my shoulder with so much force I think it'll leave a bruise. The kitchen is empty by the time I get back downstairs and her absence only makes me angrier.

The door to Buck's house opens and he slides outside a moment after I do, with James at his side. I try not to look as he smiles down at the petite blonde, lifts her chin with one hand and kisses her, grabbing a handful of her ass with the other. The kiss goes on for longer than it should and I roll my eyes, almost as annoyed by their happiness as I am Tori's cheeriness.

Slapping the roof of the truck twice, I call, "Break it up, you two. It looks bad if the chief is late to his shift."

Without even an ounce of urgency, Buck pulls back, glares at me, then turns back to James, talking quietly to her. She nods, then says something back to him, a soft smile spreading across her lips.

"Finally," I hiss as he climbs into the driver's seat and puts the key in the ignition.

"You could have just driven your own ass up to base. You don't have to wait for me."

"You could have kept the PDA to a minimum and we could have been on time," I snap back petulantly.

"What the fuck is your problem?" my brother demands, his expression angry.

"I kissed Tori," I snarl, running my hands through my hair, wishing for the first time that I had enough length to pull at.

"You what?" Buck asks, slamming his foot on the brake and stopping in the middle of the road.

"I…" Pausing, I rub at my face. "I kissed her."

"Yesterday afternoon, you were bitching about living with her and worrying about her playing Knight. How the fuck did you go from that to kissing her?" he exclaims, driving forward again.

"Fuck if I know," I confess. "She went to Knight's again last night. When she got back, we were talking and then I kissed her."

"*You* kissed *her*?"

"She was walking away and I grabbed her ponytail and then… yeah, I kissed her."

"Did she kiss you back?"

Sighing, I scrub my face again. "Yes. I don't know. Fuck, I don't know."

"So, what happened after you kissed her and she possibly kissed you back?" It's obvious he's amused, but I ignore his tone.

"I left."

"You left?"

"What the fuck else was I supposed to do?" I cry.

"Did you tell Knight?"

"No. I planned to. I left my room to go to his place… then…" I stop talking. My brother is my closest friend and confidant. But I don't think even we're close enough for me to admit that I stood like a creep with my ear pressed to her door, listening to her masturbate and then came in my pants. "I couldn't do it and I went back to my room."

"So, what happened this morning?"

"Nothing."

"Nothing?" he parrots back at me.

"Nothing. She just acted normal, like nothing happened. She was cheery as fuck, like she is all the fucking time. She asked me if I wanted a croissant, then sat at the table and ate breakfast like nothing had happened at all."

"Obviously, she knows it was a mistake too, and she didn't want to make a big deal out of it." Buck shrugs as we pull off the road and onto the dirt track that leads to the base.

"Obviously," I say, bitterness lacing each syllable. What I don't say is Tori and I kissing *was* a fucking big deal and how pissed I am that she dismissed it so easily. I don't mention that my dick was, and still is, hard from the sounds she made. Nope, I don't say any of that, but my thoughts swirl with those words, over and over, taunting me with the knowledge that as much as I don't want to admit it, even to myself, kissing Tori definitely wasn't nothing.

Chapter Eight

Tori

Sunday is my day off, and although I always get up early, I usually go back to bed for a lazy morning to catch up on my TV shows or read a book. But my normal plans have gone to crap in the aftermath of Hurricane Nero. Even a day later, it still feels like my hands are shaking as I park my car on the street behind the bakery. It took everything I had to stay calm and nonchalant in the kitchen yesterday morning. I'm not sure what I was expecting from Nero, but silence and badly disguised disgust definitely wasn't it.

He kissed me. He. Kissed. Me. And then he left after acting like it never even happened. What exactly am I supposed to do with that? Yesterday, I got up early like I usually do, then hung around the kitchen like an idiot until I heard the sounds of him moving around upstairs. I thought maybe we'd talk about the night before or at least laugh it off as a joke, mistake, or drunken mishap.

But instead, when he finally sauntered downstairs in his Rockhead Point Fire Department T-shirt and utility pants that clung to his thick, thick thighs, he didn't even glance at me. When I offered him a croissant, his lip curled like I had just suggested he spread dog shit on his cornflakes, and when I sat down opposite him at the dining table, I honestly thought he was going to get up and leave.

I don't know why his attitude bothers me so much. When he kissed me the night before, when his lips were on mine and his tongue was tasting me like I was his favorite dessert, I had a glimpse of what it must feel like to be owned.

My ex-boyfriends—and there have only been two— never ignited more than a tingle anywhere except in my pants. Both were attractive men who were pretty good in bed, but they never made me feel like my world started and ended with them or that they felt the same about me.

I honestly don't get how Nero made me feel that in thirty seconds with a single kiss when I've never got there in the past after good sex and a serious relationship. Urgh. I hate how much I'm questioning myself. He started all this. He kissed me and then he acted like it was nothing, but I can't forget it, or dismiss it, or pretend it was a joke, because I don't understand why he did it in the first place.

Throwing open the back door, I stow my stuff, turn the radio to an angry rock station, and get to work. I hurry through the simple batch muffins quickly, then decide to make some sweet loaf breads just so I'll have an excuse to work some of my tension out kneading and mixing.

By the time Mrs. Yates enters the kitchen, I'm singing along loudly to an older, angsty song and straining to get the dough to the consistency I want for the sweetened loaves I'm making.

"Is everything okay, dear?" Mrs. Yates asks, turning down the volume on the radio.

The moment the music lowers to a normal level, I snap out of my frustrated haze and blink rapidly, bringing me back to the present. "Oh, I'm sorry, Mrs. Yates. Yes, everything's fine. I'm just having a few teething issues with my new roommate and it has me a little frustrated."

"Oh." She smiles. "I was wondering if we could have a word when you have a minute?"

"Of course, let me just get these in to prove and I'll come up."

"Perfect. I'll make coffee."

Quickly transferring the dough into bowls, I cover them and then slide them into the large proving drawers. I clean up in double time, then head upstairs to the office, nervous butterflies fluttering around in my stomach.

"Come in, dear," she calls the moment I appear in the doorway.

"Is everything okay?" I ask cautiously.

"Sit," she says, only making me more nervous.

"I'm not going to beat around the bush. I've been approached by a chain of bakeries to purchase the store. They're looking to expand into the tourist towns and thought this place would be a good addition."

"What?" I shriek. "We had a deal. We're supposed to sign the papers this week."

Mrs. Yates lifts her hands in a consolatory gesture. "I know. Which is why I told them no. But I feel like I need to make you aware that if they decide to look for another store here in town, you might find yourself with some competition from a well-known brand."

"Oh," I say, all the air bursting from me in a puff.

"I didn't want to let you buy the store and then be completely unprepared for this to happen. I also want to give you the chance to back out of the purchase with no hard feelings. A chain bakery could cause huge problems for you, especially with the tourists who tend to stick with something familiar rather than seeking out local businesses."

"Oh," I say again.

"Take some time, discuss it with your lawyers."

"Oh, I don't need to do that," I say, waving her concern away. "I'm not worried about a chain bakery, even if they do move to town."

"Dear, I think that might be a little shortsighted—" she starts.

"Mrs. Yates, I haven't told you this because I didn't want you to think that I wanted to buy the store and then immediately change things, but my plan is to expand into patisserie goods and make the shop more of a bespoke, high-end eating experience. I'll still offer the popular items we sell the most of, cupcakes, muffins, cookies, but as well, I plan to offer macarons, tarts, and other traditional French patisserie cakes."

I tense, worried that this woman who has been so sweet to me over the last three years is going to be upset, but instead, a bright smile spreads over her face. "Oh, Tori, what a wonderful idea. Goodness, how fabulous, and you're such a talented pastry chef, the store is going to be such a success. I'm so excited for you," she gushes.

"You're not upset?"

"Upset? No, of course not. Since the day you interviewed for the position here, I've worried that you were wasting your talents making cookies and birthday cakes, but you said this was what you wanted and I knew that you were hoping to buy the place when I retired. Knowing how you plan to transform the store into a high-end delicatessen makes me so happy."

"I'm so relieved." I laugh.

"Me too." She giggles, looking ten years younger than she did when I stepped into her office. "Let's see if we can get the paperwork signed earlier. Then I can take you out to celebrate and you can tell me all about your exciting plans."

Excitement distracts me for the rest of the day until it's time to head to the lawyer's office and sign all the paperwork. I'm almost vibrating as I listen to my lawyer when he speaks to me through the computer screen. I'm nodding in all the right places, but I'm barely listening to a word. I've read the contract back to front, consulted the law firm my brothers all use and I know Mrs. Yates isn't trying to screw me over. Once I sign on the dotted line, I'll own the business, all its assets, and the building Yates Bakery is currently housed in. I'll be up to my eyeballs in debt, but I'll be a business and property owner and everyone involved agreed this is a good deal for both me and Mrs. Yates.

An hour later, I've signed my name so many times my arm hurts, but all the t's are crossed and the i's dotted, and it's all mine.

"To Le Petite Patisserie," Mrs. Yates and her husband say in unison, lifting their champagne flutes into the air and toasting me.

"Wishing you all the success in the world," Mrs. Yates says from across the table at the restaurant where they brought me to celebrate.

"Thank you both." I smile, tapping the edge of my glass against hers, unable to keep the grin from my face.

"I'm just so excited for you," she gushes. "Tell me your plans."

So, I do, explaining my vision for the store while she nods, enthuses, and offers her advice. We eat delicious food and drink champagne, then we walk back to *my* store and they bid me good night.

I know I should go home, but instead, I open the door to the dark, empty store and step inside, locking it behind me. The glass counter is empty, and the place is eerily quiet, but I can't help throwing my hands into the air and letting out a happy, girly shriek.

Dropping my purse to the floor, I rush through the storefront, kitchen, storeroom, then upstairs into the office and finally the apartment. When I've touched practically every surface, claiming them all as mine, I push open the door to the roof and step out. Biting my lip, I tip my head back and yell, "It's mine," into the cool night air, declaring my ownership for the whole town to hear. Running back downstairs, I grab my purse, then head back up to the roof with a pad and pen and start to plan.

It's well after midnight when I push through the door

and into the house. The silence of the empty space has a frightening quality, but I ignore it, locking up, then heading to my room.

I fall asleep with recipes, menus, and color schemes racing through my thoughts while Nero lurks at the back of my mind, present but not a part of everything exciting that's happening. I just wish I wasn't thinking about him at all.

The next couple of days are a whirlwind of activity. Mrs. Yates and I sit the bakery staff down and explain about the sale and how I'm the new owner. Daniel, the other two part-time counter staff, and Hannah, who does the deliveries, all seem excited for me. Jean, the only full-time staff member who has spent the last three years regularly explaining why I'm doing everything wrong, throws a fit. It's been clear since my first day that she believes she should have been promoted to chef when Mrs. Yates decided to take a step away from the kitchen. I think she assumed if she undermined me enough, I'd eventually leave, and she'd get my job.

She's actually not a bad home baker, but she is incredibly set in her ways, and after several occasions when she refused to abide by the health and safety rules set in place, Mrs. Yates, on my advice, relegated her to cupcake frosting and working the counter.

"I quit," she declares loudly, looking to Mrs. Yates like she expects her to beg her to stay.

"Okay," I say with a smile.

"Okay?" she shrieks, looking at Mrs. Yates again. "I've worked for you for five years."

"Jean, I no longer own this business. Tori has absolutely

no obligation to retain any of the bakery's current staff, although she said she would do so as long as everyone was happy to work under her as the new owner. As you're obviously not happy with the situation, all I can say is thank you for all your hard work over the years, and good luck in your future endeavors."

Jean's jaw drops open, then she spins around and glares at me. "You can't fire me, you stupid child."

"I didn't fire you. You quit," I tell her calmly.

"No… I… Mrs. Yates," she says, whining like a child.

"I'm so sorry that this hasn't worked out. As you don't have an employment contract with me, there's no need to worry about notice. You can just grab your stuff and go," I say with a sickly sweet smile.

"I… No… I…"

All eyes turn to Jean, whose face has heated to a glowing red color before she stomps out of the kitchen, grabbing her bag from the storeroom and slamming the back door as she leaves.

Turning to the rest of the staff, I smile softly. "I'm sorry about that. What Mrs. Yates said is true. Your jobs are safe if you want to stay working here with me. If you do, then I'll have new employment contracts drawn up and we can carry on as normal."

"Now that she's gone, is there a full-time position available?" Daniel asks coyly.

"I guess there is." I chuckle, shrugging.

"I'd love more hours if they're available."

"Perfect." I laugh. I can't believe how easy this worked out. I got rid of Jean and got Daniel full time in less than five minutes.

"Well, I need to grab some things from my…" Mrs. Yates holds her hands up with a chuckle. "*Your* office, and then I'll get out of your way. I'm just on the end of the phone if you need me, not that you will. You'll do fabulously."

Leaning in, she hugs me tightly, then ten minutes later, she leaves, and all of a sudden, I'm the boss. My first official day as owner passes so quickly that it's late by the time I've finished up everything, and rather than drive up the mountain, I decide to stay at the store. The floor is hard and cold and I order myself a bed to be delivered the next day, before the sun has fully risen in the sky.

Time flies by in a blur of baking, planning, and calling up all the suppliers to change the bakery's accounts into my name. The business side of running the store takes more time than I expected because, at the moment, I'm still running things the way Mrs. Yates did, and I'm not ready to make all of my changes immediately.

What I do change is the archaic till for a new computerized EPOS system connected to my computer. I add a full stock list and start adding the recipes for each item so I can work out the exact costs for each product, the profit margins, and what sells out first. It might take me a few months to be in a position to have a full cost analysis, but once I do, I can figure out what to change and when.

I know that being a success isn't just about making great cakes, so I need to be smart and savvy about how to make the most profit while having the best product, service, and reputation. Losing Jean has been the best loss I've made so far. She was on the highest wage and not having to pay her salary is the perfect initial business move. Daniel is a much better option; his wages are lower, even at full time, and he has much more flexibility than Jean did in the hours he wants to work.

After a night on the floor, I cleaned out the apartment and moved all the equipment that was being stored up there down into the basement before setting up my new bed. I haven't decided if I'm going to move into the apartment here permanently, but at least now I have somewhere more comfortable to sleep than the floor.

After spending a couple of hours taking photos of all the kitchen equipment Mrs. Yates has been hoarding, I list them for sale on Craigslist, eBay, and some commercial kitchen sales groups on Facebook, then decide to go home.

The bathroom in the apartment above the shop is in need of a seriously good clean and I don't want to have to remove a colony of spiders before I can take a shower. It's late again, but I feel more excited than exhausted, regardless of the long days I've been putting in.

It's almost one a.m. when I park my car outside the house, and my limbs are tired and dragging as I open the door and step inside.

"Where the fucking hell have you been?" Nero demands.

Chapter Nine

Nero

Tori fucking Hoffman is driving me crazy. I haven't seen her in four days, but that hasn't stopped my brain from constantly thinking about her. I taste her on my lips, her scent has permeated my clothes, and my dick is constantly hard remembering the sounds she made when she came.

I've tried to speak to Knight half a dozen times since he got to base four days ago, but every time I open my mouth to broach the subject of my maddening roommate, I go mute. The idea of telling him I kissed her and that I'm sorry makes me nauseous because I'm not sorry.

I'm not sorry I kissed her, I'm not sorry that I listened while she came, and I'm not sorry that my dick hurts because she makes me so damn hard. I'm not sorry, and if I tell him I am, I'd be lying.

The pair of them have been constantly on my mind. If they're together, he hasn't mentioned it, and I haven't seen him even touch his cell at all in the four days we've been on shift together. Clearly, whatever they have is new and maybe not even exclusive. He might not care that I pressed my lips to hers and demanded entry into her mouth with my tongue. But if she were mine, I'd care and that pisses me off even more.

In the past, at this time of year, it'd be quiet. Peak wildfire season has passed, and usually, we'd have some much-needed downtime before we move to a local precinct for a few months during the late fall and winter months.

Since our department got the funding to stay here all year round, I was assuming it'd be an easy life with lots of maintenance and training. Only for the last four days, we've barely had time to clean the equipment and restock the supplies from one incident before being called out to the next. Luckily, most of the call-outs were small fires that were easily manageable, but we had one incident in a town about an hour from Rockhead Point where a barn full of animal feed and hay had set alight. It had burned so fast and so wildly that the owner was worried his house would be caught in the flames before we could get there. Thankfully, we got there in time to save his home, but he lost all of his winter feed for his animals, his barn, and a couple of other small outbuildings.

By the time Buck and I are climbing into his truck, I'm dragging my feet and more than ready to take a hot shower and crawl into bed. But before I can do that, I know I need to make things right with Knight.

My brother is practically bouncing by the time we pull into Jumpers Row, slowing to a stop outside his house. "See you in a few days. I need to be inside my woman for a week to make up for being away from her for this long," he growls, not bothering to wait for me to reply before he's out of the truck and striding through his front door.

Scanning the small group of houses, I look for Tori's car, but it's not there. She was home from work at this time when I was off shift last week, but I guess she could be working late. Grabbing my bag, I open the front door and take my stuff upstairs, emptying out the clothes that I washed and dried up at base and unpacking them back into my closet.

When I'm done, I look around, trying to find an excuse to delay me from going to speak to Knight, but when nothing jumps out at me, I exhale, find my balls, and head to my buddy's home. Knocking on the door, I shove my hands into my pockets and lower my chin, feeling the weight of my betrayal sitting heavily on my chest.

"What's up?" Knight says, opening the door.

"Hey, sorry, I know we just got home, but I need to talk to you. Is it okay if I come in?"

His expression stays as neutral as always as he steps back and gestures for me to enter. All the houses in the row have the same layout, so I head into the kitchen, standing awkwardly by the breakfast bar as he follows me in.

"Look." I sigh. "Fuck, I'm just going to say it, okay?"

"Okay." He nods.

"I kissed Tori. I didn't plan it and it didn't mean anything. She didn't instigate it and I'm not sure if she even kissed me back. But it happened and I shouldn't have done it," I blurt in a rush.

Knight's brows pull together slightly. "Okay."

"I mean, it's not. Obviously, it's not okay. You're my buddy and you and her…" I trail off, hoping he'll fill in the gaps and tell me what exactly they are to each other.

"Okay," he says again.

"Seriously?" I snap, getting angry now. "I kissed your woman and all you have to say is *okay*?"

"Tori's not my woman. I don't have a woman," he says simply, his voice monotone.

"I assumed you guys weren't exclusive yet, but still."

When he stays quiet, my fingers clench into fists.

"I mean, you're dating and I kissed her, bro. Don't you have anything to say about that?" I demand, confused as to why he isn't bothered.

His expression changes. I don't really know what the look he's giving me is, but it's different from his standard, neutral face. "Tori and I aren't dating."

Something inside of me goes pop and my ears fill with static. "What?"

"Tori and I aren't dating," Knight says again.

"She's been coming to your house. I carried her stuff to your house," I snap, arguing.

"She's been using my kitchen."

Squeezing my eyes closed, I blink them open and furrow my brow as I squint at him. "What?"

"She uses my kitchen and she makes me dinner."

"That's a date," I say slowly. Knight isn't your average dude. I've never asked questions about what his deal is because it's not my business, but I get the impression he's not neurotypical. Or he could just be someone who doesn't give a fuck about all the bullshit I'm slinging at him right now.

"I asked her and we agreed it wasn't a date," he tells me, passing me a beer while he twists the lid off his own bottle and brings it to his lips.

"So, you asked her out?" I ask, even more confused now.

Sighing, like he's being incredibly patient while I ask stupid questions, he says, "I confirmed it wasn't a date and she agreed."

"So why the fuck is she using your kitchen when we have a perfectly good kitchen at our place?" I growl.

"You'd have to ask her that," he says elusively.

Elusively? When the fuck is Knight elusive?

"So, you don't want to date her?"

"No," he agrees.

"And you don't care that I kissed her?"

"I'm confident you don't need my permission to kiss anyone. But no, who you or Tori kisses is none of my business. Although I like her, so don't touch her again until she gives her permission. I'd hate to have to hurt you." His eyes flash with a darkness I've never seen from him before and it's enough to make me take pause. Nodding, I hold out my hand to him. "Thanks."

"You're welcome," he says, his voice back to his dry, disinterested tone.

"You like her?" I ask.

"Yes. She's…" Knight pauses as though he's searching

for the right word. "Calming and easy."

"Tori?" I laugh. "There's nothing calming about Tori. The woman never shuts up."

Knight's brow wrinkles again, and a very un-Knight-like expression changes his face. "I really would hate to have to hurt you," he says.

Not knowing what to say to that, I stay quiet and after a few moments of silence, I fidget. "Well, I should go."

He nods, not speaking, as he follows me to the front door, shutting it without another word the moment I'm outside. Somehow, even though he alleviated my guilt by ensuring me he and Tori are not dating, I somehow feel even more confused over their relationship and why she's been going to his house in the first place.

More so, how could Knight possibly find her calming and easy? I can think of a lot of words to describe the woman I haven't been able to stop thinking about for the last four days, but calming and easy definitely wouldn't be in my top hundred.

The house is still empty and Tori's car is still missing when I let myself back in. Crossing to the refrigerator, I'm surprised to find that almost empty too. Even after clearing out space for me, I noticed that Tori keeps the kitchen stocked with plenty of food. To find only a couple of yogurts, some cheese, butter, and a few other bits seems a little out of character from what I know of her so far.

My shelf is pretty sparse too, but I have the fixings for a sandwich, so I throw one together, grab a soda and slump down onto the couch to watch TV. When eight p.m. comes and goes, I start to wonder where Tori might be. Since we've lived together, she's never been this late home.

By the time ten p.m. rolls by, I'm starting to get a little worried, and I even consider texting or calling her. But she's a grown woman who doesn't have to explain her movements to me, so as much as I don't want to, I keep my cell in my pants.

When midnight passes and she's still not home, I start to get angry. Surely, it's common courtesy to let your roommate know if you don't plan to come home. But then, when I went out the other night, I didn't let her know I was going to be late, so it feels unreasonable to expect her to do the same.

When her car finally parks outside the house at just after one a.m., I'm livid. It's the middle of the fucking night. Where has she been until now, and why didn't she come home? I have no right to know the answers to these questions, but the words fall from my lips on a growl the moment she steps inside.

"Where the fucking hell have you been?" I demand.

Startling, she stumbles back a step, blinking at me owlishly, like me being here is a surprise.

"What?" she croaks.

"You heard me. Where the hell have you been? It's the middle of the night."

Lifting her wrist, she glances at her watch, then back to me. "It's hardly the middle of the night and I was at work. I lost track of time."

"You were at the bakery, on your own, in the middle of the night? What, was there a rush on croissants and cookies? I mean, what the fuck, Tori?"

Her brows pull together and then she smiles, the sound of her chuckle filling the air. "No, smart-ass, there wasn't a rush on pastries."

"Then what the fuck were you doing until now? It's not safe for you to be driving the mountain roads in the middle of the night."

A bewildered smirk spreads over her lush lips.

"Why the fuck are you smiling?" I demand, sounding like a demented caveman.

"I'm not," she says, trying and failing to smother her expression. "I just... I... Err... What is happening here?" Shaking her head, she laughs and smiles again. "I'm too tired to do this right now. I need to go to sleep. Night, Nero."

I open my mouth to speak, but she just turns and leaves before any words make their way past my lips. Something inside of me urges me to go after her, to demand she tell me where she was and who she was with, but the more rational side of my brain reminds me that it's really none of my business, even though it feels like I want it to be.

Deciding to listen to the rational part of me, I eventually go to bed, but my dreams are filled with thoughts of Tori. In my head, instead of walking away, when she smiles at me, she turns, braces herself against the couch and offers her ass to me. In my dreams, she begs for more as I fuck her, reddening her ass with my palm while she promises never to make me worry about not knowing where she is ever again.

The house is quiet and empty by the time I get up the next morning, and for reasons that I'm unwilling to explore, I'm pissed. I fight the urge to drive down to the bakery all morning, but by noon, I'm seething with unexplainable anger. Normally, when I'm agitated or stressed, I go for a long run or spar with Buck to burn off my excess energy, but five miles later, I'm still just as pissed as I was before I left.

Tori isn't my girlfriend; hell, we're not even friends, but since my lips touched hers, I've had this inexplicable need to know where she is and what she's doing. But that doesn't really make sense to me either. I'm not the possessive type. I've never had a relationship where I've wanted or expected to be a part of every aspect of the woman's life. Honestly, it's normally the complete opposite. I work a lot, so my exes have all been the type of people who don't want someone to be clingy and intrusive.

Easy, light, and part time is what I normally go for. It's why I stayed with Miranda for so long, even knowing she was sleeping with other guys too. So why the fuck do I feel so growly and possessive over a woman that I barely know and don't even particularly like?

I'm sweaty and frustrated when I strip off my shorts and shirt and step into the shower, sighing as the hot water pelts my skin. Closing my eyes, I try to clear my mind, dipping my head back until the water streams over my face.

The moment my eyelids close, her face pops into my mind and my dick swells to life. Tori isn't my type. Her body is curvy, yet athletic, tight, but she still has plenty of tits and butt. Her hair is sort of beachy, brown with blonde bits that look like she spends all her time in the sun, and her skin is covered in freckles that my fingers tingle to touch and trace with my tongue.

Okay, she's absolutely my type.

I know I shouldn't do it, but I reach down and palm my

dick, gripping my length and grunting slightly. In my head, Tori slowly strips off her clothes and my length twitches in my hand. This is so fucking wrong, but I imagine her tits bouncing free, her nipples high, pink and begging to be bitten.

Time slows in my perverted daydream as she wiggles her full, round butt and slides her panties down her thighs, revealing a peek at her pink pussy when she bends and kicks her underwear off completely.

My mouth waters, and I jerk my dick in earnest as I imagine her sliding her hand between her thighs, coating her fingers in her arousal, then offering them to me like a gift. The moment I imagine leaning down and sliding her fingers into my mouth, hot cum explodes from my dick.

My eyes crash open, and reaching out a hand, I brace my palm against the tile as I blow my load into the bathtub, the evidence of my fucked-up fantasy washing down the drain. When my dick jerks for the last time, I exhale, hanging my head as shame and messed-up acknowledgment settle over me.

I have a thing for my annoying fucking roommate.

The reality of my admission haunts me as I dry myself with a towel and get dressed. It stalks me through the house as I pace around, wasting time while I try to decide what the fuck to do. It follows me as I make dinner, subconsciously making enough for two, while I wait for her to get back. And it hangs on me like a fucking angry monkey when she still hasn't gotten home by the time I force myself into bed after one in the morning.

Waking up angry is a new experience for me. I'm not an

angry person by nature, or at least I wasn't until I met Tori fucking Hoffman. For some reason that I still don't fully understand, she makes me fucking miserable. Everything about her annoys the crap out of me, and facing the reality that I might be reacting to her so strongly because I have some kind of attraction to her is only annoying me even more.

The house is quiet and empty, and I debate packing up a bag and heading to the lake for the day, but instead, I find myself in my car, driving down the mountain and slowing to a stop on the street outside the bakery.

It's still pretty early, barely even nine a.m., and the store is just opening up. The same guy who was in there when I called in last week is stocking the glass counter while a young girl is doing something with the till. There's no sign of Tori and unexpected concern lands quickly in my chest.

I'm starting to realize how little I know about the woman I share a house with. I've driven here, expecting to find her serving at the counter, but for all I know, she could be taking deliveries or be in charge of the paperwork in an office somewhere.

A fresh bout of—what is starting to feel like familiar—guilt settles on me. I've been an asshole to her and she's done nothing to deserve it, apart from moving in to help her friend feel more settled.

Determined to make more of an effort, I climb out of my car and stride toward the store. A bell dings when I push open the door and the guy behind the counter lifts his head and smiles at me. "Good morning. We're still setting up, so there's more stuff to go into the counter if you don't see what you're looking for. Our new muffin of the day is maple chai pumpkin. Sounds weird, I know, but they're delicious."

"Err," I say, my eyes glancing to the counter as I consider ordering something and leaving like a fucking pussy. "Actually, I was wondering if Tori's here?"

The guy's brows arch upward and his eyes run down my torso to my feet, then all the way back up to my face again. "I can go check if she's available. Can I say who's asking for her."

"I'm Nero, her…" I cringe slightly, but I don't know why. "Roommate."

"Okay." He elongates the word before turning and disappearing into the back.

"Nero?" Tori says when she steps out into the front of the shop, wiping her hands on the towel that's tucked into the apron she's wearing over a chef's tunic. "Is everything okay?"

She's a chef. A mix of surprise and the knowledge that, at the back of my mind, I think I already knew that washes over me. Makes sense why she has so much cooking stuff and why she mentioned experimenting the day I bitched her out for taking over the refrigerator.

"Nero?" she calls again.

"Sorry." I snap back to the present. Tori and the guy are standing side by side, arms touching, both looking at me with matching confused expressions. They look good together. He's taller than her, blond to her brunette, but still compatible.

Fresh anger surges to the surface at the idea of them being a pair. A couple. Together. Fuck, I need to get it together because right now I'm standing here, scowling at them, while I fight the urge to grab that fucker's shirt and haul him away from her.

"Are you having a stroke?" Tori's voice snaps me out of my violent internal rage.

"What? No. I was hoping to talk to you," I finally say.

"Oh," she says, her brow furrowing even deeper, like me wanting to have a conversation with her is more shocking than me having a stroke. "Err, why don't you come on back? We can talk upstairs."

She turns and heads into the back of the store and I walk around the counter, straightening to my full height as I pass Counter Dude. Her brow is still furrowed as she waits for me at a door off the kitchen, opening it and waiting for me to catch up. We climb the stairs and go through another door into what appears to be a small apartment. "Sorry, it's a bit of a mess up here," she says as I spot a bed through one of the half-open doors. "We can sit in here."

I follow her into an office and watch as she perches her ass on the edge of the desk, motioning for me to sit on a chair to the right of her. "Is everything okay? Is James okay? I only spoke to her a couple of days ago and she was fine. I figured she and Buck were busy, so I deliberately haven't called her since he got back off shift. Has she gone AWOL again?" she asks in a rush.

"James is fine as far as I'm aware. That's not why I'm here."

"Oh, thank goodness." She smiles, pressing her palm against her chest. "I was panicking there for a minute. So, what's up? I was shocked when Daniel said you were here. I honestly didn't know you even knew where I worked." She giggles, her smile bright.

"Of course I know where you work," I snarl, more anger in my tone than is warranted, considering I was only thinking how little I know about her less than five minutes ago.

"Okay." Her smile becomes a little forced but doesn't fade.

"I wanted to see if you wanted to have dinner together. It seems like we should make a little effort to get to know each other, considering we live together."

"Oh." For the first time, her smile vanishes, but a second later, it's fixed back in place and I'm left wondering if I imagined her reaction to me inviting her to dinner. "That's a nice idea. When did you have in mind?"

"Tonight."

"I actually have plans tonight."

"What plans?" I snarl.

Her smile disappears again, flashing back a moment later. "Knight and I are having dinner."

"You and Knight?" I say slowly, my tone dark.

"Yes."

"He said you're not dating," I blurt.

Smile gone. Smile back. I wonder if she even realizes she does that or that her microexpression is more telling than any of the words coming out of her mouth. "We're not dating, we're friends."

"Why?" I demand.

"Is this because you think I'm planning on playing sex bingo with your teammates?" Her smile is still firmly fixed in place, but her tone has turned frosty.

"I didn't say that," I grit out.

"Look, I'm not sure dinner is a good idea. I appreciate you making the effort, but it's clear that we're never going to be friends."

My feet force me to a standing position so I can look down at her rather than up. "What the fuck does that mean?"

Following my lead, she stands too, but she's so small. She's not really any higher than she was sitting on the desk. "You haven't hidden the fact that you don't like me. I don't get why. I'm nice. But you don't, and I have to learn to live with that. What I don't have to do is spend time with someone who clearly thinks so little of me."

"I—" I start.

"I have to get back to work," she interrupts, turning like she plans to leave.

I don't know why I do it. I don't plan to, but instead of letting her go, I curl an arm around her waist and pull her to me, making a small grunt burst from her as she slams into my chest. Leaning her back, I press my lips to hers and kiss her like she's not the most infuriating woman in the world. Or maybe that's why I'm kissing her. Because it's better than listening to her twist my words and talk around me in circles.

Forcing my tongue between her lips, I expect a knee to my balls or for her to bite me. Instead, she kisses me back almost as desperately as I feel. She tastes like sugar and vanilla, and I grab her hair, twisting my fingers into her ponytail, controlling her movements and positioning her just how I want her so I can push the kiss deeper.

My thigh slides between her legs, pressing against her hot core and for a second, she grinds against me. Then her hands that have been fisting my shirt start to push my chest, and I reluctantly release her, opening my eyes and bracing for her reaction.

Her gaze is heated, fire flashing in her depths, and her lips part like she's going to speak, but she doesn't. Instead, she turns on her heel and leaves *just like that*.

Chapter Ten

Tori

My feet move on their own, rushing me down the stairs as I cling to the handrail, hoping that I don't fall in my haste to get away from Nero. He kissed me. Again. He kissed me and just like before, I kissed him back. I have no idea what's happening between us, but I know I need to be away from him.

Entering the kitchen, I turn right and merge into the storeroom, heading for the cold storage. We don't really need a walk-in refrigerator, but Mrs. Yates bought it at some point and right now, when I pull the door until it's almost but not quite closed, I'm grateful for a place I doubt anyone would think to look for me.

Running away feels incredibly childish, but honestly, I have no idea what to do or say to him. He's been pretty open about disliking me. He's suggested I would cock hop through his teammates and even went to the effort of asking Knight about my and his relationship to make sure we weren't dating.

I don't get it. I don't get him. But fuck, my body reacts to him. I understand attraction, but usually, for me, attraction is almost equally about emotional connection as it is about physical compatibility. I've never openly disliked someone that I've desired before and it's messing with my head.

Sex is good. No, sex is great. Great sex is even better, and maybe the reason I've never had a life-altering relationship is because I've never felt this kind of burning, all-consuming need to be fucked before. But why? *Why* did the first time I experience that have to be with Nero?

When Daniel came and told me that Nero was asking for me, I was confused, then worried something was wrong. But for him to turn up here to ask me to have dinner with him just seems odd. Why didn't he just text me? The last time we kissed, he acted like nothing had happened, but then he kissed me again and God… I kissed him back again. Is the reason he wanted to have dinner because he thinks I have feelings for him?

No, that doesn't make any sense. But then, nothing to do with Nero makes much sense. To distract myself, I tidy and organize the shelves, checking the expiration dates on all the food and bringing the things that expire first to the fronts of the shelves. I even have a burst of inspiration for a cake I can make when I find some fruit I forgot I'd ordered and that would have spoiled.

By the time twenty minutes have passed, I'm cold and

feeling like a coward for hiding. Pushing open the door, I tiptoe out, closing and locking the walk-in behind me, shivering when the warm air coats my chilled skin.

Cautiously, I make my way back to the kitchen, sighing with relief when it's empty. The tray of cupcakes I was frosting when he arrived is gone, so someone must have finished them. I have a little mermaid-themed birthday cake to make this afternoon, and now, because of Nero's impromptu visit, I'm behind on my schedule.

Pulling out the cake pans, I place them down on the counter with a little more force than I intended and Daniel pokes his head in from the front counter. "Everything okay? Your roomie didn't look too happy when he left."

Sighing, I roll my eyes. "He hates me," I say bluntly.

"What?" Daniel gasps. "Why would he hate you? You're lovely. Literally, everyone loves you."

"Jean hated me," I point out, pouting.

"Jean was jealous of you. That's different."

"Nero definitely isn't jealous and I honestly have no idea why he dislikes me. Gah, I don't even want to think about him. Are we running low on anything? I need to make a birthday cake, but I have time to throw a few batches of stuff in at the same time."

"The mille-feuilles you trialed today have all gone."

"Really? We've been open less than an hour. Did you push them?"

"Nope, I've been pushing the muffin of the day, but everyone was cooing over how pretty the fancy pastries looked and they went fast."

Nero woes forgotten, I smile brightly as all my thoughts

go to the beautiful French cakes that just sold out in less than an hour. My mind whirs with thoughts of what patisserie I can offer tomorrow and if it'll be as well received as the mille-feuilles were.

"That's better." He smiles.

"What?"

"You're smiling again. It's rare you're not, and I hate that your roommate made you frown."

"Me too." I laugh.

The bell on the door jingles and Daniel heads back to serve. Sliding back into my happy place, I bake and decorate a mermaid birthday cake for a five-year-old, a wide, familiar grin permanently etched onto my face.

Once the cake is done and ready to be collected, I head up to my office and get up to date on my paperwork, moving as much as I can into digital format. Of course, I saw all the business's books before I agreed to buy the place, but I had no idea how archaic her filing and paper trail were until I took over dealing with it.

When I spoke to all the suppliers, most were relieved to be able to provide me with paperless billing and ordering, and after the initial time involved with changing everything over, I'm confident it'll save me hours of unnecessary writing going forward.

Last night, I tackled the disgusting bathroom, so instead of going home and facing Nero before I meet up with Knight, I head into the shower, changing into one of the outfits I brought here for when I stayed late.

Knight is still the only person I've told about buying the store outside of the staff and my family. I haven't even told James and I don't know why. No, that's a lie. I know exactly why I haven't told her. It's because she has so much going on in her own life right now, and although owning the store is a big deal to me, in comparison to her falling in love, losing all of her surrogate family, then having a mini meltdown and getting engaged, a new business doesn't feel like that much of a big deal.

She knew I'd hoped to purchase the bakery when Mrs. Yates retired, but I didn't want to jinx things by telling anyone until the sale went through.

My folks and my brothers all know. Felix and Atticus asked when they could come and see the place, but I told them not to come until I've finished the rebrand and have a grand reopening as Le Petite Patisserie. Jude and August are about to start their hockey season and even though I know they want to visit, unless I fly to a game, it's unlikely they'll get home until Christmas.

Mom and Dad have visited before, they're not too far away and I know if I called on them to help, they'd be here in a hot minute, but a part of me wants to do this on my own. Maybe to prove that I can, or maybe because it won't feel like it's really mine unless I do it without their help.

All of my family offered to lend or give me the money to buy the store. Jude and August make more in a month than it cost me to buy the whole business and the building it's housed in. And Felix's pieces self for tens of thousands of dollars, sometimes more.

None of them understand why I'd want to have a large mortgage hanging over my head when they could help me, but it's important that this be mine, and although they don't understand it, they've respected my wishes. Atticus is the only one who really gets why I feel this way. He could buy a shop and set up as a tattooist, but he wants to work hard and build up his reputation before he puts his name on the door of his own studio.

Running a brush through my hair, I fluff the wet strands with my fingers and then give up. I don't have a hair dryer here, and brushed and not covered in flour is a vast improvement on how it looked before my shower.

Smoothing down the soft cotton fabric of my dress, I pull my leather jacket over the top and slide my feet into white sneakers. I'd planned to make mac and cheese for him, but now the sale is complete, Knight is coming to see the store, and then we're going to get tacos and Mexican beer from the pop-up food truck that's in town for a couple of days.

I told him to text me when he got here. I haven't installed a doorbell or anything on the door that leads to the alley at the back of the store. When my cell beeps, I check the screen, then rush down to the main doors, unlocking them and letting him into the dimly lit storefront.

"Hey." I greet him with a smile.

"Hi." His eyes are moving from side to side, taking in the small but welcoming space.

"Want the tour?" I ask.

"Sure." His simple monocyclic answers make me smile, and the small amount of tension I was feeling before he came melts away. Following me through the door into the kitchen, he asks insightful questions as I show him the workspace and storage rooms. When we head up to the apartment, he comments on the half-empty rooms and even offers to help me haul the larger bits of equipment that I couldn't move on my own down to the basement.

When I open the door onto the roof, he actually smiles and just like when Felix smiles, it feels like I've won a prize.

"This is a great space," he says.

"Right! I'm going to plant an herb garden and get some proper patio furniture up here. I think it could be a really great relaxing area," I gush, rushing around to show him where each part could be.

"You could even build some raised beds and have a small greenhouse to grow some fruit," he suggests.

"Oh my gosh, that would be awesome. I hadn't considered having anything bigger than pots, but I could have beds running along that whole edge of the building. I could have berries and maybe I could even get some fruit trees up here." My mind starts moving, imagining all the produce I could grow and then use in my cakes. Having locally grown produce is always a great thing, but being able to boast that they're organic and grown on the premises would be even better. The winters in Montana would be too cold to grow much, but with a greenhouse, I could focus on soft fruit and berries which produce in the spring and summer.

"You're happy," Knight says, and I'm not sure if it's a question or an observation, so I answer anyway.

"This is my dream. It's why I came to Rockhead Point, why I started working here. Everything I've done in the last five years was working toward owning my own store. Now I just have to make it work. I have to figure out how to make a town that seems to live for nothing more exotic than a blueberry muffin, want to buy high-end French patisserie," I say with a laugh.

"If you make it, they will come," Knight says.

Blinking, I bark out a laugh. "Did you just quote *Field of Dreams*?"

His lips twitch and he gifts me that half smile I've seen a handful of times now.

Locking up the store, we stroll down the sidewalk, side by side, toward the food truck. There's a line like I knew there would be, but Knight doesn't seem concerned with waiting.

"Nero told me he asked you about us," I blurt, not intending to mention it but unable to hold the words in.

"He seemed concerned," he said matter-of-factly.

"I don't get him." I sigh.

Knight is the wrong person to talk to about my ornery roommate too. If he's anything like Felix, he'll have very little time for gossip or dealing with other people's drama. So he shocks me when he says, "He asked if we were dating. I told him we weren't."

"I don't know why he seems to think it's so odd that we're friends. As far as I know, he hasn't given the other guys a hard time about hanging out with me."

Knight doesn't offer any more commentary and we wait in companionable silence until it's our turn to be served. Once we both place our order, Knight pays before I have a chance to and I look up at him. "You didn't need to pay for mine."

"You've cooked for me twice. I'm not a chef." He

shrugs.

Knight isn't a simple man, but the simplicity of his thought process is refreshing and so easy that I know it could become addictive. A part of me wishes I was attracted to Knight. I could easily see myself sliding into a calm, low-maintenance relationship with him. But I want more. I want what James has with Buck. I want the awe-inspiring love, lust, and need that they share, and Knight and I will never have that.

We eat in peaceful silence and when I'm finished, I enjoy just being with someone who is happy to exist in the same space as me without ever asking for anything. On the way home, we call into Barney's for a beer and then Knight helps me sort and move more of the junk from the apartment.

"We can ride home together. I get up early, and I can drive you to work in the morning," Knight offers.

"No, it's fine." I wave away his concern. "I want to sort the rest of the stuff in the living area and then I have a recipe for a twist on a key lime pie that I want to try while it's still clear in my mind."

His normally neutral expression changes. "I can wait and follow you home. I don't think I like the idea of you driving the mountain roads in the middle of the night."

His words are eerily similar to the ones Nero barked at me the other day, and I can't help but smile. "No worries, I'll probably just stay here tonight."

He relaxes. "Okay. Will you still need to use my kitchen?"

"Probably not as much. But I can still make you dinner

on one of your nights off after your next shift rotation," I suggest.

"Yes." He nods.

"Good. Have a good shift if I don't see you before you go back to work. Stay safe."

"Lock up after I leave. I'll wait," he says, a hint of the forcefulness of his personality peeking through.

"I will." I smile, following him downstairs and loudly locking the door behind him while he stands and watches me. Exhaustion washes over me as I climb the stairs back up to the now half-empty apartment. I know I should keep going; the sooner I can get this place livable, the sooner I can move away from Nero. But I don't feel like I've sat down for longer than a minute since I signed the paperwork and officially took ownership of the store.

Without most of the junk and free of furniture, the small living room/kitchen feels airy, but I know it'll be cramped once there's a couch and TV in here. I make a halfhearted effort to open and sort through a box, but after five minutes, I decide to call it a night and go to bed.

For a moment, I consider driving home. My bed at the house is much more comfortable than the cheap one I bought for the apartment, but I'm so tired my body doesn't care, and I fall into bed, fully dressed. I'm asleep less than a minute later.

When my alarm goes off at six a.m., I groan, having to untangle my dress from the sheets before I can sit up. I don't remember putting my cell on to charge, but I must have because it's attached to a cable and sitting on the floor beside the bed. Reaching down, I silence the alarm, rubbing at my eyes tiredly as I try to focus on the screen.

My brothers have no concept of appropriate text etiquette and regularly send me messages at all times of the day and night, so it's not surprising to find I have unread messages. What is surprising is that four of them are from Nero.

A twinge of guilt fills me. It's probably good manners to text your roommate if you don't plan on coming home, but it's not like we're close or that I even expected him to notice that I wasn't there.

NERO
Where the fuck are you?

NERO
We need to talk.

NERO
WTF! Knight said you're not coming home. WHERE THE FUCK ARE YOU?????

NERO
This is bullshit, Tori. You need to get home, right now.

Is he seriously ordering me to go home? What am I, fifteen? Unbidden anger swirls to life in my stomach, my ire rising as I read and reread his messages. We're not friends. We're barely acquaintances. Who the hell does he think he is, ordering me to come home and interrogating my friends to find out where I am?

Does he really think kissing me twice gives him some right to intrude into my life? Gah, why is his growly, angry text tone kind of hot?

Nero Henderson is so confusing. He doesn't like me,

yet he kisses me. He avoids me when I'm at home, then demands to know where I am when I don't come home. What does he want from me? My feelings for him are equally confusing. I thought I wanted to be his friend, but now I'm not so sure. I hate that he doesn't like me, but that might just be because my pride is hurt.

But then he kissed me and I kissed him back. It certainly didn't feel like he hated me when his fingers were yanking my hair and his tongue was in my mouth. It didn't feel like I disliked him either when I was making myself come thinking of him.

My cell starts to ring while my fingers are hovering over the screen, debating what—if anything—I should reply. His name flashes and I fumble, almost dropping my cell and answering as I grip it tightly so it doesn't end up on the floor.

"Hello," he shouts, his voice tight.

"Err. What? Sorry. Hello," I ramble, finally lifting the cell to my ear. "Sorry, I almost dropped my phone."

"Tori," he snaps.

"Hi."

"Where the fuck are you? You didn't come home last night."

"I know," I say, deliberately answering vaguely. I don't know why I don't want to tell him about the store. Maybe it's because I'm not sure what he'll say, or maybe I'm just not ready to worry he might be an asshole about it.

"You know?" he barks. "So, what the fuck happened? Where are you?"

"Nero, we're not friends. You don't like me, remember?"

"Where the fuck are you?" he says through what sounds like gritted teeth.

"I'm fine. I'm at work."

"It's barely six in the fucking morning. Have you been at work all night? What the fuck is going on? Why the fuck would you need to be at work all the hours you have been the last couple of days to make fucking cookies?"

His easy dismissal of my job finally ignites my ire. I'm a chef, but the ease that he reduced my passion to baking cookies pisses me off.

"Look," I say coldly. "I don't need to explain myself to you. We're roommates and nothing more. You don't get to demand to know where I am and what I'm doing because I'm none of your business."

"The fuck you're not," he hisses, his words low, rough, and threatening.

"What?"

"You're my business," he growls.

"I'm really not."

"My tongue was in your fucking mouth yesterday. So yes, Tori, you're my fucking business. Tonight, we're going to talk, so make sure you're home at a decent time, or else I'll hunt your ass down and force you home over my fucking shoulder."

This is the first time either of us has mentioned the kisses we've shared and I don't know how I feel about it. He ran from the first kiss, and I ran from the second, and both of us have continued to act like nothing happened, so why is he bringing it up now?

"Tori, tell me you hear me and that you understand," he

demands.

"What is happening?" I ask, but I'm not sure if I'm asking him or myself.

"I have no fucking clue," he answers. "Tonight, Tori, no fucking excuses." Then he ends the call, leaving me bewildered and thoroughly confused.

Chapter Eleven

Nero

Ending the call, I stare down at the cell in my hand. My knuckles are white from gripping it so tightly and I'm amazed I haven't shattered the screen or thrown the fucking thing across the room.

Dealing with this woman is infuriating. She's the one who didn't come home and then she acts like I'm the freak for wanting to know where she is. Kissing her again yesterday was a mistake, but she has this effect on me and I seem to lose all reason and sense when I'm around her for too long. She's annoyingly upbeat and that constant smile is infuriating. But I can't stop thinking about the way she tastes, the spicy cookie scent that seems to cling to her, and the way my dick jumps to life the moment I even think about her.

I want her. There's no point denying it. I want Tori. I want her naked, beneath me, on top of me, full of me. I want to bend her over, spank her ass, and fuck her until she's so wrung out she doesn't have the energy to smile.

I want to watch her choke on my dick until tears fill her eyes. I want to fuck her until she's so full of me she loses the veneer of cheerfulness and I get to see the real person she is beneath.

Watching Knight leave his house to go to dinner with her was a lesson in self-control. It's only the fact that both of them confirmed they're not dating that kept me inside and not beating the shit out of him, so he wasn't capable of leaving.

A part of me wondered if she'd go to his place when they got back last night if maybe they were lying or denying the real relationship. But watching him come back alone was somehow worse.

I didn't even try to stop myself from banging on his door when she wasn't back an hour after he got home. When he answered, I demanded to know where she was, but he wouldn't give me details. He just told me she wasn't coming home.

Even now, I honestly don't know if I'd rather she be with him than be somewhere I don't know about, maybe even with someone I don't know about.

A growl slips past my lips and I really do throw my cell, hearing it hit the wall, then the floor with a thunk. I've been so worried about Knight that I hadn't considered she could be with someone else.

Would she have kissed me back if she was seeing

someone else? Miranda did. She kissed multiple other men, but at least I knew about them right from the start. With her, it was almost a relief to know she wasn't sitting around waiting for me or resenting my career and the time it stole from us.

Could I share Tori with another guy?

No.

The answer comes immediately, along with a barrage of anger that makes me want to find my cell and throw it again. I wouldn't, couldn't share her. I won't share her. She's mine.

Fuck.

She's mine.

What the hell am I going to do now?

Normally, I enjoy my days off. I visit my sister and nephew, hang out with my brother and make the most of my downtime, but today is an endless eternity, with every minute that passes making my skin itch with needy anticipation.

I try to think about what I'm going to say when I see her, but my mind is swirling with a mix of anger and lust that have meshed into an intense desire to fuck her or spank her, or maybe spank her while I fuck her.

By the time six p.m. rolls around, I'm a bundle of pent-up aggravation, contemplating if I'm actually willing to hunt her ass down like I said I would.

Keys turn in the front door before I have to make a final decision, and she steps inside wearing tight jeans and a pink tank with a black leather jacket. Her feet are clad in white sneakers, her hair is in a ponytail high on the back of her head, and her skin is free of makeup.

My dick twitches to life, eager to get closer to her and inhaling sharply, I send a silent message to it to back the fuck off. Tori and I are barely civil at the minute. There's no way she's going to let my dick anywhere near her.

Standing up from the couch, I take a step toward her and as if my movement pulls her attention, she turns her head and looks at me. "Hey," she says, her lips wide in her ever-present smile.

I don't know what happens or why I do it, but I close the distance between us in three long strides. One hand finds her nape, gripping tightly as I grab her ass with the other, pulling her to me until we're touching chest to chest, my dick grinding into her pussy.

Dipping my head, I claim her mouth with mine, kissing her like she's my salvation when, instead, I'm almost certain she'll be my demise. I won't stop this time; I won't let her go or walk away. I want her too much, and even though I'm confident this isn't what either of us needs, I can't stop.

Lifting her off the floor, she wraps her legs around my waist and I position her so the seam of her pants is directly over my cock. There's no way she could miss how hard I am. My dick wants her, and unless she pushes me away, I'm going to give in to this ridiculous need.

Walking away isn't an option. This moment, right now, is a bubble, and I won't be the one to burst it and allow reality and rational thought to stop me from claiming her. I press her back against the closed front door, pushing her jacket off and lifting her shirt, kissing her until the fabric separates us. Ripping it over her head, I reclaim her mouth while I fumble with her bra, unclasping it and freeing her tits.

Dragging my mouth from hers, I pull the cups of her bra off, only allowing myself a moment to take in the perfection of her full tits before I lift one up and pull her tight, pink nipple into my mouth.

Not trying to be gentle, I scrape my teeth over the tip, then bite, soothing the sting with my tongue. My dick swells when she moans like a porn star. She's the most dangerous kind of perfect and I want to destroy her almost as much as I want to cherish her.

Swapping to the other breast, I bite, suck, and tease, leaving tiny bruises on her tits, so there will be no doubt that I've been here by the time I'm done.

"Nero," she gasps when I leave a hickey on the swell of one breast.

"Pants off," I growl, lowering her to the floor and immediately fumbling with the button on her jeans. This is her chance, the opportunity to say no, to push me away, but instead, her pupils dilate and she bats my hands away, unfastening the button while I free the zipper and push her pants down over her hips.

Her sneakers fly across the room when she kicks them away and she wiggles the jeans off her ankles, leaving her naked except for a pair of white cotton panties. The sweet, innocent underwear is so at odds with this moment, and my lips curl into a grin. Reaching out, I slowly wrap my fingers around her throat, pushing her head back against the door.

For the first time, there's no damn fucking smile on her bee-stung lips and I love it. I don't want her to be happy and smiling. I want her desperate and feral and just as fucking angry about this as I am.

Because wanting her now isn't a choice, it's a compulsion.

Her lips part and I know she's going to speak, so I grip her throat a little tighter, cutting off her words. "The only word you get to say is no. Say it and this all stops. Otherwise, you stay fucking silent. Nod if you understand."

Fire smolders in her eyes and I revel in it. She's not fucking happy, but I've never seen her look more alive. Her chin moves up and down and I exhale, slowly and silently.

Reaching down, I roughly cup her sex, and the heat practically sears my palm as I grind the heel of my hand against the wet cotton. Grinning wider, I slide my fingers beneath the fabric, stifling a moan when I touch her bare sex.

Parting her folds, I plunge two fingers into her and her arousal instantly coats my hand. She's soaked, and a depraved part of me wonders if I ripped off her panties and forced her to widen her legs if her arousal would actually drip from her cunt. The idea makes a tiny burst of cum seep from my cock.

Her eyes are screaming at me to move, to plunge in and out of her, or replace my fingers with my tongue or cock, but I don't. Instead, I still. Two fingers fill her, my other hand around her throat, tight enough to feel the movement every time she swallows.

A whimper falls from her lips and I push my fingers in deeper. A part of me wants her to say no, to tell me to stop. At least then, I'll have no choice but to walk away, but when she leans into my hand at her throat, I know she isn't going to.

Neither of us wants to admit that we want this, but it's palpably clear that we're both willing to make this stupid decision together, and I want her too much to allow reason to push away any of my furious lust.

Slowly, I pull my fingers almost all the way out, then push them in deep, fucking her hard and slow while her cream drowns my hand. I want to taste her, but I'm not willing to pause this moment or look away from her eyes when she's this wildly beautiful.

Her breaths are ragged, even though my hold on her isn't restricting her breathing. Her cunt is gripping my fingers, clenching around them and tightening as she tries to hold me in place.

My dick is weeping and if I don't get inside of her soon, I'm going to blow my load in my pants, but I want to watch her fall apart. I want to see the inferno in her eyes as I make her come all over my hand.

I need to stretch her, but my hands are big, and as much as I want to push her limits, I don't want to hurt her. Instead, I move my hand faster, fucking her in frantic thrusts until her cunt becomes a clamp. She comes on a broken cry, her whole body shaking with the intensity of her release.

Unable to wait a moment longer, I pull my fingers from inside of her and rip her panties down. Ignoring the sound of the fabric shredding, I roughly shove them down her thighs, leaving her to kick them off as I rid myself of my own pants.

My dick is so hard it hurts, and my fingers fumble as I try to unbutton my jeans. Small hands join mine, and she helps me, her fingers trembling as she pushes the denim down and over my butt. The moment there's space, my dick pops free, precum eagerly dripping from the tip.

I've got a big dick. It's not scary huge, but it's big enough that I feel Tori's gulp when she sees it. If her cunt wasn't so greedy and wet, I'd have to find lube and put in some serious foreplay time to make sure she can take me, but I'm confident she's ready.

She whimpers again when I let go of her throat. My kinky little ray of sunshine likes it when I collar her. Gripping her hips, I lift her into the air and she wraps her legs around me again. I want to watch as I fill her cunt for the first time, so I press her back against the door, tilting her hips and holding her in place with one arm while I palm my dick and bring the head to her entrance.

Pausing, I lift my gaze from between her legs to her face. Her mouth is open, the fleshy part of her bottom lip imprisoned between her teeth. I don't plan to, but I lean forward and bite her, dragging her lip into my mouth and sucking on it lightly before kissing her and swallowing her taste.

When my senses are consumed by her scent and taste, I pull back, refocusing my gaze to where the head of my cock is teasing her entrance. Rolling my hips forward, I fill her in one slow glide, watching the lips of her pussy part to accept me.

A stifled groan falls from her lips, and her cunt strangles my cock. She's struggling to take me, but her muscles are so tight it's like she's refusing to let me go. I silently curse at how fucking perfect she is, hot, wet, and achingly tight.

Glancing up from between her thighs, I almost come

from the mesmerizing look on her face. Her eyes are glazed and wide with lust and just a hint of pain. Her cheeks are flushed, her chest rising up and down, tiny tremors ricocheting through her arms and legs as she struggles to stay in place.

My dick twitches, threatening to unman me, so I ease my pace, grinding my dick before withdrawing slowly until only the head is still inside of her. Like everything with Tori, I don't *plan* to slam back into her, but my body takes over, instinctually needing to claim her.

Her pussy tightens, but I force my way in, filling her while she whines and moans, her fingers digging into my shoulders. "Oh fuck, how fucking big is that thing?" she shrieks when I start to fuck her in long, deep thrusts.

Watching her cunt spread wide around my dick is addicting, but this is about more than just what I can see. My eyes drift upward, over her soft stomach and her full tits that are bouncing from the force of my movements to her face. She's beautiful normally, but like this, raw, wild, and free, she's stunning. I dip my head and find her lips again, pushing my tongue into her mouth.

Tori isn't what I was expecting. She's so wrong and so fucking right all at the same time. Night and day, heaven and hell, life or the most delicious kind of death. She's a vice that could so easily become an addiction, and I know I'm not strong enough to resist, not that I'm even trying.

My mouth on hers muffles the sounds that I'm forcing from her lips, so I release her, finding the fluttering pulse in her throat and dragging my tongue over it. She tastes like sweat, desire and cookies. It's a bizarre combination that I want to drown in.

"Nero, oh fuck, I'm going to. Oh fuck," she cries when her cunt becomes impossibly tight, bearing down on me and almost strangling my dick.

"Come," I growl, holding her in place while I fuck her with brutal abandon. I've fucked women plenty of times, but whatever the hell this is with her, it's a brand-new experience.

When her orgasm hits, she clenches around me so tightly that a guttural grunt bursts from behind my clenched teeth, and I have to focus on counting backward just to stop myself from coming.

My gaze locks with hers and I watch her fall apart, her long, slender neck tensing as she throws her head back and wails. In this moment, all of her sunshine has darkened to something more intense. The sun comes out every day, but right now, she's a total eclipse, rare, elusive, and breathtaking.

Heat builds low in my stomach, and as much as I want this to last, I know my resolve is fading. Slamming into her, I lean forward and kiss her again as my balls draw up and I explode, filling her cunt with my cum and claiming her as mine.

Chapter Twelve

Tori

Wave after wave of bliss washes over me, and my eyes close, squeezing shut against the onslaught of sensation. Firm, unyielding lips press against mine and he kisses me, swallowing all my animalistic sounds, his hips rolling furiously as he fucks me in a way I've never been fucked before.

I'm not a nun. I've had plenty of sex, even some good sex, but I have never had this before. In the past, even great sex was all about what was going on between my thighs. That's not a problem. I like feeling all the good pussy reactions. It's where the magic's happening, after all. Somehow, Nero has made sex a whole-body, sense-altering experience. He's not just fucking my pussy. He's fucking my mind, my sight, my sound, my aura.

The door is cool at my back, but the cold air warring against my heated nakedness is just another layer of this overwhelming experience. His movements become erratic and he fucks me with abandon, his monster of a cock destroying my pussy in the very best way. When he comes, I swallow the noises he makes this time, riding out my own high alongside his as he slows his thrusts, pulling his lips from mine and burying his face in my neck.

When the euphoria of the pleasure begins to fade, I blink away the veneer of lust and start to question what the hell just happened. Nero and I aren't together. He demanded I come home and then the moment I stepped through the door, he jumped me and now I'm naked and impaled on a very large cock.

Is this what he had planned all along? He doesn't like me; he told me that and has treated me like I was an inconvenience at best and an enemy in other moments. But I guess he has kissed me a few times. Was that what all the kissing was about? Does he think we're together now? Was this a hate fuck? Or some kind of messed-up revenge? So many unanswered questions run on a loop through my mind, and I squeeze my eyes closed tight for a second to silence the voices in my head.

"Stop," he growls, grinding his hips. His dick is softening, but I still shudder, immediately settling a little at his demand.

"Nero."

He sighs and the action moves his whole body. Slowly he withdraws his cock, the head finally sliding free, but instead of letting me go, he leans forward and presses his lips to mine once more. This kiss isn't hard or rough. Instead, it's butterfly soft and gentle, and the juxtaposition is so startling that it's almost as confusing as how we ended up in this position in the first place.

Sighing again, he slowly lowers me to the ground, holding me up when my legs shake. He seems almost reluctant, but he lets his fingers slide from my waist until finally his touch is gone, and I'm naked, his cum dripping down my thighs while he stares at me intently, his softening cock on display, wet with a mixture of both of our arousal.

"What was that?" I whisper.

His expression becomes strained. "You know what that was."

Something about the way his eyes wrinkle and narrow makes me suddenly self-conscious and I look around, searching for my clothes. My pants are somewhere across the room and I don't know where my shirt is.

Tutting, he grabs the back of his shirt and drags it off in that effortless way only hot men can do. "Here," he says, holding it out to me.

I should absolutely refuse it, but I don't. Pulling it on, I inhale his sexy scent as the cotton slides down my body. When I'm covered, I attempt to lift my gaze to his face, but I stumble at his chest, losing my train of thought as my eyes slide over the rise and fall of his toned abs.

A soft chuckle echoes through the air and my head snaps up to his face. It's the first time I've heard him laugh and I don't know how to cope with how sexy the sound is. I shouldn't be thinking about how attractive his amusement is. I shouldn't be thinking about him at all, but we just had sex up against a door, and no matter how funny that is to him, I need to know what the hell just happened.

"Nero. What?" My words dry up because how do I even start this conversation?

"I want you," he says, startling me.

"You don't like me."

"Doesn't mean I don't want you," he says bluntly.

What do I even say to that? Is he seriously telling me that he wants to fuck me, even though he actively dislikes me? "No thank you," I say.

"What?" his voice is gruff and low.

"I said, no thank you."

"What does that even mean?" he demands, all traces of amusement gone and replaced with his standard grumpy expression.

"You want me and I said no thank you."

"You weren't saying no when your cunt was full of my cock."

His bold words make my sex pulse and clench, and a fresh gush of his cum seeps out of me.

"This was clearly a mistake," I blurt.

"A mistake?" he says slowly.

"I don't even know how it happened."

"Are you trying to tell me you didn't want this?" he asks, his tone measured, like he's making sure there's no doubt what he's asking.

"I didn't say no if that's what you're getting at. This"—I wave my hand in the air—"was all consensual."

His shoulders drop in clear relief, and for a second, I feel like a huge asshole, but then I remember what he just admitted. That he wants to fuck me while actively disliking me.

"So," he says, stepping toward me, his dick still hanging out of his pants, slowly hardening again.

"It's still a no thank you," I snap.

"You want me, Tori. There's no point in lying. Your body doesn't lie anywhere near as well as you do. I bet if I was to lift that shirt, you'd be dripping, your hungry cunt more than ready to be filled with my cock. Those full tits of yours would be flushed pink again, your tight nipples desperate to be tugged, bitten, and sucked on. So, say no to me again. I fucking dare you."

His eyes have turned molten, and I swallow down the needy whine that's vibrating in the back of my throat, desperate to burst free. Like my body has been trained to react to his words, my pussy clenches, making a fresh gush of cum escape. My breasts tighten and my nipples pebble, ready to beg for his attention.

My body is a hussy for him and I'm not sure I'm strong enough to be the voice of reason.

"That's a good girl, Sunshine, lift that shirt, let me have a look at your greedy cunt. I want to see you so full of my cum that you just can't keep any more of it inside of you. Maybe then I'll fill your tight ass. Has anyone's dick been inside your ass, Sunshine? Do you like to be fucked in such a naughty place? I think you'll love it. I think you'll beg me to take you there when I've worn your cunt out for the night."

From the moment he kissed me when I walked through the door to him coming inside of me, I think he said one, maybe two words. If he'd been like that again, I think I could have coped, but dirty talk is my weakness. His spelling out each filthy little thing he wants is like verbal foreplay and I wonder if I could come just from the words. Right now, my body is vibrating and I'm not sure if it's beneath my skin or if he can see it. See how much he's affecting me.

His eyes go hooded and he steps closer again. "Answer the question, Sunshine. Has anyone's cock been deep in your ass, or is it still a virgin hole waiting to be defiled?"

My throat thickens and I know I couldn't speak even if I could find the words, so I just shake my head.

"Good girl. I love the idea of breaking your virgin ass in. I'll be careful. I'll stretch you out good with my fingers and maybe a toy or two. I bet you've got all sorts of toys you like to play with. Maybe I'll let you show me how you fuck yourself. But not now. Now I'm going to bend you over, spank your ass until it's pink and hot, then I'm going to watch my dick destroy your cunt until you're screaming. After your cunt is full of me, I'm going to fuck those perfect tits and come in your mouth."

A whimper finally escapes and I squeeze my thighs together, unable to hide the way I'm reacting to him for even a second longer.

"Oh, Sunshine, I think I like it when you try to stay quiet. But I think you like it even more when I talk. You like hearing all the things I plan to do to you. Don't you?"

I nod again, and when he smiles, it lights up his whole face. A second later, his shoulder hits my stomach and I'm airborne, his shirt falling forward and exposing my ass. His palm lands on my butt cheek and I squeal. A burning sensation ricochets across the skin of my ass, changing to a heated warmth that burns in the most delicious way. I haven't been spanked since I was a kid, and my brain is struggling to process enjoying the sensation.

Climbing the stairs, he swats my ass every few steps until he pushes open the door to his bedroom and throws me down onto the bed. My butt hits the comforter and I hiss at the sting of pain.

"Roll onto your stomach, hands and knees. I want your ass high in the air."

I absolutely know I shouldn't do as he asks, but I comply anyway, slowly getting into position and putting my ass and sex on display for him.

"Lose the shirt, I want to watch your tits bounce while I fuck you."

Sitting up, I strip off his shirt, then drop back down to all fours, pressing my palms into his plain white comforter.

I squeak in surprise when he pushes two fingers into my sex, lurching forward and almost toppling over.

"Look how juicy and wet this cunt is. So slick and coated in me. My dick's stretched you out so fucking good, I bet I could get three fingers in you now, fuck, maybe if we worked at it, you could even take my whole hand."

Fear at the idea of him trying to fit his whole freaking hand inside of me has my butt and sex clenching. A low chuckle fills the air. "You don't like the idea of me fisting you, Sunshine? I bet you'd scream and squirt until you were a filthy, wet mess. But that's okay. I have other plans for you anyway. Don't move."

His fingers pull out of me and I feel him step away.

Glancing over my shoulder, I search for him, twisting my head around to see where he is, but I can't see him.

"Nero," I call, starting to feel self-conscious at the vulnerable position I'm in. Naked and on display. Just when I decide to move and put his shirt back on again, he strides back into the room, carrying a very familiar purple dildo in his hands.

"I knew you were a dirty little girl, Sunshine. All those toys hidden in your dresser. None of those plastic cocks are as big as me, but that's okay. I like the idea that no matter how many times you get off on them, I'll always stretch you out when I make you take my dick."

All my words dry up and I just gape at him, my mouth falling open as I watch him hold the dildo in his hand, testing the weight and girth.

"Spread your knees," he orders.

When I don't move, he positions himself behind me and spanks my pussy with the soft plastic cock.

A startled gasp bursts from me and he chuckles again. "Oh, Sunshine, you dirty, dirty girl. Do you want me to spank your pussy again?"

I can't speak, but apparently, he doesn't need me to. This time, it's his palm that lands on my swollen, wet sex. The sharp burst of pain morphs almost immediately into burning heat that pulses bright and fucking glorious within me.

His fingers fill me again and he fucks me roughly for a few seconds, then pulls out, leaving me empty and needy. Twisting my head, I look behind me and find him using his hand and coating the dildo with my own arousal.

I open my mouth to protest but then snap my lips shut again when he presses the head of the toy to my sex, pushing it into me until I can feel the base of it against my pussy lips.

"Fuck, I like that. I like seeing your pussy swallow your dildo like it takes my dick. Clench down on it. I want you to hold it inside of you while I spank your ass."

Tightening my pelvic floor, I pull in my stomach as much as I can, but even though he's told me what he plans to do, I'm still unprepared when his palm lands on my ass. He does it a second and third time and my butt gyrates, arching toward his hand, silently begging for more.

He spanks me a fourth time, then caresses the skin with his fingers. "Fuck, you're already going pink."

I feel it when he grabs hold of the end of the toy and starts to fuck me with it, thrusting it in and out of my pussy.

Moaning, I move, pushing my hips back into him, fucking the toy while he fucks me with it. Before now, I'd never played with a toy with a guy. For the most part, my exes were offended by my dildo and vibrator collection, like it was a personal affront to them that I had needs and was willing to take charge of my own sexual satisfaction without them.

Filling me with the toy, Nero holds it in place, and I feel wetness drip against my other hole. I still, my whole body tensing. I've never done any kind of anal play. My ex's have never suggested it and although I was curious after falling down an anal rabbit hole on a porn site one day, I've never found someone I'd be interested in exploring it with.

Nero isn't asking permission. He's forging ahead. I feel his finger at my hole, then he pauses, not applying any pressure, just waiting. He's giving me the chance to say no, only I'm not going to, and when he realizes that, his finger presses against my ass, eventually sliding inside.

"That's it, Sunshine, bear down, let me watch you push your tight virgin asshole onto my finger."

His dirty words urge me on and I do exactly as he says, pushing slowly back, letting his fingers fill my hole. There's a burning sensation, a slight pain, then an odd feeling of fullness that surprises me when I feel my butt hit his palm.

"Look at you," he coos, low and gravelly. "How does it feel, dirty girl? I bet you feel full with just one finger. Imagine how you'll feel when I slide my fat cock into this tight hole."

His words only heighten the sensation and I grind my hips.

"Patience, Sunshine. I'll give you what you want, but only when I'm ready to give it. Until then, you'll behave."

Holding the end of the dildo, he starts to fuck me with it, hard and fast, keeping his finger in my ass but not moving it. My clit aches to be touched and I drop down to my elbows, freeing one of my hands so I can shove it between my legs.

"No," Nero snarls, pulling his finger from my ass and the toy from my sex, then spanking me hard, first one cheek, then the other. "If your fingers touch this cunt without my permission, I'll stop."

Slowly, I consider if I should just carry on. It's my body, and he can't tell me what to do. Having sex with him again is a terrible idea, but I still drag my hand from between my thighs and reposition it beneath my chest alongside my other arm.

"Good girl," he coos softly. "Are you needy, Sunshine? Do you need my dick?"

Since the moment he touched me, all of the words that I should have said have refused to burst free, but now, when I should be silent, I can't stop myself. "Yes."

"Ask me then, dirty girl. Ask me to fuck your cunt with my cock. Ask me to take you over and over until you can't take anymore."

"Please."

"You never normally shut up, so I want to hear the words. I want my dirty little sunshine to beg for my cock."

"Fuck me."

"How many times?"

"Until I can't take it anymore," I beg.

I hear the sound of fabric rustling and when he finally climbs onto the bed behind me, he's naked, the hair on his thighs tickling the backs of my legs. Slapping his hand down hard on my butt, he guides his dick to my entrance and slides easily inside, my core wet and ready for him.

Instead of jackhammering into me like I was expecting, he slowly inches in until his stomach is pressed tight against my butt and I'm so full my eyes water. One of his hands holds my hip, but the other slides around to my clit, finding it easily and rubbing in gentle circles.

My body reacts instantly and I moan, wantonly pushing my butt against him and prompting him to move.

"My dirty girl needs to come. So you're going to come while I rub your clit and you warm my cock."

Circling my clit with his finger, he works me toward an orgasm, not pushing too fast, just building me higher and higher until I'm squirming, panting and desperate.

"More," I beg. "Please."

Instead of fucking me like I want him to, he pulls back and spanks my clit with two fingers. I scream and he continues to rub again, pushing me to the edge and then slowly backing off, only to work me back up again.

"Nero, please, please, please."

"Does my dirty girl need to come?" he taunts.

"Yes."

"Tell me what you are."

"What?" I question.

"If you want to come, you need to tell me what you are."

Realization washes over me, along with a bout of humiliation that only makes me even more desperate. I never imagined I'd be into this kind of thing, but apparently, I am, and the words fall from my lips. "I'm a dirty girl."

I don't know what he does, but when his fingers move, it feels amazing, and within seconds, I'm squirming on his cock, trying to grind myself against his fingers, frantic to reach the peak before he stops again. But he doesn't stop, and I tip over the edge, free-falling into the oblivion of my orgasm, screaming incoherent words while I twitch and writhe.

"Good girl, such a good girl," he coos, talking me down as he slowly starts to glide his dick in and out of me. "Stay still, put your cheek on the comforter and take what I give you. You've been so perfect. I'm going to give you everything you need, over and over. I'm going to fill you with my cum and make you hold it inside of you."

A hand presses between my shoulders and he slowly guides me down until my chest is flat against the bed, my face turned so my cheek is resting on the comforter. I expect him to release me, but he doesn't. Instead, his fingers curl around the back of my neck, holding me down while he starts to move inside of me.

His dick fills me, then retreats in long glides, bottoming out completely and making feral grunts fall from my lips each time he forces the last of his length into my sex. It doesn't take long for the friction and sensation of being helpless to heighten everything, and my grunts become sighs and moans.

"Are you going to soak my cock, Sunshine? I can feel you tightening around me, trying to get your gift before I'm ready. Such a greedy girl," he purrs, his voice as smooth as whiskey, each word filling me and stoking the fire inside of me even higher.

I've never had an orgasm just from penetration before, so it takes me off guard, shattering inside of me and causing every one of my muscles to tighten. His dick feels even bigger and his measured thrusts become wild and punishing.

"Fuck, Sunshine, your cunt is strangling me. You're so desperate, so I'm going to give you my cum. I can't wait either."

His fingers on my neck tighten, and even though I'm not going anywhere, he pins me in place like I'm trying to escape. Slamming his dick into me, pleasure and pain mingle when he pushes into me so deeply, his hips dig into my ass with each thrust.

When he comes, it's on a groan, and he jerks as he

fills me with his cum. His weight rests on me, pushing me even farther into the comforter, but it's not uncomfortable, so I exhale, my breathing fast and labored, even though I haven't had to do anything but lie here.

I expect him to pull out, but he doesn't. After a while, he lifts his weight a little, releasing his hold on my neck but keeping a single finger at the base of my hairline, like he can't quite stop touching me there. The hand that was gripping my hip slides down and between my legs, tracing the lips of my sex where they're still spread around his dick.

The silence becomes thick between us and I have the urge to run away, like distance will make this all a dream, and I won't have had weird, kinky, sexy, unprotected sex with my roommate. Maybe I could have called once an aberration, but twice… well, I'm struggling to even explain to myself how I could have fallen and landed on his dick twice without admitting that I wanted it to happen.

The fingers that were playing with where we're still connected slide up and over my ass, a single finger finding my asshole and pressing down lightly over it.

Tensing, I try to turn and look at him, but the finger still on my neck presses down and I freeze in place. "Such a pretty little hole," he murmurs almost to himself, then he makes a noise and wetness hits my ass crack and hole.

"Did you just spit on me?" I rasp, unsure if I'm disgusted or turned on.

"Yes," he says simply. "Lube would be better, but you didn't have any, so spit will have to do for now. When I stretch you out properly, you'll need something better, but right now, I just want to play a little."

There's another wet sound as he spits again, then his fingertip presses against my ass, applying unrelenting pressure until the muscle relaxes and he slowly fills me. My pussy is still full of his dick and with his thick finger in my ass, I feel even more stretched.

"Oh fuck," I gasp.

"My dirty girl has a tight ass, but eventually, you'll take my dick in here. I can't wait to watch your hole stretch to take me." Using slow, careful thrusts, he fucks my ass with his finger, and I don't hate it. Mainly, it feels weird, in a kind of nice way. It's not going to make me come, but it doesn't feel bad or hurt too much.

Without any warning, he moves and his dick slides free of my pussy, leaving me empty and exposed. His finger pushes all the way into my ass and I gasp, jolting forward now I'm not held in place by his dick. Fingers probe at my sore pussy and I squirm, unsure if I want him to stop or to force him to keep going.

"Look at you, keeping all my cum inside of you. You're such a good girl. I want you to come for me. I want you to come with my finger in your ass so your cunt swallows my cum nice and deep."

His hand starts to move, fucking my pussy with two fingers and my ass with a third. Lifting his finger from my neck, he reaches beneath me, finding my clit and tapping it lightly over and over. The sensations are all different, but they join together like this rising tide moving to the shore. I try to move, but any direction I go either pushes me farther onto his probing fingers or into his hand that's steadily tapping my clit, making it pulse and swell.

The wave of sensation grows and grows until it's a tsunami that I know will pull me under and swallow me whole. When I come, I close my eyes, squeezing them tightly shut as I shake and scream, detonating until the whole world shatters around me and the only things that are left are me and him.

Chapter Thirteen

Nero

Fucking hell, she's magnificent. I thought fucking her against the door, wild and unrestrained was hot as fuck, but having her like this. At my mercy and loving every minute of it is life changing.

The women I've had sex with in the past have all been happy to play rough. To allow me to edge into the kinkier things I enjoy in bed. But they've more tolerated rather than embraced them. I'm not a sexual deviant, my tastes aren't even particularly kinky, but I like control, submission, a lot of ass play and a bit of degradation and praise when I'm in the mood.

Miranda enjoyed name-calling, but she wanted me to call her a slut, a whore, and a hole to be used, and none of those things are terms I'm hugely comfortable with. For me, it's only sexy if it's subtly humiliating, not out and out abusive, and until now, I've never found anyone I could truly indulge in the kink with.

I didn't plan to call Tori my dirty girl, but I couldn't keep the words inside. And when I made her say it to me, when she called herself a dirty girl and begged for my cock, I almost blew my load right then and there.

Every single thing we've done since we got up to my bedroom is the best sexual experience of my life. Having her warm my cock while I played with her clit, spanking her and fingering her ass, holding her down and forcing her to take what I gave her. Jesus, just reliving it in my thoughts is making my dick hard again.

I didn't know sex could be like this. Sure, I've had good sex. I've even had what I thought was great sex, but none of it compares to this. To her. A part of me foolishly thought if I fucked her, it would get her out of my system, that it was the wanting her and her being almost off-limits that was making her seem more appealing to me.

Then I pulled her clothes off her and ran my gaze over her naked body. That's when I realized how fucked I really am because she's a goddess. Full hips, thick thighs, an ass that I know I'll spend the next twenty years fantasizing about fucking, and tits; Jesus, her tits. Full and high and creamy skinned. I've never seen such perfect real tits in my fucking life.

I always knew she was beautiful, but now I know calling her beautiful is almost an insult. She's stunning, sexy, perfect. Mine. She's mine, and I don't even know how to start to process that.

I've never wanted a woman to be mine. I've never

looked at a woman I've been dating and thought, she's mine and I will kill anyone who tries to take her from me.

But that's how I feel about Tori. She's mine and that's that. Not having her isn't an option and after tonight, I know she feels the same way. It doesn't matter that I'm not crazy about how loud, cheerful and happy she is. I can tolerate that. Or maybe I can keep her mouth full of my dick so much I don't have to listen to her talk and talk and talk.

Reluctantly, I slide my fingers from her ass and then carefully roll her to her side while I get up and head to the bathroom to wash my hands. She's still where I put her when I get back, so I slide into bed beside her, lifting her up so she's curled up on my chest, her cheek resting against my pec.

Soon I'll need her again. I promised her I was going to fuck her tits and I still intend to. I plan to claim her over and over until she's branded in my scent, my touch, and my cum. By the time I have to go to work in the morning, I want her so sore she can barely walk, and each step will make her think about me until I get back off shift. But for now, I'm happy to lie here like this, quiet and sated.

I know the moment she comes out of her orgasm daze because she tenses, then sighs. I don't know what that means, but I don't plan on asking. Starting a conversation with her right now would be a mistake. We'll have plenty of time for her to talk to me in the future, but right now, I just want to enjoy her and how fucking perfect she is. When she falls asleep, I let her rest, stroking the side of her breast and teasing her nipple.

The fucked-up, animalistic side of me wants to lift her

leg and slide my cock back into her while she sleeps, but I manage to hold back. Soon, I'll have to wake her up, but for now, I'm happy to watch her sleep.

An hour later, my dick is rock hard and raring to go. Carefully, I roll us to the side, then position her on her back, slowly sliding my arm from beneath her. Taking a moment, I look down at her, laid out on the comforter like a present just waiting to be opened. When she sighs and moves slightly, her legs fall apart, putting her perfect cunt, still wet and glistening with my cum, on display for me. Reaching out, I slide a finger through her folds, dipping it inside of her. She's wet but disappointingly no longer sloppy and full of my cum.

That's okay. I'll fill her up again soon, but first, I need to wake her up. Shuffling down the bed, I position myself between her thighs, spreading them wide to accommodate my shoulders. Her clit is a little swollen, peeking out temptingly from the hood and I dip my head and run my tongue over the tiny ball of nerves.

She tastes like a mixture of me and her, and I don't hate it. Licking her again, I slowly pump my finger in and out of her sex, not trying to make her come just yet, just playing with her.

Her muscles tighten and I smile, flicking my tongue over her clit slowly, then faster, until her hips start to twitch in her sleep. Adding a second finger, I spread the wetness she's creating, lubing her up and making her ready to take me. I want to play with her ass again, push two fingers into her tight hole and watch it spread to take them, but I want her to love ass play as much as I do, which means making sure she's not in any pain.

When I finish my next four shifts, I'm going to fill her ass with lube, then play with it, carefully stretching her while I hold the Hitachi wand I found in her drawer against her clit. I'm going to train her brain to associate her ass with orgasms until she's begging me to fuck her daily in her tight, forbidden hole.

All the depraved things I want to do to her start to play on a reel through my mind while I eat her pussy and finger fuck her. Taking her ass is my number one, but then fucking her pussy while her ass is full of the dildo we played with earlier is definitely a close second. Having her ride me in front of the mirror, dirty talking into her ear as I tell her how much I love her being my dirty girl, is absolutely top five.

So is setting her on my cock and forcing her to watch a movie or eat dinner, not giving her what she wants, while I edge her until she's begging me to fuck her any which way I please.

Jesus, my dick is seeping precum, and I'm no longer playing with her. I'm fucking her with my fingers and sucking on her clit while her hips bounce and jerk beneath me,

"Nero," she rasps sleepily,

"Come for me, dirty girl, come all over my face."

As if I've trained her to climax on demand, her body goes tense and she cries out, whimpering and squeezing her thighs together like she can push me out of the way.

"So fucking perfect, such a good girl," I praise, pulling my fingers from inside of her and pushing them into my mouth.

Climbing over her, I straddle her waist, gripping my dripping cock in my palm. "Lift your head," I order.

Her gaze is confused, but she does as I say and lifts her head. Sliding a pillow beneath her, I position myself over her chest. "Push your tits together and open your mouth."

I'm being a bossy motherfucker, but my dick is about to explode and I plan to do it on her face after fucking her tits.

Her movements are slow, but when she finally realizes what I want, she grabs her breasts and pushes them together. Reaching my hand behind me, I shove two fingers into her cunt, collecting as much of her cream as I can, then rub it over my dick, using her cum as lube. Slowly, I slide my dick between her tits until the head pops out of her cleavage. "Open your mouth and tip your chin. I want my dick between your lips every time I slide between my dirty girl's tits."

She follows my orders like a perfect little submissive, and I start to pump back and forth, fucking her tits until I come with a cry. Streaks of white cum hit her lips, chin, and chest, and I want to throw my arms into the air and celebrate like I just scored the winning touchdown at the Super Bowl.

"I need to clean up," she says, her voice raspy.

My chest is heaving, my breaths ragged, but I move down her body until I can take her in. Her cheeks are flushed a sexy pink color. Her hands are still holding her tits together, her nipples dark pink and begging to be sucked on. But despite how sexy she is, my eyes follow the streaks of my cum that are decorating her. Pride fills my chest as I rake my eyes over how I've claimed her, marked her. It's depraved and dirty and fucking perfect.

There's a pearl of cum on her lip and I lean down, collecting it on my fingertip, then push it into her mouth. "Suck."

Her eyes are like saucers, but she doesn't argue, sucking my finger and then swallowing. A part of me wants to collect all of the cum from her skin and feed it to her, but instead, I draw a path over her skin, rubbing my release in and forcing her body to accept it. Watching me, she stays still and lets me do it, her breath hitching every time I touch her. "Let's take a shower," I say when I've finished.

Her lips part, but I don't want to listen to her chatter, so I scoop her into my arms and carry her to the bathroom across the hall. Setting her down on the counter, I turn on the shower, then pick her up again and position us beneath the stream of water.

Her expression is a little glazed and I silently pat myself on the back for sexing her so thoroughly that not only is she quiet, but she's almost subdued. She reaches for the shower gel, but I grab it first, squirting some into my hands before rubbing it over her skin. Her eyes close and she sighs when I lather her hair with shampoo and then smooth conditioner through the long strands.

My dick is hard again by the time I wrap her in a towel and carry her to my bed.

"Nero," she says.

"In," I growl, pulling back the sheets and motioning for her to climb in.

She starts to speak again, but I narrow my eyes at her, and sighing, she clambers onto the bed, her towel still around her.

"Be a good girl and get some sleep. I'm going to need you again soon," I warn her, dragging the towel from her body and pulling her on top of me again. She stays tense for longer than I'd like, but eventually, her breathing evens out and she falls asleep.

I woke her twice in the night, the first time by lifting her legs onto my shoulders and fucking her hard and fast until she was brimming with my cum again. The second time by lifting her on top of me and making her ride my dick, guiding her movements with my hands tightly gripping her hips while I sucked bruises onto her neck and tits.

The sun is almost up when I finally fall asleep; my dick too well used to consider getting hard again.

When I wake up, I reach for her, eager to start the day inside of her. Only the other side of the bed is empty, and the sheets are cold. Sitting bolt upright, I scan the room, looking for any sign of her, but there's nothing. Even the shirt she was wearing when I carried her up here is folded neatly and draped over the back of a chair.

Jumping out of bed, I head for the bathroom, piss, then barge straight into her bedroom, wondering if she decided to shower in her room, only both are empty with no sign of her.

Not bothering to put on any clothes, I stomp downstairs and glance out of the window. Her car is gone. She fucking left. Sprinting upstairs, I throw open the door to my room and search for my cell, pulling up her number and hitting dial.

"Hello," she answers.

"Where the fuck are you?" I growl.

"Who is this?"

"Are you fucking serious?" I demand. "It's Nero."

There's a pause and then she clears her throat. "Sorry, I'm driving. I can't see the caller ID on my hands-free."

"Answer the fucking question, Tori, where the hell are you?"

"I'm on the way to work?"

"Why?"

"Because I have a job," she croaks.

"It's five in the fucking morning. You don't normally leave this early."

"I have four birthday cakes being collected today."

"Come home," I order.

"Why?"

"Because I wasn't expecting to wake up alone," I snarl angrily.

"Err." She clears her throat again. "Well, you didn't get much sleep. I didn't want to wake you."

Her perpetually cheerful tone is back, and it does nothing to calm the raging anger waking up alone has caused.

"I'll see you when you get home, Tori."

"Nero, I have to work. I can't just come home."

"Sunshine, I have to go to work in a couple of hours too. I won't get to play with your pussy for another four days, so be a good girl and come home."

Her tiny gasp is audible and I smile, allowing the sound to settle some of my churning anger. I hate that she's not here and that I can't truly order her to come back. It feels like all I'm doing lately is sitting around and waiting for her, but this will be the last time I do it. From now on, I'll have her home, waiting for me to come in the door.

I want my dirty girl on her knees, mouth open, in the doorway, waiting for me after days of missing me, ready to be as filthy as I tell her to be.

Fuck, my dick is hard again and I have nothing but my own hand and depraved thoughts of Tori to help me sate my need for her. I'm tempted to beat one out in the shower, but allowing my cum to wash down the drain feels like a waste when I could be filling one of her holes with it.

"I'm sorry, I can't," she whispers, then ends the call.

Anger and proprietary need swell to a crescendo in my gut, and I reach down and squeeze my dick tightly. I don't even know where these kinky cravings are coming from. I've never cared where my cum ended up before. Most of the time, it's inside a condom or a mouth if the woman I was seeing was willing. Last night was the first time I've ever had unprotected sex and it was fucking unbelievable.

All the stuff the condom companies say about not being able to feel the difference is utter bullshit. Being inside Tori bare was a fucking revelation. In the back of my mind, a part of me knows that I should be freaking out about how many times I fucked her and filled her with my cum, but I can't bring myself to care.

Seeing her cunt coated in my release was mind altering, and I don't think I'll ever be able to bring myself to use a condom with her. I know babies are a real possibility, but instead of the idea scaring me, it only makes me harder.

There's something primal about breeding a woman, fucking her with the sole purpose of filling her with a baby, and I want it. I want to force my cum deep inside of her, so deep that it takes root and breeds her. I want to take her over and over until even fate and the laws of science and percentages don't apply to us. I want to breed her so hard; her body can't do anything but get pregnant with my baby.

Hell, I wasn't even sure I wanted kids until I saw her pussy full of me and then everything clicked into place. Now, claiming her, keeping her, and breeding her feel like my only important roles in life.

She's mine. And the caveman Neanderthal inside of me is taunting me that the only way to make sure the whole fucking world knows she belongs to me is to brand her with a swollen belly and a ring on her finger.

Pissed that she's not coming home, I leave my room and cross the hall, pushing through the door and into her room again. Her gauzy, white princess bed dominates the space, hundreds of fluffy, soft, and furry throw pillows piled artfully at the head and almost transparent white fabric floating from the tall posts, making the bed look like it would be more at home in a fairy tale, or a filthy Arabian nights porno.

Striding past the bed, I head into her bathroom and start to root through the cabinets, looking for birth control pills, condoms, or anything that hints at how she's protecting herself from pregnancy.

I don't know how long it's been since she's been in a relationship. If she's been single for a while, she might not be using any birth control, but I doubt I'm that lucky. She never said a word last night about me not using a condom, but I deliberately didn't give her much thinking time, keeping her orgasm dazed for as long as possible before my body pushed me to take her again.

When it's clear my search is fruitless, I put everything back in the places I found them and start to just peruse her things, paying attention to what she has out and what's hidden in cupboards. When I've finished in the bathroom, I look through the dresser in her room and inside her closet. Apart from the abundance of sex toys, nothing else jumps out at me.

Abandoning my search in her bedroom, I head to the now-empty third room and open the boxes she stored in there after she moved in. All but one is full of cooking books and journals filled with recipes and notes. The only box that isn't food or cooking-related is filled with well-read erotic novels. Picking one out at random, I turn it over and start to read the blurb on the back cover. "Obsessed: to be preoccupied or fill the mind with someone continually and to a troubling extent. As soon as I realized she existed, I lost the ability to look away. She was always destined to be mine."

Smiling, I turn the book over and look at the title *Obsession*. How apt. Because that's how I feel now. Obsessed.

Chapter Fourteen

Tori

Tiptoeing from the room, I cast one last glance back at Nero and his perfect body stretched out in his bed. Sneaking away from him like this is the height of cowardice, but I'm not sure what the hell will happen if we wake up next to each other. Will he hate me again in the light of day? Will he go back to ignoring and sniping at me at every turn and accusing me of sleeping with his teammates?

"Oh god," I gasp, then slap my hand over my mouth to stifle the sound. Is that what this was about? Did Nero and I have sex because he thought I was planning to sleep with his friends? Was fucking me his way of protecting his team from me? The thought makes me feel sick and I rush into my room and into the bathroom, leaning over the toilet just in time for the vomit to gush from my mouth.

As I purge the contents of my stomach, my mind replays everything that happened last night. If you discard the epic sex and just look at what he said and the way he said it, he told me he wanted me, but he didn't say he cared about me or liked me. In fact, I think he might have actually agreed when I pointed out that he hated me.

Oh god. A fresh bout of vomit surges out of me and I sink down to my knees, tears rolling down my cheeks. Was everything that happened between us a strategic move to make sure I didn't mess with his team? Am I off-limits now? Is it a bro-code thing?

As soon as I'm confident that I've finished throwing up, I turn on the shower and clean up as fast as I can, unwilling to take my time just in case he wakes up. It's barely four a.m., but I know I need to leave because if his reasons for jumping me last night are what I believe, then I know I'll fall apart when he admits what he's done and he doesn't get to see that.

The moment I'm relatively clean, I dry off and throw on athletic tights, a sports bra, and a baggy ripped T-shirt that I stole from one of my brothers' bags the last time they came to visit. Shoving my damp feet into trainers, I push my cell into my pocket, then tiptoe downstairs.

The proof of what happened last night is everywhere. My clothes are littered across the floor and my purse is abandoned by the front door. Quickly grabbing all the discarded items, I rush into the garage and shove them into the washer, setting it to go before grabbing my purse and keys and leaving.

It's barely light by the time I hit Main Street, and I

glance at the store, wondering if I should just hide out in my apartment for a couple of hours. It's a tempting idea, but Nero has already proved that the bakery is the first place he'll go to look for me, and right now, I don't want to see him.

Driving past the store, I keep driving out of town, not stopping until I hit the freeway. If I didn't have a business to run, I'd keep driving until I found any of my brothers. I know they'd comfort me, or distract me, or hell, they'd help me plan how to kill Nero so no one ever found the body. But I have to be in the kitchen making muffins and cookies for my customers in three hours, so running away to California or Nashville isn't an option.

Normally, James would be the person I turn to, but she lives next door with Nero's brother, and if I call her this early, she'll know something's wrong. I don't want to have to explain that I had epic sex with my roommate, who hates me and may or may not have slept with me as a fucked-up way of preventing me from sleeping with his friends.

I need to waste a couple of hours. Spotting a sign for a twenty-four-hour roadside diner, I pull off the freeway and park in the lot beside a couple of cars. Getting out of my car, I glance through the glass window and am surprised to see that the diner is busy. There's a mix of men sitting at the counter, a few families in booths, and then groups of people who are too dressed up to be starting their day and must have been out drinking last night and are getting food before they go to bed.

Pushing open the door, the smell of bacon hits me and my stomach growls. I didn't have a chance to eat last night before Nero stripped me naked and fucked me senseless, and I threw up any food left in me this morning.

"Sit anywhere you like. I'll be right with you," a smiling waitress says as she carries a pot of coffee in one hand and a plate piled high with food in the other.

Nodding, I wander over to a small booth for two in the window and sit down. There are mugs and glasses already set out on the table, along with a plastic-coated menu. Picking it up, I run my eyes over the choices, my stomach grumbling even louder.

"Hello there, welcome to Dirk's. Can I start you off with some water or coffee?"

"Coffee would be great, thank you," I tell the older woman who's wearing a classic diner waitress dress in mint green with white collar and cuffs.

Turning the mug on my table over, she fills it with hot black coffee. "Do you know what you want, or do you need a minute?"

"I'll have a Yankee breakfast please," I say, adding creamer and sugar to my mug and stirring.

"You want hash browns with that?"

"No, thanks."

"Okay then, shouldn't take long," she says, taking the menus from the table and darting away toward the kitchen.

The moment I'm alone again, I stretch out my legs and feel the ache between my thighs. I've never felt any kind of discomfort the day after sex before, at least not since I lost my virginity. But then, I've never had sex with a guy whose dick was as big as Nero's before. I absolutely don't want to think about Nero's dick right now, but I can't help it. My sex twinges as I unconsciously clench, my mind giving me a glimpse of a phantom orgasm just from remembering the way he took over my body last night.

He did things to me that I never even knew were part of sex. He used my body and my mind against me and I… loved it. God, I loved every single minute of it, and that only makes this worse because how the hell will I ever go back to boring, normal sex when I know how it feels to be owned so completely?

Obviously, I've done the standard stuff. Foreplay, penetration, etc. But he filled me with his cock and then just held it there inside of me, not moving while he made me come by rubbing my clit. He played with my ass, fucking me there with his finger. He called me his.

A blush fills my cheeks when I even think about it. He called me his dirty girl and the way it both humiliated me and turned me on is something I'm pretty sure I'll need a therapist to help me understand.

He held me down, completely under his control, and took from my body like it was his to use as he pleased. But the worst thing is that he made me love it. All of it. I loved being played with. I loved being dominated physically. I loved the way he made me squirm and cringe when he made me tell him I was a dirty girl who needed his cock. And God, I loved it when he spanked me.

Apparently, I'm a kinky little sexual deviant, and now I have no idea how I'll ever go back to normal when all I want to do is give myself to him and tell him to do his worst. Because I know when I explode into a million mind-altering pieces, he'll make me feel amazing even as I lose myself completely.

I'm so lost in thought that I startle when the waitress slides my food in front of me. "Here you go, enjoy. Let me know if you need anything else. I'll be back to check on you in a minute."

Nodding my thanks, I pick up my silverware and start to eat. The food looks good, but I couldn't tell you how it tastes because I'm so distracted, all my unanswered questions swirling around in my mind.

A part of me still doesn't understand how any of this happened. How does someone go from actively avoiding spending time with me and resenting my presence to demanding I come home, then jumping me the moment I walk through the door?

Does he really still hate me?

I don't hate him. If I did, I know I couldn't give myself to him the way I did last night. No, I definitely don't hate him, and that makes the idea that he still dislikes me so much harder to swallow.

Is this just a sex thing? Did he kiss me the first time because I was convenient?

No, that doesn't seem right, not even in the bizarre scenarios I've been concocting in my mind. But me being convenient makes more sense than him just being overwhelmed with desire for me out of nowhere.

Finishing my food, I leave enough cash on the table for the meal and a tip, then make my way back out to my car. I've managed to waste an hour, so if I drive slowly, I'll get to the store just before six thirty a.m. It's earlier than I normally get to work, but it's late enough that Nero won't have time to find me before he has to leave for work himself.

Climbing back into my car, I freeze when my cell rings the moment I start the engine. My car has a hands-free system connected to the stereo, so I hit the button to answer the call. "Hello."

"Where the fuck are you?" a male voice growls through the car's speakers.

Oh fuck. "Who is this?" I ask, knowing exactly who it is but really hoping I'm wrong.

"Are you fucking serious?" he demands on a snarl. "It's Nero."

My throat closes and I swallow, trying to dislodge the lump that's formed. "Sorry, I'm driving. I can't see the caller ID on my hands-free."

"Answer the fucking question, Tori, where the hell are you?" He sounds mad, but that doesn't make sense. Who wants to deal with a woman the morning after a weird one-night stand? And that's all this can be… right?

"I'm on the way to work?" It comes out like a question and I slap my hand over my mouth when I realize I sound like I'm asking permission. Like, if he refuses, I'll turn around and go back home. Like a good girl. Fuck, that's what he called me last night too. His dirty girl, then his good girl. I am so fucked up.

"Why?"

"Because I have a job," I say, hoping that he can't hear the shakiness in my voice.

"It's five in the fucking morning. You don't normally leave this early." Why does he care? Was he hoping for a repeat of last night? Honestly, I'm not sure my pussy can take another night like that. We had sex five times in one night. Five times in a week is a lot, and with the heavy load he's packing, once was hard work on my poor vagina. Round five would have just hurt if he hadn't wound me up so tightly by making me tell him I was his dirty girl over and over while he bounced me on his dick until he came *inside of me*.

"I have four birthday cakes being collected today," I say in a rush.

"Come home," he says, the order clear in his tone.

"Why?"

"Because I wasn't expecting to wake up alone," he says angrily, his tone rough and gravelly, and is that hurt I hear?

"Err." I clear my throat again. "Well, you didn't get much sleep. I didn't want to wake you." It's utter bullshit, but I smile while I say it and hope it at least sounds like a plausible explanation for my running away from him while his cum was still drying on my thighs.

"I'll see you when you get home, Tori," he says slowly, each word a whiskey-soaked caress that has my thighs squeezing together and my sore pussy weeping with excitement.

"Nero, I have to work. I can't just come home," I squeak.

"Sunshine, I have to go to work in a couple of hours too. I won't get to play with your pussy for another four days, so be a good girl and come home."

"I'm sorry, I can't," I whisper, then end the call. Dead. I'm dead. Gone. My mind is bouncing around like a squirrel on ecstasy is holding a rave in there. I hadn't even noticed that not only did I put my car in drive and pull out of the space I was in, but apparently, I also stopped. And now I'm stationary in the middle of the diner's parking lot, having a meltdown because Nero Fucking Henderson called me a good girl and ordered me to come home to him.

Quickly pulling to a new space at the back of the lot, I put my car in park and sit for the next twenty minutes while I wait for my hands to stop shaking enough to drive. What the hell is this man doing to me? I need some advice, but I can't talk to James because she might say something to Buck and then he'll absolutely say something to Nero.

But I don't have any other female friends that I'm close enough to discuss my fucked-up, newly discovered sexual preferences with. Maybe I could talk to James but not tell her who the guy is. As long as she doesn't tell Buck I fucked his brother, that could work, and right now, I need to talk to someone.

Even though it's far too early to call on a Monday morning, I hit dial and wait for her to answer.

"Hello," she says sleepily.

"I need you," I hiss quietly, whispering, even though I'm alone in my car and no one else can hear me.

"I'll come over," she says, suddenly sounding more awake.

"I'm not home. But can you go somewhere Buck can't hear our conversation?"

"Sure, I'll go downstairs. Give me a minute."

I can hear the sounds of muffled voices and then her moving. "Okay, I'm downstairs. Are you okay?"

"No. Yes. Oh god, I don't know. I'm sorry to call you so early, but I'm in my head and I just need to talk to you."

"It's fine. I had to get up soon anyway. What happened?"

"I had sex," I blurt.

"Okay, who with?"

"Who doesn't matter. It was how."

"You're going to have to give me a bit more than that," she says cautiously.

"So, there's this guy. He's not my type and I'm not his. At all. Anyway, we're not close, and then, out of nowhere, he kisses me, and then he just walks away. And I think, okay, well, that was weird, but whatever, maybe it was just a fucked-up moment. Then, a day or so later, he kisses me again. This time, *I* leave, and again, whatever, right? It's just a kiss. Then the next time we're together, the moment I see him, he's on me, ripping my clothes off and fucking me against the door, like he can't wait a moment longer."

James laughs. "Tori, honey, I mean, as long as he didn't force you, there's nothing super weird about anything you just told me. He wants you and he got desperate. Sounds hot to me."

"Oh, I'm not done."

"My bad, carry on."

"So anyway, the whole time we're together, he doesn't say a word. He strips me naked, fucks me against the door, drives me insane and he's silent, like not a noise, until he finally tells me to come, like I can do it on command."

"Okay, well, that is a little odd," she says.

"I haven't gotten to the odd bit yet."

She giggles again and I smile, feeling calmer just from being able to talk to her.

"So afterward, I say, 'What was that? We don't even

like each other', and he's like, 'I want you.'"

"Well, that's good, isn't it?" she asks.

"No, that's not good. He doesn't like me, I know it, he knows it, he's not pretending, he just doesn't like me, so him saying he wants me is literally him saying he wants to have sex with me."

"And that's not what you want?"

"No," I whine. "I don't know. But the truth is, I'm not sure how much I like him either. So, I say 'No thanks.'"

"You did not?" she gasps, giggling.

"I did. I said, 'No thanks,' and he was like, 'What?' Like no one has ever said no to him before. Then he literally threw me over his shoulder like a caveman and took me to his room and he was like a completely different person. He was all about the dirty talk, he…" I pause, not sure if I should be admitting this. "He…" I try again.

"Tori, I'm starting to freak out a little. Did he do something you didn't want? Did he hurt you? Because if he did, I'll have Buck hold him down while I castrate him, then I'll call the cops and have his ass thrown in jail."

"No, no, I was all green light the whole time. It's just…"

"Sweetie, you know all about the things I like in the bedroom. If he did something freaky-deaky to you, I swear I won't be weirded out by it," James assures me.

"Oh god," I whine. "He held me down."

"That's hot," she coos.

"He played with my ass."

She makes a sound of understanding.

"And he called me names and made me use them too." The moment I finish speaking, I brace, expecting to hear disgust.

"Names?" she questions. "Like mean names? Did you like it?"

"No, not mean names."

"Sooo." She elongates the word.

"I swear if you ever tell anyone about this, I will reveal all the stuff I know about you."

"I won't tell a soul, not even Buck. I promise."

Inhaling sharply, I tip my head back and look up at the roof of my car. "He called me his dirty girl, and then he made me beg and call myself a dirty girl."

"Oh wow," she gasps. "That's…"

I brace again.

"Hot."

All of the air rushes out of me. "Oh my god, it was so hot. It was humiliating, but at the same time, I was so turned on, but now I don't know how I feel about it," I confess.

"Do you feel bad about it? Because you shouldn't. Liking something during sex isn't the same as accepting something in everyday life. God, I should know. Since Buck and I made up, I find myself letting him make more and more of the decisions, but I'm still a total girl boss at work, and I would never allow a colleague to interfere with me doing my job."

Tension I hadn't realized I was holding falls from my shoulders. "So, you don't think it's weird? I've never done that before and I wasn't expecting to like it as much as I did."

"It's not weird at all if you enjoyed it. I love the squirmy, uncomfortable feeling I get when Buck orders me around. I think that's part of the appeal."

"That's exactly it. He'd call me a dirty girl and my stomach would do somersaults, but it wasn't like a barf feeling. It was a *this is wrong, but I like it* feeling. He called me a good girl too, which is almost more humiliating, but I liked that just as much."

"Oh, I love it when Buck calls me a good girl."

"Have you…" I falter.

"Jesus, Tori, at this point, just ask whatever you're building up to asking." She laughs.

"Have you and Buck done anal?"

"No, not yet. He's mentioned it and he's played with his fingers, but we haven't gotten to full-blown anal yet. Did you do anal? I thought there needed to be prep. Buck's dick isn't like monster big, but he's thick, so I guess we'd need to work up to it."

"He played with his fingers, but he didn't just try and shove his dick in there, there's no way it'd fit, he's huge. Biggest I've ever seen in real life."

"So, are you together now? Or was it just a one-night thing?"

"We're not together. I think maybe he wants it to be a regular thing, but I don't really know. We didn't do a lot of talking last night," I confess.

"Do you want to be together?"

"I don't think so. I'm not sure I could even have a sexual relationship with someone who doesn't like who I am as a person. I'm nice and I've never done anything to make him dislike me. I don't really understand why he'd even want to do anything with me when he so openly hates me."

"Maybe he's just pretending to not like you, to hide the fact that he's secretly in love with you. Or he could just want to fuck you. Men find it easier than women to separate sex and relationships."

Shaking my head, I remember that she's on hands-free, not video call, and she can't see me. "He's definitely not in love with me," I scoff.

"So, are you freaked out that you had sex with a guy who doesn't like you or that you discovered a few quirks you didn't know you liked?"

Letting my head fall back against the headrest, I sigh again. "God, I don't even know. As soon as he fell asleep, I left."

"You left?" She giggles.

"Yep, snuck out of his room naked, then got in my car and just drove off."

"He doesn't know you're gone?" She gasps.

"No, he knows. He called me right before I called you."

"Was he mad you left?"

"He wasn't happy." I shrug.

"So, when are you planning on admitting you had wild monkey sex with my future brother-in-law last night?" she asks bluntly.

"What?" I shriek.

"Your car was outside the house when I got home from work last night, and it was still there an hour later and when we went to bed. You were home all night, sweetie, so unless you suddenly got a new roommate or invited a random dude who isn't your biggest fan to your house, the only person we could be talking about is Nero."

Panic surges through my veins and I frantically try to think of a lie I can tell her that would be plausible but come up empty. "Urgh, fine, I slept with your future brother-in-law," I admit quietly.

"What are you going to do?" she asks.

"Honestly, I have no idea. He hates me. I don't know why, but he really does. Last week, he accused me of trying to sleep with Knight as a way of then working my way through the rest of the guys on the team. When I told him Knight and I were just friends, he asked Knight if we were dating, like he thought I was lying."

"Maybe he's jealous."

"Of what? Knight and I are friends. He's a great guy and he let me use his kitchen when Nero got mad at me for using more than my allotted shelf in the refrigerator. There is absolutely nothing between me and him except quiet comradery. And it's the same with the other guys. I like them and they're fun. But Nero thinks I'm this femme fatale or firefighter groupie who's trying to tick each guy off after I take their dick for a test drive. The first time he's done more than scowl and hiss at me was when he was calling me a dirty girl and making me beg for his cock." The words fall from my lips in a rush, and I let my head fall forward until my forehead is resting against the steering wheel.

"Tori."

"I think he might have had sex with me just to stop me from having sex with the other guys," I confess in a shaky whisper.

"No. He wouldn't do that."

"Wouldn't he? Because I'm honestly not so sure. The

only thing I'm one-hundred-percent confident about is that he likes having sex with me and his dick keeps getting hard. Other than that, I have absolutely no idea what he'd be willing to do to protect his teammates from the threat he seems to think I am."

"Tori."

"Don't feel sorry for me. I had a great time. Probably the best sex I've ever had."

"Where are you? Come to me. The guys are leaving for work soon anyway, but I'll get rid of them until they go. I'll send Buck to Nero. I'll call into work and you have the day off. We can have a girls' day, drink too much wine, watch a sad film and you can cry it out."

"I can't. I have to work today, and this is your last chance to spend time with Buck before he goes back on shift. We can do a girls' night once they're at work. Enjoy your time with him. I know how much you miss him when he's gone."

"I miss you too. I feel like I barely see you anymore. I've gone from spending all my time with you to nothing at all," she says softly.

"I know, but you have that big ole beautiful man of yours keeping you busy. We can catch up in the next couple of days and you can tell me how blissfully happy you are while I try to forget the other Henderson brother exists."

"He's not an idiot. It won't take him long to recognize what a gem you are; then you can be as happy as I am."

"Hmm," I agree noncommittally. "Go back to bed, but please don't tell Buck about this. I don't want anyone to know."

"Of course I won't. I love you."

"Love you too," I say, hitting the button to end the call and exhaling tiredly. The part of me that was freaked out about the new kinks I unlocked last night feels better after talking it out with my bestie. But the part that's a little bit broken about Nero wanting me in spite of his dislike for me is still raw and hurting.

Sex doesn't have to be anything but sex, but for me, it usually is. I've never been the type of girl who did casual hookups. The guys I've gotten into bed with have always meant something to me, even if they never inspired big love feelings in me. And now I can't help feeling a little bit dirty after last night's sexcapades with Nero.

I know I shouldn't. There's nothing wrong with owning my own sexuality and desire to sate my needs in any way that I want. But the more I think about having sex with someone who is so blatant in their dislike for me, who could possibly have used sex as a weapon to protect his friends from me, the more icky I feel.

Not wanting to repeat this morning's vomit incident, I put my car into drive, lower the window all the way down and pull onto the freeway. Thirty minutes later, my nausea has settled and I slow to a stop outside my store.

Warmth fills my chest the moment I climb out of my car, and by the time I reach the back door and unlock it, I push all thoughts of Nero out of my head, inhaling the lingering scent of cinnamon and sugar that never seems to fade.

Chapter Fifteen

Nero

Waking up alone after the single best night of sex I've ever had in my life sucks. Sitting around with a hard dick while I wait to see if Tori does as I asked, and comes home, is fucking worse.

The moment I spoke to her, I knew she wasn't coming back. I should have chased her down into town and brought her home, but a part of me hoped she'd come back because she wanted to. By the time the clock hits six thirty a.m. I'm so fucking angry I honestly contemplate driving down to the store and dragging her home by her hair. Only, as much as I want to, I know I can't do that.

Apparently, my ballsy little ray of fucking sunshine is a runner. It makes sense. She's been running from me since the first time I kissed her, so I guess I should have been prepared for her to run after what happened between us last night.

Next time, I'm going to have to tie her to me *or the bed* just to make sure she's still there when I wake up, but that's no hardship. To be honest, the idea of cuffing her to me while we sleep is kind of fucking hot.

Maybe I can just keep her cuffed to me all the time, at least then I'll know where she is and I won't spend all my time waiting around for her. I could get her a collar and a leash? Nope, pretty sure if I suggested that, the next time I woke up, it'd be without at least one of my important appendages.

I don't really get why she's running now. Last night, I made it really fucking clear that I own her body. Sure, we didn't get into feelings or any of that stuff, but I made it clear how much I wanted her, and her body told me exactly how much she wanted me.

Heading to my bedroom, I open the door and inhale deeply. My room smells of sex and my dick hardens the moment the scent fills my nose. I need to change the sheets, but if she's not here to help me dirty them up again, I want to be surrounded by the scent of how fucking fantastic last night was for as long as possible.

I haven't fucked a woman over and over since I was a teenager and perpetually hard, but I couldn't get enough of Tori last night. Even thinking about it now, the craving for her roars back to life, and I reach down and palm my cock, silently commiserating with it that it won't be back inside her for four days. Her cunt is perfect. Hot, wet, and tight, but what makes it so different is that her cunt is mine.

I've never had that before; I've never wanted it. But since the first time I kissed her, I've been fighting the urge to beat my chest and drag her around by the hair so that everyone knows she belongs to me. Tori is a beautiful woman and I know guys notice. Hell, my teammates sure as fuck noticed. But I won't stand for them looking at her now or even fucking talking to her. The "group chat, games night, come hang out at my place" bullshit is going to stop. She's mine and I have no interest in sharing her with anyone else.

Stripping out of my boxers, I lie down in bed, gripping my dick and slowly stroking. I absolutely shouldn't be hard. So much of my cum went in and on Tori last night that my balls actually hurt when I woke up this morning, but I can't help it. I still want her.

I need to leave for work in half an hour, so closing my eyes, I imagine how many times I can make her come in thirty minutes. Once on my fingers, again on my tongue, once with my dick stretching out her cunt, and maybe even again with my fingers in her ass, while I bend her over the bed and punish her for leaving me without her today.

For the first time in a really long time, I don't want to go to work. Not being able to be inside of her for four fucking days feels like an eternity, and I want to gorge myself on her, keeping her chained to me metaphorically, or maybe even physically, until this overwhelming need feels sated. I'm not in love with her. I'm not even sure I want to be with her beyond this intense physical connection we share, but I want to be propriety over her. I want to make sure that no one else even contemplates touching what's mine and she is *mine*.

Squeezing my dick tighter, I imagine her falling to her knees and parting her lips, offering me her mouth. *Does my dirty girl want to taste my cock?* Pupils dilating, she nods, shuffling forward until her cheek is resting against my thigh. *Open wide then, Sunshine.* Grabbing a handful of her hair, I pull her head away from my leg, so I can look down and watch as she parts her lips and opens her mouth wide, ready and eager to swallow my dick.

That's as far as I get into my fantasy before my dick swells and I come, coating my hand and stomach in my release. Jesus, I don't jerk off that much, but when I do, I usually need a hell of a lot longer than two minutes and the intro to a BJ to get me to come.

Climbing out of bed, I grab my boxers from the floor and clean as much as I can, then flop back down, my arms behind my head as I stare up at the ceiling. The scent of sex surrounds me, combined with a faint cookie smell that prompts the memory of pulling her on top of me last night, our skin slick with sweat and a mixture of our releases. She was a mess, pupils blown wide, heavy tits heaving up and down while she tried to catch her breath, and cum dripping from between her thighs.

I've never seen a woman look so depraved and still fucking adorable before. Maybe that's why I can't stop thinking about her. Maybe it's the fucked-up mix of vixen and virgin that's luring me like the idiot sailors of old, who steered onto the rocks and certain death just to get a glimpse of the sirens calling them to their watery grave.

Tori isn't my type. She's not what I want or what I need.

But none of that seems to matter when my bed feels empty without her. The house we share is quiet and lifeless. Each moment that passes is long and boring, and even the pale morning light feels desolate and void of joy, all because she's not here, filling my world with noise.

The thought of leaving and not seeing her again until Friday makes a weight I don't fully understand settle into place on my chest. I'm not someone who constantly craves company, and hell if I were, Tori would be the last person I'd seek out. It must be the sex. It's the only explanation that makes sense. We fucked several times and it was epic. Life affirming, maybe even life altering, and it's totally reasonable to crave that again.

Sex that good isn't something that lasts, so I need to make the most of it while it does. Although thinking about her as a fling doesn't sit right. But not seeing her for a few days will only make the sex when we're together even more explosive, so this break might actually be a good thing. I need to stop pining over her not being here when I should be appreciating the extended foreplay this forced separation will give us.

Nodding to myself, I smile. This is perfect. I can spend the next four days edging my dirty girl to teach her a lesson for running from me today. I'll get her so worked up that she'll be the one jumping me when I get back from my shift on Friday.

My dick hardens again, but I ignore it, and instead, I pull out my cell and type out a text.

ME

My dick wishes you were here.

I can still smell us on my sheets and when I close my eyes, I can see you pinned beneath me, begging for my cock.

Such a dirty girl.

All three messages change to read and I smile, watching the screen to see if she replies. I doubt she will, at least not straight away, but that's okay. I'll punish her for ignoring me when I see her later in the week.

Flicking into a game on my cell, I waste some time waiting for her to reply, but just like I anticipated, it never comes. As little as I know about her, some things about Tori are incredibly predictable and when she runs, she runs. But that's okay, I don't mind chasing, at least not chasing her, because we'll have so much fun when I catch her.

I have to leave soon. If she'd come home, we could have showered together. I could have bent her over and fucked her against the tile. Fuck, I could have used the showerhead to tease her asshole while I slammed into her cunt. Or maybe I could have taken my own pleasure and left her wanting to teach her why she shouldn't run from me.

Ignoring the ache in my balls, I throw back the covers and climb out of bed. Showering quickly, I get dressed then head downstairs. Setting the coffee machine to brew, I open the refrigerator and peruse the contents. It's looking pretty sparse. Since the day of our argument over the shelves, Tori's barely been here, and instead of foil-wrapped parcels and containers full of various foods, her shelf has been mundane and kind of empty.

A pang of discomfort pulls in my stomach. I was an asshole that day and I still haven't apologized to her. In my defense, when we argued, I was still a little bitter about living here with her, but that's no excuse for being a little bitch to her when she didn't do anything wrong.

Pulling a carton of milk out, I make oatmeal, then stand at the counter and watch the front door. I already know she's not coming, but apparently, I'm a fucking glutton for punishment, so I pull out my cell and type out a text.

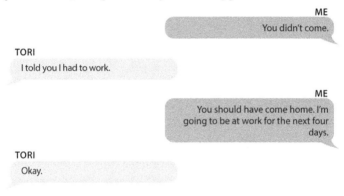

ME
You didn't come.

TORI
I told you I had to work.

ME
You should have come home. I'm going to be at work for the next four days.

TORI
Okay.

Okay? That's it? Okay? I'm not going to see her for four fucking days and she's just saying okay like she doesn't give a crap. I get this is just sex, but even so, it's great fucking sex. Is she pissed at me? I don't remember doing something to make her mad, but clearly, she is.

Before I even realize what I'm doing, I'm dialing her number.

"Hey," she answers on the third ring, sounding out of breath.

"Are you mad at me?" God, I sound like a pussy.

She's silent for a long moment. "Err. No."

"Then why didn't you come home?"

"I'm at work, Nero."

"We're not going to see each other for four fucking days, Tori."

"Okay," she says easily.

"Okay," I parrot back.

"Okay," she says again.

Neither of us speaks again and the silence stretches until it's so uncomfortable I think she might have ended the call.

"I have to go. I've got three different batters in the mixers and if I don't get them out, they'll overmix," she whispers like she's not sure she should actually break the epically awkward silence we have going.

"Make sure you reply to my texts, don't leave me on fucking read," I growl, not saying what I actually want to, which is that I want to see her, taste her, kiss her, fuck her and I'm disappointed I won't get a chance to until later in the week. "See you on Friday, Sunshine."

"Bye, Nero, be safe."

Chapter Sixteen

Tori

Ending the call, I stare down at my cell in my hands. What the hell even was that? I wasn't expecting him to call, but then I wasn't expecting the texts he sent me earlier either. Running from him this morning was cowardly, but I'm finding that when I'm dealing with my confusing feelings for Nero Henderson, I'm a total wimp.

I have no idea how to deal with him now we've had sex. Part of me just assumed we'd ignore what happened like we did when he kissed me. Is Nero assuming that we're fuck buddies now? Is that still even a thing? My stomach clenches when I think about him using me as a superconvenient booty call, but I guess it's both super easy and super complicated when your hookup sleeps in the room next door.

Will he be dating other women? Am I supposed to date

other men? I don't understand the rules, and the more I think about it, the more sick I feel. I don't want to be his hookup, I don't want to be his convenient vagina next door, but I'm not sure I want to be anything more either.

A part of me still feels like the only reason we had sex is so he could stop me from having sex with his teammates, and nothing he's said or done so far has dissuaded me otherwise. But my body hasn't gotten the memo that having sex with him again is a bad idea.

Unable to resist, I open up my text app and read the messages he sent me.

NERO

My dick wishes you were here.

NERO

I can still smell us on my sheets and when I close my eyes, I can see you pinned beneath me, begging for my cock.

NERO

Such a dirty girl.

My stomach does that squirmy thing James and I talked about again. I didn't reply to him, but I've lost count of how many times I've read and reread his words. I barely slept last night and I feel ragged, like my skin is too sensitive and my mind is fraying. I wasn't expecting him to call me again this morning and just hearing his voice has set off a chain reaction of electricity to rush through my body. I don't know what that means or what I'm supposed to do about it, but the idea that I'm reacting to him so strongly bothers me.

Throwing myself into work, I make all the usual counter cakes and goodies, then throw myself into macarons and elaborate meringues that I'm not sure will sell. By the time Daniel and Emma arrive to open up, a tray full of colorful macarons and fluffy-looking pink and white meringues is waiting, ready to be displayed in the counter showcase.

"Morning, boss," Daniel says, poking his head through the door from the front of the store and into the kitchen. His eyes widen when he sees all of the trays ready to fill the counter. "Are we late?" he asks, pulling his cell from his pocket and looking at the time.

"No." I force a laugh. "I just got here a little early this morning to get a head start on today's stock. We have chocolate, vanilla, pistachio, rose, lavender, white chocolate macarons and white and pink meringues. Muffin of the day is carrot cake and you can whip up whatever you like as the drink of the day. I know you've been holding back."

"Wow," he breathes. "Err, okay, this all looks amazing. But is everything okay? You look…" he trails off, clearly trying to decide what to say.

"Like shit," I answer for him.

A laugh bursts from his lips, and I can't help it. I smile.

"I was going to say tired." He grins.

"Yeah, I didn't sleep well. But baking is my stress relief, so I actually feel a little better now. Well, no, that's not true, but I have three celebration cakes and a giant cookie to make, so I'll be fine after that."

Daniel nods, but he doesn't look convinced. "You want me to make you a drink once the machine has heated up?"

Sighing, I nod. "That would be great. I set a plate of the macarons and meringue aside on the counter for you and Emma to try so you know what you're pushing on the customers today. I'll add them to the EPOS in a minute."

"I'm pretty sure they'll be gone quick. They look delicious." Smiling, he disappears back into the front of the store and I exhale, heading to my office to add the new stock item to the sales list on the EPOS.

Grabbing my tablet, I head downstairs again and count how many of each flavor there are, adding it to today's stock list. It's an easy way for me to check how sales are going during each day without having to actually count stock.

Quickly counting up the rest of the counter stock, I add it to the spreadsheet, then empty the dishwasher when it beeps to say the cycle has finished. Without realizing I'm even doing it, I open my text app and read Nero's texts again. God, why can't I just forget them and ignore everything that happened between us?

His texts are so casual, and I wonder how many times he's sent that kind of text before. The thought bothers me and I don't know why. I don't want him sending me sexts, but it irks me that he could have sent them to other women. God, I'm such a cliché. I don't want him, but I don't want him to flirt with other people either.

Turning my cell to silent, I place it on the counter and force myself to turn away from it. Baking is my happy place, so that's what I do. By ten thirty a.m., I've baked all of the cakes that are being collected today and the cookie cake is in the oven. Daniel has brought me two hazelnut praline mochas and I've got all the decorations ready to go as soon as the cakes are cool enough to frost.

"Hey, boss," he calls, stepping into the kitchen.

"Hey, is everything okay?"

"Just sold the last of the macarons."

"What?" I blink.

"Almost everyone who's been into the store today has bought at least one and we've only got a handful of the meringues left too. All this fancy French stuff you're making is flying off the shelves."

Pride swells to life in my chest and the first genuine smile in what feels like hours spreads across my cheeks. "Really?"

"Yep, everyone loves it."

Clapping, I bounce about like an idiot, launching myself at Daniel and hugging him tightly. "Ahhh, I can't believe it. They really sold that quickly?"

"Yep, and Emma and I have hardly had to push them at all. We've sold more macarons than we have snickerdoodles and they've always been a bestseller," he says, not letting me go but pulling back enough that he can look down at me.

"It's happening. I'm going to make this work, aren't I?" I ask him.

Cupping my cheek, he smiles. "You're absolutely going to make this work. Le Petite Patisserie is going to be a roaring success."

His pupils dilate and his breathing hitches as he looks down at me, amusement fading into something else. Oh shit, is he going to kiss me? An image of Nero pops into my mind and clearing my throat, I step back quickly, untangling myself from him and turning away. Daniel is close to my age, maybe a couple of years younger. He's attractive, in a soft, sweet sort of way, but I'm not attracted to him, and I have enough man drama with Nero. I don't need to add any with Daniel into the mix.

"Thank you for letting me know about the macarons and for all your help since I took over. I really appreciate it."

Straightening, he nods, his expression going sad, then resigned. "Of course, I'm always here for you, for anything you need. We all want this place to be a huge success."

"Thanks, Daniel. I'm almost done with these cake orders, so I'll whip up another batch of something for the counter."

"Okay, boss," he says, slipping back into the storefront without another word.

The rest of the day goes quickly. I make some cream scones for the counter, which sell out almost as quickly as the macarons, and I vow tomorrow to half some of the stock that hasn't sold as well since I started introducing patisserie recipes and replace them with more of the items I plan to sell moving forward.

Somehow, I've managed not to check my cell all day. Waving goodbye to Daniel and Emma, I lock the door behind them, then pick up my cell from where I've studiously been ignoring it and swipe the screen to bring it to life. I have ten texts and a slew of emails. Opening the email app to avoid having to check my texts, I quickly delete all of the junk mail and reply to any that need a response.

Then I open my texts. One from James, one from Felix, one from Atticus, a notification of a new message in the family group chat that I, my brothers and my folks use, and six messages from Nero.

I know I should open the ones from my family first, but I don't. His name lures me in and I'm clicking into his messages before I can stop myself.

NERO

> Can't get the image of you bouncing on my cock out of my head. Every time I close my eyes it's all I see, and the moment it's quiet, I remember the way your cunt squeezed me tight while you screamed my name.

NERO

> Are you still sore? I hope so. I hope your cunt reminds you of how well you took my dick every time you move.

NERO

> As soon as I get home, I'm going to put you on your knees and make my dirty girl beg me to fuck her mouth, then you're going to swallow all my cum and thank me when I'm done filling your throat.

NERO

> I'm going to fuck you in every room in the house. I'm going to bend you over your fucking princess bed, and finger fuck your ass until you beg me to fill it with my cock.

NERO

> I'm going to ruin your cunt, Sunshine. I'm going to fuck you so much my cum will be dripping out of you for days.

NERO

> Don't make me punish you before I fuck you, Tori. Leaving my messages unread is worse than leaving me read and not bothering to reply. If you make me, I'll spank your ass red and edge you until my dirty, dirty girl is begging for my dick in any hole just to make the craving stop.

My head spins and my mouth goes dry, but it's the only part of me that is dry because between my legs is throbbing and gushing with arousal at each of his potent threats and dirty words. I shouldn't like him talking to me like this. I really shouldn't, but I do like it.

I like the way it makes me feel uncomfortable. How the things he's saying he wants to do to me feel so brazen, so wrong, but excite me all at the same time. This isn't the first sext I've received, but it's the first time that I actually feel like I need to go and get myself off, just from words.

But if I make myself come, it'll be to the scenario he created and as much as I want to, I know I shouldn't be so turned on by anything he says. This thing that happened between us was purely sexual, so maybe I'm wrong. Maybe it's completely okay to react so strongly to him. It doesn't mean I want him beyond sex. In fact, it's almost enforcing the realization that this thing between us is purely hormone based.

Rushing upstairs, I strip out of my clothes and dive under the bedcovers, finding my clit and rubbing it while I push a single finger into my soaking-wet sex. Adding a second finger, I sigh when I start to find the friction I need. Circling my clit, I pump my fingers in and out while I imagine him doing all the things he just texted about.

Me on my knees, begging him to fuck my mouth and feed me his cum. Bent over, my face crushed into the softness of my comforter while he finger fucks my ass until I'm writhing and begging him to fill me with his cock. Him spanking me while I lie over his lap, my ass burning, begging him to fuck me or make me come, or do something to sate the need his touch has created in me.

I come with a cry, my body tightening on my fingers as spasms of pleasure jolt through me. The orgasm is a pale imitation of the way he made me climax, but it's taken the edge off the frantic need I was feeling only minutes ago. When my muscles unclench, I relax, sliding my hands from between my legs and opening my eyes, staring up at the ceiling while my breathing slows.

Humiliation washes over me when I think of the things I just fantasized about. Begging him over and over again. Is that what I like now? It's not something I ever thought I'd do, but I did it for him. I begged for his dick and I liked the way it felt when he made me call myself his dirty girl. I liked it a lot, and I have no idea what to do with that. Jumping out of bed, I dart into the bathroom, stepping under the shower the moment the water starts to fall, and scrub all evidence of my orgasm from my body.

I don't know why I'm reacting so strongly to this. After James and I spoke this morning, I felt more at peace with the things Nero and I did and how much I enjoyed them. But now I'm alone, and post-solo-masturbation session, I feel weird and oddly ashamed.

Once I'm clean and my skin is pink and a little raw, I wash and condition my hair and then turn off the shower, wrapping myself in a towel. Sitting down on the edge of my bed, I remind myself that nothing I do with any guy is wrong as long as it's consensual, safe, and not going to leave any lasting damage on either of us. There's nothing wrong with me enjoying a little mild humiliation and degradation in the bedroom. But even as I'm thinking the words, I don't really believe them.

Maybe it's because it's Nero, or maybe because it's only extremely casual sex with no feelings behind our relationship, but it feels dirty in an icky, unpleasant way, and I don't like it. Grabbing my cell from where I dropped it in my haste to get naked, I pull open the text app with shaky fingers and delete all the texts he's sent me in the last twenty-four hours.

I can't do this with him. I can't be his casual fuck and play these games.

I need to move out.

Chapter Seventeen

Nero

Four fucking days. I've been on shift for four fucking days and it's been four fucking days since she started ignoring me. I've texted and called, but she stopped reading my texts on Monday night and she's been blanking me ever since.

It's driving me absolutely fucking insane. It shouldn't matter. I shouldn't care that my roommate, and fuck buddy, is pretending I don't exist, but it's driving me crazy that she won't talk to me or even reply to my texts.

I've tried flirting, demanding, ordering, coercing, and honestly, on occasion, even begging. But it doesn't matter what message I send. She doesn't read them, and when I call, she sends me to voice mail.

At one point, I actually worried that she was hurt or ill or something, so I called the store and asked to speak to her without telling them it was me. She answered, laughter in her voice and I cut off the call without speaking. She's fine. She just doesn't want to talk to me.

The group chat she's in with the guys has been a hive of fucking activity. Apparently, she can text with all of my team, but when I contact her, it's radio fucking silence. Watching the clock, I count down the minutes until the second shift arrives and I get to go home and hunt down my wayward fucking roomie.

Over the past ninety-six hours, my excitement has morphed from anticipation and lust to fear and anger, and now I'm just downright furious. How fucking dare *my sunshine* bestow her light on everyone but me? I accused her once of wanting to take turns fucking all the members of my team and she vehemently denied it. But now I'm starting to question if that's why she's ignoring me. Because she's ticked me off her list and she's moving on to her next target.

Fury swells inside of me just thinking about her touching one of my friends. I'll kill them, then I'll tie her to my bed and never let her go. She's mine and I refuse to share her. The moment the guys turn up, I rush through handover, then march out to Buck's truck and stand by the passenger door, impatiently waiting for him to get out here.

"Finally," I hiss under my breath when he exits the building and slowly saunters over.

Pressing the button on his key fob, he disengages the lock and I scramble in.

"You okay?" he asks.

"Just eager to get home."

"Why?" His brow furrows. "Hot date?"

I scoff. "Hardly."

"Miranda and her guys still blowing up your cell?"

"No, I blocked them a few weeks back. For a while, they were using prepaid numbers to call and text me, but I think they've finally figured out I'm a lost cause and given up."

"So, who's the girl?" my big brother asks.

"There's no girl." I shrug.

"Then what's bugging you? You've had a face like someone pissed in your Wheaties for days."

I try to stay quiet, thinking out a reasonable explanation for my blatantly increasing agitation that's been building for four fucking days. "I fucked Tori." Well, shit, I didn't mean to say that.

"You what?" Buck splutters, turning to gawk at me.

"I fucked Tori on Sunday night."

"So are you guys…" he trails off, waiting for me to fill in the blanks.

"It's sex."

"That's it. Sex. Just sex?"

"She's noisy," I blurt, apparently unable to stop any words from just falling from my mouth. "And always fucking happy."

"Okay. And that's a good thing?" Buck asks cautiously.

"No, it's not a good thing," I snap. "Who the fuck wants to be around someone who's that fucking happy all the fucking time?"

"I'm confused."

"Me too," I confess.

"So, you don't like that she's happy and… noisy? But

you had sex?"

"Yes, and yes." A minute ago, I couldn't stop talking, and now, apparently, I have nothing to say. What the fuck is wrong with me?

"So are y'all together?"

"No," I snap.

"But you fucked?"

"Yes," I huff, annoyed. "We fucked on Sunday night, and she's been ignoring me for four fucking days," I hiss, my anger reigniting.

"Did y'all agree it was just a one-time thing?"

Rubbing my forehead, I drop my gaze.

"Did you talk about it at all? I mean, you live together; you didn't think fucking her was going to make things awkward?" Buck asks, his voice getting louder with each word.

"It wasn't exactly a talk about it moment," I say through gritted teeth, hating that he's pointing out how messed up this could be.

"Were you drunk?"

"No, we weren't fucking drunk. And no, we didn't talk about it. We fucked. It was insanely good, like best sex of my fucking life good," I tell him angrily.

"So, if it was so good, why is she ignoring you?" he deadpans.

"I have no fucking clue."

"What happened the next morning? Please don't tell me you left before she woke up."

"No," I hiss. "She did."

The car is so quiet, you could hear a pin drop, then my

asshole brother laughs. "She left?" He chuckles.

"Yep." I seethe.

"And you haven't seen her since? Have you spoken to her?"

"I called her when I woke up and realized she was gone."

His shoulders shake as he fights to hold back his laughter. "Let me get this straight. You and Tori had sex. Sex that, according to you, was so good it was life altering. But she left before you woke up and didn't come home before you left for a four-day shift and has been ignoring you ever since?"

"Yes." I force the single word past my gritted teeth.

"Bro, I love you. But I think it's pretty clear she's not interested."

"She's interested," I growl.

"Women that are interested don't run before the guy wakes up."

"She's fucking interested. She was losing her mind, screaming my name, begging for more and coming all over my fingers and cock. She's everything I ever wanted in bed, rolled into one sexy fucking package."

"If it was that good, why aren't you together?"

"It's not like that. In bed, she's my type one hundred percent because I can keep her quiet with my dick or focused on screaming and begging. But she's not the type of woman I could be in a relationship with."

"Dude, if I wasn't driving, I'd punch you in the face right now. What the fuck is wrong with you? Tori's great. She's snarky, witty, fun, hell, half the team would wife her up in a hot second if she showed even an ounce of interest," Buck says, his tone serious.

"What?" I snarl. "Who?"

"Oz, Warrick, Danny, maybe even Knight."

"Her and Knight are just friends," I snap.

"Who told you that?"

"He did."

"You asked?" Buck says incredulously.

"Yes, I fucking asked."

His laugh is so loud I grimace at the sound.

"What is fucking funny?"

"Nero, I love you, baby brother, but the bullshit that just spewed from your mouth is fucking hilarious. You fucked Tori. You asked our team brothers if they were interested in her. You're pissed that she's ghosted you for four days, and you're still trying to tell me y'all aren't together?"

"I don't want her like that," I insist.

"Whatever you need to tell yourself. Fuck, Beau warned me the Barnett legacy would move on to someone new now all the Barnetts had found their woman. Looks like it made its way to us. Me first, now you. I just wonder how long it'll take you to pull your head out of your ass and claim Tori. Don't wait too long. A woman like that, some dude is going to see her and snap her up."

My teeth grind together as I clamp my jaw tight, refusing to comment on anything my asshole of a brother just said. I don't want to date Tori; I just want to fuck her. Over and over and over. Blood rushes to my dick and I will it away. I will not get hard in the car with my brother sitting next to me just because I'm thinking about fucking my roommate.

Neither of us speaks as we turn off the road and onto the drive that leads to our houses. It's not even nine a.m., but I know Tori will have left for work already. Just like I expected, our house is dark and her car is missing when Buck slows to a stop.

"I need to head into town later if you want to come," Buck says.

"No thanks, I'm going to do some laundry, then go to the grocery store."

Tapping the roof of his truck, he nods, then turns to walk up the path to his house while I cross the small front yard and open my door with my key. The moment I step inside, something feels off.

Kicking off my boots, I glance down, noticing that the shoe rack Tori bought is missing from beside the door. Dropping my bag at the bottom of the stairs, I step into the living room, glancing at the couch and finding the bright cushions she'd put on there gone too.

The house feels empty, but not in a way that suggests someone just left. Instead, it feels cold and dull, like it's been longer than a few hours since the house was awakened by someone moving inside of it.

My steps are slow as I cross to the kitchen and look around. At first sight, it all seems normal, with everything still in its place, but then I open a cabinet and find it empty. The cooking equipment that filled the space only a few days ago is gone. One by one, I open the cabinets that she claimed as hers and find them all clean but empty.

She told me she was going to buy some racking for the garage, but I didn't expect her to take everything out of the kitchen and store it out of the way. Shutting the cabinet doors, I make my way upstairs, pausing outside her closed bedroom door.

Goose bumps pebble across my skin as I stare at the wooden door and before I can second-guess myself, I turn the handle and push it open, revealing… nothing. The room is empty. Her ridiculous four-poster princess bed and the thousands of throw pillows she had covering it. The dressing table, shelves, photos. All of it gone. And the room is immaculately clean, like she was never even here.

I don't know why, but I open her closet, hoping to find it full, that maybe she'd gotten rid of her bed so she could use it as an excuse to sleep in mine, but like the rest of the room, it's empty too.

Not bothering to check her bathroom, I storm to my room, throw open the door, and almost step on the folded sheet of paper that's lying on the floor. Bending down, I grab the paper, unfold it and read the handwritten words.

Nero,

As you may (or may not) have noticed by now, I've moved my stuff out of the house. Sorry for leaving without any notice, but I've sent you enough money to cover my half of the rent for the next three months, which should give you enough time to find a roommate of your choice if you decide you don't want to live alone.

When Buck and James asked me about moving in, I said yes because I knew James needed me to and because I thought it would be fun to be close to her and be surrounded by hot firefighters. I never considered that it wasn't something you were okay with, and for that, I'm really sorry.

I think it's been pretty obvious the last couple of weeks that us sharing a house isn't something that either of us is super comfortable with, so when another apartment became available to me, it made sense for me to move out.

James doesn't know yet because I didn't want you to find out from someone else, but I'll call her and explain in a few days. I'm pretty sure I managed to get all my stuff, but if you find anything I've left behind, please pass it to James to pass on to me.

See you around.
Tori

Turning the paper over, I look for more words, but there aren't any. That's it. *Sorry it didn't work out, bye.* That's it? I know I should be relieved. A week ago, I was the one thinking about moving out, so her leaving should be a good thing. But that was before my fingers and cock felt the inside of her cunt. Before I came inside her multiple times. Before I made her mine.

Now, she doesn't get to walk away unless I tell her to go. She doesn't get to just fucking leave. She doesn't get to dismiss what happened between us like it was nothing. Hell fucking no.

I don't realize I've moved until I'm downstairs and shoving my feet into my boots. Throwing the door open, I grab my car keys, slamming the door shut without looking back.

"Bro? Everything okay?" Oz shouts, calling my attention from a few doors down.

"No," I growl.

"Whoa," he says, jogging over. "What's happened? Where you going? Do you need me to drive?"

"I'm going to find my woman and spank her ass until she's crying and begging me to stop while promising never to ignore me or run away from me again," I growl.

"Your woman?" Oz asks, shocked.

"Yes. My fucking woman. Tori's off-limits, so spread the word."

The look of shock on his face would be funny if I had time to stop and enjoy it, but I don't, so instead, I push past him, climb into my car, and drive off, ready to find my woman and make sure she knows she doesn't ever get to leave me again.

Chapter Eighteen

Tori

It probably makes me an asshole that I waited until I knew James had left for work to arrange for the movers to go in and collect my stuff. But the truth is, I don't want to have to explain why I'm moving or listen to all the reasons she thinks I should stay.

Living with Nero was a mistake and sleeping with him was a brain fart that I intend to ignore. That's if he'll let me. He's been blowing my cell up with calls and texts for the last two days, but I've managed to stop myself from answering or replying. Last night, I almost slipped and read the messages he had sent me. That was when I decided to block his number.

Sleeping with Nero was a really dumb decision, but there's no way I can live with him and pretend like it didn't happen, or worse, let it happen again. So, really, moving out was my only option.

Handing the movers a tip, I close the door behind them and lock it, sliding the dead bolt into place. I really need to get a decent lock put on this door, then I can use it as the entrance to my apartment, so I don't have to keep coming and going through the store. Turning, I look at the piles of boxes they just unloaded in my small living room and exhale a weary sigh.

I got here early enough to make all of today's stock, plus the tarts I experimented with at Knight's place. The counter is full and I don't have any orders for any cupcakes or celebration cakes that I need to bake, so I get stuck unpacking and organizing my small apartment.

If I hadn't been in such a rush to move, I'd have taken the time to redecorate the place before I moved my stuff in, but the need to get out of Nero's place was greater than my desire to get rid of the ugly beige walls.

Ignoring the bed that's sitting in the middle of the small living space, I build my princess bed in the now empty bedroom and haul my mattress onto it, remaking it with fresh sheets and adding all the comfy throw pillows I boxed up ready for the movers.

The only good thing about moving twice in less than a month is that I've gotten really good at packing and unpacking, and by the time my stomach is growling, reminding me that I haven't eaten since breakfast, the apartment is looking almost livable. I don't have a couch yet, so I push the other bed sideways against the wall, cringing at how dorm room it looks, but it'll do until I can go shopping for more furniture.

Because Mrs. Yates only used the apartment as an office and storage space, everything is outdated and in serious need of a revamp, but it's clean, and when I have the money, I can redo the kitchen and bathroom and decorate. Right now, it feels like an oasis because Nero won't be in the room next door.

I'm not stupid. I know I can't avoid him forever, but I don't need forever. I just need long enough for our weird but enlightening night of sex to become a distant memory. A few weeks will do, and I can stay away from him and his team that long if it makes things less awkward when we're forced to see each other.

He'll move on, and maybe I will too. There hasn't been anyone in town that I've been interested in before, but maybe I could get online and see if I can find someone else who gives me that nervous, excited feeling the way Nero did.

Ordering Chinese takeout, I shower and change into my pajamas, then rush down to the front of the store just in time for the delivery guy to arrive. Not bothering with a plate, I eat straight out of the box in bed while halfheartedly watching a crappy Netflix show on my laptop.

When I wake up the next morning, my new room smells like stale Chinese food, and I'm exhausted after tossing and turning, my dreams hampered with reruns of mine and Nero's night together.

Crawling out of bed, I head for the bathroom, then turn on my coffee machine before heading downstairs and turning the ovens on to preheat. Guilt about not telling James I've moved gnaws at my stomach and I sigh, feeling a little sick. Part of me worries that this stuff with Nero will all blow up in my face, and James will get caught in the cross fire. If the brothers force her to pick a side, I know it won't be mine and I guess I wouldn't expect it to be.

She and Buck are engaged, and Nero will be her brother-in-law. If he makes things weird, I'll be the one who doesn't get invited to parties and events. I'll be the one who gets phased out, not him. It's why I need to pretend that our night of madness didn't happen and why I need him to pretend it didn't happen either.

I get dressed while the coffee brews, then take a mug downstairs with me and get to work. Just like always, I lose my worries at the bottom of a mixing bowl and by the time I've finished slicing the traditional French chocolate opera cake, I feel lighter and almost relaxed.

Since I started slowly offering some of the classic French patisserie cakes I plan to sell in the shop, the response has been better than I ever could have expected. Every day, the patisserie items are the first to sell out and it's such a relief to know this isn't a stupid idea and that this kind of food will sell here.

My life kind of feels a little adrift right now, and this store is the only thing keeping me afloat. Speaking to my family via text and video chat is great, but it only reminds me how much I miss my brothers and how long it's been since we were all together. Growing up, I didn't have a lot of close girlfriends. Having four hot brothers didn't make forming genuine friendships with girls easy. I never struggled to make friends, but it was always hard to know who was genuine and who was looking to use me to get closer to my brothers, so once I hit high school, it became easier to keep everyone at a distance.

My brothers and I have always been a team, and not having them here, when the foundation I've relied on for the last three years has gotten a little shaky, is harder than I expected. We speak all the time, but it's not the same as being in the same room as them or spending real time with them.

Nero will be home from work in the morning and he'll know I moved out. I don't know if he'll be upset or relieved, and honestly, I'm not sure which is better. As much as I know the best thing for both of us is to forget the other night even happened, my body isn't in sync with my mind.

The moment I fall asleep, my dreams are hampered with memories of him and every night since I left him asleep in his bed, I've woken up in the middle of the night, hot and bothered and on the edge of release. Dirty dreams aren't something new for me. I've always had an active imagination, but what is new is not being able to make myself come.

The moment my eyes crash open, my orgasm withers away and neither toys nor my fingers can satiate the need the memories evoke. My body feels wrung tight, and I have no idea what to do to relieve the tension.

"Morning, boss," Daniel says, stepping into the kitchen and running his eyes over the trays of cakes waiting to be displayed in the counter showcase.

"Morning Daniel, how was your evening?" I ask, refilling my mug from the coffeepot I brought down from upstairs.

"Could have been worse. I had to take Monty to the vet because Kara fed him chocolate. I swear my baby sister is going to be a nightmare when she's older."

Smiling, I chuckle softly. Daniel dropped out of school to move back home and help his dad look after his sister after his mom passed. She started kindergarten in the fall, which is why Daniel was so pleased to be able to get full-time hours after Jean quit. "Is Monty okay?"

"He's fine. The vet gave him something to make him sick, so the house smells like dog barf, which is always fun." He laughs.

"Urgh." I grimace.

"Tell me what all this deliciousness is. Take my mind off all the vomit." He smiles, bracing his hands on the doorframe above his head and flashing me a glimpse of his surprisingly toned abs.

"Err." Fumbling for words, I swallow, then force my eyes to lift from this exposed stomach. "Muffin of the day is pistachio and rose and these are chocolate opera cakes," I tell him, pointing to the green muffins and the indulgent slices of layered opera cake. "I whipped up a batch of lemon madeleines, and I've taken the lemon muffins off the list for today, so let's see how the madeleines do and if anyone asks for the lemon muffins, let me know."

"Am I pushing the new stuff or just seeing if they sell?" he asks. It turns out Daniel is a great salesman and had almost finished a marketing degree before he quit school to come back home. Even without his degree, he's had some great suggestions about the new stock I've been carefully introducing, and I'm grateful for his advice and ideas.

"Don't push them, but maybe mention them when you mention the muffin of the day. Let me know how they're going midmorning, and next week, I'll start adding more patisserie lines and see how they fare against each other."

"Sounds good to me. Want me to come up with a drink of the day, or did you have something in mind?"

"Nope, go wild."

Smirking, he nods, grabs a tray of cakes, and then disappears back into the front of the store. I have a three-tier sweet sixteen cake to make, so I quickly pull together the ingredients and put them into the oven to bake before heading up to my office.

The moment I sit down behind the desk, my cell rings. Looking at it cautiously, I brace myself for it to be Nero before I remember that I blocked him. My screen says Atticus and I'm smiling even before I answer.

"Hey," I say.

"Little sis, how you doing?" Atticus says, his gravelly familiar voice making tears fill my eyes.

"I'm good," I say, forcing myself to sound upbeat.

"What's wrong?"

"Nothing's wrong."

"Then why are you about to cry?" he demands, in the way only my big brother can.

"I just miss you," I say as the first tear falls.

"I miss you too, Little Bit. Why don't you come visit? I can send you a ticket and have you here by tonight?"

My brother is a fixer. He always has been. Over the years, he's cleaned up all of the carnage Felix leaves in his wake. Picked up the pieces of broken hearts, stupid mistakes, and even a couple of pregnancy scares. He's the best big brother, and right now, I wish he could fix me just by sending me a plane ticket.

"I can't. I have the store. I only just took over, so I can't take a vacation because I miss my brothers," I wail pathetically, tears rolling down my cheeks.

"Sure you can. That's the joy of being the boss." He chuckles.

"Att, it's a bakery and I'm the chef. If I'm not here to bake the cakes, we don't have anything to sell."

"So, employ another chef," he says like it's the most obvious thing in the world.

"I plan to once I have the rebrand done and I've proved to myself and the town that there's a market for classic French patisserie in small-town Montana."

"You'll get there, Little Bit. No one can resist your food."

"How's things?" I ask, diverting the conversation away from me.

"Good, I'm busy, but Donovan is still pissed about that article in that magazine and about me turning down his stupid reality TV show. Apparently, he'd pitched me working here and Jude and August making regular cameos to the producers, and since I told him I wasn't interested, he's being a little bitch about it. Guess he thought he was hot shit, but without me and my NHL star little brothers, they weren't interested."

"Did he really think you'd say yes? You've worked with him for what… five years? He must know that you don't talk about the guys and what they do. None of us have ever capitalized on Jude and August's fame."

"I know. Hell, he's never even met them. They've never even been to the shop. If they want new ink, I go to them, or we do it at my place. If they hadn't tagged me in the stuff they've posted on social media, he wouldn't have even known we were related. But I don't know how much longer I can deal with him. I like the shop and all my clients, but I keep my own appointment book and I'm too busy to do walk-ins. I think it might be time to find somewhere new to work out of."

"I'm sorry, Att. Do you think you'll set up your own shop?" I ask.

"I don't know." He pauses. "No. I'm not there yet. I don't want to be the boss. I want to do my art but have the space to be there for Felix when he needs me. He has a huge exhibition coming up at that gallery in New York and if I had my own shop, I wouldn't be able to travel with him. I want to be able to set my own hours and clients and I can't do that if I'm the one in charge."

Even though he can't see me, I'm nodding. "Are you going to look for another shop to work out of?"

"Maybe, or maybe I'll look for a few guest spots in some of my friends' studios. I have clients that travel from all over. I'm pretty sure they'll still come, even if I'm on the East Coast for a while."

"You could always come home. Montana is a great state, and me and Mom and Dad are here. Jude and August could get a trade to Idaho or something and we could all be together again."

His laugh is soft and low. "We all miss home, Little Bit.

I'll put the feelers out and see if anyone knows about any guest spots near home. After Felix is done in New York, I could find him a space to work from close by. He doesn't care where it is as long as the light is right."

"Seriously?" I shriek.

"Yeah, a few months of family sounds good to me. Maybe I could make it work for the same time as the guys' offseason and we could all be home for a couple of months."

"Don't threaten me with a good time, Att. Are you seriously serious? Do you think you could make that work?"

"Don't I always fix it, Little bit?" he asks.

"Yes." I sob, my emotions bubbling over and exploding out of me.

"Little Bit," he sighs.

"I'm sorry, it's just been. It's been a tough few weeks," I confess.

"Tell me," he demands.

"No, it's fine, it's nothing really."

"Tell me, Tori. Now, or I'll have to call Jude."

I'm close to all my brothers, but Jude is the one out of all of us who refuses to deal with bullshit. If Atticus calls him and tells him I'm not okay, he'll either call or show up and he won't leave until he knows exactly what's happened. He's a bloodhound when it comes to filtering through all the platitudes we tell one another to protect the others when one of us is having a tough time.

It's funny, but when I think about it, my brothers and I all have our roles. Atticus is the fixer, Jude is the asshole, Felix is the peacemaker, August is the fun one, and I'm the nurturer. Maybe that's why we work so well, why we're

222   GEMMA WEIR

close and rarely, if ever, fall out.

"Urgh, don't call Jude, he's busy with hockey and I'm fine."

"Bullshit. I can't fix it if I don't know what's wrong, so spill."

Sighing, I open my mouth and tell him everything. About James meeting Buck, about her moving in with him and me agreeing to move in with Nero. I tell him about Nero hating me and how much Knight is like Felix. Then I tell him about Nero kissing me, about him running, then him kissing me again and me running. And finally, I tell him about Sunday night.

The whole time I'm talking, he stays quiet and lets me speak, not interrupting, just letting me spew words at him without trying to offer anything. When I finish, I feel lighter. I don't tell him all the details about the sex, or the kinky bits, or the way they made me feel. We're close, but not close enough for him to want to know intimate details about my sex life.

"Okay, so here's what I've got from all that," he says. "This Nero dude is either a fucking asshole who I need to beat the shit out of, or the guy's in love with you."

I scoff. "Well, he's definitely not in love with me, but you can't beat him up either."

"The hell I can't. If he thinks he can have you as a live-in booty call, I can and will beat the crap out of him."

"I don't really know what he wanted from me," I confess. "And it doesn't matter now anyway because I moved out."

"But he doesn't know that?" Att clarifies.

"By now, he should," I say quietly.

"Twenty bucks says the guy is banging down your door before lunch." He laughs.

"He doesn't know where I've moved to. The note just said that I'd moved out."

"You left the poor guy a note?" Att laughs.

"Hey, it was a nice note," I protest.

"Jesus, Little Bit, he's going to lose his ever-loving mind. If you were mine, I'd spank your butt until you couldn't sit down."

A shocked, choked gasp falls from my lips. "What?" I splutter.

"Fuck, Little Bit, it's only a spanking, don't be a prude."

"No. No, it's not that. I guess I'm just a little shocked. I mean, are you… are you a Dom?" I ask, cringing as the words come from my mouth.

"I'm not Christian Grey." He laughs. "But I enjoy a certain amount of control and a little discipline," he says, keeping it vague enough that I'm not sick to my stomach.

"So, you and Kim?" I ask, mentioning his ex-fiancé.

"No," he replies quickly. "She didn't. That wasn't her thing."

"Is that why things didn't work out?" I ask. Att and Kim split up a couple of years ago, but it came out of the blue. One minute they were together, the next they weren't and he hasn't had a serious relationship since.

"One of the reasons, yeah. I wanted things she wasn't interested in doing, and she wanted me to cut Felix out of my life."

"She what?" I snarl angrily.

"She thought we were codependent and that it was

"unhealthy."

"You're twins. You shared a womb, a sac, for goodness' sake. What did she think was going to happen, that you'd just never speak to your other half again?"

"Pretty much. But we're not talking about me. Kim and I have been over for years. Right now, we're talking about you and this Nero guy."

"I'm pretty sure he'll be glad I'm gone. Plus, this way, hopefully, it won't be too awkward at parties and things. We had a crazy night, but then we just forgot about it and carried on like nothing happened. It's the best thing for everyone."

"Unless he doesn't want to forget about it," Att says, clearly amused.

"Why wouldn't he want to forget? He wants sex and I'm not interested. The night we shared was fun, but that's all it was."

"Who are you trying to convince, Little Bit? Me or yourself?"

"I'm not. Urgh, I hate you," I whine, exhaling loudly.

"Do you like him?"

"I don't know. I know I don't like that I know he doesn't like me. Does that make sense?"

"Are you sure he doesn't like you? Not many dudes go around fucking women they don't like in real life."

"He told me he wanted me, so I said, 'You don't like me,' and he said, 'Doesn't mean I don't want you.' I can't have sex, no matter how good it is, with someone who is literally only there for the sex. It icks me out."

"Hmm," Att says, sounding out his agreement.

"Look, he won't care that I've moved out, and I'll be

fine. Plus, you agreed to come home for a while and I can't wait. I have my new business; James is happy, and if you can convince Jude and August to come home in the offseason, I'll have you all here and that's literally everything I'll ever need."

"Little Bit." He sighs.

"I mean it. I don't have time to deal with man drama right now. I'll sign up for online dating or whatever once the store is running like a dream. Until then, I'm going to focus on my career."

"If he doesn't like you, he's an idiot. You're the fucking best, Little Bit, total wife material, the holy grail, and if he doesn't see that, it's his loss, not yours."

"Love you, big bro."

"Love you, Little Bit."

"I have to work," I say reluctantly.

"Me too. Felix and I will come visit soon and we'll do our usual video chat this week, all of us."

"Okay."

"Take care. Let me know if I win that bet."

I laugh. "Yeah, I wouldn't bank on that money. I'll collect my winnings from you the next time I see you."

He ends the call and even though I always feel better after I speak to one of my brothers, I feel worse too. A part of me thought he'd be a little more on my side about this whole Nero thing and he wasn't. I'm not saying I need my big brother to fight my battles for me. And there isn't a battle here anyway, but I kind of expected him to be a little more fire and brimstone about the whole thing.

Most of the time, Atticus's advice is awesome; he's

always been able to read people and situations better than the rest of us. But he's wrong about this one. There's no way Nero will be banging down my door trying to find me.

"Tori," an angry male voice yells from downstairs.

Well fuck.

Chapter Nineteen

Nero

Turning the key in the ignition, my car roars to life and I pull away from the house, spinning the wheels as I slide along the path and onto the road. The twenty-minute journey down into Rockhead Point passes in a red haze that tinges my vision and seems to make the minutes move both too fast and too slow.

There's nothing safe about the way I speed down the winding roads, but right now, I don't care. I'm too eager to get to Tori and fucking throttle her, or maybe spank her, or just fuck her until this rage is purged from my body.

I was pissed the day Miranda brought her two lovers with her on our date, and the three of them tried to convince me to become the fourth member of their poly group. But the anger I felt then has nothing on the pure, unadulterated rage I've been feeling since I read the words she thoughtlessly wrote on that slip of fucking paper.

She didn't even leave me a forwarding address, but although I don't know where she's living, I do know where she works. Turning up at her job is an asshole thing to do, but right now I don't care. I need to see her, need her to explain what the fuck she thinks she's doing and then I'm taking her home.

Haphazardly abandoning my car in a space across the street from the bakery, I march along the sidewalk and throw open the glass door with more force than I intend. It shatters against the frame, sending shards of glass skittering across the floor to the gasps and horror of the customers who are waiting to be served inside.

"What the—" the guy who's been here the last two times I've been here says from behind the cash register.

Ignoring him, I stride behind the counter, intent on getting to the kitchen and Tori.

"Sir, stop. You can't go back there," he says. "Hey."

I'm not gentle when I barge past him. I'm a big guy and I have at least six inches and fifty pounds on him, so there's no way he's going to stop me from getting where I want to go.

I vaguely hear him telling someone to call the cops, but I don't stop. When I step into the kitchen, it's empty, the counters and workspace immaculately clean, the steel-topped tables shining with nothing but a covered cake cooling on a rack.

"Tori," I yell. "Tori, get out here," I yell again when she doesn't appear.

It takes me a moment to spot the door she led me

through the last time I was here when she took me upstairs to a small office. Grabbing the handle, it turns beneath my grip and I pull it open, stomping up the stairs.

"Tori, you better get out here, woman."

"Nero?" She appears from the room we were in before, her brow furrowed and confusion laced across her expression. "What are you doing here?"

A dry, angry laugh bursts from my lips. "Are you fucking serious right now? I've been at work for four days, then I get home to a note saying you've moved out. Where the hell else was I going to be?" I yell.

Instead of the guilt I was expecting, somehow, her expression gets even more confused.

"Sunday night, my cock was buried deep in your cunt, filling you up with my seed while you begged to be my dirty girl."

"Okay," she says.

"Okay?" I snap.

"I'm just not sure what you're getting at. We had sex, but that doesn't explain why you're here," she says slowly, like I'm too fucking dumb to understand her words.

Taking a step closer to her, I watch as her breathing becomes shallow and her eyes go wide. "We didn't just have sex. I had you pinned down, begging for me to fuck you while I played with your ass until you came screaming my name. We didn't just have sex. You had my handprint on your skin while you strangled my cock and begged for more. We didn't just have sex, you submitted to me and you loved it just as much as I did. We. Didn't. Just. Have. Sex. We had a mind-altering claiming. I told you I wanted you. I told you you were mine."

Sighing, she looks away, not giving me her full focus. Snapping my hand out, I pinch her chin between my finger and thumb and drag her face back until she's forced to look at me. "Eyes on me, Tori. I want you looking at me when I speak to you so I know you understand me."

"Nero."

"You don't get to leave. You don't get to ignore me. You don't get to pretend like what we shared was nothing. Do you fucking understand me?"

"No." Her head moves like she's trying to shake it and deny my words, but my grip holds her tight.

"Wrong answer, Sunshine," I say, lowering my head to take her lips with mine. Forcing my tongue into her mouth, I don't give her a chance to protest, demanding entrance and refusing to allow her to pull away. The hand that was holding her chin drops to her throat and I collar her with my palm, feeling her swallow beneath my grip. My free hand tangles with her ponytail, giving it a sharp tug as I swallow her hiss of pain down my throat.

For the first time in days, my heart starts to slow and my tense muscles begin to relax.

"Police," a loud male voice shouts.

Reluctantly pulling my lips from hers, I keep my hands on her as I turn to look at the two armed deputies who are pointing their guns at me.

"Step away from Miss Hoffman, hands in the air," one of the deputies says.

Slowly, I release my grip on her throat and hair and lift my arms into the air.

"Deputies," Tori starts.

"Are you okay, ma'am?" they ask.

"I'm fine. There's no need for this," Tori says, defending me.

"We got a call that a male perpetrator smashed the store's door, then barged his way into the kitchen, screaming and hollering for you."

"You smashed the door?" Tori shrieks, turning her attention from the cops who are pulling my hands behind my back and securing them into cuffs.

"I opened it with a little too much force. I'll pay to replace it." I shrug, not even remotely repentant.

"For goodness' sake, Nero, you couldn't have called? Or just left me alone?"

"Nero?" The second deputy says, pushing forward to look at me.

"Hi Cameron, how you doing?" I ask Cora's older brother.

"Better than you." He laughs. "Want to explain what the hell this is all about before we have to take you in?"

"She's mine," I tell him with a shrug.

"I am not," Tori gasps.

"Yours?" Cam says. "Jesus, tell me this isn't happening again. I thought we'd seen the last of this love-at-first-sight bull when Cody got married. You telling me this is a Barnett legacy or myth or whatever situation we have going on here?"

"No fucking clue," I tell him honestly. "All I know is that this woman, Tori Hoffman, is mine and I have zero intention of staying away from her."

"Tori, do you want to press charges against this knucklehead?" Cam asks with a sigh.

"No," she answers, her bottom lip pulled between her teeth.

"Is there somewhere a little more private we can talk for a spell?" he asks her.

Nodding, she glances at me before she motions Cam into the small office, closing the door behind them.

Gritting my teeth, I stare at the door. I know Cora's brother. We're not friends, but we're definitely friendly acquaintances. But right now, I don't give a fuck who he is. If I wasn't in handcuffs and being restrained by a cop, I'd be storming in there and kicking his ass for being holed up in a room with my woman.

Until the last few weeks, I wouldn't have ever considered myself a jealous person, but when it comes to Tori, I'm finding that I'm a raving fucking lunatic. It feels like forever until the door opens and a smirking Cam steps out with a tense Tori behind him.

All of my muscles bunch tight and I test the cuffs, straining against them and finding myself unable to move. I need them off and I need to have my hands on my woman, so I can make sure that Deputy Cam fucking Cunningham remembers she belongs to someone else and to keep his hands to himself.

"Uncuff him," Cam says with a chuckle, waving his hand toward me.

The other deputy releases the cuffs and I pull my arms forward, flexing my hands to get the blood pumping again.

"Lucky for you, Tori doesn't want to press charges.

She also confirmed that you haven't hurt her or touched her without her consent. I don't like to get in the middle of domestic disputes, but I think the best thing to do right now is for you to go home and cool off. I'll give Cody a call and have him get some guys in to board up the door until he can order in a replacement one. I'm going to let him know that he'll be billing you for the damages and for a nice new coat of paint for the whole of the front of the store."

"Fine, but I'm not leaving. We haven't finished our conversation," I tell Tori, looking at her intently and saying so much more with the intensity of my gaze than my words.

Dropping her chin, she refuses to meet my eye, and I inhale sharply, clamping my jaw together to stop myself from demanding she look at me.

"Nero, just go," Tori begs quietly.

"Come on, big guy," Cam says, his voice full of amusement and doing nothing to quell my urge to punch him.

"Fine. But this isn't over. Remember what I told you. You are mine."

Unable to look away, I watch a tremor rack her body. She might be sending me away, but there's no way she'll be able to deny what my words have done to her. Smiling, I turn and head down the stairs with the two cops following behind me. They shadow me through the kitchen, through the store, past the shattered front door and shocked employees and all the way across the street to where my car is abandoned.

"Look, Nero, I like you. I mean, we're basically family, what with both of our sisters being married to the Barnetts. So, listen to me when I tell you that if you cause a scene like this again, I won't have any choice but to take you in. Tone down the crazy. I don't pretend to know what the fuck is in the water up on that mountain, but if we have a whole new bunch of men who are going to lose their minds over their women, then I need to let the sheriff know. In the meantime, just give Tori some time and try not to do anything too insane."

"I'll try my best," I growl, holding out my hand to him.

Gripping it, we shake, his grip firm but not as firm as mine when I squeeze a little harder than necessary. Releasing me, he pulls off his hat, rubbing his head as he chuckles, slapping his colleague on the shoulder before they both turn and walk away.

Standing beside my car, I spin until I'm facing the store, my butt leaning against the trunk. Crossing my arms, I stare up at the windows above the storefront and scoff. That's where she's living. I'd lay money on it. The last time I was here, I glimpsed a bed in a room, but the rest of the place looked more like storage than a home. She must have cleared the space out or maybe just moved in with it still packed full of junk.

Lifting my wrist, I look down at my watch to check the time. It's barely ten a.m. She usually works until at least four. I'm pretty sure the asshole who works the counter and who would definitely fuck her if he had the chance will call the cops if I go in there again while the store is open.

Resigned to having to wait, I push off my car and walk down to the coffee shop to order a large coffee, then head to Grannie Annie's diner and order a breakfast sandwich to go. Armed with food and coffee, I walk back to my car and get comfy, watching the store.

Cody and a couple of his guys arrive an hour later. They get busy patching the broken door up with planks of wood and taking measurements to order either a new door or replacement glass. When Cody glances my way, spotting me leaning against my car, he takes a moment to speak to his guys, then jogs across the street to me.

"Heard I'm sending the bill for this to you. That right?" he asks.

"Yep," I answer coldly.

"Want to explain what that door did to piss you off? They're not cheap to replace, so I need to know if I should order in more than one if you plan to break it again."

Narrowing my eyes, I turn to look at him.

"Oh fuck." He laughs. "I recognize that look. Who is she? The girl behind the counter? I don't recognize her, but since I found Betty, I don't really see other women anymore."

"Tori," I growl, reluctant to tell him but eager for as many people as possible to know she's mine.

"Tori." He whistles. "I don't know her well, but Betty likes her. Apparently, she knows Tori's brother. He's a tattoo artist in Cali or something. Kind of a genius from what Bett told me."

"Brother?"

His laugh is full of familiar amusement. "You didn't ask her about her family?"

I shrug. "We haven't spent much time chatting."

"I'm guessing that since you're out here watching the store like a stalker, and I got a call from the sheriff's office, things aren't going too well."

"We're working things out," I snarl.

"Does she know that?" He laughs.

I open my mouth to tell him to fuck off, but he speaks before I can.

"Dude, I'm sorry. It's just I've had this exact conversation with basically every single one of my brothers, and they've had it with me too. I know you haven't asked for my advice, but I'm going to give it to you anyway. There are two routes you can take here. You can go for the tried and tested Barnett bulldozer method, where you force your way into her life and ignore all of her protests. Or you can behave like a normal, rational person and give her some time to process things. Date her, woo her, whatever the fuck you want to call it. Either way, going in as angry as you look right now isn't going to win you any points."

I hate admitting that he might be right, but I also don't know how to release any of the pent-up anger I'm feeling if I'm not fucking it out.

"Which option did you use?" I ask.

His chuckle is full of amusement. "I'm a Barnett." He shrugs.

"But the bulldozer option clearly worked for you."

"It did and it didn't. Bett ran and I had to spend three months without her. Longest ninety-one days of my life. After that, I bulldozed even harder. It took a baby and some real come-to-Jesus moments, but it all worked out and we just found out we're expecting our second kid. Now, looking back, I do wonder if a slightly more finessed approach would have worked better."

"I'll take that into consideration," I say reluctantly, blowing out a tense breath.

"If you do decide to take the bulldozer route, you should know she's living upstairs and there's an entrance to the apartment down the side alley." He winks. "She just asked me about fitting a lock for it, so the door will be open in, say, an hour or so once I've gotten her a lock, which you're also paying for."

"Anything else she needs, you send the bills to me from now on," I agree, smiling for the first time since the cops made me leave. "Thanks."

"No thanks needed. But before you do this, think really fucking hard about if she's yours forever or just for right now. If it's right now, then you need to leave her the fuck alone, I won't help you fuck her, but we have to stick together when it's *the* woman. You understand?"

Inhaling a slow, measured breath, I think about Tori. A week ago, I'd have said I wasn't interested. Four days ago, I only wanted her body. A couple of hours ago, I was telling Buck she wasn't someone I wanted a relationship with. But now, it's pretty obvious I was lying to myself because this feels like so much more than just lust. I still want to fuck her, but having her ignore me and then move out has made this insane, primeval urge inside of me flare to life. I don't want her to ever be able to ignore me again. I want her desperate for me, in the same way I feel almost crazed for her. I want her thinking about me, texting me, missing me when I'm not with her. I want everyone to know that she's not available, to know that she belongs to me.

Do I want her forever? I'm honestly not sure, but then

I also can't imagine ever wanting to give her up. Will that change once she's mine? Is this about her leaving rather than about her?

"I can see you asking yourself a hell of a lot of questions, so I'll leave you to your thoughts. The side door will be open in an hour or so while I'm working on fitting the lock. But if you decide to step through that door, and you end up changing your mind and you hurt that girl, I'll beat the shit out of you, then I'll let her brothers know exactly who and where you are and they'll hurt you too. Barnetts might be bulldozers, we might do fucked-up things to get our women, but we're also protective motherfuckers and not a single one of us would hesitate to take care of you for her."

Anger swells inside of me again. "She's mine," I growl animalistically.

"Perfect, then I won't need to look out for your woman. See you in an hour." Straightening, he walks away, smiling and whistling as he goes.

I'm clenching my fists so tight that my fingers start to tingle. The anger that I was already feeling has been reignited by my chat with Cody, and being forced to stand outside on the street while my woman hides from me isn't doing anything to help me calm down. I'm jittery, on edge, and ready to sate my anger on Tori's luscious body.

When Cody asked me, I wasn't sure if I was ready to call Tori my forever, but if the idea of another male just looking out for her makes me feel this furious, I can't even imagine how feral the thought of her being with someone else would make me.

My thoughts run away from me as I stare at the first-floor windows. Tori might be mine, but she's still one of the most annoying women I've ever met. Wanting her doesn't make her any quieter or any less cheerful, and I don't know if I can look past that. But part of me wonders if I'm just finding fault with her because since she moved her sunshine into my house, it feels like my life has completely altered and shifted in a different direction.

Finishing my coffee, I drop my trash in the can and then return to my spot watching the store and the apartment upstairs. Time slips past as I try to decide if I can imagine my life without her in it. How would I feel if I never got to touch her again? Not everything is about sex, but right now, our sexual connection is the main thing I share with Tori. Because I haven't made any effort to get to know her. In fact, I'm pretty sure I've been an unmitigated asshole to her and this feeling of impotence right now is my punishment.

When it's been an hour since Cody left, I push off my car and stride toward the bakery. Not entering the store but heading down the alleyway between the buildings to where Cody is cutting a hole for a lock in a shabby-looking door up a flight of metal stairs.

When he sees me, his lips tip up into a smile and he nods, then turns and disappears inside, leaving the door invitingly open and unprotected. Being guided purely by instinct, I climb the stairs and walk into her home. The small apartment is mostly empty, and I scan the space, noting the lack of furniture and that most of the equipment I spotted the last time I was here is gone. I don't know where Cody went, but I'm not stupid enough to call out to him. Instead, I silently open doors until I find her bedroom and slide inside, closing the door behind me.

The room smells like her. Until this moment, I'd thought she smelled of cookies, but it's actually a rich vanilla with just a hint of spice and chocolate that lingers in the air. Her princess bed is just like it was at home, covered in fluffy, soft throw pillows and a white comforter, only she's wound strands of twinkle lights between the posts and frame forming a light canopy above the mattress.

Translucent white fabric is draped along the frame and the whole thing combined looks like it would be more suited to an Arabian Nights–themed hotel than a tiny, shitty apartment above a bakery.

Despite the sparse and shabby state of the place, there's something about the room that makes me smile. The paint is dull and stained, the carpet in need of replacing, but the time and effort she's put into making this bed ethereal and decadent makes me question if I know anything at all about the woman I'm claiming as mine.

Does Tori want to be treated like a princess or ravished like a kidnapped concubine? Maybe she wants both. My eyes run over the posts of the bed, and for a moment, I consider all of the things I could do to her, all the ways I could make her beg if she was tied to the corners. My dick hardens and I reach down and cup it, squeezing and silently warning it to calm the fuck down.

Sighing, I kick off my boots and flop down onto the mattress. The bed is a queen, too small for us to share without her lying on top of me, but at least if she was on top of me, she wouldn't be able to move away from me in her sleep or disappear before I woke up. Needing to be quiet,

I turn my cell to silent and close my eyes, ready to wait in here for the rest of the day until everyone has left and the store has closed. Once we're alone, I'll force her to have the conversation we started earlier.

I doze, snoop through her things, and mess about on my cell, but at some point, I must fall asleep because by the time I wake up, it's after two p.m. and I'm sprawled out on her bed, her mounds of throw pillows scattered across the floor. My cell is beside me and I have three missed calls from my brother. Unwilling to call him back, in case Tori is upstairs in the office, I open up my text app and write him a message.

> **ME**
> Hey, can't call right now, is everything okay?

I'm not expecting an immediate reply, so I close the app and drop my cell back to the comforter. When it vibrates, I look down at it, surprised.

> **BUCK**
> Heard a rumor you got picked up by the cops today. Want to explain????

Scoffing to myself, I type out a reply.

> **ME**
> Just a slight mix-up with me and Tori, no harm, no foul.

> **BUCK**
> No harm, no foul? She called the cops.

> **ME**
> She didn't call the cops, the dick she works with did.

BUCK

I heard you smashed the glass on the front door to the store and then barged through to the kitchen.

ME

I didn't smash it, I opened it a little too forcefully and the glass shattered. I'm covering the costs of the repairs and a fresh coat of paint for the front of the store for the trouble.

BUCK

So, things are all good between you guys? I haven't seen James in days, I don't want to have her stressed over you and Tori's drama.

Smirking, I type…

ME

No drama here, Tori's mine.

His reply comes in seconds.

BUCK

Yours? This morning she was annoyingly cheerful and loud.

ME

Well things change.

BUCK

Don't hurt her. I will not allow James to be forced to pick a side, so do not piss off my fiancé's best friend.

ME

I don't tell you how to handle your woman, don't tell me how to handle mine. Might not be home for a couple of days, text me if you need me.

Dropping my cell back to the comforter, I exhale, trying to lessen the tension speaking to my brother has caused. He's the second person today who's warned me not to hurt

Tori. I don't need any other man to tell me how to treat my fucking woman. What I need, more than anything, is for everyone to mind their own business.

For the first time since I heard the stories, I'm starting to appreciate why the Barnetts have such a hard-on for kidnapping their women. If the two of you are in the middle of nowhere alone, there is no chance anyone else will start sticking their noses in.

Unfortunately, kidnapping Tori right now isn't an option. So, I need to think of something that forces her into my orbit and won't give her a chance to run away or build up any walls against me. An hour later, an idea comes to me and it's so fucking obvious I wonder how I didn't think of it earlier.

Now, I just need to wait for her to finish work and I can put my plan into place.

Chapter Twenty

Tori

I've never had a stalker, but if having this constant feeling of being watched is what it's like, then I wouldn't survive. Since the cops escorted Nero out of my apartment, I've constantly felt his eyes on me.

Not wanting to feel like I'm hiding, even though I'm absolutely hiding, I take refuge in baking and decorating the cake I'd left to cool before Nero decided to barge in. But even in my kitchen, which is normally my sanctuary, I can feel his palpable anger permeating the air all around me.

Throwing myself into cake decorating, I speak to Cody Barnett and his team when they arrive and even remember to ask him about fitting a lock on the apartment door. When I've made the celebration cake as beautiful and elaborate as I can, I head upstairs, hoping that focusing on paperwork will banish all thoughts of Nero from my mind.

Instead, I find myself drawn to the front windows and spot him immediately. There's no sign of the furious anger he was filled with earlier as he leans against the hood of his car, staring straight up at me. Dropping the drapes, I stumble away from the window and hide in my office. When I've exhausted every piece of paperwork, I head back down to the kitchen and throw myself into pastry prep for some classic French pastries so they're ready for the morning. But my nerves don't calm for the rest of the day.

After a while, Nero disappears, but his car remains parked across the street, taunting me every time I glance outside. I send Daniel home early and man the counter, needing to occupy myself so I don't have any time to think about everything Nero was saying earlier.

Unfortunately, serving customers doesn't keep me as busy as I need to be to block out the thoughts that attack my brain.

She's mine.

He told the cops that I was his, like it was normal, like laying claim to someone is usual. Although, in this town, after the Barnetts, maybe it is.

He seemed so angry about me moving out. Which makes no sense because why would he care? *Because he thinks you're his,* my pesky inner voice shouts at me. But that makes no sense either because Nero and I haven't ever had a civil, two-way conversation. Either I've talked at him while he's grunted and scowled, or he's bitched at me in his gruff, grumpy tone.

We have never, ever talked about us being a couple or even wanting to be a couple. Sure, we had sex—great sex—

but sex doesn't equate to a relationship, and it definitely doesn't give him the right to barge into my home and business, shouting and throwing his weight about.

Annoyed, indignant rage intermingles with lust-soaked memories of the night we shared and fills my thoughts for the rest of the day. By the time I finish cleaning and lock the makeshift door Cody's guys boarded up, I'm horny and pissed about it.

Turning off the store lights, I step into the kitchen and take a minute to straighten the bowls of prepped dry ingredients I've set out for the morning. I'm procrastinating, but I don't know why. A part of me expected Nero to turn up again, demanding to speak to me in that sexy, authoritarian tone he sometimes uses. But he hasn't. His car is still across the street, but he's been missing since this morning and I don't know if I'm upset about that or not.

Sighing, I check that the back door in the stockroom is locked, then turn off the lights and head upstairs. The stairwell is dark, but I feel my way up the steps until I reach the door at the top. Cody fitted an electronic lock on this door for me too, so the apartment is completely secured from the store now, but I asked him not to lock it when he left and to leave me the master keys for both this door and the outside door on the kitchen counter.

Turning the handle, I step into the apartment, wishing I'd asked him to put the light on before he left so I wouldn't have to walk into a dark room. Ignoring the goose bumps that pebble across my arms, I step forward, running my hand along the wall and searching for the light switch. When I feel the heat of someone behind me, I freeze, my breath dissolving in my lungs as fear consumes me.

Rocking back on my heels, I tense, ready to run, when darkness explodes into light at the same time that a strong arm bands around my waist, pulling me back into a firm body.

A scream rips from my mouth, like I'm the doomed heroine in a horror movie, and I battle to get free.

"It's me," a familiar voice says, making me pause in my bid for freedom for a split second. Taking advantage of my melee, a second strong arm bands around me, holding my flailing arms to my sides and immobilizing me.

"Calm down, Sunshine, it's me, Nero."

"Nero?" I croak.

"Shhh, it's just me. I didn't mean to scare you," he croons, pressing a soft kiss to the skin beneath my ear.

"You didn't mean to scare me?" I shriek. "Then why on earth would you creep up on me in the dark?"

"I didn't creep up on you. I walked. You seemed to be having an issue finding the light switch. I flipped it for you."

"Why the hell are you in my apartment? Put me down," I demand.

"No."

"No?" I echo back at him.

"I think I like you like this. Plus, we need to have a conversation without you running away from me. So, it's either with me holding you to me like this or impaled on my cock. Personally, I vote for option two, but I think we need to get a few things straight before you bend over and present that perfect cunt for me."

"Let me go and get out before I call the cops," I hiss,

trying and failing to sound intimidating.

"How are you planning to call the cops, Sunshine?" he mocks, sliding one of his hands under the edge of my shirt and caressing my bare stomach.

"Nero, this is crazy."

"Completely, certifiably crazy."

"Then stop this, go home and we can pretend this never happened."

"I wish I could. I wish I could pretend that we never met. But I can't. I can't forget how your lips taste. I can't forget the way your arousal coated my dick or the sight of your cunt full of my cum. I can't forget any of it or the fact that even though I don't fully understand it, I know that you're mine."

"Nero." His name is a desperate gasp, and when he hums against my ear, I feel slick arousal pool in my panties.

"Mine," he rasps against my neck, his hand on my stomach, sliding up to tease the underside of my breast over my bra.

"No," I argue weakly.

"Are you wet, Tori? If you're not, I'll leave. I'll walk away and leave you alone."

Before I can protest, the arm banded over my chest tightens while the other moves down my stomach and beneath the waist of my pants.

"I bet this needy little pussy is all wet and desperate," he growls as his fingers push beneath the fabric of my panties.

I make a lackluster attempt to move out of his hold, but instead of pulling his hand free, Nero shoves his fingers between my legs, cupping my sex and feeling the shameful truth. That I'm soaked.

"There she is," he rasps. "My dirty, dirty girl, wet and greedy."

A whine bursts from me and heat fills my cheeks.

"I should make you beg me to fill you up, but I need you too much."

As he speaks, he inches two fingers to my entrance, the fabric of my pants digging into my hips painfully as his thick arm maneuvers to allow him more room to move.

"The night we spent together, I didn't make it clear, so I'm going to spell it out for you."

Two fingers plunge into my sex, stretching me and pushing me up onto my toes.

"The moment I touched this cunt, it became mine. No one touches it but me, and yes, my sweet little dirty girl, that includes you. The only things going inside this pussy are my fingers, my tongue, any toys I decide to use on you, and my cock, nothing else."

Restricted by the tight fabric of my pants, he finger fucks me in short, shallow thrusts that stretch me but don't provide me with enough friction to come. His thumb finds my clit, and he starts to rub in slow circles.

"This clit is mine. No one but me gets to rub it or lick it."

His fingers pull out of my sex and slide farther between my legs until they're pressing against my ass, rubbing over the tight ring of my asshole.

"This tight little virgin asshole is mine. Only I get to play with it, stretch it out and fuck it. No one else."

Without me realizing it, his arm that's been holding

mine down has loosened, and instead, he's cupping one of my breasts.

"These full, perfect tits are mine. No one but me gets to see them or touch them or taste them."

His one hand plucks at my nipple over my clothes while he fills my sex with two fingers again, using his other hand. "Do you get me?" he asks slowly.

"Nero," I gasp as he tries to push a third finger into my pussy.

"I asked you a question. Do you understand what I just told you?"

"No." I shake my head, denying his words, not interested in what he has to say when he's yet to make me come.

"You're my woman, Tori Hoffman. You belong to me. Mine to fuck, mine to own, mine to claim. When we're done with your lesson, we'll be packing up your shit and taking it home."

It takes me a moment to understand what he just said. The rhythmic pumping of his fingers inside of me distracts me from his words. "No," I gasp.

"No?"

"Not moving," I gasp as he pushes my pants and panties down and over my hips until they fall to my feet and I can clearly see his fingers sliding in and out of me.

"My woman lives with me, not in a shithole apartment above a store."

"No," I half growl, half moan when he slides one finger free of my pussy and pushes it against my asshole, applying enough pressure to slip past the tight band of muscle and slide inside of me.

"Yes. We're going home and then you're going to spend the next three days sitting on my cock, so I know where you are. When we fall asleep, it'll be strapped together, my fingers or my dick buried inside of you."

His talented ambidextrous fingers thrust into my sex and my ass at the same time, his free hand rubbing my clit until I'm teetering on the edge of release.

"Nero," I cry.

"Does my dirty girl want to come?"

"Please," I beg, too far gone to care what I have to say to get the orgasm I'm on the verge of.

"Tell me you're my dirty girl."

"I'm your dirty girl," I parrot back, all shame washed away in my desperation to claim the release he's preventing me from finding.

"This greedy cunt and this tight little ass haven't been properly taken care of, have they? But don't worry, I'm home now and I'm going to keep them both full of my cum."

A second finger pushes into my ass and the stretch hurts almost as much as it feels good. But the pain and his voice saying filthy things against my ear tip me over the edge and I scream out my release, soaking his hand when my muscles tighten on his fingers, trying to hold him inside of me.

Aftershocks are still ricocheting through me when I become aware that I'm moving. My stomach lands against the edge of the spare bed I've shoved against the wall of the living room as Nero rips my jeans and panties off my feet. Positioning me how he wants me, I barely have time to catch my breath before his hard dick finds my entrance and slams inside of me.

"Fuck," I scream, my eyes flashing open as he pummels into me, railing me at a brutally fast pace. Unable to move, I lie bent over the edge of the mattress and take it while he fucks me, his hands gripping my ass to pull my cheeks apart.

"My dick's going in that tight ass soon," he snarls, leaning forward and spitting against my hole. His pounding pauses for a moment before he moves again, and the feeling of his cooling saliva rolling between my cheeks adds to the torrent of sensations I'm experiencing.

Opening my mouth to protest, I'm shocked when a moan comes out instead of the insult I'd intended to scream. I shouldn't be enjoying this. I'm not even sure I consented, although I don't want him to stop. Once again, that squirmy feeling fills my stomach as my body and my brain war against each other.

In the end, my body wins and an orgasm crashes over me. Screaming, I claw at the mattress, desperate to find some purchase to hold on to while wave after wave of intense, pain-filled bliss implodes inside of me.

My mind quiets, and all I can hear is the thudding beat of my heart. Everything slows, and the world shrinks down to just me in a bubble, with him on the outside. The silence allows me to think without the invasion of the judgy voice inside my own head.

I can still feel him fucking me, feel the way his dick fills me each time his pelvis hits my ass. But everything is muted, like I'm seeing it all from beneath water. Closing my eyes, I try to process how I'm feeling, but the truth is that I just don't know.

My body is alive, each nerve ending electrified and charged, but if I could hear it, I know my inner voice would be chiding me for enjoying the way he's using me. And that's what this is. *He's* fucking me. *He's* using my body to sate his own need and anger. Right now, as good as everything he's doing feels, it's about him, not me or us. This isn't romance or love; it's raw, depraved, carnal sex, and even though I don't think I should be enjoying it, I am. It feels startling when I admit to myself that I love feeling used, like he's made me a toy for his pleasure.

The world speeds up, and suddenly I'm back in the present, aware of each slap of his thighs against my butt and the squelching sound of my wetness, greeting him every time he slides into me.

"You're so fucking tight. Even when I'm pounding into you, this cunt is still desperate, gripping me hard enough to drag the cum right out of my balls. You're mine, Tori. My dirty little sunshine. My cunt to fuck, and fill, and breed. I'm going to keep you full of me. I'm going to pump all of your holes full of my cum until it's dripping out of you, and you're exhausted and sore but still so greedy for more that you beg me to keep going."

His words and the gravelly timbre of his voice tip me over the edge and I come again, a slow, burning orgasm that rushes from my toes and engulfs the rest of me as it spreads upward.

His powerful thrusts lose rhythm and become stuttering jerks, interspersed with hip-shattering slams until he comes with a guttural, animalistic grunt. Falling forward, his weight pins me to the mattress, my chest squashed, while his hips keep gently rolling, his dick twitching inside of my tender core.

"Nero," I rasp.

"If you try to run, I'll tackle you to the ground and fuck your ass raw," he warns lowly.

"You're crushing me."

His weight instantly lifts, and I drag in a deep breath, reinflating my lungs.

The mindless bliss only lasts a moment, then reality slips in. I'm not sure what happens now. Last time we had sex, it all felt very spontaneous, like we lost control and neither of us could help it. But tonight, he was in my apartment, waiting for me when I opened the door.

I don't even know how he got in. The door that leads into the alley at the side of the building has been locked since Cody showed me how to program the electronic keypad lock he fitted for me. Nero must have come in before then, which means he's been in my apartment most of the day.

His being here isn't a knee-jerk reaction, and what just happened between us wasn't a spur-of-the-moment incident. It was planned.

Before I have time to think any more, Nero slides his dick out of me, then flips me over, placing me down on the mattress on my back. Grabbing my thighs, he drags me down the bed, but instead of pushing his dick back into me like I expect, he slides two fingers into my core.

"Do I have your attention?" he asks, curling his fingers and making my sore, well-used sex twinge.

I nod.

"Words, Sunshine. I need to hear the words."

"Yes."

"Yes what?"

"You have my attention," I croak, my throat dry.

"Good, because I'm only going to say this once more. You're mine. We're together, boyfriend and girlfriend, or husband and wife if you want. We're going to pack up your stuff and go home, and then I'm going to spend the next three days fucking you raw for ghosting me while I've been at work. After that, you'll go to work, then come home to *our home* every night at a decent hour. You won't flirt with the fucktard who works with you. You'll delete the group chat with my teammates, and you'll make sure they all know you belong to me. If they don't figure it out, I'll arrange a game night and have you sit on my cock while they all watch, so none of them ever question who you belong to again. Do. You. Understand?"

Squirming, I try to move out of his grip, but he pushes his fingers in a little deeper, keeping me immobile, while his other hand presses down on my stomach to hold me in place.

"Do you understand, Tori?" he asks again.

"No," I shriek. "I don't understand any of this."

An expression of sheer incredulity spreads across his face. "What the fuck don't you understand?"

"All of it. We don't like each other; we barely know each other. I literally have no idea what's going on or how any of this happened."

"Your cunt is full of my cum. I'd say we know each other pretty well," he sneers.

"We fucked. That doesn't mean we have a relationship;

it means you put your dick in me and moved back and forth until we both came," I gasp, throwing my arms into the air, then covering my face with them.

"We didn't just fuck. I claimed you."

"This isn't a medieval romance novel," I hiss. "You don't get to just claim me."

"Tell that to the Barnetts."

"You're not a Barnett."

"Well, apparently, I am an honorary Barnett. Because I don't understand this either. But the one thing I am sure of is that you are mine."

"And you think that gives you the right to break into my apartment, accost me, and then stick your dick in me?"

"Yes," he snarls, his eyes blazing with feral heat. "I'd say it gives me a hell of a lot of rights, including me taking you home."

"I live here now."

"Why the fuck would you want to pay rent for this shithole?"

"I don't pay rent."

"What? Your boss lets you stay here for free?" His brows furrow, his expression oddly, adorably confused.

"I don't have a boss, and I don't pay rent because I own the whole building," I blurt before I can think better of it.

"You what?" He blinks, clearly shocked.

"Look, it's pretty clear we know absolutely nothing about each other. I'm not moving back up the mountain with you. I have to be here to run my business. I don't think I did, but if I gave you the impression I was looking for a boyfriend or whatever the hell it is you're offering, then you misunderstood and I'm sorry. The sex is awesome, but a relationship requires a lot more depth than I think you're capable of."

Bitch does not come naturally to me. James has ice queen badass down to a *T*, but for me, it's weird to hear so much unpleasantness come from my own mouth.

The truth is, I do think Nero has the capacity to be a nice guy. I've just never seen it because when it comes to me, he's a grumpy asshole.

"If you won't come home with me, then I'll just stay here with you," he says like he didn't hear anything I just said.

"No, you can't."

"Sunshine, my fingers are holding my cum inside of you right now while your cunt clenches around them, begging me to shove my cock back in you. Stop pretending you don't want me."

Choking on my own saliva, my eyes feel like they bug out of my head as I stare at him.

"Don't look at me like that," he chides. "I told you if your pussy was dry, I'd walk away and leave you alone. But it wasn't dry, was it? It was soaking wet, dripping with your need for me." His jaw clenches and he spits, "Or was all that cream for someone else?"

Looking away, I try to avoid his penetrating stare, but he releases his hold on my stomach and grabs my chin, forcing me to look at him. "Tell me," he orders. "Was your cunt gushing for me or someone else?"

My eyelids flutter closed, but he pinches tighter, refusing to allow me to hide behind silence and avoidance.

"Answer the question."

"You," I whisper, ashamed to admit the truth but aware that he won't stop until I'm honest.

"Words. Use your fucking words."

"You, it was for you," I say louder.

"Tell me."

Swallowing thickly, I inhale, then shout, "My pussy was wet for you."

"Good girl," he croons, softening his hold on my face. "Don't ever fucking lie to me again."

"Lots of guys make me wet, but my body having a reaction to someone doesn't mean they have some claim on me. I almost came in my panties the first time I watched *Aquaman*, but it doesn't mean I belong to Jason Momoa."

Chapter Twenty-one
Nero

Burning, fury-filled rage surges through me so quickly my vision actually goes red at the edges, like my anger may make me explode or pass out.

"You belong to me. You don't even get to think about having sex with other guys," I say through gritted teeth.

Her eyes go wide, and I know I'm being entirely irrational, but the proprietary ownership I feel for her has apparently sent me off the edge into insanity.

"Nero," she scoffs.

"I'm fucking serious, Tori. I will spank your ass until it's burning, then fuck it until you know exactly who owns you. And I'll keep doing it until all thoughts of any man other than me are banished from your mind."

"Are you on drugs?"

"What?" I choke.

"I'm serious. Are you on drugs? Or are you in the middle of some kind of psychotic episode? Because those are the only two explanations I can come up with that rationalize your crazy behavior. Unless maybe I'm the one who's had the mental breakdown and none of this is real. Me losing my mind feels like a more likely reality than you pulling a Barnett and deciding we have some kind of make-believe relationship."

"Tori," I growl, my lips slipping into a scowl.

"Can you take your fingers out of me please?" she asks, oddly calm.

"No."

"I'm not sure we can have a rational conversation while you're inside of me in any way. I think I should maybe call James. She'll be able to figure out if it's you or me who's lost their mind."

"Neither of us have lost our goddamn minds," I snap, losing my patience. Reluctantly, I slide my fingers out of her cunt, staring briefly at the white cream that's coating the edges of her pink and puffy pussy.

Dragging my shirt over my head, I offer it to her. "Put on my shirt. You can call James when we get home."

"I live here," she tells me again, denying me and pissing me off.

"You don't even have a fucking bathtub. This place is a shithole."

"It's not a shithole," she protests, pulling my shirt over her head, hiding her body as she scoots backward, away from me.

"Look around you, Sunshine. The paint's flaking, the carpets are worn and stained. The whole place needs renovating just to be habitable. We have a really nice house already; we're not living here."

"You're right," she says quickly. "*We're* not living here. I live here. And yeah, it needs some fixing up, but it's a work in progress, and it's more than habitable. I think you should leave."

"The only way I'm leaving is if you come with me," I tell her, crossing my arms over my chest.

"I'll call the cops."

"Call away. I already told them you're mine. Do you think they'll bother turning up again, when, with one look, they'll see just how well fucked you are, with my cum still drying on your thighs?"

"You're an asshole," she hisses, curling her legs beneath her and scowling at me.

Shrugging, I don't deny her words. What's the point? I am being an asshole right now. The truth is, if she called the cops, I'd probably get arrested, or at the very least, they'd handcuff me and take me to the station. But right now, I'm not against telling her what I need her to hear, and that's that I'm not going anywhere and there's no one, including her, that can do anything about that.

"I need to take a shower," she says wearily.

"We can take one together."

"I'd rather not," she sighs.

"I didn't ask for your opinion. We shower together, or you don't shower at all."

Closing her eyes, her lips move, but no sound comes

out. "Nero, this is ridiculous. You should go."

Anger swells inside of me again, but I pull in a breath before shaking my head. "Not happening, Sunshine. If you won't come home with me, then I'll stay here with you."

"I don't want you here," she argues, shuffling across the bed that I'm guessing she's using as a makeshift couch.

"I told you not to lie to me again. I don't like hearing all that bullshit coming from those pretty lips of yours, Sunshine. Do you need me to prove to you how much you really want me here? I'm more than happy to help your body show you just how much you don't want me to go."

"Insane, absolutely insane," she mumbles, shaking her head as she climbs down from the mattress.

"Hold out your hand, Sunshine."

Grumbling, she looks at me, then at the door behind me. Silently surveying her options, she exhales shakily before lifting her hand out, palm up.

"Ask me to help you shower."

"Are you serious?" she snaps.

"Deadly."

Her eyes narrow and fire fills her gaze. "Oh, enormous douchebag, who broke into my home and refuses to leave, will you help me shower?"

I can't help it. I laugh. Even when she's trying to be a snarky bitch, she can't quite commit to it. Her insults almost sound… nice.

"I'd love to help you shower, although I kind of enjoy how dirty you are right now. Before we go, why don't you lift up that shirt and show me how messy I've made you?"

The sound of her gasp of shock goes straight to my

dick, and all my blood rushes downward until I'm hard, my cock standing proud.

"Do as I say, Tori, show me that messy little cunt," I order.

I don't know why, but it's like my words flip a switch in her and the angry woman from only a moment ago disappears, replaced with a sexy little kitten who remembers how good I can make her feel. Her full lips part and her gaze lowers to my hard cock. Reaching down, I grip my length, slowly sliding up and down until a bead of precum pools at the head of my cock.

I'm not sure she's aware she's even moving when her fingers curl around the hem of my shirt, and she lifts it just enough that I see a peek of her pussy.

"Higher. I want to see your swollen clit and well-fucked cunt."

Dragging her lower lip between her teeth, her eyes stay fixed on my hand, slowly jerking my cock, while she lifts my shirt all the way up so her sex and stomach are exposed.

"Spread your legs and then use your other hand to pull your lips apart."

She follows my orders like she was made to do it, her pupils blown wide, lost to the urge to submit to my demands. It's clear this is new to her. I doubt she's ever fucked anyone as sexually controlling as me. But then, I've never wanted to exert my dominance over anyone the way I want to with her either.

"Why do you need to shower, Sunshine?" I ask.

Her brow furrows in confusion, so I help her along. "Dirty girls, whose cunts are messy with cum, need to clean up before they get dirtied up again. So why do you need to shower?"

I watch her throat move as she swallows thickly. This hint of humiliation is something I've secretly fantasized about before but never actually done in real life. The first time we fucked, I hadn't intended to call her my dirty girl, but seeing her react when I did, only proved how sexually compatible we really are.

The fabric of my shirt is too thick for me to see if her nipples have hardened, but I bet they have, and I'd lay money on the fact that her pussy is drooling at the idea of having to say the words I'm prompting her to say.

"Who are you?"

"A dirty girl," she whispers.

"My dirty girl," I agree, praising her. "And what are you?"

A shudder runs through her as she blurts, "Messy with your cum."

"Such a good girl," I coo. "So why do you need to shower?"

"Because I'm a dirty girl who's messy with your cum," she says, her chest heaving, even as a gush of cum mixed with her arousal escapes from her sex.

Smiling, I close the distance between us in a single step and scoop her into my arms. Holding her close, I find her lips with mine and kiss her until we're both breathless. When she's pliant and soft in my arms, I carry her into her tiny, dated, but clean bathroom and lower her to the small counter while I kick off my clothes and turn on the shower.

"What are we doing?" she asks quietly.

"Just showering, Sunshine. I know this is a lot, but we'll figure things out."

"You don't like me," she whispers, like it's the biggest obstacle between us and happily ever after.

"Yeah, well, we'll figure that out too," I tell her, lifting her back into my arms and underneath the warm spray.

She's quiet while I wash her hair and body. Her breath hitches when I drop to my knees in the cramped stall and thoroughly clean her pussy and ass before dirtying them back up with my tongue.

By the time I turn off the water and wrap her in one of the new fluffy pink towels she's got stacked on a shelf over the sink, her eyes are drooping and it's clear she's exhausted.

"I need to feed you," I say, wrapping a towel around my hips and growling with annoyance when it barely covers me.

Carrying her into the living/dining space, I set her on the kitchen counter, then open her refrigerator, frowning at how empty it is. "Why is your refrigerator empty?"

"Because I haven't had a chance to go grocery shopping. I planned to go tonight, but then I got accosted by you. Let me get dressed and I'll go out and get some supplies."

"Not happening, Sunshine. I'll order us some takeout."

"You can't actually keep me a prisoner up here, Nero. I have to work in the morning," she says tiredly.

"I don't plan on keeping you a prisoner. I'm just not giving you a chance to run from this again. You did that once already and it won't be happening again. There's something between us, Tori. You're mine. My woman. And I won't let you dismiss that just because we didn't start out the way you imagined we would."

"I'm not denying that there's definitely a sexual connection between us. Physically, it's clear that we're…" She pauses, obviously trying to find the right word. "Compatible. But sex is only one aspect of a relationship. Or have I misunderstood all this growling *mine* stuff and you're just looking for a hookup?"

"Not a fucking hookup," I snarl, gritting my teeth hard to stop myself from declaring that she's mine again. I wonder if the Barnetts had this much trouble getting their women to understand what it meant when they claimed them.

"Okay. But if you think this is more than a hookup, how are you planning on getting past the fact that we're not friends?"

"Not looking to be friends either."

Huffing, she hoists the towel up and holds it around herself more firmly. "But friendship is the basis of a good relationship. I've never met two people who lived happily ever after when their relationship started with them annoying the hell out of each other so much they couldn't stand to be in the same room."

"I can stand to be in the same room as you," I argue.

"Really? When did that happen? Because we shared a house for literally less than a month and I don't recall us having one single conversation that didn't start or end with an argument. You openly admitted that you don't like me. Which is frankly bizarre because I'm generally considered to be super nice."

"You're loud." I shrug.

"I'm loud?" she shrieks loudly.

"And you talk too much."

Her mouth opens and closes, but no sound comes out as her eyes practically bug out of her head.

"I like you a lot more when you're quiet," I confess, grabbing my cell from the bathroom and calling through an order for pizza.

"You didn't ask what I wanted on my pizza," she says when I step back into the living room.

"I got a pepperoni, extra cheese, and a bacon and mushroom."

"What if I'm a vegetarian?"

"You're not," I sigh. "The last time you got pizza with my team, you asked for bacon and mushroom, then ate three slices of the pepperoni."

Her shoulders sag and she tilts her head to the side, assessing me. "How do you know that? You were there for maybe ten minutes before you left."

"I didn't leave."

"Huh?" her brow furrows.

"I didn't leave. Oz lit the firepit in the yard. I was out there."

"You sat outside on your own rather than with your friends?"

"I don't always want to be social."

"Huh," she says, clearly bemused by my confession. "I need to get dressed."

"Why?"

"Because I'm in a towel."

"So?"

"So, this"—she motions between us—"is weird enough

without me being naked."

"I like you naked."

Her brow furrows even further. She looks like a little confused kitten, and it's oddly cute. Holding the towel with one hand, she shuffles to the edge of the counter, then drops down. Following, I trail her into the bedroom, my own towel doing nothing to hide my growing erection.

"What are you doing?" she asks.

"Watching."

"Well, don't. Go and put some clothes on."

"I only have the stuff I was wearing earlier."

"Go home then."

"Apparently, I live here now," I say with a sarcastic grin.

Spinning to face me, her expression is part indignant, part outrage. Her fingers release her hold on the towel to prop on her hips. "You do not live here."

"But you live here?" I ask.

"Yes."

"Then I live here too," I say, arching my eyebrow and daring her to argue with me.

"You're insane," she shouts, throwing her arms into the air and dislodging her towel that unfurls and slithers to a heap on the floor.

Her body is beautiful, soft and full, begging to be used, and my dick hardens fully, the towel doing nothing to cover me.

"Oh my god," she gasps, dropping to the ground to grab for the towel.

"Leave it," I order, striding toward her, my hard dick

leading the way.

"Nero," she whines, but she does as I say, her fingers tangled in the fabric but not lifting it.

"You say you don't want this, but we both know that's a lie. Stop fighting and start enjoying how perfectly we fit together. You were made for me. Just as filthy and dirty and depraved as I am. Tell me you don't like the way I make you feel."

She's still crouched on the floor when I reach her. Curling my fingers under her chin, I lift her face until she's looking up at me from beneath her long lashes.

"Nero," she whispers.

"Just be honest, Sunshine."

"The sex is good," she says nonchalantly.

Chuckling, my lips tip into a smirk. "Just good?"

"I mean…" she trails off.

"It's more than fucking *good,* Tori. My dick has never been so hard and I've never come so much or as often as I do when I call you my dirty girl. I've never felt as desperate as I do when I tell you exactly how I plan to use you in the most humiliating detail, and you gush with arousal. You're everything I had no idea I was craving in a sexual partner. You're strong and confident but soft and sexy too. You like to submit to me, but you do it with defiance shining in your eyes. You're all the dirty fantasies that I never knew I could have in real life. We are fucking perfect. So, calling it good is like saying the Grand Canyon is a pothole. It's like saying Vegas has a couple of lights. It's like saying the sun and the moon are just bits of rock. Us together is so much more than fucking good."

Her chest is heaving, her eyes wide and shining with need, desire, and the defiance I love so much. A part of me wants her to argue, to fight and deny just so I can subdue her. But I want her supplication even more. "Do you have any idea what I want to do to you right now?"

She shakes her head slowly and I move with her, my fingers caressing along her jaw. "I want to pry your mouth open and shove my dick down your throat. I want to hear you gag on me but keep going anyway, and then I want to come on your tongue and face and chest. I want to watch you kneel at my feet, covered in my cum, and then I want you to thank me for making a mess of you."

I watch her reaction as I speak, noticing when she swallows, when her breathing hitches, and when her thighs squeeze together. She gets off on dirty talk. She gets off on the hint of humiliation she feels when I tell her what I want and all the ways I plan to use her. Because she wants to be used, it turns her on.

She's fucking perfect.

Her tongue slips out of her mouth and she licks her lips.

"Open your mouth, Sunshine."

It takes her longer than I'd hoped, but she wiggles into a more comfortable position, curling her legs beneath her before she slowly parts her lips and opens her mouth.

"Do you want to taste my cock?"

She looks at me like she's waiting for something from me, so I smirk and her shoulders sag. Then she nods.

"Such a good girl," I praise.

Her eyes go hooded and a visible tremor vibrates through her. She likes to be praised almost as much as she likes to be embarrassed. Cupping her jaw with my hand, I grip my cock with the other hand and guide it to her mouth.

"Eyes on me," I order as I push the head of my cock between her lips, slowly filling her until I hit the back of her throat.

Chapter Twenty-two
Tori

"**P**erfect, that feels unbelievable," he croons, tangling his fingers into my hair to guide my head up and down his intimidating length.

He said he wants to feel me gag on his dick, but I'm really hoping that's just dirty talk because I'm pretty sure the only women who can actually deep-throat are porn stars, and if he tries to shove his mega dick down my throat there's a strong chance I'll puke all over him.

Getting into a rhythm, I lick and suck on his dick, feeling myself getting more and more turned on every time he tells me how good I feel, how amazing I am at sucking his dick, and how dirty I am for clearly loving every minute of being on my knees for him.

Nothing about this should feel good to me. I'm at his

feet, naked, exposed, and yet again, I'm not entirely sure I agreed to any of this. But my body is alight with sparks of energy rushing through my veins. He's barely touching me, one hand in my hair, the other still holding my jaw, but my sex feels heavy and swollen, and I can feel my own arousal coating my thighs.

A strong wind or a single flick of my clit would send me over the edge and tumbling into orgasmia, and the new but now almost familiar squirmy feeling that seems to be coming more and more often fills my stomach.

When his grip on my hair tightens until it's painful and he's fucking my mouth in careful strokes, I squeeze my thighs together, fighting the urge to play with myself while he uses my mouth for his pleasure.

His groan is audible, sexual cyanide, and my core tightens, heating with need. My fingers start to move between my thighs, but before I can touch myself, he comes with a pained grunt and hot cum fills my mouth. After the first burst of release, he pulls his dick from between my lips, letting the rest of his cum hit my cheek, chin, then my chest.

"Swallow," he orders, his voice even more gravelly and rough than normal.

I do as he says on instinct, and the salty, disgusting taste of him coats my tongue and throat. I try not to grimace, but when he smirks, I know I failed. Instead of commenting, he lifts the hand that had fallen to his side and smears the cum on my face across my lips with his thumb.

"Fucking perfect. My perfect dirty girl."

His voice is full of… pride, and I react, warmth building from the outside in, blossoming from his praise. Dirty isn't a word I would normally associate with a compliment, so I honestly don't understand why when he uses it, it feels like the highest honor he could bestow. My inner feminist is burning her bra and piling her antitoxic masculinity soap box so high it could rival a skyscraper. And yet here I am, on my knees, covered in cum and feeling like I've achieved something.

God, what the hell is wrong with me?

"Do you have something to say to me?" he asks, his voice smooth and sexy, like whiskey and ice.

My mind is full of static, my psyche warring with itself about whether it's okay to enjoy the way he's treating me or if I should be outraged and appalled. But apparently, my lips didn't get the memo that the rest of me isn't sure how to feel about all of this because words tumble free before I can stop them. "Thank you for making a mess of me."

His smile is raw, male pride, filled with so much possessive ownership that I'm pretty sure I feel a brand appear over the skin of my heart. I don't want him to be right. But in this moment, it really does feel like I'm his, and I have no idea if that's the best thing that's ever happened to both of us or a natural disaster waiting to strike.

His eyes slip closed for a second, and when they open again, they're brighter and sparkling with intensity. It's clear my acquiescence has affected him, so I don't fight him when he lifts me from my knees and kisses me, his cum still smeared across my mouth and face.

"Fucking perfect." He smiles. "I really want to leave you coated in my cum, but the pizza will be here in a minute, so let's go clean you up again. If the pizza guy sees you like this, I'll have to fucking kill him."

Lifting me completely off the ground, like I'm weightless, he carries me into the bathroom, then wipes all of his release from my skin with a washcloth. For a moment, I consider offering to do it myself, but it's his mess, so I let him clean it. When he's done, he frames my face with his hands, leans down and kisses me.

Unlike the other kisses we've shared, this one isn't frantic or spur of the moment. This kiss is soft and playful. It's his reward for playing this game we both seem to be a part of. And no matter how much I try to deny it, what just happened between us makes me an active player, not a pawn being dragged along for the ride.

I don't know if this will work or if I even want it to, but either way, the train has left the station, and I'm on board until we stop or fall off the tracks and explode in a fiery ball of flames.

Pulling away from my lips, he presses a sweet kiss to the tip of my nose. Bending down, he pulls on his pants, not bothering to fasten them, and retrieves his shirt from the floor. "Put this on."

"It's dirty," I say, wrinkling my nose.

"I want you in my clothes and this is the only thing I have here right now. I'll get Buck to drop some more of my stuff off in the morning, but this will have to do for the minute."

"Or you could just go home," I say with a shrug and a smirk.

His eyes narrow and his lips turn down into a frown. "Sunshine," he says, the single word a clear warning.

"Fine," I sigh, rolling my eyes. "But I'm not putting on your dirty shirt. I have clean pajamas in my dresser."

"It's my shirt, or naked."

"You're being ridiculous."

"Naked it is," he says, dropping his shirt to the floor again before dipping down and hoisting me off the counter and over his shoulder, my naked ass pointing at the ceiling.

"Put me down," I shriek, clawing at his arm.

Ignoring me, he carries me out of the bathroom, through the living room and to the doorway that leads down to the kitchen and store downstairs.

"What are you doing?"

"I just got a text. I'm assuming it's telling me the pizza's here, so I'm going down to get it."

"I'm naked," I yell, wiggling to get free.

"I gave you the chance to wear my shirt and you refused."

"You said you'd have to kill the delivery guy if he saw me with no clothes on," I say, trying to get him to put me down so I can get dressed, but instead, he shrugs, carting me down the stairs and into the kitchen.

"You'd better make sure he doesn't see you then."

Finding the light switches effortlessly, he flips them on, and artificial daylight fills the space. My kitchen is immaculately clean, but in the harsh overhead beam, it feels almost clinical and creepy.

Nero slides me down from his shoulder and I panic. "Don't you dare set me on the counter. I refuse to put my bare butt on any surface in this kitchen," I screech manically.

Freezing with me dangling halfway down, he turns us

and lowers my feet to the floor next to the counter. "How much cleaning would we have to do if I fucked you in here?" he asks seriously.

I feel the horrified expression take control of my features.

"Okay." He laughs, holding his hands up in mock surrender. "So, fucking you in your kitchen is a hard no. Duly noted. What about in the front? I could pin you to the glass and fill you with my cum while your tits were pressed against the window, waiting for someone to walk past and see the show."

His suggestion is as appalling as it is titillating. Apparently, I just unlocked exhibitionism on my kink scoreboard. What the hell is this man doing to me?

Laughing lightly, he chuckles. "Dirty, dirty girl. Stay here while I get the pizza."

I'm pretty sure my brain has short-circuited because I don't move while he steps through into the store and collects the pizza. I'm still in the exact same position, naked and barefoot, in my kitchen, when he returns with two steaming pizza boxes in one hand and a paper bag in the other.

"Let's go, Sunshine," he orders, nodding his head toward the stairs and motioning for me to go ahead of him.

It isn't until I step back into the apartment that my mind seems to click back into focus. "How did you open the door?"

"What door?"

"The store. How did you open the door to get the pizza?"

"With the key," he says, putting the food down on the kitchen counter before opening and closing the cabinets until he finds plates and silverware.

"How did you get the key?"

"You dropped your keys on the floor when you first came up here. I picked them up."

"Oh." I guess that makes sense. I was holding my keys when he accosted me in the dark and scared the shit out of me. "How did you get into my apartment?"

His expression goes purposefully blank. "The door in the alley was open. I walked straight in, then waited in your bedroom until after the store closed."

His words are almost believable, but from the way he looks like he's trying to make me believe him, it's pretty obvious he's lying. "How—" I start.

"Let's eat before the pizza gets cold," he interrupts, putting two slices on a plate for me, then eyeing the bed he fucked me over earlier. "Why do you have two beds and no couch?"

Taking the plate from him, I frown down at my nakedness. "I can't eat pizza naked. It's a one-way ticket to a burned nipple."

"I'll get you my shirt," he smirks, striding into the bathroom and returning moments later, holding out the shirt I refused earlier.

"I have clean pajamas."

"I gave you your choices, Tori. Hot-cheese-burned nipples or my shirt. Pick. And answer my question. Why do you have two beds and no couch?"

"Fine," I huff, snatching the shirt from his hand and pulling it over my head. "After I realized that the floor is really fucking hard, I ordered a bed to keep here for when I was working late."

"You slept on the floor?" he growls. "Why the hell would you do that?"

"Because I stupidly moved in with my bestie's fiancé's brother and it turned out he was an asshole who couldn't stand me," she deadpans.

"Are you trying to tell me you slept here on the floor because of me?"

He sounds horrified, like I just told him I sold an organ on the black market, not like I confessed to spending a single night on the floor before I ordered a bed.

"Well, I guess you're not the only reason, but yes, you were a factor. But it was one night. I had a bed delivered the next day, so it's hardly the end of the world. When I moved in properly, I had my real bed delivered, so I pushed the spare bed up against the wall as a makeshift couch until I have a chance to go and pick out a new one. Once I get it delivered, I'm going to get a waterproof cover for that bed and drag it up onto the roof."

"The roof? Why the fuck would you need a bed on the roof?"

"I'm going to plant a roof garden up there. Having a bed as a sun lounger or a place to lie and watch the stars is going to be epic."

We both fall silent while we eat the pizza and drink the sodas he bought. By the time I can't eat another bite, I'm tired, the stress of him and a long day taking their toll on me. Yawning, I reach up and pat my tangled hair. I never even brushed it after our shower, and it's going to be a rat's nest by the morning, but I don't seem to be able to find the energy to care right this second.

"Let's go to bed, Sunshine," Nero coos. Taking my plate from me, he puts it on the side in the kitchen, closing up the pizza boxes and putting the empty soda bottles in the trash before coming back to me and scooping me into his arms.

"Nero," I sigh tiredly, trying and failing to find the energy to argue.

"I'm not going anywhere, so save your breath."

Exhaling, I let my head rest on his shoulder. Tonight, I'll let him have his way, but tomorrow I'll think of a better argument why us being together when we have nothing in common, except how well his dick fits in my vagina, isn't a good idea.

The million throw pillows I keep on my bed are already askew when he lowers me to the mattress. Apparently, his hiding out in my bedroom wasn't a lie. Grabbing handfuls at a time, he throws them all to the floor, not taking care to stack them or put them away tidily.

"Hey," I protest.

"You're lucky I'm not throwing them out the window. Who needs this many fucking cushions?"

"They're soft and it's the aesthetic."

"They're fucking ridiculous. Arms up."

"What?" I say sleepily.

"Put your arms up so I can take this shirt off you."

"Why?" I yawn. "I thought you wanted me to wear your stinky clothes."

"While you're wandering around the apartment, you can wear my shirt, but in bed, you'll be naked."

"You're insane," I protest, but I still lift my arms into

the air and let him drag his shirt up and over my head.

"When it comes to you, you have no fucking clue how insane I am," he murmurs quietly.

I watch as he crosses the room and opens the bottom drawer on my dresser. "What are you doing?" I ask.

"Finding this," he says, holding up the soft chiffon scarf I wear as a hair band sometimes.

"What do you need a scarf for?"

Walking quickly back to the bed, he kicks off his pants, leaving them in a heap on the floor, then climbs onto the mattress. Grabbing my hand, he entangles our fingers, then wraps the scarf around our wrists, binding us together.

"What the fuck?" I shriek, trying to pull my hand away, only to be stopped by his unmoving grip. "Nero."

"The last time we shared a bed, you snuck off in the middle of the night and I woke up alone. That won't be happening again. If you need to get up, you'll ask for permission."

"I'm not a child or a prisoner. This is ridiculous."

"You running off without a word was pretty childish," he jabs. "Now you'll either be bound to me or the bed every night until you earn my trust and prove you'll still be where I put you in the morning."

"I am not sleeping tied to you."

"It's late and you have to be up for work in the morning. I'm not arguing about this, but if you keep pushing me, you'll sleep bound to me, with my cock in your ass."

Heat fills my face, but I'm not sure if I'm horrified or aroused by his threat. The now all-too-familiar squirming sensation is back and I don't know if it's how my wrist is tied to his or the fact that he's told me I have to ask permission to leave the bed. Or the threat of anal—that I don't hate anywhere near as much as I should—that's causing it, but either way, I'm turned on and ready to call the cops at the same time.

"I thought my cock in your ass all night might be a punishment, but from the look on your face, maybe it'd be a reward. If you want it as much as your expression says you do, you'd have to be a really good girl to earn my cock inside one of your holes while you slept."

Burning need vibrates in my core, but I try to keep my face neutral and not show him how he's affecting me. I try to think of something scathing to say, anything that will push the attention away from how well he seems to be able to read my expressions. Instead, he pins our joined wrists over my head and slowly climbs over me, forcing my legs apart with his knees.

His free hand pushes between my thighs to cup my pussy, and a low, rough groan falls from his lips when he finds me wet, my sex dripping with arousal.

"Look at all this cream. Is this for me?" he questions.

I shake my head, although I don't know why. Denying it's him that's turning me on is completely futile, but I just can't stop.

"Don't lie to me, Sunshine. Is your cunt drooling because of me?"

Swallowing, I nod.

"Is it because my dirty girl likes being tied to me, or because you want me to push my big cock into your tight ass and then keep you stretched around me all night long?

I won't fuck you; I'll just use your hole to keep my dick warm, keep you impaled on me, ready to use if I want."

A whimper bursts from my throat and a triumphant grin spreads over his beautiful lips.

"You're so fucking perfectly filthy," he coos, pushing two fingers into my soaked sex and slowly pumping in and out. "I wasn't going to touch you again tonight. I don't want you to be too sore, but you need it, don't you? You need me to dirty you up again so you can sleep. If you beg prettily, I'll finger fuck you until you come, then I'll slam my cock into you and use your cunt until I fill you up with my cum. Do you want that, Sunshine?"

I know I shouldn't, but I can't help it. It's like he's brainwashed me or hypnotized me because I want what he's suggesting so much I feel almost desperate. "Yes," I pant.

"Then beg. Tell me exactly what you want and how much you want it. If you ask prettily enough, I'll give it to you. If not, I'll leave you unsatisfied after I cover your cunt and ass in my cum."

"Please, please, Nero. Make me come, then fuck me," I blurt quickly.

"That wasn't begging. I'll give you one more chance," he offers, pushing a third finger into me and stretching me until I'm not sure if it hurts or feels amazing, but either way, I'm on the edge of an orgasm.

"Please, I need you, please, please, please. I'll be your perfect dirty girl. I need you to finger me until I come, then I need your cock inside of me. Please, Nero, please fuck me. I need you." This time, I'm not begging. I'm pleading. I feel mindless, nothing more than a junkie desperate for their next fix.

"Good girl. That's more like it, my beautiful, sexy, perfect, dirty girl. My Sunshine. Come on my fingers, show me how much you need it."

Rolling my hips, I ride his fingers as much as I can from beneath him and within moments, I come, a guttural cry bursting from my throat as I convulse, coming harder than I ever have before.

Tears fill my eyes, spilling over and rolling down my cheeks as he replaces his fingers with his cock, slamming into me and triggering a second wave of release that has my toes curling, my back arching, and my eyes squeezing closed so hard it feels like they'll never open again.

"Look at me," he demands, grabbing my other arm and pinning it above my head too, keeping me immobile while he fucks me with wild abandon. Lifting my legs, I curl them around him, locking my ankles together at his back to keep me as close to him as I can while he thrusts in and out.

Dipping his head, his lips find mine, and he kisses me possessively, his tongue filling my mouth and dominating me while his body brands mine as his. I come so hard, my muscles hurt, but his lips swallow every sound I make until his thrusts start to stutter, and hot cum bathes my sex, heating my ravaged core.

"Mine," he growls, pulling back from my mouth just enough to nip at my bottom lip with his teeth.

Something is happening between us. I don't know what it is, but I don't try to move when he rolls us to the side, his dick staying inside of me while he tangles our limbs together.

My cheek is pressed against his chest, one of my legs clamped between his, the other draped over the top of his thigh and held in place with the hand that isn't tied to mine. We're a human knot, but instead of hating it, I feel oddly… protected. Like he'll keep me safe from the world and all the hard edges of life.

It's not a sensation I've ever experienced before, but as my eyes get heavy and my sore, satisfied body melts into Nero, I fall asleep wondering how I'll cope if I never get to feel this way again.

Chapter Twenty-Three

Nero

It feels like I hold my breath all night as I wait for her to try to get up and leave me, but she never does. She sleeps peacefully all night, her body mashed so close to mine I can feel her heart beating and each breath she takes.

Every single moment with Tori feels different from any other woman I've been with. It's like she's in 4D and the women in my past were in black and white. I don't understand why it's not the same, but this feeling that she's mine thrums so hard in my chest I feel like there are jungle drums chanting it with every beat of my heart.

In the hours I spent in her room, I nosed through her stuff, but I also tried to think of how to claim her in a way that wouldn't ever allow her to leave. I'm confident that serial killers put less thought into how to pursue their victims than I have, trying to find a way to bind Tori to me without actually kidnapping her.

In the end, the only thing I could think of was making her fall in love with me or getting her pregnant. Her iPad was on the bedside cabinet, and I managed to use a picture she had of her and James to open it. Her calendar shows she gets the birth control shot, but her reminder to book an appointment to get the next one isn't for another three months. Unfortunately, Dr. Google says there isn't a way of removing it from her system any quicker, so filling her with my kid isn't an option right now. Which only leaves getting her to fall in love with me as a way of tying her to me indefinitely.

I want Tori more than I've ever wanted a woman in my life. I know she's mine. That she belongs to me, but I don't love her. I barely know her. I feel something for her. Something that's strong enough to compel me to hide in her apartment for several hours and refuse to leave, but I don't think that's love, or at least not in the way I expect love to feel.

I love my mom. I love Buck and Juni. I love my nephew Austin, and I've had love-adjacent feelings for women I've dated over the years. But I don't know if I've ever been in love before.

When I first met Miranda, I felt like she could be someone I could eventually fall in love with, but her harem of men and my unwillingness to push for exclusivity meant I never developed deep feelings for her.

Trying to figure out how to make Tori fall in love with me has been a weird experience. Movies suggest that gifts and grand gestures are the way to go, but other than orgasms and my dick, I don't know what Tori likes.

The Harlequin romance books my mom loves usually have the woman falling for the bad guy, but I'd say I'm a pretty decent human being. I pay my taxes, I recycle and I donate to a handful of charities, so I'm hardly a bad boy.

The romance books that are in Tori's Kindle library, including one called *Property of the Mountain Man*—which could almost be a retelling of the way the Barnetts woo their women—suggest that shock and awe tactics work best. So that's what I've decided to go with. I knew there was no way I was going to get her to come home with me last night, but I had to try. When she refused, I told her if she was staying here, I was too.

I have three days until I have to be back on shift. Hopefully, if she's not in love with me, she'll at least be so drunk on all the orgasms I plan to give her in the next couple of days that she won't completely block me out when I have to leave.

If forced proximity is what it takes to make Tori realize that she's mine and that I'm not going anywhere, then that's what I'll do.

Her alarm goes off a little after five a.m., but she doesn't even stir until a second alarm sounds ten minutes later. Her body unfurls like a sleepy kitten, and she stretches as much as she can until she realizes how close she is to me. Freezing, her eyes snap open and she looks up at me with an unfocused gaze.

"Morning, Sunshine."

"Hey," she croaks, her voice gruff from sleep and all the

screaming she did last night. "Urgh, I feel like I only just closed my eyes."

"Can you sleep a little longer?" I ask, dipping down and pressing a kiss against her lips.

"What time is it?"

"Five fifteen a.m."

"I have to get up. I have to make all the stock, then I have a four-tier wedding cake being collected later. They wanted red velvet cake and frosting, not icing, so I'm having to make it and decorate it all on the same day."

Pulling away from me, she sits up, forgetting about her wrist still being bound to mine, until she tries to shuffle to the edge of the bed. "Oh my god, you seriously kept me tied to you all night?"

"Yes."

Rolling her eyes, she reaches with her free hand and tries to untie the knot, but I cover her fingers and stop her. "Do you need to ask me something?"

"What?" her brow furrows. "I need to get up. I need to shower and get the ovens on."

"You don't leave this bed without my permission. So do you have something you want to ask me?"

"Are you serious?" She glowers.

"Deadly serious. You're not getting out of this bed until you ask, and I've got nothing but time."

"Can you please untie me so I can get up for work?" she says through gritted teeth.

"I think maybe you're looking for a reminder of who's in charge in this relationship."

"We're not in a relationship," she shrieks. "And if we

were, you wouldn't be in charge."

I laugh. I can't help it. "Oh, Sunshine, we both know you love it when I'm in charge. Your cunt gets all wet the moment I start ordering you around and making you squirm. Now ask me again, with a little less saltiness. It's too early for margaritas."

Inhaling sharply, she closes her eyes and then exhales, letting her shoulders relax a little. "Nero, I have a very busy day, which I'm now running late for. I don't understand what's going on between us, but I'm sore, tired, and confused, so can you please untie me so I can try to just carry on and pretend like I'm not living in the twilight zone right now?"

Grabbing her chin between my fingers, I turn her to face me. "I know this is a lot, but you want this. You want me. I'll bet you'd feel a lot better if you stopped trying to fight this so hard because deep down, you know we're as inevitable as I do. Let's get up and shower, and then you can tell me what I can do to help. But tonight, we sit down and talk. We work this out so we both understand we're together. You hear me?"

Her eyes are tired, but she nods and I nod back, leaning in and kissing her quickly before I untie our wrists. "I'll get the water started," I say, climbing out of bed and giving her a moment. She could run, this could backfire on me, but I don't think she will, and even if she does, I'll track her ass down and just tie her tighter to me next time, literally and figuratively.

Counting to twenty in my head, I wait for the water to heat, hoping she'll come to me on her own. When she finally appears in the bathroom doorway, she's wearing a robe and an uncomfortable expression.

"Take off the robe, Sunshine, and come get in the shower with me. I dirtied you up. It's my job to get you clean again," I tell her, my voice low and quiet.

She stalls a couple of times, her fingers toying with the sash before she finally unknots it and slides the robe off, hanging it on a hook on the back of the door.

"Good girl," I praise, holding my hand out to her.

When she places her fingers against my palm, I curl my hand around hers and guide her into the shower first, then step in after her, closing the door to the stall behind us. Grabbing the shower gel, I squeeze some into my hands and gently wash her, starting at her shoulders and working my way down, avoiding her ass and sex. I wash her hair, then run conditioner through the ends before quickly washing myself.

When I'm done, I grab more soap and slide my hand between her legs. Her gasp makes my dick instantly hard and I press myself against her back, making sure she can feel what she does to me. I wash her folds, then bring my soapy fingers back to her clit, rubbing the tiny bundle of nerves in slow, easy circles.

"Nero," she whines breathily.

"I'm not going to fuck you, Sunshine. I don't want you smelling like sex when you're around that asshole that works the counter. But I want to make you feel good and stretch you out so you feel me with every step you take."

Lifting one of her legs, I hook it over my thigh, then carefully guide my dick into her entrance. I don't miss her slight wince as my girth stretches her, but she settles once I'm fully seated inside of her.

"I thought you said you weren't going to fuck me," she says.

"I'm not, but I want you full of my dick while I rub your clit until you come."

Her body somehow both relaxes and tenses when I work her clit, rubbing until her breath is nothing more than ragged gasps, and she comes with a cry, her muscles clenching on my cock as her release barrels through her.

Sliding my dick out of her, I'm rock hard and close to coming after feeling her cunt clench around me. "Turn around," I order.

Her knees seem weak, but she turns to face me, watching as I grab her fingers and wrap them around my length. Covering her hand with mine, I move it up and down, working my dick until I explode all over her hand and stomach.

She's quiet as I wrap her in a towel and carry her into the bedroom. But instead of her silence being nice, for the first time I find it unnerving. She lets me dry her, then I step back, watching her with something that feels like fear prickling under my skin.

I wait for her to talk, for her normal, unending chatter to kick in and drive me crazy. But she doesn't speak as she brushes her hair, twisting it up into a bun on the top of her head, nor while she pulls on tight yoga pants and a baggy sweater with just a thin pale-pink bra underneath.

Moving silently around the small kitchen, she takes two bowls out of the cabinet and pours in granola into them, spooning Greek yogurt over the top. Pushing a bowl to me, she grabs spoons from a drawer, then eats standing up at the counter, her gaze weary and uncomfortable.

For the very first time since I met her, I want her to talk. Tori's quietness seems unnatural and it screams at just how uncomfortable things are between us when sex isn't involved. Naked and touching, we're explosive and compatible. Fully dressed, we're two virtual strangers who have nothing to say.

I'm not really a talker. I'm not a mute either. I talk when I need to, but I'm not someone who wastes words. I doubt anyone would ever call me verbose; at times, I might even be called a grumpy asshole, but for the most part, I just save my commentary for when I have something valuable to say rather than chattering away for the sake of it.

The day I met Tori, her constant need to fill any moment of silence with noise made me crazy. Right now, I'd give anything to hear her mutter about random sunshiny shit. Anything she had to say would be better than this tense, charged silence.

When she's finished her food, she washes our dishes and spoons, drying them with a dish towel before putting them away. Until now, I've never considered how tidy she is. The house was always immaculate, but I guess I just assumed she lived in chaos while I wasn't there and cleaned up before I got off shift.

I follow her downstairs when she heads for the door, watching as she methodically preps and mixes several different recipes at once, her brow furrowed with concentration while she multitasks like a boss.

Two hours later, the kitchen smells amazing and trays of muffins, cookies, pastries and some things that I don't recognize but really want to try line the cooling racks she has set up against one of the walls.

When we first got down here, I offered to help, but Tori shook her head, waving away my suggestion, and beyond the sounds of the mixers, spoons and other cooking paraphernalia, neither of us has uttered a single word in hours.

I hate it.

I hate her silence.

I hate not hearing her voice.

I hate the fact that her lips slip into a smile as she works, but the moment she looks in my direction or even remembers I'm here, it fades away and a frown replaces it. The longer she stays quiet, the more I feel the need to fill the void with sound, only I have no idea what to say.

"What are they?" I finally force out, pointing at a tray of fluffy-looking circles of cake that she's filling with cream or custard and slices of strawberry.

She jolts at the sound of my voice, which seems so much louder in the silent room. "They." She clears her throat. "They're miniature fraisier cakes."

"What is a fraisier cake?"

"Err." She clears her throat again. "They're genoise sponge, filled with crème patisserie and strawberries with a strawberry jelly glaze on the top."

"I had no idea this place sold this kind of stuff. I guess I thought it would be more muffins and cupcakes," I say.

Her hand shakes slightly as she squeezes the cream stuff

from a bag in perfect circles onto the tiny circle of cake. It's the first time this morning that she's shown anything but confidence and I know it's because of me. I'm making her uncomfortable.

"Before I took over, that's all we really sold. I've been slowly introducing some classic French patisserie dishes to see how they're received."

"Took over?" I ask.

She averts her gaze, dropping all her attention to the cake.

"You said you own the building?"

"Yes," she answers, even though I haven't really asked her a question yet.

"But are you running the store too?"

Her sigh is the most Tori-ish sound she's made all morning, and something about her annoyance is fucking perfect. I'll piss her off all day, every day, if it means I get a reaction from her.

"I bought the building." She pauses. "And the business. This is my store now."

I let her words filter through my mind. She bought the bakery and the building it's in. Property in Rockhead Point isn't cheap, especially prime retail space right in the center of town. I have no idea how much an established business and a building of this size would cost, but my guess is a lot. "How can you possibly afford to buy a business and a whole building?" I blurt, wishing I could swallow the words back the moment I say them.

"It wasn't a whim; I've been planning this for years."

"What do you mean?"

"I'm a classically trained chef. When I graduated, I had my choice of job offers, including Michelin-starred restaurants. Baking birthday cakes and snickerdoodles isn't why I spent four years in culinary school and trained in France. I came here because I saw huge potential in this place and Mrs. Yates and I had an agreement that when she retired, I'd get first refusal to buy the business."

My eyes widen as I realize I completely misjudged the woman I consider mine. I assumed she sliced cookies from a roll of dough and sold cupcakes behind the counter. It never crossed my mind that she was a real chef, especially not one capable of cooking in a top restaurant.

I'm an asshole.

"So you plan to sell fancy cakes like those?" I ask, pointing to the stunning creation she's just finished with a perfect circle of red shiny glaze on the top.

"Among other things," she says, clamming up.

"Do you think Rockhead Point has a market for anything more adventurous than pumpkin spiced latte and red velvet cake?" I'm being deliberately combative because I want to make her bite at me. This morning has made me realize if all she'll give me is anger, I'll take it any day over her silence.

"I think you'd be surprised," she snarks, pressing her lips together as she turns all her attention to what she's doing and falls frustratingly silent once again.

No matter how many obnoxious questions I ask, she barely gives me more than one-word answers as she decorates and frosts and does things with cakes and cookies that I've only seen on cooking shows on TV.

By the time someone knocks on the storefront, there are

more cakes and desserts in the kitchen than I've ever seen in real life at one time.

Wiping her hands on a cloth, she tosses it to the counter, then heads to the front of the store to open the door and let whoever is working today in. To my annoyance, the asshole dude who has been here every time I've been near the place follows her back into the kitchen, his eyes firmly on her ass, until he notices me and his expression darkens.

"Okay, so this morning, we have the usual stuff: banana, blueberry, and cranberry orange muffins. The muffin of the day is sour cherry and chocolate. There are milk and white chocolate chip cookies, the usual Danishes, then I've made a few more macarons, key lime, salted caramel, Nutella and coconut. These"—she points to the fraisier cakes—"are fraisier cakes, they're genoise sponge, filled with crème patisserie and strawberries, then topped with a strawberry glaze."

His gaze keeps darting to me, then back to Tori. "Those look amazing. They're going to fly out of the counter. Did you price them yet?"

"Yes, I've added them to the system. You'll just need to write out a counter card," she says, all business, despite the hot looks the asshole keeps flashing her.

"Okay, no worries." His eyes move to me again and a frown turns down the corners of his lips. "I'm sorry, I don't think we've been introduced. I'm Daniel," he says, taking a step toward me and holding out his hand.

"Nero Henderson." I nod, taking his hand and squeezing harder than I need to, not letting go until he allows his discomfort to show on his face. When I release him, I move closer to Tori, curling my arm around her waist and pulling her back into me in a blatantly claiming move that I know is going to piss her off.

Looking over her shoulder, she flashes me a part-furious, part-disgusted look before turning back to the asshole. "There are also pain aux chocolat and croissants, and I made some almond croissants too. I have the Walsh wedding cake to make today, so if you're running low on the basics, let me know and I'll try to throw a few batches of something simple together, but hopefully, with all the standard stuff, plus the new items I'm trialing, you should be good for the day. If anyone comes in wanting custom stuff, tell them they'll need to book an appointment. I've added my shared calendar to the EPOS system, so you can check dates to see what I have booked in, then add all their details and arrange for them to come in next week to discuss."

"Okay, boss," Daniel says with a flirtatious smirk, grabbing a tray of cookies and heading back into the front of the store.

For a while, Tori, the asshole and a young girl who goes bright red when she spots me, work together to carry all the stock through to the front of the store, filling the huge glass counter showcase. I try to help, but when it's clear there's a system that I don't understand and no one seems willing to explain, I step back, fill the coffeepot in the kitchen, and set it to brew.

"Coffee?" I ask Tori when she passes the last tray of delicious-looking cakes over to Daniel.

"Oh." She spins around like she forgot I was here. "Yes, please."

"How do you take it?" I ask, cringing yet again that I don't even know how my woman drinks her coffee.

"Creamer and sugar, please."

Nodding, I make her coffee, then pass it to her. "You do this every morning?" I ask.

"Do what?" She blinks, lifting her mug to her lips and taking a sip.

"Get here before six a.m. and cook the entire stock fresh each day."

"No, well, until I took over, I used to start a little later and Mrs. Yates used to have me prebake the stock for the days I didn't work, but it always made me cringe to think they were selling day-old goods. But yes, since I started here three years ago, I've been doing this every day."

"What happens if you're ill or on vacation?"

"Before, Mrs. Yates would step in. Now, eventually, I'll employ someone to help, but for the moment, I can't get ill, and I don't plan to take any vacations."

I nod, but the idea that she's working every day with no break or backup makes me want to take care of her in a way I've never experienced before. Since Buck and James got together, he's tried to explain his need to control her, including taking over her care and ensuring she looks after herself to me, but until right now, I never really understood.

I'm sure I don't feel it to the extent he does. I want Tori to do what I tell her, but it's more of a sexual thing, for the most part. I don't want to take over her life. Except when it's to do with guys, then I plan to take over completely and make sure everyone with a dick in a fifty-mile radius knows to keep their hands to themselves.

"I usually take my coffee up to the roof once the counter stock is done," she says quietly. It's not quite an invitation, but it's close.

"Then let's go," I say, placing my hand on the base of her spine and guiding her up the stairs, through her apartment, and up onto the roof, with her leading the way.

The moment we step outside into the morning light, Tori inhales deeply and then visibly relaxes. The roof space is pretty empty, with waist-high walls edging the whole way around the building, creating a safe and mostly private terrace.

There are a couple of lawn chairs and a small camping table set up in the middle of the space and I guide Tori over to them, sitting down and pulling her into my lap when she tries to sit in the empty seat.

"Nero," she says with a groan.

"Just go with it." I smile, turning her sideways so both of her legs are draped over mine, her butt perched on my thigh. "You're quiet this morning."

"You say that like it's a bad thing. I thought you'd be happy I wasn't constantly making noise."

"I thought I would be too," I confess. "But I think I've gotten used to your chatter."

"You're an asshole," she snaps, going to climb off my lap.

"I'm sorry, that came out wrong. What I'm trying to say is that I don't like it when you're *this* quiet. It feels like I'm making you uncomfortable."

"Nero, you barged your way into my business and my home and declared that I belong to you, then you orgasmed me into not calling the cops, and now you won't leave. I'm not sure if you've lost your mind or I have. Either way, this is a lot. Right now, my life is busy enough and I don't think I need all this drama too."

"I know it's fast and I know it's a lot, but I feel it in my gut that you're mine, that we're meant to be together. Don't you think that a once-in-a-lifetime connection like this is worth fighting for?"

She doesn't answer, and again, I hate the silence.

"I guess the sex is great," she grudgingly says.

A laugh bubbles through my chest and I pull her into me, pressing my lips to hers and kissing her like it's the most natural thing in the world because that's what it feels like. Like I've been kissing her all our lives and that I'll keep kissing her until the end of our forever.

She doesn't fight me. She just kisses me back, her fingers tangling in the fabric of my shirt, holding on to me while our tongues move together in the world's oldest dance.

"I have to get back to work," she says, pushing my chest until I allow her just enough distance to speak.

"Tell me you know you're mine and I'll let you up."

"I know *you* think I'm yours," she snarks, twisting my words.

"Every inch of you is mine, Sunshine. Do you want to know why I'm so sure?"

"Yes," she whispers.

"Because I feel it right here in my chest." I smack my chest over my heart. "Because I don't think I could leave you, even if you called the cops to haul me away. Because from the moment I woke up without you the other morning,

I haven't been able to think about anything else but you. And because being in our house without you made the place feel like a prison cell. I can't really explain this to you because I don't fully understand it either. But I'm sure because nothing has ever felt so right as holding you in my arms and knowing I'll never let you go."

Her body goes soft and she lets herself sag into me, her ribs and shoulder resting against me. I don't know what it was that I said that made her relax, but I'm glad it did. "Those were the perfect words," she admits, sighing as she rests her head on my shoulder.

"Look, I know this all seems like it's come from nowhere, and I know I was an asshole to you when we first moved in together, but can you just give this a chance to see if this feels as right to you as it does to me? Don't run from something that could be so amazing just because I'm a grumpy asshole who makes a terrible first impression."

"Okay," she says so quietly I'm not sure I've heard her at all.

"Okay?"

"Yes, okay, I'll give this a chance."

Grabbing her chin in my fingers, I turn her to me and claim her lips with mine. When my dick is so hard it must be stabbing her in the leg, I reluctantly pull back. "Later, I'm going to make you beg for my touch, then when you're squirming and so needy you don't know how you'll function if I don't give it to you, I'll make you come so many times you'll go hoarse and my dirty, dirty girl will be filthy with a mixture of sweat, tears, and our cum."

A shudder ripples through her and she exhales a shaky

breath. "Nero," she whimpers.

"Yes, Sunshine?"

"Is it weird that…" she trails off.

"Is what weird?"

"Is it weird that I like it when you talk to me like that? I've never… No one has ever—"

"No one has ever dirty talked to you before?" I question.

"No. I mean, yes, I've heard dirty talk before. I'm not a virgin or a nun. But no one—"

"No one ever made you blush while arousal gushed from your cunt, by telling you exactly what they planned to do to you?"

"Never."

"No one ever made you beg?"

"No."

"No one ever made you desperate to beg? No one ever made you tell them exactly how filthy you want them to be?" I ask, deliberately embarrassing her.

Clearing her throat, she wiggles on my lap, trying to squeeze her thighs together. "No."

Sliding my hand between her thighs, I turn it, forcing her legs apart. "But you like it when I talk to you that way, don't you?"

Her cheeks are flushed a vivid shade of pink when she nods.

"I need to hear your response."

"Yes, I like it," she says, looking away from me. "Is this something… is this something you've always been into?"

"No," I say immediately. "I've thought about it, but the only person I've ever… It's just been with you. I didn't know…" This time, I'm the one to trail off, unsure how to tell her that the only person I've ever spoken to like this is her, that I crave *her* submission, that *her* humble humiliation is the sexiest thing I've ever seen in my entire life.

"Oh. Me either," she mumbles.

Squeezing her chin, I wait until she looks at me again, needing her full attention. "It's another reason that we're so perfect for each other. Neither of us knew this was a kink we'd enjoy until we found it together. I had no idea sex and intimacy could be like this until you. I'm addicted, and later I'm going to make you bend over and ask me to turn your ass as pink as your face is right now."

Her breath hitches, and I can't help it. I smile. "Perfect," I whisper. "Come on, you need to get back to work before I decide that bending you over the edge of the wall and fucking you out here isn't as stupid an idea as I know it is."

The rest of the afternoon passes quickly. I call Buck and ask him to pack me a bag and bring it down to the store for me. When he arrives, he has James in tow, who immediately drags Tori off to the storeroom. When they come back five minutes later, James is grinning from ear to ear and Tori looks a little shell-shocked.

"Everything okay, Precious?" Buck asks his fiancé.

"Apparently my bestie's been keeping secrets. She bought a business and a building and moved out, all without telling me. So, we're going to be having dinner tonight, so she can fill me in on all the stuff she's been keeping from me," James says, in that cool, no-nonsense tone she slips into sometimes.

"No," I say, capturing everyone's attention.

"I'm sorry?" James says.

"Tori and I have plans tonight."

"She's my best friend," James argues.

"She's my woman," I say back.

"How 'bout we have dinner together?" Buck suggests, trying to keep the peace.

"Fine, we'll bring takeout and Tori can show us around the building she bought," James says, her tone snippy.

"No," I say again.

"Nero," Tori whispers, her eyes wide, her expression… worried.

Walking away from my brother and James, I grab Tori carefully by the upper arm and guide her back into the storeroom, closing the door behind us. "Sunshine—"

She immediately interrupts me, "It's only dinner and she's right. I have been keeping things from her. She deserves an explanation."

"You're mine."

"You're being unreasonable," she argues, crossing her arms over her chest.

"You're mine," I say again.

"Nero, you asked me to give this a chance, but I'm not like James. I have no interest in letting a man take over my life or order me around. If that's what you think is going to happen between us, then you might as well just leave now."

Sucking in air, I grit my teeth to stop myself from growling anything that will piss either of us off any further. "Fine, we'll have dinner with them, but you'll sit on my lap during dinner, no panties, wearing a plug."

"What kind of plug?" she asks, but she's practically

panting.

"A butt plug, filling your tight virgin hole."

Her cheeks go so red I know if I grazed her skin, she'd be burning to the touch. "I, I, I don't have a plug," she whispers.

"I ordered you some. They're being delivered this afternoon."

"You ordered me a butt plug?" she whisper-yells, her eyes wide in lust-drenched arousal.

Smirking, I chuckle. "Plugs, plural. I had a good look through your stash of toys when I was hanging out in your room yesterday and I noticed that there was nothing for anal play, so I ordered some things for us to use. I know how much you like your ass being played with."

"Plugs? Why would I need more than one?"

"I'll show you later when I put one in your ass before we have dinner and I'm forced to share you with my brother and James."

She swallows so hard I actually hear it. If anyone else came in here right now, I'm sure they think I'd said or done something awful to her. Her pupils are blown, her body is tense, and she's red-faced and trembling. But only she and I know that she's not scared or angry. She's humiliated and so turned on I'd lay money on her panties being soaking wet.

"Let's go," I say, taking her hand with mine and tugging her back to the door that leads into the kitchen.

"I can't go out there looking like this," she gasps.

"You look fine, a little flushed, but otherwise beautiful and entirely unravished."

Her lips part and her brow furrows, but I don't ask her

why she's looking at me like that. I just lead her back into the kitchen and smile at my brother. "We'll see you at eight."

"Tori," James says.

"Don't bother getting takeout. I'll cook," Tori says, forcing a smile to her lips.

"No, you won't. You can cook next time. You started baking at six this morning and you're still decorating this ridiculous wedding cake. We'll have takeout tonight; you can cook on a day when you're not so busy."

James's expression morphs from pensive to a wide grin in seconds. "We'll grab Chinese food," she says, nodding at me. "See you guys later."

"Come to the door up the stairs at the side of the building," I tell them as Buck curls his arm around James and leads her out of the kitchen.

Once they're gone, Tori goes back to work, cutting out tiny flower shapes and sticking them one by one to the enormous, four-tier wedding cake.

"Parcel for you," Daniel says with a sneer, holding out a cardboard box to me.

"Thanks," I say, stepping forward to take it from him, glad that I prepaid the tip for the driver when I ordered it yesterday.

The moment Daniel disappears back into the front of the store, Tori looks at me. "Is that the…?"

"Yep." I smirk.

Her cheeks heat again and I smile, placing the box on the counter while I watch her work.

Chapter Twenty-four

Tori

By the time I slide the huge white cake box into the back seat of the soon-to-be Mrs. Walsh's SUV, I feel like I'm crawling out of my skin. It's been two hours since that freaking box was delivered and instead of opening it, Nero left it just sitting on the counter while he watched me cut out hundreds of stupid flowers for this monstrosity of a cake.

"What else do you have to do?" Nero asks, watching me with intense, heat-filled eyes.

I can't help it. My gaze darts to the box, then to him. "Err."

"Tori," he calls.

"Oh. Err, I have to measure out the dry ingredients for the morning, then lock up once Daniel finishes cleaning up the front."

"Can I help?"

It's the same question he's been asking me since six a.m. when he followed me down here and he's been here all day with me, watching me patiently and asking questions while not interfering or getting in my way. For the most part, he's stayed at viewing distance, not forcing himself into my personal space. At least he hadn't until Daniel popped his head into the kitchen earlier, then Nero suddenly found a need to touch me and pull me into his huge, hard body.

A part of me is still confused as to why he's here, but every time I ask, he gives me the same answer. That he's here because he knows I'm his, and he wants me to know it too. Every time I hear the words, the more honest they feel, but it still doesn't resolve the fact that until yesterday, I was pretty sure he seriously disliked me.

I'm starting to wonder if the dislike he was feeling toward me was actually repressed lust because he doesn't even try to hide how much he desires me now. Our chat on the roof this morning was humiliating but also sexy, honest and real. I don't think he was lying when he said that the whole embarrassing, name-calling, dirty-talk thing is something he's only done with me. If that was something he'd enjoyed in the past, I think he'd have admitted it, and oddly, it made me feel reassured to know that this is something unique and new that the two of us share.

He asked me to give this thing between us a chance, and the moment I agreed, it settled the niggling worry that's been wiggling in my gut since the very first time he kissed me. I'm still dubious that we have any kind of real connection beyond the physical, but I'm allowing myself to be open enough to explore if we do and I think that's really all he's asking of me.

My gaze darts to the innocuous brown cardboard box, then to him, my mind fighting to remember what he just said to me. "No, thanks, it won't take me long to do prep, then I just need to do a final clean and I'm done."

"Okay," he says simply, stepping back and crossing his arms over his impressively large chest.

It takes me twice as long as it normally would to weigh out the dry ingredients because my thoughts are consumed by the contents of that stupid box. Surely, he didn't really buy me a butt plug?

I'm not stupid. I know plugs exist. I've even perused the section on the online sex toy store where I got my vibrators and things from. But I've never thought about buying myself one because anal play feels like something guys are into and women tolerate. But the more I think about how embarrassing it would be to have my ass plugged while I did something asinine and normal, like eating dinner with my bestie, the more appealing the idea is.

"Right, I'm done," Daniel says, stepping into the kitchen, his eyes immediately searching for Nero and scowling when he finds him.

"Thanks, Daniel, you're off on Monday, aren't you?"

"Yeah, I'll see you on Tuesday though."

"Have a great weekend. Thank you for all your hard work this week," I say with a smile.

"You too. Bye, Tori." He smiles back, then it falls when he looks at Nero. "Goodbye, Nero."

"Bye, Daniel," Nero says, draping his arm possessively

over my shoulders.

"I'll come and lock up after you," I say, ducking out from under Nero's arm and following Daniel to the boarded-up door. Once I slide the dead bolt into place, I move behind the counter and flip the switch to turn off the lights.

"You ready to head upstairs?" Nero asks with the box gripped in his hand when I step back into the kitchen.

"I have to do a little paperwork."

"Okay," he says, gesturing for me to head up the stairs ahead of him.

When I open the door to the apartment, he follows me in, then places the box down on the kitchen counter. "I ordered us some groceries; they'll be here soon. Why don't you go do your paperwork and I'll take a quick shower and change before the food gets here."

This is the first time he's allowed me any distance or alone time all day and it feels odd. "Okay," I agree, but the moment I sit down behind the desk in the office, I can't concentrate, my mind firmly fixed on him naked in the shower and the contents of that fucking box.

After a while, I force myself to push all thoughts of him away and concentrate on my paperwork. I'm excited to see that the French patisserie items have been my best sellers every day since I started introducing them. The price point on them is a little higher than the standard original stock, but that doesn't seem to be affecting sales, and every day, they've been the first thing to sell out.

Actually, seeing my classic French dishes selling reaffirms my confidence that I can make my dream of a French patisserie work here, and by the time I finish loading the cash into the safe in the floor beneath my desk, I'm standing straighter and walking with a little pep in my step.

All my thoughts come to a crashing stop when I find Nero shirtless, in gym shorts, reaching up to put something in a cabinet, the muscles in his back tensing and flexing in a way I didn't even know was sexy to me until literally this moment.

"Holy fucking sex sticks," I mutter, consciously closing my mouth just in case a little drool seeps out.

My words must have been louder than I thought because he spins to face me, and I get the glorious view of his chest, his firm pecs and washboard abs suddenly seeming very… lickable. Obviously, I've seen Nero naked before, but there's something about him being just in shorts that is very, very tempting and my body perks up and screams *take me* in a very dramatic fashion.

"You all done, Sunshine?" he asks, his voice low and rough.

"Yeah," I squeak.

"Why don't you go have a shower. Buck and James will be here in an hour."

I'm not sure why I thought he'd jump me the moment I was done with my paperwork, but the fact that he's basically dismissing me is a little mortifying. And not in a sexy squirmy way, but in a cringy "I'm horny, and he's clearly thinking I'm a hot mess and need to clean up" way. Since the moment that box arrived, I've been on high alert, anxious to see if he really did buy me a sex toy and actually expects me to wear it. But now that he's sending me to shower alone, when he hasn't allowed me more than a few moments separation all day, I feel foolish.

Cheeks blazing, I scurry to the bathroom, locking the door behind me and then leaning back against it, letting my face fall forward into my hands. I've never met a guy who makes me feel as off-kilter as Nero does. Even though he's spelling out what he wants from me, I still feel like I'm second-guessing both his and my actions because I've never experienced this kind of relationship before.

In the past, my exes have been nice guys who became my friends, then my boyfriends. It was all very civilized and nice and I got bored and dumped them. James meeting Buck and introducing me to a whole group of sexy firefighters was the most exciting thing to happen to me in the three years since James and I moved in together.

Turning on the shower, I let the water heat until the small room is full of steam. Stripping off my clothes, I spend too long beneath the water, soaping my tired body and washing and conditioning my hair until I'm so relaxed I'm pretty sure I could go straight to sleep instead of having dinner with James and Buck.

Earlier, I gave her the CliffsNotes version of everything that's happened in the last month or so, but I know she's going to expect all of the details of me buying the shop and everything that's happening with Nero. It's actually the first time she hasn't known everything that's happening in my life since we met, and it's felt strange not to have her as a sounding board all of the time.

I might have moved up the mountain to help her transition into her new life away from town, but I've tried to keep my distance so she doesn't feel the need to keep trying to be James and Tori, when she should be focusing on being James and Buck. I've been so busy it's been easy to stay away, but as tired as I am, I'm excited to have a chance to get her take on all things Nero Henderson.

Reluctantly, I turn off the water and wrap my hair into a towel, twisting it up on my head. Grabbing another towel, I dry myself off, then secure it around me, opening the bathroom door and crossing the small apartment to the bedroom.

My feet stumble to a stop when I find Nero lounging on my bed, his chest still bare and his long, thick legs crossed at the ankle.

"Feeling better?" he drawls.

"Yes, thanks," I say painfully politely.

"You took so long; I opened your gift without you."

"Gift?"

Picking something up from the comforter beside him, he smirks as he holds it up for me to see. "Yes, your gift."

It takes me a moment to identify what the metal object is, but when I do, my heart pounds in my chest and my breathing becomes labored.

"Come here." He smirks.

"No." I shake my head slowly from side to side.

"Are you scared?" His tone is soft, almost gentle.

"I've never." I clear my throat. "I've never."

"You already told me you've never used a plug before. But don't worry, we can start small."

"That's not small," I say, lifting my hand and waving it toward the plug.

"This is tiny, just big enough so you'll feel it, but not

big enough to do more than remind you it's there and stretch you a little."

"Nero."

"Come here and look properly," he coaxes.

Deciding not to move, I look down in horror as my feet shuffle forward of their own volition, taking me to him and the fucking butt plug he wants to put in my ass.

"My dick is going to be rock hard all night thinking about this plug buried deep in your ass," he growls, swinging his legs over the side of the bed and pulling me to him the moment I'm close enough. "You don't need this," he murmurs, untwisting the towel around my body and throwing it toward the hamper. "Or this." Carefully unwrapping the towel from my hair, he adds it to the pile, then gently finger-combs my tangled strands. "Much better."

"Naked is better?" I ask, my voice a little shrill.

"Naked is always better. I think maybe the house should be a clothes-free zone, then I can keep you naked the whole time."

"You can be naked there as much as you want, but I live here, and here we wear clothes," I say, arching my eyebrow. Baiting him.

Not saying a word, he yanks me forward, toppling me off balance and into him. Taking advantage of my momentum, he turns me, lowering me down and over his lap.

"Nero," I snap. "What the fuck?"

The first slap of his hand against my ass cheek makes me freeze. Before Nero, I had never been spanked and even though I know it won't hurt, I wait for the pain. Just like I remember, none comes. Instead, there's the familiar warmth that blooms across my skin in the most deliciously addictive way.

He spanks me again on the other cheek and the same sensation intensifies, heat pooling low in my belly as I allow a wanton whine to fall from my parted lips. Arousal trickles from my core and I don't know if I should clamp my thighs together or spread them and beg him to touch me.

"You live wherever I live. For now, that's here, but when we move back to the house, neither of us will be wearing clothes, so I always have access to this sexy ass."

He spanks me again, once on each butt cheek, then rubs the skin, helping the warmth to spread until it's a glow that permeates my entire lower body. "Fuck, Sunshine, I want to do so many filthy things to you when I have you in this position," he rasps.

Before I can stop myself, I wiggle my legs apart a little, needing him to touch me and stem this tide of arousal he's created. "Nero," I moan.

"Do you need me?"

"Yes."

"Then you know what you need to do."

It takes me a moment to process his words. Then, a moment longer to decide if I'm willing to beg him in the way he wants me to. "Please," I whisper.

"You can do better than that, Sunshine," he coaxes.

"Please touch me, Nero. I need to come. I…" I swallow past the lump of mortified, shame-filled lust that's lodged in my throat. "I need you to touch me."

The hand that has been rubbing my ass moves and then air hits my asshole as he pulls my cheeks apart and leans down, spitting against my hole. His fingers dip down to my pussy, pushing inside of me easily and fucking me in deep, slow thrusts.

"Look at all this mess," he says, pulling his fingers from me, then wiping my own arousal against my ass, mixing it with his saliva. Pushing his fingers back into me, he continues the slow, intense thrusts, curling his fingers inside of me and finding the spot that makes arousal gush from my core and my stomach twist.

When he pushes at my asshole with a probing finger, I tense. "Relax, you like my fingers in your ass. You love how dirty it makes you feel, don't you?"

His probing stops, and I hear the click of a bottle lid being opened before cool liquid drips against my hole.

Squealing in surprise, I tense, clamping my ass cheeks together and lifting my hips from his lap, but he just parts my cheeks again. "Relax," he orders.

I try to relax, I really do, but the moment someone tells you to relax, the more you want to do the opposite. The sexy burn of humiliation has faded and been replaced with icky discomfort that is a major turnoff.

As if he's sensing my emotions, he leaves his finger pressed against my ass but doesn't try to probe any deeper. Slowly, pulling his fingers almost all of the way out of my sex, he pushes them back into me again, fucking me in a slow rhythm, rubbing circles on my ass cheeks and occasionally spanking me to reignite the heated burn all across my skin. "Your ass is the perfect shade of pink, Sunshine. Not dark enough to bruise, but hot enough that you'll feel the warmth when you're perched on my lap while we eat."

He's not trying to make me come, and I'm not chasing my release, even though I know I could get there if I tried. But with each touch and each word, I relax, settling back into the moment with him.

"That's a good girl, lying over my lap with your ass pink while I finger your sopping cunt and play with your tight hole. I wish I had my cell so I could take a picture of you like this. I'd use it to jerk off to while I was at work, then I'd make you fuck yourself over video chat while I watched."

Each word that falls from his sinful lips pushes me higher, and by the time his finger is circling my ass, I'm ready to come around his fingers, tongue, or his dick. I don't care which as long as he's touching me.

More cold lube drips onto my ass, but I don't flinch this time, I moan.

"Soon, you'll beg for my big dick in this tight little hole. You'll beg me to fill it full of my cum."

The moment his finger breaches my ass, I gasp, then moan. It doesn't feel good, but it doesn't feel bad either. But the idea of him fingering me there heightens all of the deliciously humiliating emotions I'm already feeling from lying over his lap and listening to him dirty talk.

"So fucking tight," he groans, impressing me with his ambidextrousness as he fucks my pussy with one hand and works his finger into my ass with the other. The finger in my ass pulls away and I hear him squeeze more lube, the tip of the bottle brushing across my hole.

"Next time, I'll use my cum as lube before I stretch you out and plug you, but we don't have time for that right now because I want this plug settled deep in your ass before my brother and James get here."

The reminder that he plans to plug me and expects me to wear it while we host dinner pushes me over the edge and I come around his fingers, my pussy clamping and tightening as my orgasm pulses through me.

"Perfect," he praises, replacing the single finger in my ass with two, stretching me and filling me until it feels like I can't take any more and a second pulse of pleasure detonates from my ass, bursting forward until my entire core is swirling with bliss.

My mind struggles to process the pleasure when I feel something cool and foreign press against my ass. Even though I know it's the plug, I still panic. "Nero," I gasp.

"It's okay, Sunshine, it's only small, barely as big as my fingers. Deep breath in, then exhale."

I follow his instructions, dragging in a shaky breath, then exhaling. The moment I allow the air to push out of my lungs, he slides the plug into me.

"Oh god," I pant, unsure how I feel about having a foreign object inserted into my ass.

"Relax. Once it's all the way in, it's going to feel so fucking good, just like when I push my finger into you."

I try to breathe in and out again, but with each exhale, he works the plug deeper into me until I can feel the broad head pressed between my cheeks.

"Fuck, Sunshine, seeing that pretty jewel between your ass cheeks is the sexiest fucking thing I've ever seen. After dinner, I'm going to fuck your cunt while you're wearing it. My dick's rock hard just thinking about it."

"I don't," I mutter, my voice weak and unsure.

"How does it feel?" he demands, cutting off my protest.

"I… Err… I…?" I can't find the words. It feels wrong but right in a messed-up, taboo way that I didn't know was a turn-on until I met Nero. Now I find myself craving that discomfort and the way it feels forbidden but exciting all at the same time.

"I'm going to stand you up," he warns, rolling me to my side, then onto my feet in a way that seems somehow effortless, even though I know I couldn't have been that graceful without him lifting me.

"Fuck," he growls, his hands finding my ass and turning me fully so my back is to him.

Warm palms pinch my already heated skin and he parts my ass cheeks, making me flush, my face heating so quickly I go a little lightheaded.

"I wish you could see what I see. These full plump cheeks, red and hot from your spanking, the jewel on the base of the plug just peeking out. Move around. How does it feel?"

Taking a tentative step forward, I gasp when the plug moves with me. It doesn't hurt, but it constantly reminds me with every breath that it's inside of me. I'm not sure it feels good, not like those balls you push into your cooch that are supposed to make everything tighter and somehow make you feel like you're going to spontaneously come. But the plug feels… naughty.

"I asked you a question, Tori. How does it feel to have my plug buried in your ass?"

"Dirty," I whisper, the word slipping completely

unbidden from my lips.

I'm not sure what I'm expecting, but when his lips spread into a wide, mischievous grin, I can't help grinning back. I honestly never ever thought I'd consider a butt plug a bonding moment between us, but it kind of is. We'll both know I'm wearing it, we'll both know he put it there while I lay over his lap after he spanked me. We'll both know I came hard, but no one else will. No one else will know that I'm still being his dirty girl, even while we're having a civilized meal.

"I love that look on your face," he says reverently. "My naughty, dirty girl."

Spinning me around, he pulls me down and kisses me, his fingers finding my nipples and toying with them while he dominates my mouth with his tongue. Moaning, he swallows my sounds and I melt into him, allowing myself to stop fighting, to stop questioning this, and to just enjoy this messed-up, lust-drenched moment.

When he pulls back, he makes a pained moan, closing his eyes and sighing before opening them again and looking at me. "We should get dressed. If my brother sees you naked, I'll have to kill him."

Scoffing, I smile. "Dramatic much?"

"That's not funny, Tori, and I'm not fucking joking. You're mine and if a guy sees you like this, I'll be forced to kill them, then fuck you until I put my baby in your belly and everyone sees who you belong to."

"Has anyone ever told you you sound like a psycho caveman?" I chuckle.

"Never felt this way before, so no."

Rolling my eyes, I push out of his hold, looking for the towel I was wearing before he ripped it off me. "Were your exes all Amish? High necks and long sleeves, never wore a bikini in their lives?"

"No," he snaps. "But I never felt about any of them the way I feel about you."

His words freeze me to the spot. It's basically the same thing he's been telling me since his *you belong to me* revelation, but for the first time, I actually hear him. "You weren't a crazy over-the-top jealous, possessive alphahole with them?" I think I know the answer, but I need to ask anyway.

"No."

"Why?"

"Because I never saw forever with them. I have a tough job, long hours, evenings, weekends. I never lost my mind over any of them because I never saw something serious or permanent."

"But… now you do?" I ask slowly, making sure each word is clear.

"Yes, Tori, I see permanent, serious, ring-on-your-finger, baby-in-your-belly forever with *you*."

I don't know why I'm shocked. This might be the first time he's spelled it out in a way I've heard and acknowledged, but he's been telling me this in a roundabout way since the first time we had sex at his place.

"Oh," I say, like a fucking idiot.

"Oh." He smiles.

He's smiling. It isn't the first time, but he's not the type of guy who's perpetually happy. In fact, for the first few weeks, I don't think I saw him do anything but scowl, but here he is smiling… at me. Is that because he's happy? Or because he thinks I'm amusing? It can't be because he's satisfied because his dick is rock hard and tenting his shorts.

I wish I knew him well enough to understand what his smile means, but we haven't given each other a chance, have we?

"This is weird," I blurt.

His smile grows even wider and a soft chuckle slips from his lips. "Why?"

"Because it feels like we're having an important moment and I have a plug in my ass," I blurt.

Throwing his head back, he laughs, a full belly laugh that is so free sounding and full of the kind of mirth I honestly didn't think he was capable of. "Jesus, Tori, you're fucking adorable. Come on, we need clothes."

Standing, he scoops me off the floor and over his shoulder in one fluid movement like I weigh nothing.

"Nero," I shriek.

Ignoring me, he's still laughing as he deposits me onto my feet outside my closet. "Pick a dress or a skirt," he orders.

"I can't wear a skirt with this in my butt," I whisper-yell.

"No panties either, so make sure it's long enough that my brother won't see your wet cunt."

"Nero," I gasp, scandalized and, once again, pink with embarrassment.

"Fuck, I hope you never stop blushing like that," he says, cupping my face and running his thumb over my cheek.

"If you make me prance about in a dress with no underwear and a fucking butt plug in my ass, then yes, I'm pretty sure I'll be permanently red-faced."

"That sounds like the perfect life," he says quietly.

His words don't sound playful; in fact, he sounds almost serious, and I turn to look up at him. Parting my lips, I plan to say something sarcastic. Something to dissolve the sudden tension his confession has dropped over us, but instead, I say, "Sounds good to me too."

Dipping his head, he kisses me softly and I let my lids flutter shut as I fall into the kiss, not fighting him or overthinking. I enjoy the sensation of his lips on mine and the way it feels to be surrounded by him.

The sound of a cell phone ringing drags us back to the present and Nero sighs. "Dress or skirt, no panties," he warns, reaching past me to grab a T-shirt and pulling it over his head before he leaves, walking into the living room.

My eyes stumble across the clothes hanging on the rail, stuttering to a stop when I see some of his clothes hanging beside mine. I know he had Buck bring him a bag when he came earlier, but I didn't expect him to unpack or to make himself at home in my closet.

I've never shared space with a guy before. When my boyfriends slept over in the past, they just kept their stuff in a bag, the same way I did when I stayed at their places, and there's something about him unpacking that just reaffirms this permanence he keeps talking about.

Normally, I put thought into my outfits. I'm not a fashionista, but I like wearing clothes that make me feel good. But instead of perusing my closet for the perfect thing, I grab a black bodycon midi dress that fits snugly against my body and hugs my curves. It's not something I'd normally wear in the house, but it's the only dress I have that's long enough and tight enough that I can be one-hundred-percent sure I'm not going to flash the plug stuck up my ass if I bend over.

The dress has built-in bra support, so I slide it over my naked body and smooth it down, turning to check my reflection in the mirror and make sure there's no way Buck or James could know what I'm hiding beneath it.

The plug feels strange. I'm not sure it's a sensation I particularly enjoy, but it doesn't feel bad either. Walking carefully back into the bathroom, I run my brush through my hair before pulling it up into a bun on the top of my head.

"Sunshine," Nero calls, stepping into the doorway, his feet bare, shorts baggy, T-shirt tight enough to show off his toned arms and firm, thick chest.

Looking at him in the reflection in the mirror, I watch his eyes dip down to my ass, then up again, smirking when our gazes lock.

"Buck and James are on their way. James said she knew your food order and that she was grabbing wine, but to let her know if you need anything else."

"Okay." I nod, looking down at my makeup and debating if I can be bothered to put any on.

"You're fucking stunning just the way you are," he says, stepping up behind me and wrapping his arms around my waist, resting his chin on my shoulder and staring at me in the mirror.

"Thank you. I don't think I can be bothered to put any makeup on."

"Then don't." His lips dip into the hollow of my neck, kissing the skin where my neck meets my shoulder. "I like you in this dress."

"Thanks."

"It's going to take everything I have not to kick my brother and James out so I can spend the rest of the night inside of you."

"I don't hate that idea," I confess, wiggling my ass back into his hardening dick.

We're interrupted by a loud knock on the door. Sighing, he pulls me in tight, turning my head and kissing me fast and hard. Then he steps back, the warmth of his touch fading away as he leaves.

"Hey guys, come on in," I hear him say.

Bracing my hands against the basin, I pull in a sharp inhale, then slowly exhale, staring at myself in the mirror as I do. My eyes look too bright, my cheeks are flushed and there's a small bruise on my neck. I look like a hot mess who just got ridden hard and put away wet.

I look like James did the first night when Buck brought her home and ravished her in his car outside the house. I was a little jealous of her back then. Not of her and Buck, but that she had a man capable of making her lose control enough to allow him to dry hump her in his car. Now that it's me who's encountered the type of man who makes me do things I would never normally do, I'm a little shell-shocked and unsure if I should encourage his bad behavior or try to tame him into something I'm a little more familiar with.

Taking a step back, the plug moves and I gasp, remembering that Nero isn't the type of guy you tame. He's the type of guy you barely survive.

"Tori," James calls.

Plastering a smile on my face, I ignore the foreign sensation in my butt and go to greet my friend.

Chapter Twenty-five

Nero

"Hey," my brother says when I open the apartment door for him.

"Hey guys, come on in." I step back to allow Buck and James to walk through the large doorway that leads out from the alley at the side of the building and into the tiny apartment.

As much as I hate that Tori is here and not in the house we share on the mountain, this tiny apartment is growing on me. I like that no matter where Tori is, I can either see or hear her. There's no way she can hide from me when I can walk from one end of the space to the other in about fifteen steps.

Closing the door, I trail them into the small living room, remembering for the first time that Tori doesn't really have any furniture in here other than the spare bed she has pushed against the wall and a small, chipped coffee table.

"Where is she?" James asks, her eyes roaming around the room, taking in the shabby, marked walls and dirty painted woodwork.

"Bathroom," I say, forcing a smile for my brother's fiancé. It's not that I dislike James, quite the opposite; actually, I think she and Buck are a great fit for each other. But James and I got off on the wrong foot when I reacted badly to the news that she'd been married in the past. I didn't mean to make a big deal of it, but when I did, she took it very badly. Even though we've both apologized, it still feels like we're walking on eggshells around each other and I don't know if me and Tori being together will make things better or worse.

"Tori," James shouts, eying me cautiously.

"Hey guys," Tori says, stepping out of the bathroom with a bright smile etched across her lips.

"What the fuck is this place?" James demands.

"This is my apartment," Tori tells her, smiling even wider.

"So, you actually did it. You bought the store?"

"I did. Mrs. Yates came to me a while back and said she'd decided to start looking for a retirement place out in Florida and that if I was still interested in buying her out, she'd get the business appraised."

"But you own the building too?" Buck asks, placing a bag of food on the counter in the kitchen.

"That's right." Tori nods. "Originally, she wanted to retain ownership of the building and have me pay rent, but I didn't want to have to worry about what would happen to the building if she got sick or when she got older. So, I told her that I wanted all of it or none of it. It took a while to sort out all the particulars and I didn't want to jinx it by telling anyone, just in case it all fell through."

"I get not making it public knowledge, but you could have told me." Some of James's iciness bleeds through into her voice and Tori stiffens, reacting to her friend's butthurt demeanor.

Stepping closer to my woman, I brace myself to piss off my soon-to-be sister-in-law once again, but Tori says, "If I'd have told you, I'd have gotten my hopes up, and I was worried it wasn't going to happen, so I kept it to myself."

I don't know which part of what Tori just said affected James, but the air that felt charged and tense just moments ago morphs when the girls are suddenly hugging.

"I'm so happy for you," James gushes, wiping under her eyes with one hand while she hugs Tori tightly.

"I can't believe it's really happening," Tori half sobs, half laughs.

Feeling redundant and a little confused by the girls' reaction, I shove my hands into the pockets of my shorts and lurk behind Tori. I don't know why, but it's taking all my restraint not to drag her away from James and into me. Because I'm feeling confusingly jealous of their closeness. I know that the girls don't have a sexual connection—or at least I'm hoping they don't. I have no issue with lesbians. I'm a man, and if two other extremely attractive women were hugging each other tight and they happened to start rubbing up all over each other, I'd be more than happy to be an attentive audience. Or even in the past, a willing participant in anything they had in mind. But watching Tori being held that tight by anyone, even James, makes a surge of possessive heat well up inside of me.

Rationally, I know they're friends and that women are generally more tactile than men, but she's mine and I'm feeling super fucking territorial. By the time they separate, my hands are balled into fists in my pockets and my back teeth are clenched together so tightly I'm honestly concerned I might break one.

Apparently, I really don't like my woman touching anyone, not even her friend.

"Should we eat before it gets cold?" I grit out, stepping up behind Tori and draping a possessive arm over her shoulder the moment she's far enough from James that it's not super obvious I'm separating the two of them.

"Err, I don't have a crazy amount of furniture right now." Tori laughs, crinkling her face up adorably. "We could take the food downstairs and eat at the table in the store."

"Why don't we get some of the million and one throw pillows off the bed and we can sit around the coffee table?" I suggest.

Tori's face lights up at my suggestion and she nods, a wide smile spreading across her full lips.

"I'll help," James offers, kicking her shoes off, then padding barefoot after Tori into the bedroom.

All the calm I've managed to reclaim from touching Tori dissolves the moment the two of them step into the bedroom. I know I'm being completely irrational right now, but I just can't help it.

"What the fuck is up with you?" my brother asks.

"What?" I ask, swinging my head around to look at him.

"You're growling, bro."

"I am not."

"You are. Did you and Tori have a fight or something?"

"No."

"Then what the fuck is up with you?"

"I…" Swallowing, I rub my jaw with my hand. "Apparently I don't like other people touching my woman."

"Who the fuck touched her?" Buck growls, instantly indignant on my behalf, like the fucking good brother that he is.

Incapable of finding the words to admit just how crazy I am right now, I wave my hand in front of me to the spot where the girls had just been hugging. Buck's brow furrows, then his eyes widen, his lips spread into a smile, and the motherfucker laughs. "Are you serious?" the asshole asks.

"She's mine," I growl.

"Women hug, bro, they're not fucking, get over it."

"You think I don't know that? But I still don't fucking like it."

Reaching out, I punch him in the shoulder a second before the girls step back into the room, their arms full of the stupid fucking pillows that normally decorate Tori's princess bed.

"Here, let me get those," Buck says, rushing forward to take the pile from James's arms. I do the same, pulling the ones from Tori's hold, then dropping them to the ground beside the coffee table.

"Can you get the rest, please?" Tori asks as she bends down to position the pillows, her eyes going wide when the plug moves inside her ass.

"Sure thing, Sunshine. Everything feeling okay?" I ask quietly with a smirk.

Color instantly fills her cheeks and she glares at me. Chuckling to myself, I grab the rest of the cushions and bring them back into the living room, handing them to Tori one by one as she positions them around the table, making a surprisingly cozy-looking seating area.

Heading into the kitchen, I get plates and silverware, handing them to Buck when he reaches for them. "Grab a corkscrew and some glasses. James picked out wine for the girls, and there are some beers for us," he says.

Nodding, I search the cabinets, finding wineglasses, but coming up short on the corkscrew. "Sunshine, any idea if you have a corkscrew?"

Her face wrinkles and she grimaces. "I have no idea where it is. I swear I packed it, but it wasn't in the boxes with my other kitchenware. I need to get a new one, but I haven't really had a chance to go to the store."

Carrying over the food, I place it on the table, open the bag and lift out the bottle of wine. Examining the top, I peel off the metal wrapper, then head into the bedroom and grab my multi-tool from the pocket of my bag. It doesn't have a corkscrew attachment, but I still carry it back into the living room, grab the bottle and bury the small penknife into the cork.

Lifting James's shoe from the floor, I bang the sole against the bottom of the bottle until the cork starts to push free. Once it's halfway out, I grab hold of the tool, gently pulling and twisting until the cork comes free with a pop.

"That was the coolest thing I've ever seen." Tori giggles.

"You're like a Boy Scout for drinkers," James agrees, smiling up at me from her position on the pillow pile on the floor.

Smirking, I sit down on the floor and pour wine into two glasses, passing one to Tori, then to James while the girls lift out the boxes of Chinese food and open them.

"Do you want me to make you a plate?" Tori asks as James starts dishing things up onto her and Buck's plates.

"Sure, that'd be great. I'll eat anything. I'm not picky."

The girls and Buck chat amiably for a while, but I just sit back and watch, enjoying the way Tori's ass is wiggling around as she leans over the table.

"Here you go, bro," Buck says, sliding a beer across to me.

"Thanks." Twisting the top off, I lift the bottle in a silent salute, bringing it to my lips and taking a long pull. When I'm done, I place it on the table, shuffling closer to Tori and curling an arm around her waist, pulling her down until her butt is resting on my thigh.

I know the exact moment the plug pushes against my leg because she lets out a shocked gasp.

"Are you okay?" James asks Tori, her brow furrowed.

"Yep, I'm just aching a little. I had a huge wedding cake to make and decorate today and this place doesn't have a tub," Tori says too quickly.

James smirks and nods, but it's painfully obvious she knows Tori is lying. We make small talk about the food, then everyone goes quiet as we all start to eat. Tori tries to wiggle off my leg, but I tighten my hold on her, happy to eat one-handed if it means she keeps her ass on my lap, where I told her she needed to be.

Her muscles tense, but she stays put, her back straight, tipping her weight forward and off the plug in her butt.

"Soooo." James elongates the word. "Want to explain how this"—she waves her fork between Tori and me— "happened? Because last I heard, you guys didn't get on."

"We found some common ground," I growl, not really wanting to answer questions.

"Oh really? Would that commonality be dick-shaped?" James asks, grinning.

"James," Tori admonishes lightly.

Clenching my jaw, I do my best not to tell my soon-to-be sister-in-law to shut the fuck up, but it takes every ounce of self-control I have.

"She's mine," I say through gritted teeth.

"So you guys are a couple now? Like together, not just fucking?" my brother asks, a smirk on his lips because he already knows this.

A beat passes and Tori stays stoically silent. "Yes," I growl. "We're together... a couple." The word feels wrong on my tongue and James notices, her brow wrinkling as she stares assessingly at me.

"Huh," she says, dipping her eyes to her food.

I hate that Tori didn't confirm that we're together to her fucking bestie. She promised to try, but at the first test, she stumbled and failed, and it bothers me more than it should. The food is completely tasteless, but I choke it down, needing to do something so that I don't become a growling, brooding caveman. The urge to drag up the teasingly tight dress Tori's wearing and flip her over so my brother and James can see the plug that's buried deep in her ass is far stronger than it should be. I want them to see the plug that I put there after I spanked her butt and fingered her until she came all over me.

Would she still stay silent then? Would she have anything to say if I put my own version of ownership on display? Showed them how she submitted to me? Because she belongs to me, and her body knows it.

I don't even realize how tense I've gotten until Tori tries to edge off my lap. The movement snaps me from the spiraling rage that's rushing through my veins and coating my blood in anger and frustration.

Clamping my arm around her, I drag her off my thigh and fully onto my lap, her butt on top of my hard dick, my arm holding her in place tight enough that the only way she'll be able to get away from me is to make a huge scene.

A shuddering gasp falls silently from her lips as I hold her in place. The tension in the room is palpable, but I don't speak, unwilling to make inane small talk about nothing when I'm furious at the woman in my lap.

My brother is the first to break the silence. "Do you have any plans for the store, or are you intending to keep things as they are? I've never actually bought anything from here, but there are always people in here whenever I come into town."

Tori's voice is shaky when she speaks. "I actually plan to make it into a French-style patisserie."

My brother, James, and Tori chatter politely while I stew in my own anger, refusing to allow Tori more than an inch of distance from me, barely enough room to reach her plate on the coffee table. She makes a feeble attempt to loosen my hold, but when she realizes I have no intention of allowing it, she sits stiffly in my lap. By the time the food is gone, I feel like a bomb on a hair trigger.

"Excuse us a minute," I say as politely as I can muster. Lifting Tori off my lap, I lead her out of the living room and into the bedroom, closing the door behind us.

"What the hell, Nero?" she whisper-yells the moment the door clicks shut.

Snapping my hand out, I grab her chin, squeezing her jaw and silencing her. "Pull up the dress, turn around and bend over."

Her eyes go wide with a mixture of shock and fury. Fighting my hold, she shakes her head from side to side and I lose my motherfucking mind. Lifting her off the ground, I carry her to the bed, forcing her down, her chest pressed to the mattress, my palm pressed into the middle of her back, holding her in place.

"Nero," she whisper-screams.

Ignoring her, I drag her dress up until her ass and the sparkling plug are bared to me.

"We had an agreement, Sunshine. You said you'd try. You said you were mine. You begged for my cock in your greedy cunt, then the first time you're asked if we're together, you have nothing to say. You're lucky I didn't do this out there where everyone could see you like this. Dripping wet, your tight asshole stretched around my plug."

"Nero."

"Oh, now you have something to say. Now your ass

is on display and your pussy is dripping for me. Do not fucking move. If you do, I'll fuck you right here until you're screaming so loudly there won't be a single person in a ten-block radius who will ever question how much you belong to me."

"Nero, I just…" she starts.

"You just what? Forgot what we agreed? Didn't want to admit it to your friend?"

"No, I just…" she trails off again, but she doesn't move when I lift my hand from her back. Reaching out, I yank open the drawer in the tiny bedside table and grab the box of training plugs I bought for her.

"What are you doing?" she asks.

"Apparently, you need a more impactful reminder of who owns you."

"Nero, no," she gasps, pushing her arms underneath her.

"I've already told you what will happen if you move another inch, Tori. I have no issue fucking you with my brother right outside the door. I don't give a crap if he hears me fucking my woman raw. Do you feel the same?"

Her eyes are like saucers, wide and full of disbelief, but there's a hint of arousal beneath the horrified understanding that I'm not bluffing. I mean every word I'm saying. I'm losing my goddamn mind, and exerting my authority and claiming her in any and every way is the only thing that's keeping me from imploding.

"Nero, please. I just froze."

Grabbing a bigger plug from the box, I'm thankful that I washed them all earlier, not just the smallest one that's currently buried in her ass.

"Then this will act as a reminder," I snap, forcing her legs wide and unceremoniously pushing the bigger plug into her soaking pussy.

"Oh god," she whines at the invasion.

"I didn't plan to use this one on you today. I thought you'd wear the smallest plug tonight and then maybe for a few hours tomorrow to stretch you out slowly. But clearly, my plug in your ass and your ass in my lap isn't enough to make you understand that you are mine. Let's see if this bigger plug helps you understand a little better."

Grabbing the base of the plug in her ass, I twist as I slowly pull it until the widest part is stretching her hole. Pushing it back in, I fuck her with it a few times until she has to bury her face in the comforter to stifle her moans. Her asshole is soft and accepting when I pull the plug all the way out, dropping it onto the comforter beside her head.

Leaning down, I look at her stretched hole, the muscle not immediately closing tight, then I spit into it. Her whine is fucking music to my ears, and some of the anger I was feeling lessens. Reaching for the bottle of lube, I squeeze more onto her ass, then pull the larger plug from her cunt and rub even more lube over the metal, adding it to her own arousal before I push the tip against her hole.

"Nero, please," she begs.

"What do you want?"

"They're out there. We need to go back."

"I don't give a fuck if they're out there. I'll open the door and invite them in. Maybe if they saw you like this, bent over the bed, ass up high, asshole begging to be filled, pussy gushing with cream, they wouldn't be asking you questions and you wouldn't have to worry about *freezing*." I spit the word out and she keens.

"I'm sorry. I'll tell them we're together. Let's just go back out there and I'll tell them," she cajoles.

"You're not going to tell them. You're going to show them," I order, slowly pushing the new plug against her ass. The tip easily slides into her, but this plug is much bigger and broader and I watch her muscles struggle to stretch enough to accept it. "Stop fighting this. I don't want to hurt you."

"It's too big," she pants. "It won't fit."

"You can take it. Deep breath in, then exhale."

Following my orders, she inhales, and on the exhale, her muscles relax, allowing the plug to slip farther inside of her. Slowly, I start to fuck her ass with the plug, pushing it in farther and farther with every thrust. Pushing my hand between her thighs, I find her clit, rubbing it in firm circles until her hips are swiveling as she chases her release. Moaning and gasping, she pushes back onto the plug, fucking herself onto it as she gets louder and louder the closer she gets to release. I feel the moment she crests the peak and slide the plug all the way into her ass until the jewel is pressed tightly between her cheeks.

Lifting my fingers from her clit, I smile at her sound of outrage. Her climax ripped from her the moment I stopped.

"Nero," she demands.

"Only women who know they belong to me get to come."

"You're an asshole," she hisses, reaching a hand down to touch herself.

"No," I snarl, slapping my palm against her ass right over the top of the plug.

Her squeal of shock is music to my ears and loud enough that even if Buck and James hadn't heard her moans and whines, they would definitely have heard that.

"You can't leave me like this."

"I can and I will. Every time you move, you'll feel this plug stretching your ass wide, and it won't be like before where it was a fun naughty secret. Now, you'll feel the weight of it inside of you with every breath. You'll need to clench your ass to keep it inside of you, then every time you clench, it'll feel even bigger, teasing you and reminding you that you are mine. You don't get to freeze and pretend that we're not together. You don't get to stay silent. Because if you do, I have another four plugs I can punish you with, and I won't allow you to come again until every fucking person in this town knows exactly who you belong to."

Panting, her gaze is locked on mine as I pull her up from the bed, turning her to face me. Bending down, I take her lips, pushing my tongue into her mouth and forcing her to kiss me back. We've been in the bedroom less than five minutes, but it feels like hours. My dick is so hard I could probably come from a strong gust of wind or a single touch from the woman standing in front of me, who has turned me from a normal human being into an enraged psychopath.

Pulling away, I cup her face gently with my hands. "How does it feel, Sunshine?" I ask.

Cringing slightly, she fidgets. "Big."

"Does anything hurt?"

"My clit," she sasses.

"Good."

"You're an asshole." Her words are mean, but her expression isn't. She's frustrated, but her pupils are blown wide and her cheeks are flushed red with lust.

"Who do you belong to, my dirty little sunshine?"

Sighing, she fidgets some more, probably trying to find a position that will lessen the intensity of the plug, but she won't find one. It's not as big as I'm sure it feels, but it's big enough to feel foreign and probably be driving her a little crazy in an hour or so.

"I said I'd try, Nero, but this is…" she trails off.

For a moment, I wonder if I'm pushing her too hard. But she never at any point told me no or asked me to stop. If she'd done either, I would have, but she didn't. She's embarrassed, clearly overwhelmed, and maybe a little conflicted, but she's also turned on and as into this as I am.

"Tell me you don't like this. That you don't enjoy the way I've taken ownership of your body. Tell me no. Tell me to stop." I'm giving her an out. It's a risk, but I need her to admit to herself, as much as to me, that she wants this, even if she's conflicted about it.

"I don't…"

I brace.

"Fine, I'm yours," she says quickly.

My smile is instant and blinding. "Turn around," I order.

"Are you taking the plug out?"

"No, but if my brother sees your pussy, I'll have to fucking kill him, so going back out there with your skirt pushed up to your belly probably isn't the best idea."

Chapter Twenty-Six

Tori

My cheeks flare with a heat so intense I'm honestly concerned my skin might actually set on fire. I don't know how long it's been since Nero dragged me into my bedroom, but it feels like hours, and it could have been because the moment he gets his hands on me, time seems meaningless.

I hadn't meant to not say anything when James had asked if we were together, but even though I was in his lap, without any panties and wearing a plug courtesy of him, I still wondered if he'd confirm we were a couple. A part of me is still unsure, and after twenty-four hours, I don't think that's unreasonable.

Apparently, Nero disagrees.

Slowly, he drags the hem of my skirt down over my ass, his fingers stroking over the base of the new plug before he covers me up and turns me around to face him again.

"Come on, Sunshine."

The moment he tugs me forward, the plug moves and I hiss. It's not exactly painful, but unlike the other plug, this one feels huge. I try to step gingerly, but he doesn't allow me to, leading me quickly out of the bedroom and back into the living room, where James and Buck are still sitting on the floor. The Chinese food has been cleared away and in its place is a golden pie with a pint of ice cream sitting beside it.

Buck averts his gaze from me to his brother, but James arches a brow at me, her lips twisted into a sly smirk as I waddle back into the room. My cheeks are in full bloom now, but Nero seems completely unaffected as he strides confidently over to the pile of cushions, sinking down into them and pulling me into his lap.

The plug seems to double in size the moment I'm sitting down, but before I even have a chance to think about getting back up, Nero curls his arm around me, holding me in place. I'm tense and stiff as I try—and fail—to stop my full weight from resting on my butt, but Nero is relaxed and smiling as he asks Buck and James about their wedding plans, like he didn't just drag me into the bedroom and force a huge plug inside of me.

"So, are you going to give me the full tour?" James asks after we've eaten the pie and I've squirmed through every mouthful, doing everything I can to try and relive the damning ache in my ass.

Her expression is amused and she does nothing to hide it.

"Why don't you show her the roof?" Nero suggests amiably, finally allowing me to move as he lifts me off his lap. "Buck and I can clean up, then we'll follow you up there."

The moment I'm on my feet, the ache from the plug lessens and I blow out a relieved breath. Following me up, Nero crowds me, wrapping me in his arms and kissing me. His hands drop to my butt cheeks and he squeezes tightly, causing a lust-drenched whimper to fall from my mouth.

He swallows the sound, taking it inside of him as he relishes in my discomfort. This is, without doubt, a punishment, and even though I'm annoyed that I'm acting like an army of ants has invaded my metaphorical panties, I can't help being incredibly turned on by the humiliating way he's turned my body against me.

Releasing me, he turns me toward James, slapping my ass with unrelenting accuracy. "Nero," I snap, turning to glare at him, but instead of being even slightly remorseful, the asshole is fucking smiling.

"Okay, fess up. What the hell is going on with you?" James asks the moment we step out the door and onto the roof.

"Nothing, I'm fine," I lie.

"Bullshit. I know you, Tori. I've seen you dating guy after guy, coming home after each one to dish the dirt about how boring they were, how they sucked their silverware when they ate, how they undertipped or overtipped. But in the three years since we've known each other, I have never seen you act like"—she waves her hands up and down dramatically—"this."

"Nero is… Well…" I squirm, moving my weight from one foot to the other, trying to find a comfortable way to stand that lessens the effect of the plug. "He's…"

"Oh my god, Tori, are you high or something? I mean, look at you. You can't stand still. You've been fidgety since we got here and what the hell were you doing when he hauled you into your bedroom?" she demands.

"It's not—" I start.

"Do not lie to me, Tori Hoffman, or I swear to god I will punch you in the tit and then I'll call Atticus and tell him there's something wrong."

"You wouldn't," I gasp.

"I will if you don't tell me right this second what the hell Nero has done to you."

"I'm wearing a plug," I blurt.

I watch as a full range of emotions flash across my best friend's face. She cycles through shock, to discomfort, to curiosity, to blatant amusement, and then the fucking bitch laughs.

"Don't laugh, you cow," I snap, but there's no real heat in my voice, and a moment later, I find myself chuckling along with her.

"You're wearing a butt plug?" she whisper-yells.

"Yes," I say, cringing even as I giggle.

"Right now, you have a plug…" she pauses, covering her mouth to stifle her giggles, "Up your butt."

"Yes," I hiss, lowering myself into one of the ancient lawn chairs and then immediately jumping up the moment my weight moves the plug.

"Oh my god." She laughs louder. "You're fidgeting like

a junkie desperate for a fix because you have a plug shoved up your butt."

"Stop laughing," I shout.

"I'm sorry, I'm sorry." She laughs, inhaling deeply and holding her breath in an attempt to suppress her laughter. "So, is this like a thing?"

"Is what a thing?"

"You know." Her eyes dip below my waist.

"I really don't."

"The other week, after you did a fuck and chuck on Nero, we talked about anal, remember? Back then, you'd never… I'm assuming that's changed?"

"No, it hasn't."

"Oh my god, Tori, give me the ten-second rundown before they get back up here and we have to make polite conversation while you have a plug in your ass."

Inhaling, I scoff, then shake my head. "Fine. You know we fucked, you know I left, then he kept calling and texting and I… well, I don't know, it felt weird, so after the sale went through and I had this place, I moved out."

"You didn't tell him?"

"No, I just had movers come in while he was at work to get my stuff and bring it here. Anyway, he found out I'd left, barged into the store and up to the apartment. The cops got called and he told them I was his. They made him leave and when I finished work for the day, I found him in my apartment. He won't leave. He insists I'm his, and he asked me to try to see if this works between us. But honestly, he's kind of crazy."

"He's definitely intense," she agrees. "But I bet the sex

is crazy hot."

Grinning, I nod.

"I knew it." Lifting her hand into the air, she holds it up and I lean forward and slap my hand against it to high-five. "And the plug?" she asks.

"While he was in my apartment, he snooped through my sex toy drawer, he saw I didn't have anything for ass play, and apparently, he's a fan, so he ordered me some plugs. He's a tad possessive, and the only way he'd agree to this dinner was on the condition that I sit on his lap, no panties, and wearing a plug." My cheeks heat, but it's not from embarrassment. It's more from fear that James will think I'm a freak or something.

"Wow, that's actually kind of hot," she says, sitting back in her lawn chair and bringing her wineglass to her lips contemplatively. "So, how does it feel?" she asks, nodding to my crotch again.

"The first one—"

"The first one?" she gasps, her eyes going wide. "Please tell me you don't have more than one plug up there because that seems dangerous for an amateur."

Scoffing, I roll my eyes at her. "He…" I clear my throat. "He put the smallest plug in before you guys got here. That one wasn't too bad. It felt kind of… well, kind of nice."

"Nice?" she questions.

"You know, naughty and sexy."

"So what's changed? Why are you squirming about like you have to pee?"

"He was upset that when you asked if we were a couple, I didn't say anything."

"That's why he dragged you off to the bedroom? We could hear you, you know. We just thought you were fucking. I'm guessing not?"

"Err, no." I shake my head. "He took the small plug out and put in a bigger one."

"How big?" Her eyes go wide.

"I don't know. I didn't see it, but it feels big."

"Can I see?" she asks.

"What?" I shriek. "James, I love you, but I'm not into girls."

"Urgh." She scowls. "We both know if I was a lesbian, I'd have you pussy whipped in a hot minute. But… can you see it if you look behind you?"

"If it's like the other one, you can see the base. The last one had a pretty jewel on the end."

"Like jewelry?" she asks, a thoughtful look crossing her face.

"Well yeah, I guess if things that go in your butt can be considered jewelry, then yeah."

"Let me see."

"No," I snap.

"Come on, it's not like I expect you to bend over and cough. I just want to see if you can see it through your ass cheeks."

"Fine, but if Nero comes up here and sees you looking at my ass, I'm going to kill you because he has a whole selection of plugs and I'm not willing to piss him off and have him try to shove anything any bigger in my ass."

"He's not like…" She inhales, sobering a little. "He's not forcing you or anything, right? I know you said before that he was pushing your boundaries a little, that you were experimenting with some kinkier stuff. But, like, he's not pushing you to do things you don't want to, right? Because big guy or not, future brother-in-law or not, I will always, no questions asked, be on your side. You're my ride or die, and I will kick his ass if he's not treating you right."

Love, warmth, and reassurance swell in my chest, heating me up from the inside out. "I love you so much," I blurt, throwing my arms around her.

"Love you too," she cries, hugging me back.

When we pull away, I smile. "He's definitely pushing, but it's not more than I can handle. I…" I struggle to find the words to explain. "I figured I was basically vanilla. Sex has always been fun, but it's only ever been a physical thing. Bodies fitting together in a way that feels good. But with Nero, it's a total body, mind, and soul thing."

"I get that. That's how it is with Buck too. He gives me something I've never had before and he does it in a way that's so much more than I could ever have even fantasized about. It's scary, but it's the fear that makes it so good."

Sighing, I carefully sit down on the chair beside hers. "He's so intense. He hasn't given me a moment to calibrate my thoughts since he barged into the store and smashed the glass in the front door yesterday morning. I'm confused and overwhelmed and a little scared."

"Why are you scared?"

"Because we're basically strangers and he's treating this like it's this fated connection, and I just don't know if I should throw myself into the fire and enjoy the burn, or if I should run for an extinguisher, then douse myself in ice to stop the feelings from smoldering back to life."

"I wish this was easier for you," James says. "I can still kick his ass for you though. Buck will hold him down and I'll whale on him, if you want."

"Buck won't hold his brother down so you can beat him up." I laugh.

"He absolutely would. He might love Nero, but he loves me more, and I'm the one sucking his dick. Fiancé trumps brother any day of the week," she says with a smirk.

A wave of jealous envy pulses through me at her certainty that Buck loves her more than even his own flesh and blood. They haven't been together that long, weeks rather than years, but their love for each other is so palpably obvious it'd be impossible for even a skeptic to deny.

I can't imagine ever being that confident in Nero's feelings for me. He wants me and his dick gets superhard for me, that's indisputable, but I can't imagine a world where I'm ever as certain as James is.

Sighing wistfully, I try to smile. I shouldn't be comparing me and Nero to James and Buck. What they found was an instant, enduring connection. Love at first sight. That's not what Nero and I have and that's okay. Maybe it'll grow into something that feels more concrete and permanent. Maybe it won't. But wishing it was something it isn't, or pretending it's not exactly what it is, would be a one-way ticket to disaster.

"He's so sure," I admit.

"Buck told me that Beau thinks his family legacy has moved to the jumpers now that all the Barnetts are married and multiplying."

A dry, scoffing laugh falls from my lips and I shake my head. "I know the Barnetts sold that story pretty well, and all the girls bought into it. But the idea that this love at first sight legacy has just moved on to a new group of hot guys seems a little far-fetched, even for Rockhead Point."

James shrugs, unrepentant. "It happened that way for me and Buck and now Nero is smashing doors and telling anyone who'll listen that you're his. Far-fetched or not, there's no denying that it's happening."

"Or maybe it's just a boys' club excuse to go all caveman over a woman they want to fuck without people calling them a psycho."

"You think Nero's a psycho?" she asks tauntingly.

"Abso-fucking-lutely. He's insane."

"But it's hot insane, right?" she laughs.

"Crazy hot. You might even say he's… on fire."

We both burst out laughing at my terrible pun.

"Come on, show me before the guys get up here."

"You might be my bestie, but I'm not sure we're *that* close," I drawl.

"If I had a plug in my butt, I'd absolutely show you." She pouts.

Sighing, I cautiously push myself out of the chair. "Fine."

Clapping excitedly, she shuffles to the front of her chair and waves her hands at me to hurry me up. Turning away from her, I grab the hem of my dress and shimmy it up my legs, dragging it over my butt and holding it in place at my hips.

"Oh wow," James breathes. "It's like a jewel."

"What color is it?" I ask.

"Like a pale-lavender color."

"What the fucking hell are you doing?" an angry male voice yells.

Chapter Twenty-Seven

Nero

"**B**ro, if you don't relax, you're going to crack your jaw with how hard you're clenching it right now. They went upstairs. She's not going anywhere."

"I'm fine," I argue.

His laugh is derisive and low. "You are so fucking far from fine. I figured after a day locked up with her, you'd be a little more fucking relaxed, but you look more wound up than you did when she was still ghosting you."

"She's been working."

"Ahh, so that's what it is, we're cockblocking you right now? But you literally dragged her into the bedroom thirty minutes ago. Your balls can't be that blue when you just had a quickie."

"I didn't fuck her."

"You didn't?" My brother's eyebrows arch in surprise. "Well, that was a fucking noisy chat if you weren't fucking."

"I'm not going to discuss how loud my woman is when I fuck her," I tell him coolly.

"Fair enough. But tell me what's going on. Why do you look like you've been ready to explode all night?"

"Things aren't going... how I expected," I admit.

"Well, what were you expecting?"

"She's mine."

"Okay."

"I told her she was mine. I told her I felt it, all the way down to my core."

"But?" he asks.

"I never expected to feel this way, but now that I do, it just seems so fucking simple. She's mine, we're together, that's it. I know that physically we're compatible, but she's just acting like it's all just normal."

"Normal how?" he asks slowly.

"Like nothing has changed."

"Her ass has been on your lap all night and she let you do" —he waves toward the bedroom door—"whatever you were doing in there. How else were you expecting her to act?"

"Juni, Bonnie, Cora, all the Barnett women and James, they all act like they're as into it as the guys are. Tori seems like she just wants me to leave her alone," I admit.

"Brother, a week ago, you couldn't stand the sight of the girl. Now you're barging into her home and hanging around her work. Honestly, I'm surprised she didn't let the cops haul you off yesterday."

"James was all in from day one," I protest.

"She fought some, but the truth is that maybe James and I are a little different because she was looking for something. Her needs had never been fulfilled until we met and I think that made it a little easier for her to just go with it. To be honest, Tori was a big help too. She helped James see that it was okay to need what she needed and that she never had to apologize for it."

"So, what do I do to get Tori to act like she gives a fuck?"

"Maybe stop being an asshole to her. Try spending time with her. Get to know her. Do things that require clothes. I don't know, figure out what she needs and give it to her. That's what I did. I'm not saying you won't have ups and downs, but nothing that's worth having comes easy."

"We have to go back to work in a couple of days, and I'm worried that being away from her for four days will ruin everything. Right now, I'm not giving her the time and space to rebuild the walls I've destroyed, but when I'm gone, I don't know if I'll have to start all over again with her when I get back."

"I don't really know Tori well enough to know what she needs. But with James, we might have had physical time and space between us when I had to work, but I never allowed her any emotional distance. I told you about Beau and Bonnie, right?"

I furrow my brow, but he carries on talking.

"They have this thing, a mantra or whatever you want to call it. No space, no distance. I asked him about it when James went AWOL, and he said it reminds them both that he won't allow things like work or life or anything else to come between them. James and I have something similar and maybe you and Tori need to find your thing, something that reminds you both what you're fighting for."

We fall into a contemplative silence, working side by side to wash the dishes and put all the throw pillows back into the bedroom. Buck doesn't comment when he sees the discarded butt plug on the comforter and neither do I, dropping the pillows onto the bed before heading back into the living room.

"Shall we go see what the ladies are up to?" he suggests.

"I'll grab some drinks. I've not been onto the roof at night before, but Tori says it's pretty up there."

Armed with wine and beers we climb the stairs, and I push open the door that leads onto the roof. The moment I step outside, I freeze to the spot as I watch James lean forward on the edge of her chair while Tori stands in front of her, her dress pushed up to her waist, her naked ass and my plug clearly on display.

"What the fucking hell are you doing?" I yell.

Tori jumps at the sound of my voice, snapping her head around to me, her eyes wide with shock. Giggles fill the air and both women burst into laughter, but I don't think it's fucking funny.

Storming forward, I close the distance between us in a few strides, grabbing her dress with my hands and shoving it down her legs, ignoring the sound of ripping fabric as I cover her up.

"Nero." Tori giggles.

"Brother," I growl, not turning around to address Buck

or his giggling fucking fiancé.

"Come on, Precious, we should go," I hear him say.

"Bye, babe," James calls.

"No," Tori protests, still giggling as she tries to lean around me to speak to her friend.

"Bye, James," I say, grabbing Tori by the throat to keep her from moving. Everything goes quiet until I hear the sounds of the door to the stairs opening and closing.

"Want to explain why the fuck I just walked up here and found you with your skirt around your waist and your ass on display?" I growl.

Tori's eyes are big, but instead of concern, they're filled with amusement. "James wanted to know why I'd been squirming all night, so I told her about the plug. She was curious and asked to see."

"So you got naked," I hiss through gritted teeth.

"We're girls who used to live together. She's seen me naked a million times."

"But back then, you didn't belong to me. Now you do and I won't share you."

"Jesus, Nero, we weren't fucking, she just wanted to see what it looked like."

"If you were fucking, I'd have to really piss my brother off when I killed his woman."

Her laugh is high, sexy and happy. It's the happiest sound she's made since the first time we met. Back then, I found her laugh and everything else about her annoying as fuck. Now, something claws at my stomach that I haven't done anything to make her sound this free before.

"You sound insane. I flashed my butt to my girlfriend; I

didn't strip off and start swinging on a pole in front of your buddies. You're overreacting."

Spinning her around in my arms, I grab two handfuls of her butt and squeeze. "This is mine. I won't tolerate anyone seeing what's mine."

"You're such a caveman," she says, rolling her eyes.

"There are three plugs bigger than the one inside your ass right now, waiting in the bedroom. Keep rolling your fucking eyes at me, Sunshine, if you're ready to find out what they feel like."

"Err, no thank you," she gasps, pushing at my chest to get away from my hold.

"No one gets to see what's mine. So I don't give a fuck how close you and James are, you keep your fucking clothes on around her, you get me?"

"You're being ridiculous, Nero."

"So you're saying if I whipped my dick out and started swinging it around, you wouldn't give a fuck?"

Her gaze stays on me, and then she shrugs. "In front of your buddies, I guess, no, I wouldn't care."

"Well, why the fuck don't you care?" I demand. I sound like a petulant child right now, but her blasé attitude is driving me crazy. She should care. It should bother her; she shouldn't want to share me, and I don't know how to cope with the fact that she just doesn't.

"I'm not really a jealous person, Nero."

"Well, neither was I. Until you," I bark. "Everything is different with you. I hate sharing you, even with my brother and your friend. You're mine and I want all of you to be *just* mine."

Something in her gaze softens and she stops pushing at my chest, relaxing into my hold and letting her body rest against me. "Baby, James is my friend. I wasn't sharing anything with her. It was just girls being girls. We talk, we're open about sex and pretty much everything else. I told you I'd try and I meant it. I'm all yours."

She's reassuring me, and even though it feels good to hear her call herself mine, it's not enough. I thought keeping her here with me would satisfy my need to claim her, but I need more. I need everyone to know, to see. Word travels fast in this tiny town and even faster on the mountain, and maybe if everyone in Rockhead Point knows about us, it'll be harder for her to forget about me when I have to leave her.

"I like it when you call me baby," I admit.

"You do?" she asks, surprised.

"Do you like it when I call you my dirty girl?" I coax, letting my voice go quiet and low.

She shudders in response and I smile.

"Yes," she breathes. "I like it when you call me Sunshine too."

"Let's sit for a while." Loosening my grip on her butt, I offer her my hand and she takes it without thought. Lowering myself to one of the lawn chairs, I pull her forward, but she hesitates.

"Can you take out this plug?"

"Does it hurt?"

"No, not really."

"Then no," I say with a smirk, yanking her forward. Stumbling, she falls into me, her eyes going wide as the plug finds my thigh.

"Jesus, fuck," she hisses.

"When we finish our drinks, I'm going to take you downstairs and fuck you on your ridiculous princess bed with that plug in your ass and you're going to lose your fucking mind," I whisper into her ear.

Her shudder is perfection and I smile, turning her a little more sideways on my lap.

"Why culinary school?" I ask.

"When I was a kid, I used to bake with my nana. It wasn't anything special or fancy, just cookies and cakes and things. But I loved it. I thought about going to college, getting a degree and a corporate job, but it all just sounded so dull. I was more interested in experimenting in my mom's kitchen than I was in writing college application essays about how I overcame my biggest hurdle in life. My dad was actually the one who suggested I go to culinary school, and the moment I saw the brochures, I knew it was exactly what I wanted."

"You trained in France too?"

"Yeah, I did a gap year and applied for this internship in a Michelin-starred restaurant over there. I got the job and spent a year training under their chefs, learning French techniques in every position in the kitchen. It's what cemented my love of pastry and really inspired me. They actually offered me a full-time job once I graduated, but although me and my brothers are spread all over the states, I knew I didn't want to be on the other side of the world from them."

I feel like an asshole that even though I'm distantly aware that she has siblings, I've never really asked her about them. "Are they older or younger than you?"

"Both. Atticus and Felix are three years older than me and Jude and August are two years younger."

"You have four brothers?" I ask, arching my brow.

"Yep."

"And you're close?"

"Incredibly close. We text pretty much every day and we have a video group chat once a week."

"So when are they going to threaten to kill me if I don't treat you right?" I chuckle.

"Err."

"They know about me, right? If you text every day."

"Err, sort of."

Anger barrels through me and she must sense it because her body goes tense.

"Where's your cell?"

"Downstairs."

"Then let's go downstairs and you can text your fucking brothers and let them know you have a man."

"I can't do that," she chokes out.

"You can and you will. You're mine and I want everyone to fucking know it." Lifting her off my lap, I drag her downstairs, then stand over her while she types out a message and scowls at me before hitting send.

The moment she's done, I nod, then pull out my own cell and send a text to my sister.

ME

Hey little sis, I need a favor.

Her reply is instantaneous.

JUNI
What do you need?

ME
I need you guys to host a barbeque or something tomorrow. I'll pay for all the food or whatever.

JUNI
Why? It's not a problem, but I need to know why first.

ME
Tori's mine, we're together and I want to spread the word that she's taken.

JUNI
Yours? As in YOURS???

ME
Mine.

JUNI
Well holy shit, big bro, that's awesome, Tori is great. But I have to be honest, I'm a little shocked, you didn't seem like you were her biggest fan when we first met her.

ME
That was then, this is now. Can you host or not?

JUNI
Of course. I'll engage the Barnett telephone tree, see you tomorrow, say 5.00 p.m.?

ME
Love you, little sis.

JUNI
Love you too, big bro.

Looking up from my cell, my eyes are drawn to Tori; her brow is furrowed in consternation and her fingers are moving fast as she types on the screen of her cell.

"You good?" I ask.

"No. I'm getting the inquisition from all my brothers. Thanks for that." She scowls.

"They needed to know."

"They really didn't," she argues.

"Tell them good night. Do you have to be up in the morning?"

"No, the store is closed on Sundays."

"Good, we can lie in a while then. My sister and the Barnetts are hosting a barbeque tomorrow afternoon though."

"Oh, okay, well, I should do some work anyway." She shrugs.

"You're going with me," I tell her decisively.

"No, I—"

"I wasn't asking you, Sunshine; I was telling you. We're both going to my sister's tomorrow afternoon to spend time with my family, and then we can let everyone know we're together."

"Meeting the family is not a day two activity," she says, her expression wary.

"You've met my family."

"Not as your…" Her words dry up as if she's struggling to find the right label.

"Girlfriend, woman, fiancé, any or all of those work. Pick one."

"Girlfriend," she squeaks.

"That will do, for now." When her jaw drops open, I can't help it. I smirk. "Come on, let's go to bed."

She's quiet as I check the door locks, then lead her into the bedroom. Stripping the dress off her, I push down my shorts and drag her into my lap. Just like I promised her, by the time she collapses onto my chest, our skin is clammy with sweat, and she's almost hoarse from screaming my name.

Chapter Twenty-eight

Tori

My body is deliciously sore as I stretch my legs, blinking my eyes into wakefulness. Last night was crazy. Having dinner with my bestie wearing a butt plug was one of the weirdest experiences of my life, but riding Nero's cock with it still firmly in my ass was unbelievably hot.

His dick is big to start off with, but add in the size of the plug and it felt like I was being stretched and filled in the most titillating way. I came so many times I could barely speak by the time I collapsed into sleep, our wrists bound together again and my head resting on his chest.

The weight of his body feels nice behind me. Nero is a cuddler, which I wasn't expecting. For some reason, I thought he might roll to the edge of the bed and fall asleep with his back to me, but instead, he's curled himself around me, the perfect big spoon.

My muscles are tight, and I know I'll feel the crazy amount of sex we've had in the last couple of days the moment I get up. For the first time since I closed the door to the house up the mountain, I wish I was back there. If I was, I could run myself a bath and soak my well-used pussy in some Epsom salts. Instead, I'll have to make do with the crappy, tiny shower in my ugly, dated bathroom.

The screen on my cell lights up, and I don't need to look at my notifications to know I'm going to have ten million messages waiting for me in the sibling group chat. After Nero demanded I inform my brothers about him, I'd reluctantly typed out a message.

ME

> Hi guys, I miss you all. Thought I should let you know; I've sort of met someone. It's super new, but he has a thing about wanting everyone to know I'm "his" and insisted I tell you. I'll fill you all in properly on our video call. Love you all LB xoxo

I knew the vagueness would drive them all crazy, but Nero is a lot to explain via text.

It only took about ten seconds for the first message to come through.

ATTICUS

> Name, address, social security number if you have it. Also, you owe me twenty bucks 😉

JUDE

> Who the fuck is this dude?

AUGUST

> He tells people you're his? Hell fucking no! Dude's dead.

I don't like it.

Instead of giving them the information they irrationally demanded, I quickly typed out a reply to all of them.

ME

No one is killing anyone, although he asked when he should expect the death threats from all of you, so I doubt any of you will scare him off with your mean-mugging. He's James's fiancé's brother, he's a decent guy, even though he's a total caveman. I'll tell you more later. Speak soon xoxo

Closing down my cell, I followed Nero into my bedroom and once his hands were on me, I never even thought about looking at my messages again. Now though, the reality of having to deal with the fallout of dropping the boyfriend bomb sits heavily on my chest. My brothers are all overprotective alpha males, even Felix, who doesn't seem like he'd have a dominant bone in his body. I know they're going to demand to know every little detail about Nero, but honestly, I'm only just getting my head around the idea of us being together myself. Having to try and defend a guy that I'm not one-hundred-percent sure about just sounds exhausting.

"What's got you thinking so hard?" Nero asks, his voice gruff with sleep. "I can practically hear your brain ticking."

Sighing, I roll over so I'm facing him. "I'm just wondering how many hundred messages I have from my brothers." I force out a laugh, but it's a weak noise.

"Are they giving you a hard time?" he asks, his voice instantly alert.

"No. They just want to know your social security number so they can have someone investigate you."

"It's—" he starts, but I immediately cut him off.

"I'm not going to give them your social security number. Don't be crazy."

Shrugging, he reaches out and brushes a strand of hair away from my face. "I don't care if they run a background check on me. I have nothing to hide and I'd rather they get it over and done with. I won't allow their suspicions to affect you or come between us, so I'm happy for them to do what they need to do. I'll speak to them when you have your video chat."

"You will not," I hiss, outraged.

"Why the fuck not?"

"Because the idea of you pissing them off or them pissing you off is more stressful than convincing them to tone down the crazy big brother routine. I'll deal with them. It's fine."

His brow furrows and it's clear he isn't happy with my answer, but he doesn't argue and I'm grateful for the reprieve. Instead of talking, I rest my head on his bicep, inhaling his sexy scent of sweat and sex. It should be gross, but it's not and as I relax into him, I close my eyes and fall back asleep.

The next time I wake up, the sun is bright, beaming through the shitty blinds covering the window and filling the room with light. My stomach growls before I even have a chance to speak, and Nero's chest vibrates with the sound of his throaty chuckle.

"Hungry?"

"Starving."

"Let's go out for food then."

"Where do you want to go?" I ask, stretching out again and wincing slightly at the ache in both my ass and my pussy.

"You sore?" Nero asks, tipping my chin up with a fingertip so I'm looking into his concerned eyes.

"A little, nothing a Tylenol and shower won't fix."

"You sure? I know we both enjoyed the push and pull yesterday, but if anything ever hurts, I need to know you'll tell me."

His expression is earnest and although I'm not shocked to know he doesn't want to do anything to cause me actual pain, it's sweet that he looks so worried about it. "I will. And I…" I pause, swallowing. "I do like it. All of it."

"Even the plugs?" He smirks.

"Even the plugs. Although there's no way anything any bigger than the second one is going inside of me."

"My dick is going in there soon."

"There's no way," I gasp.

"You can take it, maybe not today, but eventually I'm going to slide my hard cock all the way into your tight virgin ass and you'll love it. You'll beg and scream and come for me over and over and over."

"Nero." I shudder, excited by his husky words.

"I loved watching your ass stretch around that plug yesterday. It was one of the sexiest things I've ever fucking seen. Then pushing into your cunt and feeling how soaked you were, knowing it was because the plug had been edging you all night. Knowing that my dirty girl was plugged and stretched for me. It was fucking perfect."

My aching core twinges and I seriously consider climbing onto him to sate the itching lust he's just ignited in me. But before I have a chance, he rolls upright, unbinds our wrists and shuffles to the side of the bed, his long, hard cock bouncing against his stomach when he stands.

"Come on, Sunshine, let's go shower so I can feed you."

The rest of the day is a lesson in teasing. Barely there touches as he washes me in the shower. His knuckle scrapes over the side of my breast as he drapes his arm over my shoulder when we walk to the diner. The dirty words he whispers into my ear while we wait for our food to arrive.

Apparently, Nero is a huge fan of PDA. From the moment we leave my apartment to the time we get back, his hands never leave me, his lips claiming mine at every given opportunity. I've never been someone who felt the need to make out in the middle of the street, but with Nero, my self-control has left the building.

The moment his lips touch my ear, and his whispered voice tells me to be his dirty girl and spread my legs, I'm moving without even realizing it. Something about the way he affects me makes me feel like a puppet on strings, waiting for him to control me.

It's as exciting as it is terrifying because I'm not sure how far I'll allow him to push me—especially if, after only a couple of days, I'm already so consumed with his dominating control that it feels like I'm starting to crave the squirmy way he makes me feel.

Not that anything he's asked me to do has been that bad. He told me to forgo panties again after our shower and the idea of being naked beneath my leggings made my cheeks warm and my body tighten with excitement. When he pushed his finger into my mouth, then down the back of my pants to play with my ass while we sat in the booth at the diner, I honestly worried I might come, just from the knowledge that he was doing something so naughty in public.

He's kept me on edge the entire day, my cheeks pink with perpetual mild embarrassment. My stomach feels like a swarm of wasps has moved in, and the anxious anticipation of what comes next is so titillating it feels like I'm going to come out of my skin.

Before Nero, I never knew that foreplay could be such a mindfuck, and honestly, I don't hate it.

I'm also not unaware that while I'm vibrating with need, he's calm, relaxed and… at peace. Watching Nero Henderson smile, laugh, and just be happy is a beautiful thing. I don't know if it's a new feeling for him or if he's just been a miserable asshole because of the circumstance surrounding how we met. But today, he feels like a completely different person.

The moment we step into my apartment, I jump him, throwing myself into his arms and assuming he'll catch me as I press my mouth to his, kissing him like the world might end at any minute and I want to die with our lips joined. His tongue in my mouth.

His arms band around me, tight and sure, and he kisses me back. But unlike me, he's not wound tight. He's relaxed and amused, his mouth smiling even as we kiss. "Sunshine." He chuckles, dragging his lips from mine.

"Need you," I pant between wet kisses.

"What do you need?" A hint of that sexy, gruff rasp fills his voice and I kiss him harder, needing to be closer to him to relieve the itch that only he can scratch.

"I need you to fuck me."

"You're sore."

"I'll be fine."

"Sunshine, I take care of what's mine. I'm not going to ruin your perfect pussy just because you're needy. I'll fuck you later. After you've had a soak in the tub."

"I don't have a tub," I whine. "Fuck me now."

"We have a tub at home. Grab some stuff and we'll go home before the barbeque."

"Nero," I moan into his ear, pressing my lips to the pulse point in his neck. "Please."

"When we get home, I'll eat your pussy until you're dripping, but I'm not fucking you until later."

The hand holding my weight beneath my butt slides inside my leggings and toys with my ass. "I need to check to make sure you're not too sore here too," he purrs, his honeyed rasp making me shudder as the tip of his finger presses against my hole.

My lips part and he pushes his tongue into my mouth, kissing me while he toys with my ass, not pushing inside, just rubbing circles over the sensitive skin. My needy pussy twinges with jealousy and I wiggle in his arms.

"My ass is fine, but my pussy is feeling a little neglected," I pant against his mouth.

"Don't worry, your pussy is going to get plenty of my attention later. I'm going to fill her up with my cum all night, and any that tries to escape, I'm going to push into your ass. I want every single one of your holes so full of me it's dripping out of you all day long tomorrow."

God, this man and his filthy mouth.

"Jesus, I love watching your cheeks turn pink," he snarls, lowering me to the floor and holding me until he's sure my feet are steady.

"Pull down your leggings."

Hooking my thumbs into the waist, I push them down.

"Stop."

The fabric is bunched at my knees, but I freeze, half–bent over, my pussy naked and on display.

"Show me how wet you are," he orders.

Curling back upright, the familiar wash of humiliated anticipation fills me, and I shudder in response. Sliding my fingers between my folds, I feel the slickness of my own arousal coating my skin.

"Show me," he demands, a hint of impatience and desperation slipping into his tone.

Lifting my hand up, I show him my wet fingers.

"Fucking perfect." He smiles, curling his palm around my wrist and bringing my fingers to his lips. The warm wetness of his mouth surrounds my fingers as his tongue laves the skin, sucking all of my arousal from them.

Releasing my fingers, he uncurls his palm from my wrist, then slowly drops to his knees at my feet. I expect him to dive on me, to attack me with his fingers and tongue, but instead, he shuffles forward until his face is level with my sex.

Holding my hip with one hand, he separates my folds

with the other, looking at me almost clinically. "You like it when I talk dirty to you. When I tell you all the filthy things I plan to do to you, don't you?"

"Yes," I say, my voice barely a whisper as I hold my breath, eager for the first swipe of his tongue.

"Have I told you how pretty your pussy is? Pink and swollen and always so wet. I bet your cunt knew exactly who it belonged to, even before I realized it. Did you argue with me, then slip into your princess bed and fuck yourself with one of your toys, pretending it was me?"

I shake my head. "No."

"What about after we kissed? After I freaked out and left. Did you slide your fingers as deep into your cunt as you could reach and wish it was me?"

"No," I deny, but it's a lie.

"Liar. I walked past your room and I heard you. I heard your moans, heard you coming through the door."

I flush from my hairline all the way down my body. The idea that he heard me making myself come in the shower is almost too much to bear.

"Jesus, your cunt just got wetter. Tell me what you were doing, what you were thinking when you made yourself come loud enough for me to hear you as I walked past."

"I was." I swallow thickly. "I was in the shower."

"Tell me," he demands.

"I used the showerhead," I admit.

A soft chuckle fills the air. "Did it feel good? The water pulsing against your little clit and empty pussy."

Nodding, I fight the urge to move, to squeeze my thighs together or grab his hand and force it where I need it. Instead,

I tense my muscles and stay still, both hating and loving the sense of helplessness that's almost overwhelming me.

"Do you want that now, to feel the hot water gushing inside of you?"

"No." I shake my head.

"I'd let you do it. I'd stand and watch while you made yourself come, but I wouldn't touch. It'd be all you."

"No." I shake my head more emphatically. "I want you. Please." I'm not quite begging, but it wouldn't take much more from him to have me telling him anything he wants to hear just to get him to touch me, to relieve the pressure he's building with his words.

"Fuck, you're getting wetter and wetter. I've never watched it happen before, watched a cunt get ready to be fucked. That's what you need, isn't it? To be filled with my big, hard cock, to be stretched and fucked until I give you my cum."

"Yes, please, please." Okay, now I'm begging, but I'm so tightly wound I don't care about pride or self-control. Right now, I just want him.

"Let's go home, I won't hurt you and after how many times you took my cock yesterday, I won't risk it, not yet."

His words act like a bucket of cold water being poured over my head. My heart sinks and angry, humiliated tears fill my eyes, only it's not the fun, sexy kind of humiliation we've been playing with as foreplay. This is the mean, heavy humiliation that settles over me and makes me want to kick him the hell out of my apartment.

Stumbling backward, I brush his hands away when he reaches for me, then pull up my panties and leggings, ignoring his pointed gaze.

"Hey," he calls, rising to his feet and stalking toward me. "What the fuck?"

Turning, I head for the bathroom, ignoring him.

"Tori."

I feel more than hear him follow me and when I try to close the bathroom door, he pushes it open and steps inside, making the small room feel even smaller.

"What is happening right now?" he demands.

"Nothing. I need to pee," I blurt, saying the first thing that pops into my head.

"So pee," he says, crossing his arms over his chest. His legs are shoulder width apart and he looks like a soldier, braced and ready for attack, but his face isn't calm. It's full of turbulent emotion.

"Get out, I can't pee with you watching."

"No."

"No. No what?"

"Something just happened. You need to explain what it was. You were hot as fucking hell; your cunt was dripping with arousal and now you're like an ice block, but there are tears in your eyes. So tell me, what the fuck just happened?"

"Nothing happened," I say as breezily as I can muster. "I need to get ready. What time did you say we need to be at the barbeque?"

"Fuck the barbeque. We're not leaving this apartment until you tell me what the hell just happened."

"It's whatever, I just don't like this game."

"What game?" he asks, his eyes narrowed. His voice so low it's almost gravelly.

"The one where I beg you to fuck me and you tell me you're not interested," I snap, blinking away the stupid angry tears that keep filling my eyes.

"Sunshine," he growls, snapping his hand out and palming the back of my neck.

"No," I yell, fighting to get away from his grip on me. "Let me go."

Instead of releasing me, he captures my face with his other hand, forcing me to look up at him. "Tori, there hasn't been a moment since the first time I kissed you that I haven't wanted you. I crave you from the moment I open my eyes to the moment I fall asleep and even then, I dream of you. I'm never, *never* not interested and if you ever doubt that, all you need to do is look down at how hard my dick is for you."

My muscles unclench a little as I blink, staring up at him, trying to find the lie in his gaze, but it's not there.

"I'm sorry," he whispers, stroking my cheek with his thumb. "I took it too far. I thought you'd enjoy being edged until we got home, but I pushed too hard. Let me make it up to you."

Shaking my head, I try to turn away from him, but his hold firms, not allowing me to. Humiliation is still shrouding me, like a heavy weight that's settled on my shoulders, making me want to curl in on myself to hide from him.

"Sunshine, look at me, don't try to turn away. We don't do that. Scream at me, shout, yell, whatever you need, but don't walk away."

"It's fine. I overreacted," I say dismissively.

"No. We don't do that, either. We don't pretend

something that's upset one of us is nothing. That's not how this is going to go between us. So be fucking honest and tell me how I fucked up. I'm man enough to want to learn how not to fuck things up in the future."

Clearing my throat, I sigh, then swallow, wasting time as I try to figure out what to even say. "I didn't like you rejecting me," I finally spit out, ugly embarrassment adding to the humiliation already settled in my gut.

"I need you to listen to me right now, Tori. Can you do that? Can you listen and really hear what I'm about to say?"

I don't want to. I want to leave, to block out his words and hide from the reality of being in a crazy, intense relationship with a man I barely know. But I don't. Instead, I nod, locking my gaze with his and wait.

"I didn't reject you. I'll never reject you, and I hate that I made you feel like I did, even for a second. I'm so fucking sorry. I want you so much it scares the hell out of me and I'm terrified that when I have to go back to work, you'll convince yourself that we're not together anymore, and I'll come home to you thinking you're not mine."

Opening my mouth, I wait for some words to come out, but they don't and we just stare at each other, lost in this incredibly honest moment. This feels like the first time we've shared something real that wasn't physical and I'm not sure how to handle it.

"Do you forgive me?"

I think about it for a second, weighing the words, before I nod. "Okay."

"That wasn't convincing," he says with a soft smile.

"I forgive you."

Instead of smiling like I'm expecting, his brow furrows. "Are you okay?"

"I'll be fine. It's been a crazy couple of days."

"Crazy good though." Taking a step closer, he slides the hand on the back of my neck down to settle at the base of my spine, pulling me in until our bodies are pressed together.

"We really do need to get ready," I say, exhaling and letting myself melt into him, not fighting his hold.

"Grab some stuff and we'll head home and stay there tonight. You can soak in the tub, then we can walk to Juni's and neither of us needs to worry about driving."

His tone is so careful and gentle that I nod, even though it feels strange to think about staying in his room at the house. The next hour is achingly polite. I pack a small overnight case while he follows me from room to room like he's keeping me literally within arm's reach, so I can't put any kind of metaphorical or physical distance between us.

The drive up the mountain is quiet and although we make small talk, it's stilted and awkward. The moment Nero unlocks the front door to the house and we step inside, he exhales and I watch the tension literally melt off him.

"Come on, I'll run you a bath. I'm sure I have some Epsom salts to put in it for you."

"I'm not that sore. You don't need to treat me like I'm injured," I snap.

"That pussy belongs to me. I take care of my things," he says, his eyes hooded and achingly serious.

"I'm not a possession."

"Yes, you are. You're my woman, my most valuable possession."

Even though his statement is utterly ridiculous and borderline offensive, I can't help but swoon a little at how utterly caveman a thing to say it is.

I'm smiling as I follow him up the stairs that, until a few days ago, led to the bedroom I used as my own. I don't know why I expect anything to look different than it did when I left, but of course, it doesn't. I half expect him to take me to the bathroom in my old room, but instead, he leads me to the family bathroom, opening the door and stepping inside.

Leaning over the tub, he pushes in the plug and turns on the faucet. He keeps his hand under the stream of water until he's happy with the temperature, then he straightens and moves to the medicine cabinet, opening it and rooting around until he turns back around with a bag of Epsom salts in his hand.

My eyes follow the way he moves. Considering he's such a big guy, his body isn't clunky or awkward. Nero is all fluid grace, every action purposeful and deliberate and I'm mesmerized watching him.

Pushing his hand into the bag, he pulls out a handful of salts and sprinkles them into the water. Repeating the action, he evenly distributes the salt across the water filling in the tub, then puts the bag back into the cabinet, closing it.

"I'll leave you to it. The towels are all clean. Shout if you need anything."

My jaw hits the floor, but before I can compose myself enough to ask him, *What the actual fuck?* he's gone. The door glides gently closed until I'm alone, the rushing water the only sound in the room, except the screaming in my head.

A part of me expects him to come back, to stride right back into the room, like he has every right to walk into the bathroom with me. When he suggested the bath, I'd assumed I wouldn't be taking it alone, but he never even looked back longingly before he was out the door and leaving me in here by myself.

Dropping my bag to the floor, I strip out of my clothes and climb into the hot water. I hiss through my teeth at the heat for a second before my body acclimatizes to the temperature and I sit down, exhaling a sigh of ecstasy when I'm submerged in the restorative liquid.

The water is quickly rising around me, but I close my eyes and let my head fall back against the back of the tub. I might not be fragile, but there's no doubt that the hot water does feel amazing, and I allow my muscles to relax in a way they haven't since Nero burst into my apartment shouting my name two days ago.

Has it only been two days? It feels like months ago since my roommate slash one-night stand snuck into my home and refused to leave until I agreed to be his. No wonder I'm wound so tightly. In less than forty-eight hours, Nero has turned my world upside down, but I already feel a little adrift without his constant presence.

Nero has an aura that's so still it somehow feels almost loud in its silence. In the short time we lived in this house together, I never noticed how all-consuming his attention was because I invested so much effort into avoiding him. Now that his eyes have been on me constantly for days, being alone and without his attention is jarring.

I have never in my life needed a man, and I can and

will cope without him, but I can't help feeling like maybe everything would feel better if he were here with me. This bath would be more fun if he were in it with me, teasing me and playing with me. Hell, even having him sitting on the counter asking me random questions about cooking, my family, or the bakery would make my erratic thoughts slow.

How, in only two days, have I become the woman who craves her boyfriend's company in all aspects of her life? Was it only yesterday morning that I was questioning his motives and honestly wondering if he was just using me for sex to stop me from starting a relationship with any of his teammates?

I'm pretty confident, with all the *mine* talk, that stopping me from fucking his buddies isn't the reason he's stuck to me like glue. Making sure everyone we've seen or spoken to knows that we're together. I may not have ever dated a real alpha male before, but I've read enough romance novels to have a pretty good idea that he isn't just here for the sex.

But if I look past all the orgasms and the man who I think could be equally capable of being a sweetheart as he is of being an asshole, there's still the issue that the reason our living together didn't work. He doesn't like me, and I don't see how adding sex into the mix has changed that.

I ponder that as I luxuriate in the tub, swishing my toes around and watching the ripples move across the water. Do I hope that our relationship develops to a point where he learns to like me? I'm not sure any successful relationship can be built on the basis of learning to tolerate each other. But what's the alternative? As much as I've run and fought getting to this point, here I am, tied to him in a way I never anticipated.

My mind is full of thoughts of him when there's a knock at the door. Brow furrowed, I look around me like the empty bathroom can answer the question of why the man who literally broke into my apartment is suddenly politely knocking at the door and waiting to be invited in.

"Nero?" I call.

"Can I…" He clears his throat. "Can I come in?"

What the hell is going on? We've been "together" for two days and I already know that Nero Henderson isn't the type of man who asks for permission, so why is he doing it now?

"Sure," I call, wondering if I should try to cover myself up or if maybe he assumes I'll be done by now?

The handle turns and Nero cautiously pushes open the door and takes a single step inside. "I thought you might like a glass of wine," he says, his eyes downcast and… pouty?

"What is happening right now?" I ask.

"Excuse me?"

"I asked what the hell is happening right now?"

"I brought you a glass of wine, Tori. I'm not sure what's got you all riled up."

"Fuck the wine, Nero. I'm asking what is going on with you? You knocked."

"You're acting like this because I have manners?" he asks, incredulous.

"In the past two days, you've broken the front door of my store, barging in and demanding to see me. You've stormed your way to my apartment and been escorted out by the cops. You've broken back into my home and hidden out in my bedroom, then refused to leave. You've spanked me, fucked me, put a plug in my ass and become a full-grown Neanderthal on more occasions than I can list. So, forgive me for wondering if you've been kidnapped by pod people when all of a sudden you decide to respect any of my boundaries and fucking knock." I'm breathing hard by the time I've finished, but oddly, I feel better having gotten all of that off my chest.

I'm not as angry about any of the things I just mentioned as I should be, but making sure he knows that I know none of this is normal is a relief.

"Excuse me for thinking you might like a little space after…" Pausing, he swallows. "After what happened earlier."

"So, because you upset me, you plan to tiptoe around me like we're polite, normal people?" I snap.

"Yes, because contrary to what you seem to think, I fucking hate that I upset you, and I don't want to do it again," he snarls, anger flaring to life in his eyes.

"So that's it? Caveman Nero is gone and now I have a new polite stranger to deal with?"

"What the fuck do you want from me, Tori? The way we've been behaving, me doing everything I can to make your cheeks go pink and that look of desperate humiliation glow brightly in your eyes. That's fun, but it's not worth seeing the lust fade and tears fucking replace it."

"Seriously? So, from now on, we're going to have nice, missionary sex while we avoid each other's gazes and pretend we're enjoying it?"

His eyes narrow and his jaw tenses, a muscle twitching

in his neck. "Yes, if that's what you want."

Standing up, I ignore the water that's dripping from my body and how very naked I am. "No thanks."

"I'm sorry?"

"You heard me. I said if that's what you're offering, then no thanks, I'm not interested."

"I must have misheard you?" he growls.

"I doubt it. I was endlessly polite when I said. No. Thanks. Before you, maybe I'd have taken you up on polite and normal. But not now. If that's all you're offering, then I'm not interested."

"Let me get this clear. You don't want polite?" he asks slowly.

"No."

"You don't want normal?"

I shake my head. "No."

"Then what exactly do you want?"

"I want everything we've been doing since you hid in my bedroom."

"You want me to humiliate you, to degrade you, to decide when and where and how many times you come. To spank your ass and pull your hair and control you?"

There's every chance I'll regret this argument when I'm not feeling so frustrated, but if I do, then it'll be worth any heartbreak I feel because now I know what it's like to have everything he just described. I don't think I can go back to boring, predictable vanilla. "Yes," I say decisively.

Blinking slowly, he lifts his chin, rolls his shoulders back and straightens to his impressively intimidating height. "You want to be a toy? Mine to play with?"

"Yes," I breathe, feeling some of the weight fall from my shoulders.

His blink is so unhurried it's like he's been put in slow motion. Then he smirks. It's not a smile, the corners of his lips barely tipping up at the sides. But I see it and I brace myself for what I just begged him to do.

"On your knees." He points at the floor at his feet. "Here."

Hopping over the side of the tub with about as much poise as a hippo wearing roller skates, I sink gracelessly down to the floor, water dripping from me and soaking the tile.

"Open your mouth and stick out your tongue."

I pause for a fraction of a second, allowing the buzz of embarrassment from his words to settle over me, then I open my mouth and push my tongue forward.

"Such a good girl," he praises. "I'm going to feed you my cock and you're going to suck me until I come down your pretty little throat. When you've swallowed everything I've given you, you're going to stand up, turn around, and bend over. Then you're going to reach back and spread your ass so I can check your tight little hole to make sure the plug I filled you with didn't hurt you."

Not waiting for me to agree or say anything, he unbuckles his belt, slides down his zipper and feeds his cock into my open mouth. Just like the last time I sucked his dick, he tastes clean and smells like soap and Nero.

Part of me expects him to take over and fuck my face, but he doesn't. Instead, he watches me intently, his gaze silently demanding. I keep my eyes on his as I suck the head, tasting his precum and swallowing hard as his flavor fills my mouth. His hands remain at his sides; he's not controlling my movements or dictating how I touch him. He's almost relaxed and nonchalant as he watches me suck on his cock like it's my favorite popsicle. If it wasn't for the barely visible tic in the muscle in his jaw that lets me know he's not as calm as he's pretending to be, I'd think he wasn't bothered about me being down here, but that tiny facial twitch gives him away. Sucking harder, I pull his cock farther into my mouth until the head is perilously close to the back of my throat.

The feeling of being on my knees, yet completely in control of this strong, intense man, is illuminating, but I'm not a porn star and I have a very real gag reflex. I don't try to pretend a competence at deep throating that I don't have, and instead, I wrap my hand around the base of his cock, moving my fist in time with my head, bobbing up and down until Nero's breathing becomes ragged and I hear him cursing beneath his breath.

"Fucking hell, I'm going to come and you're going to take it all," he rasps, finally grabbing the back of my head and holding me in place while his hips stutter forward and hot, salty come fills my mouth.

"Don't swallow yet," he orders, slowly sliding his cock from between my lips. Releasing my head, he lifts my chin with his finger. "Show me."

I don't know why, but his order makes my cheeks burn with such intense heat that I can barely look him in the eye when I part my lips and show him my mouth full of his cum.

"Fuck," he growls. "Such a filthy fucking girl. Swallow

me down."

I swallow, doing my best to hide the grimace as the taste of his cum coats my throat.

"Fucking perfect, but you forgot some." Dragging a fingertip up my chin, he catches some cum that's dripped from my mouth and pushes his finger between my lips.

Running my tongue over his finger, I lick off his cum and swallow it down with the rest of him that's now filling my stomach. Our gazes are still locked, but instead of the calm, relaxed look from a few minutes ago, his eyes are blazing with heat, fire and want.

Ripping his finger from between my lips, he grabs me under my arms and lifts me to my feet, turning me around so I'm facing the tub, my back to him.

"Bend over, pull your cheeks apart."

He told me he was going to do this, but I still feel the squirmy sensation of humiliation when I bend forward, reaching back and pulling my butt cheeks apart, exposing myself to him.

"Jesus, Sunshine," he rasps.

I don't see him move, but I feel the heat of his body behind me.

"How does this tight little asshole feel? Sore?"

Jumping, I let out a squeak when I feel something cool coat my hole.

"I'm fine," I pant.

"I can't wait to fuck this virgin hole. I love making your cunt mine every time I fill it with my cum, but I think I might like claiming your ass even more. Thinking about watching your tight muscles stretching around my cock makes me so hard."

I hear the sound of a lid popping and tense, jolting when cool lube dribbles onto me. The blunt end of his finger rubs the lube in, pressing gently until the tip breaches me, sliding into my ass.

"How does that feel? Any pain?"

"No," I gasp.

Slowly, carefully, he fucks my ass with his slippery finger until I'm pushing back into him, arousal building inside of me.

"Stop moving, dirty girl. Just stand there and take what I'm giving you."

A second finger joins the first and I whine at the stretch, a burning sensation smothering the pleasure.

"Relax. Let your body take me," he coaxes, his other hand curling around my hip to toy with my clit.

Rubbing my clit in gentle circles, he fucks my ass with two fingers, and as the pleasure builds, my mind struggles to differentiate between the fullness in my ass and the tingly feeling of him playing with my clit. When I come, it's a full-body experience, starting in my toes and rushing through my limbs until my vision turns white and I scream.

"Easy, Sunshine," Nero coos, catching me around the waist when my knees buckle.

"Oh my god," I rasp.

I feel rather than hear him chuckle against my neck. "You're fucking perfect for me, Tori."

"That was…" I pause, panting. "That was, Jesus, I don't even know what that was."

"Hot, it was fucking scorching, that's what it was. Did

you finish in the tub?" He chuckles.

"No, I got distracted."

Leaning us forward, he dips his hand into the water. "It's still warm if you want to get back in."

"Are you getting in with me?"

"If you want me to."

The moment I nod, my feet are dangling in the air as Nero lifts me off the floor and lowers me into the water. Sitting down, I shuffle forward and make room for him to get in behind me. Wrapping my arms around my knees, I turn so I can watch him pull his shirt over his head and kick his pants off his feet. When he's completely naked, acres of toned, firm, bare skin on display, he steps over the edge of the tub and sits down behind me. It's a tight fit, so Nero lifts me up, pushing his legs down flat and sitting me on his lap.

When I asked him to get in with me, I had these romantic notions of us twisted together, but the reality is that the tub is too small for us to both fit in here comfortably and I don't really know where to put myself.

"Lean back," Nero says, wrapping his arm around my waist and pulling me backward until my back is resting against his chest, my head against his shoulder.

Exhaling, I allow my muscles to relax. "This is weird." I giggle.

"I quite like it," he says, cupping my breast.

"You just like me being permanently red-cheeked," I scoff.

"True." I feel him shrug.

"Are we weird? Is what we do really fucked up?" I ask, a hint of panic leaking into my voice.

"Tori, there's nothing fucked up or weird about anything we do together. You like it when I dirty talk and embarrass you, and I like talking dirty to you and seeing how red and squirmy I can make you. On the grand scale of kinkiness, I'd say we're only a couple of steps up from vanilla."

Hmm, I guess I never really thought of it like that. In my head, enjoying him calling me slightly degrading names and humiliating me felt much bigger, like I was a deviant enjoying things that would make others cringe.

Maybe other people might not be into the same things we are, but that's okay. I've never condemned nor looked down on James for wanting to cede control to Buck. In fact, I gave her a whole speech about why it was okay to want what she wanted and not be ashamed of it, so why can't I allow myself the same amount of grace?

"We need to talk about what happened earlier."

"No, we don't. I had a moment, but I'm fine," I say quickly.

"Was it just me saying no to fucking you, or was it all of it? The things I said, the way I touched you. I don't want you to feel that way again. I don't want you to shut down and I won't let you walk away, so I need to know what I did to trigger you."

"I don't know what it was."

"You were with me, then you weren't. Something tipped you from needy and begging to tears, Sunshine," he says, his tone so soft my eyes fill with tears again.

Sighing, I exhale. "The last few days have just been a lot and sometimes I get in my head. I don't love the way you were edging me, but when I begged and you just said no…

You were so calm and I was such a mess and it just felt like you were playing me, not playing with me," I confess.

Soft, wet fingers hook my chin, gently turning my face until I'm looking back at him. "I wasn't calm, Tori. I haven't been calm since the first time I kissed you. You've bewitched me, ensnared me, you fucking own me. I might have a good poker face, but never mistake me for calm because the moment I touch you, I'm fucking crazed. I want you all day, every day. I wake up hard for you, tasting you, smelling you, desperate for you. After the first night waking up alone, all I think about is you. I'm obsessed with you, Tori, and I need to make you as obsessed with me."

"You're obsessed with me?" I whisper.

"Utterly, completely, consumedly."

My mouth forms an *o* shape, but no sound comes out. Warmth builds in my chest, but instead of traveling to my cheeks, it stays put, surrounding my heart with a barrier of… hope? I'm not in love with Nero, not yet. It's too new, but his words and the way he opened himself up, confessing that he wants me in a way that overwhelms him the same way he overwhelms me, has changed things.

I've been treating this thing between us like a game, assuming, at some point, the timer will run out and we'd both go back to the start, but maybe that was wrong. If this is a game, it's one I think we're both playing to win and instead of control or power, the prize is forever.

Chapter Twenty-nine

Nero

We soak in the bath for another thirty minutes, neither of us really saying anything, but the silence is comfortable, not awkward. Something has happened since Tori got upset earlier. I don't know if it's both of us being truly fucking honest or just gaining a deeper understanding of one another, but whatever it is, I like it.

From the moment I pulled up outside the house she and James used to share the day I met her, I had this preconceived notion about who Tori was. I thought she was loud, perpetually cheerful, annoyingly upbeat and, honestly, kind of shallow. I assumed her sunshiny nature was a way for her to hide the fact that she wasn't deep enough to look beyond herself, and now I'm starting to understand just how wrong I was.

There is nothing shallow about Tori and the fact that I ever assumed there was shows that I really am the judgy asshole that she accused me of being. I shouldn't use Miranda as an excuse for my behavior, but our relationship was utter bullshit. She used honesty as a way of hiding. She'd tell you a truth, then pretend it was fantasy, and I wasn't invested enough to try to untangle what she really wanted until she literally slapped me in the face with it.

I've been treating Tori like she was Miranda and when she said she thought I was playing her, a small part of me might have been. I made the assumption that her upbeat nature was fake, but it's not. She's just a cheerful person, or she was until I invaded her life. Since I barged my way into her work and home, I've barely seen the happy-go-lucky woman from the day I met her, and that's my fault.

I made no effort to get to know her and even less to show her that I didn't hate her. Fuck, I told her I disliked her, but I still wanted to fuck her. Jesus, I really am an asshole!

I've made Tori's body crave me. I know she wants me physically, but I've done nothing to make her need me, the person, not me, the hard dick.

But what the hell do I do now? I have to go back to work tomorrow.

Buck showered James with food and care packages while he was away from her, but Tori's a chef; she won't appreciate me sending her food. And she already has a drawer full of sex toys that I've banned her from using when I'm not there.

This almost overwhelming cloud of dread lands on my shoulders, and once again, I wonder if I can come inside her enough to beat the odds and get her pregnant. At least if I tie her to me, I'm guaranteed enough time to show her I'm not the asshole she thinks I am.

"Do you think I'm an asshole?" I blurt.

"What?"

"Do you think I'm an asshole?"

"Yes." She chuckles. "Do you still hate me?" she asks cautiously.

"I never hated you. I tried to, but it was just because I wanted you and I didn't understand it." The words fall from me in a rush.

"You told me you didn't like me but that you still wanted me."

Exhaling, I admit, "I know."

Fuck, I need someone to tell me how to fix this clusterfuck I've created. Physically, we're a perfect match, but everything else is so messed up. I need to show her that I love her noise, her smiles, her laugh, that I want every single sound that falls from her perfect lips. But more than anything, I need to prove that I'm not the asshole that she thinks she's stuck with.

I told her she's mine, and she is. Indisputably mine, but I want to be hers, and I have no idea how to make that happen.

"We should get ready," she says with a weary sigh.

"Yeah," I agree.

When I asked Juni to host this get-together yesterday, all I was thinking about was making sure every member of my team saw Tori and me together. I wanted to piss in a circle around my woman and make sure everyone knew she was off-limits, but now I wish I'd never said anything and just kept her to myself.

Being around other people isn't going to help me convince her I'm not an asshole. In fact, it's probably more likely to help confirm my asshole status when I snarl and growl at anyone that tries to get too close or touch her.

This was such a stupid idea, but I can't cancel now, not when I was the one who suggested this barbeque in the first place.

Climbing out of the bath, I lift her out, then wrap her in a towel, doing my best not to let my eyes linger on the water dripping from her pebbled nipples or how wet her cunt is.

"What did you bring to wear?" I ask her when we step into the bedroom.

"Oh, I left my bag in the bathroom. I'll go grab it."

"You get dry, I'll get it."

Still dripping water, I pad across the hall to the bathroom and grab her bag. Carrying it into my room, I place it down on the bed and immediately unzip it so I can see what she has inside.

"Fuck," I hiss between gritted teeth, lifting out tiny fucking denim shorts. "What the hell are these?"

"Shorts," she says with a faux-innocent smile.

"You're not wearing these," I growl.

"I am because I didn't bring anything else." She smirks, arching a brow in challenge.

My eyes narrow and I look back to the bag, pulling out a lightweight sweater, some makeup and nothing else.

"Where the hell is your underwear?"

"I figured you wouldn't let me wear them, so I didn't

bother bringing any." She shrugs, her gaze daring me to argue.

"Are you looking to get fucked and spanked? Did you want to wear these tiny fucking shorts so you could show off your red ass from my hand and your wet cunt full of my cum?"

All thoughts of civility, of proving to her that I'm not the asshole she thinks I am, evaporate. There's no way I can let her go out wearing those fucking shorts without branding her body so everyone will know she belongs to me.

"Yes," she says, smiling the biggest smile I've seen on her face since the day we met.

Moments later, she's impaled on my cock, leaning forward, riding me hard and fast while I spank her ass and the tops of her thighs. We come together, her shrill scream mingling with my own growl of release. It's messy, noisy, primal, and fucking perfect.

Rolling us to the side, I pull my dick free from her cunt, then tip her onto her back, sliding my fingers back inside her sex and pushing all of my cum back into her.

"This is all yours, I've filled up this tight little cunt just like you wanted, but now you have to keep me inside of you. You don't get to clean up, and in those tiny fucking shorts, everyone will see if you let my cum drip out of you."

"Nero," she gasps. "I can't."

"You will. You wanted to tease me into fucking you. Now you'll go to my sister's with your cunt full of my cum. If you feel like you can't hold it all inside, then you'll ask me to finger fuck any that's trying to get free into your ass."

"Nero." Her cheeks are a delicious shade of red, almost

the same color as her ass.

"Come on, Sunshine, let's get you dressed." Climbing off the bed, I grab hold of her hips and lift her, placing her on her feet.

"Oh god, Nero, I can't go out like this."

"Then you know what to do. I fucked so much of my seed into you, I'll bet it'll be dripping out of you for hours." This time, I'm the one to smirk, and her blush only deepens, the color spreading down her neck to her chest.

"Can't I just clean up?"

"Nope." I pop the letter *p*.

"Nero," she whines.

"I bet you're wishing you'd brought some panties right about now, aren't you?"

Her eyes widen and she looks between her legs where a pebble of cum is rolling down the inside of her thigh.

"Naughty girl, you're letting my gift escape. What do you need to ask me?"

"Will you…" She swallows thickly. "Will you fuck your cum into my ass?"

"Of course," I tell her with a predatory smile. "Bend over."

Bracing her hands on the mattress, I collect the line of cum from her thigh, dipping my fingers into her soaked pussy, then push them into her ass. She's still stretched from earlier and her ass opens easily, accepting my fingers and the cum I'm pushing into her.

"Good girl, you're such a good girl, asking me to finger fuck your ass. Soon you'll beg me to bury my cock in here. You'll ask over and over for me to claim this hole and fill it with my cum until all of your holes are so full of me that my cum will be all you smell and taste."

She comes on a startled cry, her ass tightening and clenching around my fingers.

After washing my hands, I dress quickly, then sit back on the bed and watch Tori get ready. The sexy blush on her face never fades, and she begs me twice more to push the cum that's dripping down her thighs back into her ass. By the time we're ready to leave, my cock is so hard, I'm worried I'll come in my pants if I turn too quickly, but I ignore my need, content to edge myself the way I edged her earlier. I plan to spend all night inside of her, so I can keep my dick to myself for an hour or so.

"I can't believe you spanked me hard enough that my ass and thighs are still red," she hisses, looking at herself in the mirror and cringing when she sees how pink the skin that's visible beneath the hem of her stupidly short shorts is.

"If you were wearing more clothes, no one would be able to see. You put my ass on display, I made sure anyone looking knows it belongs to me."

"You're such an asshole," she moans, but she's smiling.

Internally, I cringe at the word. She's right, I am an asshole. Less than two hours ago, I was promising myself that I'd figure out a way to make her want me, need me, and like me. Instead, I fucked her, spanked her, filled her with my cum, then played with her ass three times, all while she squirmed with delicious embarrassment. All of that might have made us both feel good, but none of it did anything to make her like me any more.

Intent on being the perfect gentleman until we get back

home later, I resist the urge to palm her ass as we walk up the hill to my sister's place and instead drape my arm over her shoulders.

As always, the Barnett house is full when we get there. With so many people living here, it's hectic all the time when everyone is home, but when you add in everyone's family and friends, even the enormous house feels packed.

"Nero, Tori," my sister calls the moment we step onto the patio.

"Hey, little sis. Jesus, you popped. When the hell did that happen?" I gasp, seeing the very visible baby bump that wasn't there the last time I visited.

"The ob-gyn says my body recognizes that I'm pregnant and has settled right back into baby-building mode. I still think I could be having twins though." She laughs.

"Twins!" Tori laughs. "Oh my god, I'd die."

My sister waves her hand dismissively. "Teddy wants a brood. Having two at a time would just mean it's one less pregnancy I have to go through. But I don't care how many are in here as long as they're healthy."

"Wow, a brood, you're braver than me." Tori laughs.

"You don't want kids?" I ask her, my heart racing behind my ribs.

Panic flashes across her face, then she shrugs. "I mean, I don't know."

"I want kids," I say decisively. "With you," I clarify.

"You want kids… with me?" she repeats.

"Yes. Soon. Now." Fuck, it's like I have verbal diarrhea.

"Now?"

"Yes."

"Oh." Her mouth moves, but barely any sound comes out.

"Hi, Tori, welcome to the family," Juni blurts, flashing me a WTF look before she pulls Tori in for a hug.

My dick twitches in my pants at the idea of Tori pregnant with my baby, but I silently urge it to chill the fuck out and wait with gritted teeth while my sister hugs my woman. Obviously, I'm not jealous or worried about my pregnant sister making a play for my girlfriend, but apparently, I don't like anyone touching what's mine, regardless of how much of a threat they are.

The moment they release each other, I curl my arm around Tori's waist and drag her back to me until her back is pressed against my chest.

"I'm so happy for you guys," Juni gushes, then promptly bursts into tears.

Tori's eyes go saucer wide and she looks at me like she expects me to do something. But before I have a chance, Teddy stalks through the throngs of people, hands my nephew Austin to me and pulls Juni into him.

I coo at Austin, making him giggle, while Teddy soothes Juni, whispering to her and wiping her tears away with his thumbs.

"Sorry." She half sobs, half laughs. "These baby hormones are making me crazy."

"Are you okay?" Tori asks worriedly.

"I'm fine," Juni says, smiling. "I'm just so happy for you both." More tears run down her cheeks and she turns and smacks Teddy's chest. "This is your fault. You must have put more than one baby in me this time to make me this crazy." Reaching for Austin, she props him on her hip, then stomps away.

"I should…" Teddy points in the direction his wife just went and strides after her.

"That was…" Tori trails off, clearly struggling to find a word to describe my sister's pregnancy craziness.

"Insane." I laugh.

"Really, really insane. Will she be like that for the whole nine months?" she asks with a slightly horrified expression.

"I doubt it. Last time, she was super emotional in the first trimester and then right before she gave birth, the rest of the time, she was one of those women who glow. I'm not surprised Teddy knocked her up again so soon." I shrug, then I envisage again how Tori would look pregnant with my kid.

My dick twitches and I vow to delete the reminder on her cell for her next birth control shot and put my baby in her instead.

"Let's grab a drink," I say, clearing my throat and pushing down the urge to drag her off and fuck her until the chemicals still lingering in her body and stopping my seed from taking root are put to the test.

I spot a few of my teammates, but I don't stop to speak to them, guiding Tori into the house and toward the makeshift bar that Cody is manning.

"You want wine?" I ask her.

"Please, unless they have margaritas again. They were so good the last time I was here."

"Hey guys," Cody says with a smile.

"Cody."

"Thank you again for fitting the locks on my doors. Any news on when the glass will be in for the store?" Tori asks him.

"Should be tomorrow or Tuesday, but I'll let you know as soon as we have it. I'll drop off the paint charts so you can pick a color too," Cody tells her.

"Oh, awesome, thanks. Anything to get rid of the hideous beige," she says with a dramatic cringe.

Gritting my teeth, I fight not to lose my shit and demand she stop looking or speaking to Cody. The man is happily married and completely devoted to his wife, Betty, but my fucked- up brain doesn't care. All it knows is that I'm not secure enough in my connection with Tori not to worry about her finding someone she likes better than me. Someone she doesn't think is an asshole.

Cody makes our drinks and we say goodbye and walk away, drifting over to where my team is sitting with Beau, Bonnie, Granger, and Alice. There's an empty seat, so I sit down, pulling Tori into my lap.

Alice is heavily pregnant, but she's still curled into Granger's lap, his hand resting on her stomach, her head resting on his chest. Beau's arm is curled protectively around Bonnie and although they're side by side, they're so close she might as well be in his lap.

"Hey guys," Bonnie says, looking at Tori and smirking. "Another one bites the dust, huh? I didn't really believe it when Beau said the Barnett legacy had moved on to you guys, but with Buck falling hard for James and now you pair, maybe it is true." She giggles.

"What the hell?" Oz snaps. "No way, you can keep your

voodoo legacy or myth or curse or whatever the hell you want to call it. I have no interest in falling for a woman and having no control over my feelings. No thank you."

"Doesn't work that way," Beau says in his low, gruff voice. "By the time you realize it's happened, you're too far gone to care. All you want is her, and you'll do whatever you need to, to make her yours."

"Nope, I plan to choose the woman I want to be mine, not have fate or whatever the fuck has happened to y'all choose her for me." Danny smirks. Turning to me and Tori, he says, "You guys don't buy into this love-at-first-sight bull, right? You're together because you were both hot for each other. This mumbo jumbo legacy had nothing to do with it."

I want to tell him he's right, that I chose Tori because I was attracted to her, because I liked her, but it's not the truth. The first time I kissed her, it was because I just couldn't hold myself back anymore. I didn't pick her and she didn't pick me. I just knew she was mine and that I had to claim her. "She's mine, bro. I don't really know what else to say. But when it happens to you, you'll know, and there won't be a thing you can do to stop it."

Danny waves my warning away, and the others all look skeptical. Only the Barnetts are nodding like they get it because I guess they do.

We spend the rest of the afternoon mingling with the hordes of Barnetts and their families. Every time Tori steps more than three feet away from me, I feel like I'm on the verge of losing my shit, and when she hugs every single person in the place goodbye, my hands are balled into fists so tight my fingers actually go numb.

Jealousy has never been something I've experienced before, but with her, I am a fucking madman. I hate everyone touching her, talking to her, and especially hugging her. Male, female, I don't care. She's mine and I don't want anyone to be close enough to even smell her perfume.

My ire rises with each new set of arms that wrap themselves around *my* woman, and by the time Danny goes in for a hug, I lose my fucking mind. "If you touch her, I will cut off your arms with a fucking axe," I snarl, turning wild eyes in his direction to warn him just how fucking serious I am.

The beautiful bastard smirks then lifts his hands in front of him to show me where they are as he backs away. I flash Oz and Warrick the same look, turning Tori into me and palming her ass.

"You're being an asshole," Tori hisses.

"I don't give a fuck. If they touch you, I will fucking kill them and if you allow them to touch you, I will keep you chained to my bed and fuck you over and over until you understand that you are mine and I do not fucking share."

I'm enraged, a crazed, unhinged psycho, and I have no fucking clue how to calm down, even though I know I'm acting completely irrationally right now.

We walk home in silence, my arm draped across Tori's shoulder, keeping her pinned to my side. Unlocking the door, I hold it open for her, not exhaling a full breath until she's inside the house and the door is locked behind us.

"What the hell was that?" Tori snaps.

"I have no fucking clue," I admit shakily.

"You threatened to cut off Danny's arms if he touched me."

Exhaling slowly, I nod. "Yep."

"Have you lost your mind?"

"Completely and utterly," I agree.

"I have four brothers; are you going to lose your mind and threaten to kill them?"

"Probably." I nod.

"You're such an asshole." She giggles.

Chapter Thirty

Tori

His eyes are blazing with fire and a whole lot of crazy and I don't hate it. He is unequivocally an unmitigated asshole, but the jealousy is kind of hot. I've never had a guy treat me like I was something special enough to get jealous over, and I didn't think I'd like it, but I do.

I don't know if he's wearing me down or if some kind of Stockholm syndrome has kicked in, but I really don't hate his particular brand of crazy. I like the way he pinned me to his side whenever anyone got too close to our personal space. I like the fact that he told every single person there that I was his woman. I like the fact that he was openly affectionate and didn't care who was watching when he grabbed my sore ass and whispered filthy things into my ear.

He's still an asshole, but I don't even hate that anymore either. Now, it feels almost like an endearment.

"Clothes off," he demands.

I strip so quickly I almost fall, trying to get my shorts and shoes off at the same time. Strong hands catch me, righting me, then hold me while I kick off my shoes and push my shorts off my feet.

"You're so fucking beautiful," he coos, his eyes running from my head, down my naked body to my feet and back up again.

I blush redder than I do when he makes me beg him to play with my ass, but I think it's maybe the first time he's ever told me I'm beautiful. I needed to hear it. So much of our free will has been taken by the stupid Barnett legacy, but me being attracted to him and him being attracted to me, that's real. It's not fate, voodoo or the universe's practical joke; it's just two people looking at each other and liking what they see, and I cling to that when he lifts me off my feet and carries me up the stairs.

There's a slight feeling of déjà vu when he lays me down on his bed and strips out of his own clothes. The first night we had sex, it started downstairs and then moved up here. That was the night I ran from him. I never expected that less than two weeks later, I'd be right back here again, desperate for him to lick, suck or touch me.

"Jesus, Tori, I have never wanted another woman the way I want you."

It's not declarations of love or devotion, but it's another confession that I want to hear and I soften, letting my knees fall to the side and putting myself on display for him.

"Fuck, I like that. Seeing you all sweet and willing for me," he says, crawling onto the mattress at the end of the bed.

My thighs widen to make space for his broad shoulders and he settles between them, his face level with my exposed sex.

"You smell like me," he tells me a second before his hot tongue licks from my clit to my asshole and back again.

"Holy shit," I gasp, my back arching and head rolling back onto my shoulders.

For the first time, there are no dirty words or demands, there are no orders or squirming humiliation, there's just us.

His tongue licks and teases my clit, then slides lower to push into my sex. When I come with a cry, my whole body seizes, shuddering through my release while Nero works me down, flicking my clit with his tongue until I come again all over his face.

Prowling up the bed, he positions himself over me, lifting my legs and wrapping them around his waist. There's nothing kinky about missionary, but when he guides his hard dick into my core, this position feels like the most taboo thing we've done together.

His cock slides in and out of me, deep and slow and so fucking intimate. His hands are braced on either side of my head, and his eyes hold me captive as we share breath, our lips almost touching, my hands cupping his face.

This isn't fucking. It's not dirty and hard. He's not trying to torture me or delay our gratification. This feels less like sex and more like making love, and tears fill my eyes as he pushes me to release. Pulses of soft bliss lap at my body, like waves at the edge of the sand, relentless, consistently pushing forward until the tide turns and they retreat. The sensation is both numbing and heightening and when the tears finally fall, they're from an overload of ecstasy that I've never experienced before.

"Sunshine?"

"I'm fine," I assure him. "That just. Wow, that was…" My words trail off because all the words I can think to describe how that had felt feel inadequate.

I expect him to pull out of me and do his alpha male thing where he pushes his come back into me, but he doesn't move, holding my legs in place and rolling us to the side, his dick still inside of me.

We're silent, but for once, it's not charged or angry. It's just quiet and peaceful.

I lose count of how many times he wakes me during the night. Sometimes for soft, intense sex, other times to fuck me hard, while he reminds me in every depraved way exactly who I belong to.

By the time my alarm goes off, I've had less than two hours' sleep, and my pussy has its own pulse. I'm sticky and coated in cum, and happier than I've ever dared to be. Last night changed things. Neither of us said sweet words or made any declarations, but we connected on a deeper level, or at least I did.

But despite it all, this morning feels like the end. It's Monday and the first day of Nero's shift. I won't see him for four days and it feels like this tentative knife's edge our new relationship is balancing on won't survive the separation.

We haven't spent more than five minutes apart in days,

and knowing that I'll be alone for the next ninety-six hours is jarring.

"Shower with me. I don't want to wash me off you, but even though I wish I could, I know I can't order you not to shower until I get home."

"Eww," I say, wrinkling my nose and forcing a fake smile to my lips.

We're both solemn as we shower together. My brain knows that it's only four days, but my heart hurts at the idea of not seeing him and touching him. I don't know what he's feeling, but he's quiet and brooding, his brow furrowed as he cleans first my skin and hair and then his own.

It's early, barely five thirty a.m., but I dress in the leggings I came in yesterday and one of his huge hoodies. It had seemed like a cute idea to only pack my booty shorts to tease him, but this morning, it feels like I'm doing the walk of shame going home in yesterday's clothes.

"You ready?" he asks, my bag in one hand, his car keys in the other.

Nodding, I follow him out to the car. It's still dark; the sun hasn't risen yet and we stay quiet as we climb in and he starts the engine. It's a twenty-minute drive down the mountain and I feel every single strained, awkward second that passes.

Slowing to a stop on the street outside the store, I unbuckle my seat belt and reach for the door handle. I'm not sure why I'm expecting him to stay in the car, but he kills the engine and follows me out, stepping ahead of me and taking my hand as I make my way to the stairs that lead to my apartment door.

Taking my keys from my hand, he unlocks the door and steps into the dark space. Memories of him scaring me in here just a few days ago flash into my thoughts and I tense. Light illuminates the room, and I blink up at Nero, trying and failing to find a smile.

I pride myself on being happy and cheerful, but right now, I can't find anything to smile about. I don't want him to leave. Somehow, in the four days since he declared I was his, I've become accustomed to him.

He's barely a few steps away from me, but he feels miles away, the distance lengthening with every moment that passes when neither of us speaks. His sigh is audible and it prompts me to move. Stepping past him, I turn to the side in the small hallway and head for my bedroom.

I don't look back to see if he's following me, but I can feel him behind me. Close, but still too far away. I can feel the words building in my throat. I want to beg him to stay, to make me blush, to make me come, to make me feel something. But I swallow them down.

Opening my closet, I pull out clean yoga tights and a tank and quickly change, slipping Nero's hoodie back over my head. The sweater falls to my knees, the arms far too long, but I don't care. It smells like him, and right now, it's the only thing stopping me from embarrassing the hell out of myself by jumping into his arms and refusing to let him leave.

"I have to go turn the ovens on," I whisper, finally breaking the silence.

"Okay. I have to go to work."

"Okay."

Grabbing a band, I twist my hair up into a bun on top of my head, covering it with a hair net to contain any strands that may come loose. Then I turn to look at him, pulling in a slow, affirming breath.

He's still not speaking, but his eyes are loud, screaming with unsaid words that I wish I could hear. Is he going to miss me? Does he care that we're not going to see each other for four days? Is he excited to have some peace away from my incessant cheerful noise?

"I'll call you later," he says.

There's nothing wrong with his words. It's nice to know that he plans for us to speak while he's not here, but I'm still disappointed. He told me that he doesn't always find the right words, so maybe that's what's happening now, or maybe he's trying to think of a way to tell me he had fun with this four-day-long fling but that he's done now.

No.

My own voice is loud inside of my head. No, this isn't an extended one-night stand. That's just my insecurities talking. Yesterday, he was talking about wanting to get me pregnant and he's told me again and again that I'm his, and he's never given me any indications that he's put a timescale on his ownership.

"I'll be home Friday morning."

"Okay." I nod.

"Okay."

"I really do have to get the ovens on." I motion to the door that leads down into the store, and this time, he nods. We're just two nodding, awkward idiots.

Inhaling another breath, I nod again, then move, stepping

past him and striding as purposefully as I can to the door, unlocking it, then descending the stairs to the kitchen. Nero watches as I move around, turning on lights and setting the ovens to heat as I go. The familiarity of my morning routine kicks in and for the first time since I woke up, my heartbeat starts to slow and my tense muscles slowly unclench.

This kitchen is my happy place. My kitchen, in my store. Mine. This is all mine. I did this. I bought my own business and I'm going to make it a success because I'm a strong, confident, kickass girl boss and I can't allow myself to have a meltdown because my boyfriend is going to work. I didn't need him to function four days ago, and I don't need him now.

Maybe if I keep saying the words over and over, I might eventually believe them.

"Tori."

"Yeah," I say, grabbing mixing bowls and scales from the racks and laying them out on the counter.

"Tori."

"Uh-huh."

Strong, unyielding hands grab me, spinning me around and collaring my neck, forcing me to stop and look up. Nero's expression is dark, his lips parted like he's about to speak, but instead, he dips his head and kisses me.

Stupidly, I assumed all kisses were basically the same. Lips, mouth, tongue. Boy, I was so incredibly wrong. Nero doesn't just kiss me; he says all the words neither of us has spoken this morning. He whispers and yells and owns and dominates and consumes me, all without uttering a sound and by the time he pulls back, I'm a mess again.

My hands are fisted in his shirt and my breasts are pressed tight to his chest. I feel desperate and tearful and weak, and it's all his fault. I don't understand how, in such a short space of time, someone who so openly disliked me could become a defining factor in my happiness.

Stepping back, he pries my fingers from his shirt, slowly uncurling his hand from around my throat. "I'll call you later."

I nod, my throat thick with emotion.

"See you, Sunshine."

Then, turning away from me, he leaves, heading for the stairs and the apartment, leaving the way we came in.

Exhaling, I stare at the empty space where he was standing only seconds ago and swallow thickly. My heart hurts, my head feels fuzzy, and suddenly, the room is large and cold and empty, and I hate it.

I hate him being gone, and I hate that I hate him being gone, and I hate that I've somehow ended up feeling like I hate everything just because he's gone.

No. Fuck this. Fuck him. I will not be the stupid girl crying because my boyfriend of four freaking days left. No. Nope. Not happening.

Sucking in a deep breath, I roll back my shoulders, turn on the radio, and get to work.

Ten hours later, I'm exhausted and still sad. I've deliberately not checked my cell to see if he's texted because I don't want to admit how upset I'll be if he hasn't. Instead of easing my customers into French patisserie a few cakes at a time, I half fill the counter with delicious cakes, decadent cream confections, and dainty-looking morsels that melt in your mouth and leave you eager for more.

None of this is in my very carefully considered business plan, but I needed to lose myself in baking today and making batches of chocolate chip cookies and blueberry scones just wasn't going to cut it.

"We're officially sold out," Daniel says, leaning against the doorway from the kitchen into the storefront.

"What?" Glancing up, I check the clock. "It's not even three yet."

"I know. It's been crazy. The new cakes and things have been a huge hit."

"Oh my god, I need to make something. We can't have an empty counter," I gasp.

"If you're going to make more, I'd go with the new stuff. Apart from a few customers buying the usual stock, alongside some of the new items, more people have been interested in the patisserie cakes than the familiar things."

My grin is so wide it feels like it's splitting my face in two. "Oh my god. Oh my god. Okay. I have some dough proving for some brioche buns that should be done soon. It was actually going to be a trial run, but as long as it turns out like I hoped, I'll get it in the oven. I'll whip up some choux pastry too. That's pretty quick." I start moving even as I speak, grabbing the ingredients I need.

"Congratulations, boss, I'm proud of you," Daniel says, tapping the doorframe with the side of his fist before disappearing back into the front of the store.

Thirty minutes later, the kitchen smells like cranberries and chocolate, and the choux buns are almost cool enough to fill and decorate. When I step into the front of the store carrying the tray of buns, I'm shocked to see a crowd of people all drinking espresso cups and waiting.

Brow furrowing, I look at Daniel, who smirks. Turning, I head back into the kitchen and grab two trays of éclairs, one chocolate, one raspberry, and then finally grab the tray of salted caramel choux buns.

The moment the trays are in the counter showcase, the people move forward and in less than five minutes, almost all the new stock is gone too. When the last customer leaves, I stare at the almost empty counter and then up at Daniel, who is smiling widely.

"Oh my god," I whisper-yell.

Daniel nods.

"Oh my god," I whisper-yell again.

This time, he laughs, and I laugh too, throwing my arms in the air as I scream with excitement.

"Having a good day, Little Bit?" a familiar voice asks.

Dropping my arms, I turn to look at the newcomer, screaming again as I run around the counter and jump, throwing myself into my big brother's arms. "Att, you're here," I gasp, then promptly burst into tears.

Chapter Thirty-one
Nero

Pulling my cell out of my pants pocket, I check it again to see if she's replied to any of the messages I've sent her, but just like every other time I've checked today, the texts are still unread.

Grinding my teeth, I fight the urge to text her again and demand she call me or text me, or just fucking something. Leaving her this morning was harder than I expected. I knew that I wouldn't want to go, but walking away was fucking awful. From the moment we woke up, I watched her retreat further and further from me. Building walls that I want to smash down but can't because I'm here and she's not.

In the years since I became a firefighter, this is the very first time I've resented my commitment to my job. If I worked a standard nine-to-five, I'd be on my way home right now, knowing she was waiting for me.

I could implement a rule where she greets me naked with a plug filling her ass or… no, bent over holding the plug, ready for me to work it into her ass. No… naked and spreadeagled on our bed, her pussy and ass just laid out and waiting for me to do whatever I fucking wanted. Or hell, just there waiting for me, fully dressed, cheeks smeared with flour, her hair a mess, in yoga pants and my hoodie. Fuck, I'll take her any way I can get her, as long as she's there waiting for me.

With the season changing from late summer to early fall, the number of callouts we get starts to slow. They never stop, especially because we provide emergency fire response to all the local rural communities, but the frequency slows, so we spend a lot of time maintaining equipment and training. It's still important work, but doing routine maintenance on the all-terrain trucks is giving me too much time to think, especially when all my thoughts revolve around Tori.

It's only been a few days since we officially became a couple and barely a couple of weeks since the first time I sank my cock into her perfect pussy and then woke up alone. But I've been in yearlong relationships that haven't felt as permanent as the handful of days I've spent with Tori.

Everything with her feels different. I want her in a way I never wanted the women I've dated in the past. Time doesn't seem important because I'm confident that she's my endgame. The problem is that I made such a shitty first impression with her. I'm just not sure if she feels the same way about me as I do about her.

I'm not sure if I was expecting a movie-worthy farewell scene this morning, but I guess I'd hoped for more than an

I have to get to work. See you later. Last night felt different between us and I'd woken up feeling like we'd turned a corner, like maybe we were finally on the same page and building feelings beyond horniness for each other.

Now I have no fucking clue how she feels about me, and I'm not sure I have big enough balls to just come out and ask her if she wants me the same way I want her.

Sliding my dick into her last night is the closest I've ever come to making love to a woman. No, last night I did make love to her. It wasn't about just feeling good. Although it did, it felt amazing. But when I pushed inside of her, it felt like it forged a real connection between us and I thought she'd felt it too.

Now I have no fucking clue and it's pissing me off. I'm not an emotional, metrosexual guy. I don't spend a lot of time questioning my actions or debating my motives about things, or at least I didn't before I kissed Tori. Right now, I feel like a fucking pussy, sitting here, lost in my own head, wondering if the woman I like likes me back, and checking my cell every five minutes, hoping she's texted me.

For the first time, I really understand the no-space, no-distance rule Beau and Bonnie Barnett live by. I can't help the physical space my job has forced between Tori and me, but I can refuse to allow any emotional distance between us. The last four days have been the best days of my entire life. Being with her, fucking her, watching her work, learning what makes her smile. It's been amazing, and I won't allow something as stupid as my shift pattern to ruin things.

Clicking into my text app, I reread the messages I've already sent.

> **ME**
> Hey Sunshine, how's your day going?

> **ME**
> We should pack your stuff up and move you back home once I'm off shift again.

> **ME**
> Don't ignore me.

> **ME**
> Tori!

Sighing, I type out a new message and then hit send.

> **ME**
> New rule, Sunshine, no more ignoring your cell! I know this is new, and it's easier to be 'with me' when we're actually together, but you're still mine, even if I'm not there. I'll call you once the store has shut, if you don't answer, I'll come and hunt you down. Speak to you later, Sunshine xoxo

Exhaling, I shove my cell back into my pocket and get back to work. When the base alarm blares to life, I jump up and race for the supply room, pulling on my kit while my team swarms in around me. The last thing I do before the chopper takes off is send Tori a rushed text.

> **ME**
> Called out to a job. I'll call when I get back if it's not too late. Miss you xoxo

Three days later, I wipe the sweat from my forehead with the back of my arm. The fire is still blazing all around me, but the flames are receding, the forest blackened and smoldering as we push the fire back, condensing it into as small an area as we can.

The air is full of smoke. The sound of crackling wood fire all I've heard for the last seventy hours. Taking in the carnage, I hiss angrily. All of this devastation is because some idiots watched a reality TV show about surviving in the wilderness and thought they'd like to try it out.

The dense forest and beautiful mountains pull in thousands of people looking to set up a tent and camp for a few nights, and ninety-nine percent of them have a great few days and then go home. Unfortunately, the remaining one percent end up being like the shitheads who caused all this damage. They tried to build a firepit to grill over and then lost control of it, too drunk to pay attention to the flames until a spark ignited some dry brush, setting fire to the woodlands surrounding them and resulting in a raging fire that's destroyed miles of forest.

By the time we got here, the blaze had the potential to be catastrophic, but luckily, me and my team are highly trained specialists. We might have lost more forest than any of us wanted, but we're finally starting to get the flames under control.

Usually, when I'm out in the middle of nowhere, I'm hyperfocused, thinking two steps ahead, trying to anticipate the wind, the fire, and the lay of the land. But the weight of my cell in my pants pocket is still demanding my attention. It stayed aggravatingly silent until the battery died late last night.

I know I shouldn't be thinking about my girlfriend right now, but I can't help it. Not knowing if she'll be pissed, or distant, or happy when I get home is driving me crazy. I know that not being one-hundred-percent present out here is dangerous, but I'm too distracted, my training not kicking in as I step forward.

The sound of wood splintering draws my attention and spinning around, I look up just in time to watch the heavy branch split from the blackened tree. Then, all I feel is pain.

Chapter Thirty-two

Tori

My smile is so wide my cheeks actually hurt, but I don't care. My brothers are here.

"I can't believe you're here," I say for the tenth time since Atticus appeared in my store an hour ago.

"You didn't seriously think we weren't going to come when you dropped the new guy text bombshell, did you?" he says, glancing at his twin Felix, who is sprawled out on the floor, doodling in his leather-bound sketchbook.

"You're here because I told you I was seeing someone?" I hiss, brow furrowed.

"Of course that's why. I've been worried about you since we spoke the other day and you told me about this guy, then you sent that text. Jude and August were threatening to skip their next game to come check on you. The only reason they're not here is because Felix and I said we were coming. I had to promise that I'd tell them if you weren't okay. They're worried about you. We all are."

"You don't need to worry. I'm fine," I say, trying to sound reassuring.

"Really, because you don't seem it to me. You look tired and your smile is strained."

"It's not strained. My grin is so big my cheeks hurt. I'm so happy you're both here. I thought it was going to be months before I'd get to see you. Do Mom and Dad know you're here?"

"They know," Felix says, finally closing his book and joining the conversation.

"So, how long are you here for? I'd offer to let you stay with me, but unless you want to sleep in here, I don't have a spare room."

Felix tilts his head to the side and looks at the bed that's still pushed against the wall. "Where's your couch?"

"I haven't gotten around to buying one yet. I've only been living here for a week."

"You should order one. I'll pay for it," he tells me, his eyes troubled. From his outward appearance, people assume Felix isn't overtly emotional, but his eyes tell a different story, always filled with so much turmoil.

"I don't need you to buy me a couch, Felix," I say with a smile.

"Pick something out. We can go fetch it if you can't get it delivered," Atticus says, interpreting Felix's silence in the way he's always done.

Sighing, I stop arguing. There's no point, Felix might

not say much, but he's one of the most stubborn humans alive. Now he's said he's buying a couch; he's buying me a couch and there's no point fighting him on it.

"Fine, I'll pick something." I relent, rolling my eyes dramatically, so they know I'm only giving in because I know I won't win this argument.

"So, tell me more about the guy," Atticus says, crossing his arms over his chest and staring at me pointedly.

Sighing, I glance up at the ugly, stained ceiling, then drop my chin and look at my brothers. They're so alike but so different at the same time. They're not identical. Atticus has the same dirty-blond hair as me, but his skin is more olive-toned, deepening the moment he steps into the sun. His skin is a work of art, tattoos coating his limbs from his fingers to his neck.

To me, he's a pussycat, but I could see how he might appear intimidating to someone who doesn't know him like I do. Felix is the other side of his coin; his hair is white blond and so light it almost glows. His skin is pale like mine, minus the freckles that are littered across my face. He's taller than Atticus, but where Att is thick and muscular, Felix is lean with a runner's build. But the main difference between them is that where Atticus is scary darkness, Felix is light.

Just having them here in my space lifts some of the weight that I've been carrying since I woke up this morning. "His name is Nero," I tell them.

"Cut the shit, Tor. This is us you're talking to. Tell us about the new guy," Att snarls.

"He's an asshole," I blurt.

"How?" Felix asks.

Inhaling sharply, I tell them. I tell them how he was the first time we met; I tell them how shitty he was to me when we first moved in together. I tell them about how he kissed me, then about the first time we had sex and how I ran away before he woke up. I tell them about him showing up four days ago, about him breaking into my apartment, about him refusing to leave. I tell them everything, and by the time I'm done talking, I feel like I've just shed a hundred pounds of baggage.

For the first time since I started unloading, I look up cautiously, unsure what to expect from my very protective big brothers. What I'm not anticipating is for Att to be smiling. Even Felix's lips are twitching with amusement.

"What's funny?" I demand.

"You fell in love," Felix says, shocking me.

"I did not," I hiss.

"This guy claimed you as his, broke into your home, refused to leave and has been systematically worming his way into your life, and you haven't called us or the cops. You're in love with him," Att says, glancing at Felix before turning back to me.

"I am not in love with him," I protest.

"Fine," Att says, rolling his eyes dramatically. "You're not"—he lifts his hands and does air quotes—"*in love* with him. But you really fucking like him."

An argument builds on my tongue, my muscles tensing, and then I exhale and admit, "I think I really do."

"Why is that making you sad?" Felix asks, his head tilted to the side curiously.

"Because I don't know if he feels the same way," I confess.

"Tori," Att scoffs. "You're not that much of a dumbass. You just told us everything this guy has done to claim you."

"I know he wants me. I know he thinks I'm his woman, or whatever the caveman translation is. But I don't know if he likes *me*. He was so honest about everything he hated about me. He thinks I'm too noisy, too cheerful, and too happy, and since he barged his way into my life, I've found myself trying not to be any of the things he hates. But I like talking and I like smiling and I like being excited by life and I'm terrified that I like him enough to try to stop myself from being… me."

It's the most honest I've been with myself. I've always known that his dislike has bothered me, but this is the first time I've admitted that I've tried to change who I am to try and make him like me more.

"No, fuck that. If he doesn't love you for being exactly who you are, then fuck him," Att snarls.

"But that's the thing, I don't know. I've been trying to be quiet and less… well, less me. But when I do, he tries to make me talk and make me smile and I don't know why. When he was here, we were in this bubble of us, and it was easy to just sort of fall into it. But since I woke up this morning and he's gone to work and I know I won't see him for a while, all these doubts have just surged to life and I don't know if I've been repressing myself for him or if he's just so intense and all-consuming that I haven't had to fill the gaps with chatter and fake smiles."

I'm expecting outrage, maybe anger, but instead, my

brothers are oddly quiet.

"You called him an asshole like it was an endearment," Felix says, being far more in-tuned with my emotions than he usually is. He isn't a robot; he's sweet and thoughtful and a wonderful big brother, but he's not usually intuitive because sometimes he struggles to understand why other people feel the way they feel. But right now, it's like he's inside my head, reading my thoughts.

"He is an asshole," I say. "But…" I trail off, struggling for the words to explain how I'm feeling.

"But you like him in spite of it," Felix says, once again understanding exactly what I'm struggling to say.

"Yes," I admit. "And maybe even because of it."

Both my brothers nod, like what I've said makes sense and another layer of tension melts from my shoulders. The sound of my cell buzzing loudly against the kitchen counter draws all of our attention. I brought it back up here while I worked this morning to stop myself from texting Nero and pathetically telling him how much I was missing him.

Reaching for it, I bring the screen to life, smiling when I see I have not just one but six messages from him. The first was from early this morning, not long after I hid my cell up here, and the tone of each message becomes more terse the more time that passes without me replying.

NERO
Hey Sunshine, how's your day going?

NERO
We should pack your stuff up and move you back home once I'm off shift again.

NERO
Don't ignore me.

NERO

Tori!

NERO

New rule, Sunshine, no more ignoring your cell! I know this is new and it's easier to be 'with me' when we're actually together, but you're still mine, even if I'm not there. I'll call you once the store has shut, if you don't answer, I'll come and hunt you down. Speak to you later, Sunshine xoxo

NERO

Called out to a job. I'll call when I get back if it's not too late. Miss you xoxo

"Everything okay?" Att asks.

"Yeah, he's texted me a few times."

"I'm guessing you haven't replied."

"I put my cell up here so I wouldn't be that pathetic girl checking her cell every ten seconds waiting for a text from a guy."

"You should text him back," Felix says.

"The message that just came through was him letting me know he's been called out to an emergency somewhere. He says he'll call me when he gets back." I still type out a quick text and hit send.

ME

Be careful x

***

Three days later

It's been days since I've heard from Nero, but like an addict who's jonesing for their next fix, I still pull my cell from my apron pocket and bring the screen to life, just in case a text or a call came through at some point in the last ten seconds.

I've heard nothing from him since that text saying he'd been called out to an emergency, but I've seen the reports of the huge forest fire on the local news and the videos of flames engulfing the ancient trees and anything else that got in their path.

Either Atticus or Felix or both together have spent every moment with me since they got here and I've loved it. We've talked about my store, Felix's next exhibition, and Atticus's issues with his boss. Atticus told me about the friend he knows with a tattoo studio who is looking for a guest artist. It turns out his friend is Betty Barnett and the studio is literally two blocks away from my store.

We've looked at studio space to rent for Felix to work from and an apartment or house for them to live in, and I've gotten more and more excited about the fact that my big brothers are moving here. But despite how great the last few days with them have been, with every hour that's passed, I've found myself craving Nero more and more.

I know he's working, that he's in the middle of nowhere, literally battling with a raging wildfire, but I hate that I've gone from having his constant presence for four days to not speaking to him at all for nearly eighty hours.

I miss him. A part of me expected to miss the physical stuff. Being with him is intense and constant, my nerves on high alert, waiting for his touch. But I wasn't expecting to miss *him* so much.

I expected the time and distance to increase the space between us, but instead, it's given me a chance to think clearly without the haze of lust I feel whenever he's close.

Nero isn't the perfect guy. Far from it, in fact. He's controlling, possessive, jealous, dominant, a lot fucked up and possibly a little crazy. But as much as I could write a list of all the things that annoy the hell out of me about him, I still wish he was here.

The sex is undeniably amazing. We click on a sexual level in a way I have never experienced before, but if I were to dismiss the mind-blowing orgasms and the way he knows exactly what to say and do to have me squirming with desire, I'd still feel like I was missing out on something without him in my life.

He watches me in a way no one ever has before, like everything I do is interesting. I know he thinks I talk too much, but he asked me question after question to try to learn new things about me.

He thinks I'm too cheerful and happy, but he is still playful, even though he's a self-confessed grump by nature.

Nero Henderson is in no way the perfect guy, but maybe, just maybe, he's perfect for me.

Chapter Thirty-two

Nero

Being airlifted out in the helicopter that I normally fly to rescue people is utterly humiliating. When the tree branch fell onto me, it knocked me out and then burned through my protective gear while my brother and the rest of our team scrambled to pull it off me.

The sound of the chopper blades ricochets through my skull, making the booming in my head a hundred times worse, and my ribs, stomach, and thigh are burning like a motherfucker. Oz lands the chopper on the helipad on the roof of the hospital, and despite my insistence that I can walk, the nurses and doctors force me onto a gurney and wheel me into the ER while Oz heads back to the fire to continue dousing the flames with fire suppressant.

I have some small patches of second-degree burns and

a goose egg on my head that may possibly have given me a concussion. But all in all, I've gotten off easy, considering my injuries are all my fault for being distracted thinking about my girl when I should have been focused on the fucking fire.

The doctor tells me I have to stay overnight and that he's called in a consult from a plastic surgeon, but all I can think about is Tori, how my cell is dead and that I wish she was here.

"Hey there, the doctor asked me to bring you in some water and some pain meds. Is there anything else you need?" The male nurse asks, handing me a tiny paper cup with some pills in and a glass of water.

"Do you have a phone I could use? My cell is dead and I need to call my girlfriend."

"The only phone is at the nurses' station, and we're not supposed to allow patients to use it, but if you know the number, you can use my cell," he offers, pulling out a cell phone from the pocket of his scrubs and handing it to me.

"Thanks," I say, pausing when I realize the only three numbers I know by heart are my mom, Buck, and Juni. Dialing my sister's number, I wait while it rings, praying that she answers.

"Hello." It's not my sister, but I recognize Teddy's voice.

"Hey, it's Nero."

"You okay?" he asks.

"I'm in the hospital."

"Which one?"

"Boseman."

"Okay, we'll be there in an hour. I'm assuming if you're calling, you're okay?"

"I'm fine, a few burns and a suspected concussion. You guys don't need to come. But I need Juni to get hold of Tori for me. My battery on my cell is dead."

"I'll swing by and pick her up on the way to the hospital," he says.

"Thank you," I breathe, feeling the relief of knowing I'll see her soon settle over me.

"That's what family does," Teddy says, ending the call.

The pain pills they give me must kick in because I jolt awake when the door to my room flies open and a panicked-looking Tori bursts inside, with Juni and Teddy trailing behind her.

"Nero," she gasps, her eyes filling with tears when she looks at me.

"I'm fine, Sunshine," I assure her, wincing when I try to sit up in the bed.

"You're hurt," she says, skidding to a stop beside me, her hands moving, then falling back down to her sides.

"It looks worse than it is," I say, forcing a smile to my lips as I reach for her. "Get over here."

Carefully, she sits on the edge of the bed, but I curl my arm around her and pull her to me, wincing into her mouth when I press a kiss to her lips.

"What happened?" Juni asks, her eyes raking over me.

"I wasn't paying attention, and a branch split off a tree and fell on me. It knocked me out and it took a little while for the guys to get me free. I've got some burns on my stomach and ribs and some on my thigh. Could have been a lot worse."

Tori stays by my side as my sister asks about my injuries; she's stiff, but she's here and just having her close settles something inside of me. She's quiet though, her muscles rigid and tense. I want to demand that she tell me she's okay, that four days without speaking didn't ruin everything, but I don't want to do it with an audience.

"Are you hungry?" Juni asks.

"I could eat." I nod.

"We'll head down to the cafeteria and grab us all some food and drinks. Any requests?"

Both Tori and I shake our heads, but I watch gratefully as Teddy leads my sister out of the room, leaving us alone.

"Look at me," I demand the moment the door closes.

Tori's eyes are watery when she lifts them to look up at me.

"You okay?"

"You're the one in the hospital bed. I should be asking you that," she says, her lower lip trembling.

"I already told you I'm fine. I'm worried about you. You're too quiet."

"You like it when I'm quiet," she says, a tear escaping her eye and dripping onto her cheek.

"I fucking hate it when you're quiet," I admit.

"That's not true, you told me—"

I interrupt her, "I was an idiot."

"You said—"

I interrupt her again, "Listen to me, Tori. When I told you I thought you were too loud and too happy, I was being an asshole."

Her nose wrinkles in this adorably confused way. "I don't understand. So you don't think I'm too loud and too happy?"

"Sunshine, you're loud as hell and it drives me crazy, but the moment you're quiet, I fucking hate it. I like your noise. I like the way you sound when you laugh and I love the way you say my name. I crave listening to the sounds you make when I'm touching you or fucking you or embarrassing the hell out of you."

"You think I'm too happy."

A chuckle bubbles from my throat. "Far happier than any adult woman should be. But you know what, I'd rather have you be the happiest woman in the world than see you sad. I want to watch you laugh and smile and giggle every day. Because even when I'm a grumpy, miserable asshole, if I've done something to make you smile, I want to see it and hear it and feel it."

"I don't understand," she admits.

"I fucking love you, Tori." Her gasp of shock is loud, but I keep talking, needing to get the words out. "It doesn't make an ounce of sense to me. It's fast and crazy and intense, but I feel it. I love that you drive me crazy. I love that we're so different but so fucking compatible. I love that I crave you and that you crave me just as intensely. I hated leaving you on Monday and I've missed you so fucking much. I don't want any space or any distance between us. I want you to be mine and I really, really fucking want to be yours."

I expect her to say something back when I finish speaking, but instead, she just stares at me, her eyes wide, her lips parted. Dread pools in my stomach and I wonder if admitting everything I feel for her was a mistake. But it doesn't feel like a mistake; it feels right, like just putting it all out there was exactly the right thing to do.

Seconds pass as she just looks at me. Then she lifts her hand and carefully cups my cheek. "It's far too fast and far too intense."

Bile rises in my throat and I think I'm going to be sick.

"You're grumpy and jealous and possessive and controlling. You're an asshole," she whispers, a hairbreadth from my lips. "But I love you too."

Epilogue

Tori

It turns out it's okay to love someone in spite of their flaws and sometimes even because of them. Nero and I are not a perfect couple. We argue, we bicker, and we drive each other crazy. I'm too loud and too cheerful, he's insanely jealous and a possessive asshole. But despite not fitting together in the way either of us expected, we work.

I've never enjoyed arguing with someone the way I do with him, but for us, it's almost turned into foreplay. I like knowing that I'm riling him up, and he enjoys making me squirm.

There's nothing conventional about us, but it turns out that's okay because Nero and I love to be dysfunctional together. We've become that couple who exist in their own bubble, happy to be consumed by each other twenty-four hours a day when Nero's not at work.

That day in the hospital, he told me that he didn't want any space or distance between us and when he's home, that's how we live. We spend all our time together, happily annoying the hell out of each other.

Admitting that we loved each other didn't immediately erase all the doubt we both felt about the other's feelings, but accepting that our relationship not being perfect doesn't mean that we're not perfect for each other definitely helped.

I don't know if it was the Barnett legacy, fate, or just good old-fashioned sexual attraction that led us to each other, but whatever it was, I'm glad it happened. They say opposites attract and that's never been truer than it is for us.

I'm sunshine and he's my rain cloud. I'm loud and he's my perfect silence.

At the end of the day, it doesn't matter how different we are because I'm his and he's mine.

The end.

Well, not really, the end... Two Montana Mountain Protectors down and five more to go.

Acknowledgments

How many books do you think I need to publish before I stop counting? Apparently more than I have at the minute, because this is book number twenty-four and I'm still as excited to type the end for this book as I was at the end of book number one!

Nero and Tori had a LOT to say, and honestly, it was a slog to get this couple to their happy ever after, but I love the struggle these two felt and how honest they were about it. I think sometimes it's easy to write two people who fit easily together, but I knew Nero and Tori were never going to be that couple, and it's been fun to watch them butt heads and really question if what they were feeling for each other was true love or just a lot of fucked-up lust. Their story is packed with so much sexual tension even I was a little flushed after writing it, and I honestly think this book has the sexiest sex scenes I've ever written.

When I started writing Blaze, I wasn't sure that I'd love these smoke jumpers as much as I love the Barnetts, but after finishing Scorch, I have a feeling I'm going to end up loving them more. All seven guys have such different personalities and I cannot wait to see who the women who knock them on their asses are.

As always, I have a few thank-yous to make.

Firstly, did you see this cover? Thank you to the absolute sweetheart, Chris, at CJC Photography. I fell in love with this picture the moment I saw it!

Kirsty Ann Still, I've said it before, but I'll say it again, you are a freaking genius! The covers you have done for not just this series but the entire Montana Mountain World have been honestly outstanding, and I feel honored to have had the opportunity to work with you.

As always, Sarah gets her mention. You know I love you and your constant and unending support. We're both living our dreams and I'm bloody proud of both of us.

To the lovely Sarah Goodman, thank you for loving my men almost as much as I do. Your constant enthusiasm always brightens my day.

Rosa, my lovely proofreader, thank you for making sure my wonderful American readers don't shout at me!

Last but not least, to all my wonderful readers, thank you for being on this journey with me. I have so many more sexy men to tell you about and so much more dirty sex to write.

Watch this space because there're more Montana Mountain Protectors coming soon!

About the Author

Gemma Weir is a half crazed stay at home mom to three kids, one man child and a hell hound. She has lived in the midlands, in the UK her whole life and has wanted to write a book since she was a child.

Gemma has a ridiculously dirty mind and loves her book boyfriends to be big, tattooed alpha males. She's a reader first and foremost and she loves her romance to come with a happy ending and lots of sexy sex.

For updates on future releases find her on:

Facebook

Twitter

Instagram

Amazon.

Other Authors at Hudson Indie Ink

Paranormal Romance/Urban Fantasy
Stephanie Hudson
Xen Randell
C. L. Monaghan
Sorcha Dawn
Harper Phoenix

Sci-fi/Fantasy
Devin Hanson

Crime/Action
Blake Hudson
Jack Walker

Contemporary Romance
Gemma Weir
Nikki Ashton
Anna Bloom
Tatum Rayne

www.ingramcontent.com/pod-product-compliance
Ingram Content Group UK Ltd.
Pitfield, Milton Keynes, MK11 3LW, UK
UKHW041326110425
5442UKWH00008B/23